HOPE GREENWOOD

A thoughtful explorat… e
want to be and how o… Hope's story
begins in 1969 when, at 17, she weaves herself a future in which she will be a child of the universe; artistic, free-spirited and unconstrained by others' expectations.

Hope's search for universal love puts her at odds with those close to her, leading, paradoxically, to distance and isolation. Lies, secrets and distrust divide her from her family, and she is estranged from her dearly loved sister, Iris.

Fifty years later, wiser but still defiant, Hope's pursuit of divine harmony continues to shape the way she sees the world. Now facing the loss of her own self in dementia, she is determined to dance her own way, despite the best intentions of her sister, Iris, and her daughter, Jeannie, to persuade her to accept her lot. Only her grandson, Tom, truly understands her determination to live life her own way.

When old secrets are uncovered, both Hope and Iris have to rethink the events that separated them, and both will need courage to change their beliefs about each other.

Hope Greenwood

by Helen Frances

Helen x

Published by Helen Frances Books

www.helenfrancesbooks.co.uk

Cover image by gin majka – www.ginmajka.com

Printed by Book Printing UK www.bookprintinguk.com

Remus House, Coltsfoot Drive,
Peterborough, PE2 9BF

Printed on recycled paper in Great Britain

978-1-9191767-0-3

£10.99

For you

you know who you are

PART ONE

Chapter 1

On the dew-heavy grass Hope lay prone, her mind formless in dawn mists of sunrise and silver.

She waited.

Could she but separate her self from this stubborn body and its ragged tremors, she thought, there would be bliss.

The day waited for light, and birdsong, but not, this time, for her. Discovering at last the silence beneath thought, she slipped from what passes for life.

Was it enough, to let go?

Passing the pinch-fisted backs of the Royal Crescent terrace, along Weston Road and beyond the hospital, the A4 shrugs off the city, loitering in the dark green valley of Saltford before climbing the hill to Keynsham. Here, Iris is awake before dawn, again. In the almost dark, the picture window of her pale-bricked house gazes on the long curve of semis whose leaded lights, vintage styled lanterns and stone block paving assert their identities. Iris feels drained. There is a gritty dryness in her eyes and her jaw aches where she has clenched her teeth in fitful, rolling sleep. For fifty years she has been at anchor, but of late she has wondered what it would be like to unmoor herself. Become a Greenwood again, like a sapling.

Mazed in the complexities of love and distance, Jeannie too, is awake. She has somehow alienated her son, who hasn't spoken to her since last October. And later today she has arranged to meet her aunt. She and Iris both want to talk about a care home for Hope. She's not safe to be left alone, the pity is.

Jeannie prefers to grapple the dawn. She is crossing the field below the monument, high on its Ham Stone ridge. Sometimes her mother's daughter, she feels a sense of oneness in the hill field now, as the early morning sun begins its springtime skitter across the uneven ground. Making her way back home, the moan of distant traffic ceases abruptly as she drops below the height of the village rooftops. The transition is like silence, but the air is full of birdsong, and she carries the morning inside like a blessing.

When her doorbell rings a few minutes later, she doesn't initially hear it over the sound of her coffee machine. A second, insistent ring and Jeannie is at the door, knowing, even as she draws back the bolt, that her mother is dead.

The police constable at her door was one of those very tall people who instinctively duck when going through a doorway. He was heavy too, though he moved with a gentle, almost soporific grace. Sitting down on her sofa, he looked over-sized, as if the sofa had been designed for some other type of person, not him.

'But I don't understand,' Jeannie leant forward, holding her knees tight to stop the sensation of falling, 'what was Mum doing in the park? Has she been there all night? What happened?'

As she stopped talking, her whole body was overtaken by trembling, she couldn't even stop her jaw shaking. This couldn't be true. Those endless scenarios and what ifs, the nightmares and catastrophic scenes that she and Iris had fought off for months; images of Hope lost, confused, dying. Those had been just the symptoms of their concern, surely? Human brains are designed to conjure scenes of disaster, rehearse deep fears, but only as one might practise a fire drill, or learn how to use a defibrillator. Such thoughts were for what if, not what is… Not her mother, not dead, not in this actual moment.

'I'm so sorry. A member of the public saw a figure lying on the ground in Hedgemead Park. We were called at 05:52 and your mother was already deceased. She had a bracelet…'

Jeannie nodded. She and Iris had agreed months ago that Hope should have an emergency bracelet with Jeannie's contact details on it. It was in case she forgot her address or couldn't remember her name. It had never been intended as a means to identify her body.

The police constable stood up softly.

'Let me make you a cup of tea, Mrs Trenow. And why don't you find a jumper or a blanket. You've had a shock.'

Feeling as she had aged five, the winter she'd caught chicken pox, Jeannie nodded mutely and gestured towards the kitchen. A few seconds later, the constable came back into the room.

'There, kettle on.' He looked at her carefully, 'Now, let's see what we should do next. Is there anyone you'd like to call?'

She should call Iris but couldn't. She needed to tell Tom first. She nodded at the constable, opening her mouth to speak, only to find that her tongue had forgotten how to form words.

'Well, let me go and brew that tea for you.'

The constable disappeared back into the kitchen, pulling the door closed behind him as he went. Jeannie took a deep breath, steadied herself, and took out her phone. After months of angry silence, would Tom even pick up? She eased her jaw, her voice like dry grit caught at the back of her throat.

'Tom? I'm sorry. Tom. Look darling. It's bad news. Nan is dead, Tom… No, no. I'm at home. There's a police officer here. It's all a bit…' her voice splintered, and she dried up. She could hear Tom's voice but somehow couldn't make out his voice.

'Oh Tom, I don't know what's happened. The police found her. I just don't understand. She was in the park. Near her house, I mean.'

The police constable waited in the kitchen until he could no longer hear Jeannie's muffled voice. He listened to the silence a little longer, and then carefully came back into the living room with two mugs of tea. Jeannie looked up.

'My son is driving over. He'll be here soon. Will you talk to him. I'm sorry. She has dementia. It's not as if… but it isn't bad, wasn't bad, I mean. Not really. We didn't expect anything like this. I can't understand why she was in the park.'

Waiting for Tom to arrive, Jeannie felt the day had grown old, crumpled and dissolved into nothingness. The dawn, the birdsong, even the ring on the doorbell, had taken place, it seemed, in some earlier epoch; a time before sedimentary rocks had been jostled by tumultuous waters, when ammonites and belemnites lived their unthought-of lives, swimming in water over land that had not yet risen in serried layers of stone.

And then Tom was at the door, tears running down his face, folding her in a hug, holding her hand. He guided his mother back into the living room, sitting beside her on the sofa as they both waited for this unknown constable to restart the world.

The constable recapped what he'd already told Jeannie; Hope, dead, found in the early morning by her blue yoga mat, a deep wound in her wrist. Probable cause of death.

'I'm very sorry for your loss, Mrs Trenow,' the constable lowered his head, 'and yours, Mr Trenow. And I know it's not what you want to hear, but there will have to be an inquest. We've taken your mother's body to the mortuary. I'm sorry, it's just routine in these kinds of situations.'

Tom wondered fleetingly what 'these kinds of situations' meant, as the constable continued.

'Please do try not to worry, it really is just a formality. The last thing we want is to add to your distress.'

Beside him, his mother nodded mutely. When the constable got up to leave, Jeannie rose too. The constable picked up his helmet.

'If there's anything you need,' he said, 'you just call me. You've got my direct contact details?'

Jeannie nodded.

'And I'm leaving you the number for the mortuary as well, you may want to visit. It sometimes helps. Just ring to let them know you're coming.'

The constable moved to the front door, Jeannie and Tom following him as if he were a departing visitor who should be thanked for calling.

Left alone, Jeannie and Tom handled the constable's words cautiously. The time of death, a description of the deceased, the location of the body. Phrases that helped buffer officials from the pain of strangers. Tom wondered if his Mum would want to visit the mortuary. He couldn't ask her that. He knew he wouldn't go.

Jeannie moved around her kitchen while Tom watched her wash the used cups, wiping them firmly before putting them away. She turned her attention to the kitchen table. It was cluttered. When his dad was away, Jeannie would pile it with books, envelopes, half-completed lists. It became a sort of zone for unfinished thoughts, works in progress. Tom loved the random mix of cookery books, envelopes and half-finished sudokus, torn out from a newspaper. He saw a copy of *Dancing With Dementia* tucked under a gardening catalogue and wondered how it was that he and his mum hadn't spoken for so long.

When Peter returned from whichever Scottish Island he'd been working on, the table would be made dour and bare again. Should his dad be here, now? Tom didn't understand how his parents' marriage worked but knew that it depended on distance and a sort of emptiness that he found hard to decipher. He watched Jeannie as she sorted the clutter into separate piles, cookery books, novels, work files, note books and old envelopes. The piles were no good. He could see that. The furrows on her forehead deepened and she pushed her glasses up her nose. She took the piles and stacked them up. The novels instantly slid off, and Jeannie attempted to rebalance them. Tom jumped to his feet. Her sharp, frenetic movements were too painful to watch.

'Let me take all that for you.'

Tom's hands were already reaching to clear the table. Jeannie pushed everything towards him.

'You don't know where things go. So just leave it all by my footstool. I can sort things away later.'

Tom nodded with relief and quickly carried the pile into the living room. He stood for a moment, breathing as if for the first time that morning. Being alone was the oddest feeling. The universe had slipped, and he found it hard to believe in the solidity of the walls, the way the floor held fast. Nan would understand, he thought. To her the world was only ever a temporary fusion of illusion and expectations. We see what we think we see, she always told him, not what really is.

Returning to the kitchen, he saw his mum had the fridge door open, her eyes darting over the contents.

'More tea, Mum? I can make it for you. There's nothing else we can do at the moment. Why don't you sit down?'

Jeannie turned, indecisive.

'Please, Mum. Come and sit down. Please.'

Jeannie nodded. She pulled out one of the kitchen chairs. She sat heavily for a moment; her arms sprawled on the table. She sat up then, her fingers tapping the table, and stood up again.

'Where are those old envelopes? I need to start making some lists.'

She rescued an envelope from the recycling bin and took a pencil from her bag.

'Who do we need to tell?'

Tom's thoughts spilled over. His Nan's life had been so full of love and friendship. So many people would want to say goodbye. The prospect of telling everyone made him feel giddy.

'Oh, Mum. Let's not do that right now. Do we need a list? We only have to tell Iris and Dad, surely. No one else matters so much. Let's wait, shall we? Before we tell the world?'

Jeannie put the pencil down near the edge of the table, from where it immediately rolled away and fell to the hard tiled floor.

‘Oh no. Oh damn, damn, damn. That’ll be ruined now. Why am I so useless.’

Jeannie leant back onto the chair; her body felt inert, heavy like a sack of coal. It was if the bones in her body had been crushed into dust and she had no way of holding herself up. She sat, eyes almost closed, her head lowered.

‘Mum?’

Jeannie shook herself and looked at him, aching to ask how he’d been through the winter. How he was now. Would the shock of his Nan’s death set off his arthritis again, or send him spiralling into himself in that awful way, where she couldn’t reach him? She smiled thinly.

‘I’m sorry. I’m alright, darling. Well, not alright, but you know what I mean. It’s just the shock getting to me. I’ll be fine.’

She felt helpless. It would be a small funeral. There was nothing she could do. Mum had never really done anything with her life. Work, of course, but she’d not been close to anyone there. And when Derek and she had gone their separate ways, it had become clear that the friends they’d shared were actually his. Exhaustion flattened her. All the effort of the last year, the constant entreaties and cajoling she and Iris had had to do to keep Hope safe, and now this. Her mother's inconsequential life. This unnecessary death. Jeannie pushed at her forehead with the heels of her hands. It was too much. And here was Tom, too. After so long. She had forgotten how their row had started, just that it had been about Hope, as ever. If only he hadn't always taken sides with his Nan. Could it really have been seven months though? She spoke blindly, trying to reach him.

'Do you think we should call Derek?'

Tom was startled. Why would they tell Derek? He and Nan probably hadn't spoken for the best part of a decade. He stared at his mother, who shook her head, as if irritated.

'Well, they were together for nearly twenty years. He ought to know.'

'Let's just think about family, shall we?' Tom wanted to be diplomatic. Jeannie relaxed again.

'She was one of a kind, wasn't she? You couldn't have had a more lovely gran. And at least the dementia never really took over, did it? That's something to be thankful for.'

Tom flinched, his eyes filling with tears at the realisation that Hope would now only be spoken of in the past tense. It was too soon. He shook the tears away. He wasn't ready for Jeannie's recalibration of the world, he wanted to be outside time and space for a while, and distancing himself was the only way he could stay connected to his own feelings. More than anything, he didn't think he could bear to hear Hope's life edited into his mother's version of her. He flinched, fearing that grief would reduce everything, as if not being here would diminish everything she had been. 'Bodies and forms,' he remembered Hope used to say, 'just temporary, you know.'

'You know, I wonder if she's been going out for a while.' he said.

'Going where?'

'Hedgemead, early in the morning. She used to take her yoga mat there during Covid, didn't she?'

'But that was years ago. She promised Iris she would stop, I don't know how long ago now. She must have been confused.' Jeannie paused, her eyes dark and full of self-doubt. 'Oh, Tom. This would never have happened if we'd got her proper care. She should have been living somewhere she'd have been looked after.'

'Monitored, you mean. Twenty-four seven.'

Tom stopped himself quickly. This was not how he wanted their conversation to be.

'God, I don't know, Mum. Can you imagine Nan's life, if she wasn't free to roam about?'

Tom kept his voice light, floating above bouldered remnants of their old arguments about Hope's approach to her dementia. Jeannie could agree with that, at least. Memories lapped at her sadness like waves breaking on flat sands.

'She was always out and about, wasn't she. The same when I was little. She used to tramp me across the fields, collecting leaves and stones, and blackberries, of course.'

'Blackberries?' Tom remembered Hope calling him her blackberry boy, telling him he was the only child in the world who knew how to pick them just right. The things grandparents say, he thought.

'Good heavens, yes. Did she never tell you? She used to remind me often enough. So often that I don't know what I remember, and what is just her way of telling the tale. There was one time… I was five. She used to talk to my Bear sometimes, instead of me. She told him we were having fish bricks and green pebbles for tea.'

'Is that where that phrase came from?' Tom interrupted, 'I might have guessed.'

'Yes, but the thing is, apparently, I told her that Bear wanted to know what was for pudding. Well, of course there wasn't any, so she and I went out to get some blackberries. It turned into a bit of an expedition. We had these huge bags, and when we got to the blackberries, we had to ask them if we could take the fruit. And there was a song, too. You know your Nan. She said I wore my old red dressing gown with ribbons tied around the sleeves. Mum always told me I looked just like her when I was small. You wouldn't think it now, would you? I mean. Oh Tom.'

Jeannie's face crumpled again.

'Oh Tom, why did this happen?'

Her fragility was immense, desperate. It had never struck Tom before that the way his mum made lists and planned for everything, was nothing but a thin layer of defence. Jeannie avoided feelings as if they would inevitably lead to disaster. How did she live, so divided from herself? The thought brought tears again, and he reached over to put his arm around her shoulder. She felt empty. It was like comforting a shell, abandoned on the shore. After a few moments, he took his arm away.

'Iris?' he said.

Jeannie nodded, relieved by his practicality.

'Let's make the call together, shall we? I'll put her on speaker.'

Chapter 2

Iris was ironing when she heard the land line ring. Her morning had been ruined when Don had announced that he was going into the office that day. He always worked from home on Mondays and Wednesdays, had done ever since lockdown, and Iris planned her days accordingly. Not that she thought his decision was sensible. Surely it would make more sense to work from home on consecutive days, preferably attached to the weekend. That's what most people did. But if she offered her opinion, Don would shake his head with a subtle smile, secure in the knowledge that his alternate days represented a subtlety of managerial craft. Today was a Wednesday, but what with the Auditors in, well, he said he needed to be there. It meant she had an extra free day, as she privately called the days when Don was out all day, but she hadn't made any arrangements for her time, which made her feel put out. She answered the call, hoping it might someone who needed her help.

'Iris Fellowes.'

The news made her gasp and hold onto the windowsill for support. Hope was her little sister. This was wrong, it couldn't be so. How could she be living, and her sister dead?

After the call, the house boomed with silence like the sudden quiet after a gun salute. It was still early, and sunlight fell slantwise on her early summer roses. Iris stood, irresolute, staring through the window. Her habitual, barely conscious and fear-filled rehearsal of catastrophe was a form of defence, as if anxiety itself held disaster in check. But this, this arbitrary leap into death. This, she had not foreseen, and she felt her security crumble.

Painstakingly, slowly, as she always did, Iris gathered the frayed grey threads of logic together. Clear thinking would hold her safe. Jeannie had given her the address of the mortuary. She stared at the pad where she had written the details, reading the address again and again as if trying to make it real. There must be some error, shc realised. Hope couldn't have had a fatal accident. Her death would be found to be a consequence of her dementia. Nothing else could possibly make sense. They had all anticipated the gradual unravelling and dissolution of Hope's mind, leaving only her body to be cared for. The doctors must have missed something. She herself had been coming round to Don's way of thinking, that Hope needed specialist care, to be somewhere she was looked after and managed.

Don. Iris returned to the kitchen to find her mobile. He would expect her to call him with such news. What should she say? He would want facts, he would offer solutions, he would tell her what to do.

Hope was dead, lying in a mortuary, alone. How awful, to be alone. Iris put her mobile in her bag and unplugged the iron. Her actions preceded her decisions as, with slight frown shadowing her forehead, she gently detached the sheet of paper from the notepad and picked up her car keys. Don should have been working from home, but he wasn't there. She would go to the mortuary at once.

An hour later, sitting by her sister's lifeless form, Iris knew she had made a mistake. She picked up and held Hope's cold hand, tracing the still blue veins under the tissued skin with her fingers. Was that the proper thing to do? She looked down at her sister's face, her closed eyes and soft mouth. Hope was wearing the clothes in which she'd been found, a beautiful gauzy green shirt and lilac harem pants; the light chiffon fabric and a lacy scarf lay serenely on her still body, and on her feet, a pair of soft velvet pumps, the kind she had always loved. Someone had bandaged her wrist, Iris saw.

Her sister looked - she struggled for words - she looked comfortable. No, that wasn't quite it. It was as if being dead was somehow right for her. That Hope knew what she was doing, had achieved something momentous. Iris herself was increasingly ill at ease. She had come on an impulse. There had been nothing stopping her, and so she was here, like a walk-on character in a crime drama. The type of character that you can't really believe in, and who is, in any case, of little consequence. She felt self-conscious and awkward in her neat slacks and flowered blouse. How did her little sister come to be here? In a mortuary. Even in dying, it seemed, Hope left Iris feeling wrong-footed.

Iris withdrew her hand, gently lowering Hope's to the surface of the trolley. Iris wanted her feelings to overwhelm her. She ought to cry, grieve, feel a sense of shock, but she didn't know how to begin. Her presence was futile, she thought. She should go home.

As she reached the door, she turned again, feeling there should be something she should say, or think, some act of farewell. Unexpectedly, her gaze was snagged by the delicate green blouse, and the present was punctured by a memory that made her breathless with pain. She stumbled, almost running from the building, recalling, as if it were sixty minutes not sixty years earlier, an argument over their carefully hoarded box of dressing up clothes. How Hope had cried bitter tears when Iris had claimed a silk shirt from the box. It had been the same green. Hope had been so demanding, and how extravagant her tears. She'd wanted the shirt because she said she was a tree, filled with rustle and movement in an imaginary breeze. Iris had wanted the shirt herself. She had seen quite plainly that it was quite the sort of blouse that she would wear when she was married and had a husband and two lovely sons, and they all lived together in a tidy house. Hope had been inconsolable, but Iris had simply walked off wearing it, turning her back on the tempest that her sister so often was. Now, sitting in her car, Iris sobbed with guilt and sorrow.

Chapter 3

Back in April, two days before her funeral when Hope had been dead a fortnight, Tom had received a letter in the post from her. Turning the envelope over and over in his hands, he assumed that the letter had been delayed by industrial action. It made sense to save the letter until later, he thought, and added it, unopened, to the box of funny, odd, philosophic and crazily illustrated letters he'd received from Hope since he was a small child. After the funeral, he told himself. He would read it after that was over. But then, the funeral had been all wrong, so few people there, just immediate family and Mel, Hope's best friend. The absence of her exuberant circle of friends had stitched his grief into a patchwork of emotion; old resentments and new bitterness scattered like broken crocks amongst his love, sorrow and sense of loss. Standing under the trees, the tight grief of the living was solid, angular, discordant, and Hope simply wasn't there, not even among the leaves or in the pauses between birdsong. He'd read some lines from a Mary Oliver poem, but only Mel had wept. His mum and Aunt Iris had been efficient, taking care of arrangements with the Woodland Trust and caterers, but where were her friends, where were all the people she had held close and who she would want here, surely, to say goodbye? Even his dad, absent except for a few brief hours, had mostly been silent, locked in that inaccessible bond he and Jeannie had, that made Tom feel like he didn't really exist.

Tom didn't know, as she had chosen not to tell anyone, that Iris had in fact kept the news of Hope's death close. For reasons of her own, she hadn't wanted to tell people, telling her husband and sons that it was better to have a quiet funeral, let the news lie for a while. And so, Tom had gone back to his volunteer work at the hospice the next day, the distance between him and Jeannie chilling once again into a permafrost of misunderstanding. It was mid-June, then, when he felt ready to pull the folded sheet from its handwritten envelope.

Tuesday

Darling Tom,

I have a presentiment that you won't need this letter. You already know. Thing is, even when we tell stories the truth can stay frolicky. Funny that I can't forget that word now. Frolicky. It reminds me of you, and Jeb, and Auntie Jane in the place where the paintings are. What's it called? So, there's a word now that I have forgotten. But I don't need to stop, do I? You do know what I mean. Anyway, Joseph had a brilliant idea. He said my letters were like seeds. The ones on that wild pink flower that grows everywhere. So, here's a seed for you. He's going to look after them for me. Or is he going to bury them, oh bother, you know. In the brown stuff that smells nice. Birdie would know, I guess. Oh yes, soil. And when it's my turn, buried in the soil. Make sure you have twice the celebration. Once for me and once for Birdie.

It's not my best day now, but you and Mel and Joseph are always.

Love and blisses, Cosmic Nan

Tom felt he would drown in guilt. How could he have forgotten? He read and reread the letter, appalled and overcome by a sense of failure. It had been their last proper day out together, a train trip to Cardiff, and Hope had oscillated between intense focus and sudden absences of self. He could see again the café where they'd stopped for tea, the rosebay willowherb with its faded pink flowers, hear the clatter of trains just beyond the courtyard where they'd sat. Jeb had been with them, meeting Hope for the first time. Then, on the train back to Bath, they had talked about living funerals. Their friend had been dying and had asked her friends to arrange a living funeral for her. And how could he have failed to remember how Nan, typical Nan, had taken the idea and made it her own. "Oh, me too," he could hear her saying, "I'll have a letting go party too." She'd turned to him, "You can arrange it for me, can't you?"

Iris was part way through an assault on her kitchen when Tom rang, having decided that it was about time she emptied and scrubbed each cupboard in turn. She bent low over the dresser where she kept her parents' best dinner service. They rarely used it, but it wasn't the sort of thing you could sell or give away. She lifted the final stack of dinner plates from the back and reached into the dresser with a damp cloth. The corners of the cupboard were so grimy, she grimaced. She still couldn't really explain, even to herself, why she had gone to the mortuary that day. But she resented Don's criticism, the way he made her feel as if she had been wayward in some way. She rinsed her cloth in the bowl of soapy water and methodically ran it along the wooden struts and joints at the back of the dresser cupboard. She could do with a small brush, really. An old toothbrush would have been perfect. Don had never understood Hope, he used to say she was away with the fairies. "Irresponsible" he'd called her, more than once, especially when she'd taken Jeannie to that Ashram in India when she was still only a child. So why, now, was he making her feel that *she* was in the wrong?

There was something lodged in the back of the cupboard, a round, flat object, wrapped in old newspaper. Curiously, she reached in and pulled it out. It proved to be a small Plaster of Paris disc, imprinted unevenly with butterfly shapes. There were the indents of bubbles where the plaster had been inexpertly mixed, and the thing was painted in the most unlikely rainbow of colours. Memories stuttered like an ancient home movie. She recalled a world of pale-yellow sunshine, of sitting at a wobbly picnic table with Hope, mixing plaster and arguing about whose turn it was with the spatula. Hope had wobbled the table, stirring her own mixture too quickly, too briefly. The scene ran through her head like a silent Super Eight, and she jumped when her smart phone buzzed on the kitchen table.

'Can I talk to you about Nan for a minute?'

Although it was a question, it didn't sound like one, thought Iris. Tom had changed.

'I was just thinking about her,' Iris said, 'Remembering our childhood. We were two peas in a pod. We did everything together, you know.' Tom swallowed his surprise; he was used to thinking of Iris as almost completely unlike her sister. They had such different lives. He pressed on.

‘Well look, I know the funeral was a pretty small affair, but there’s something Nan asked me to do.’ Tom paused, wondering how his great-aunt would react, ‘The thing is, she wanted to have a party. She asked me to arrange it for her. And I want to go ahead.’

‘You mean a memorial service?’ Iris was cautious.

‘No.’ Tom persevered, ‘She wanted a party, a proper Cosmic Nan do with everyone invited. I’m thinking about everyone who didn’t get to the funeral.’

There was a silence. Impossible, Iris thought.

‘I’ll do the work. Get in touch with everyone. All the Hotwells Meditation Centre people. Nan did so much for that place, didn’t she? Then, there are her friends from university. And all the mentoring work she did. And Joseph, of course.’ Tom tailed off, but Iris still said nothing.

‘It’s what she asked me to do, you know,’ Tom’s voice was firm. ‘And that way, she can really say goodbye properly.’

After a long pause, Iris spoke.

‘What does your mother say?’

‘I’m phoning you first.’ Tom said, simply. He hadn’t steeled himself to speak to Jeannie yet.

‘Leave it with me, Tom. I’ll speak to your mother. She needs to be asked.’ Iris was relieved. She would talk to Jeannie first, knock this ridiculous idea on the head. But Tom spoke quickly.

‘Look, I’m sorry, Iris. I know you mean well. But Nan really did ask me to do this for her. And I sort of owe her, you know.’

Unable to dissuade Tom, and feeling acutely uneasy, Iris picked up her cloth and returned to her task. There must be some way to prevent this. She certainly wouldn’t tell Don; he’d only start on again about the way she hadn’t even told his cousins about the funeral. She glanced at the clock. Nearly eleven. On cue, Don appeared at the back door, removing his garden shoes and putting a small pile of mail on the kitchen counter. He flicked the kettle on and searched for the biscuits that Iris had stowed away at the back of the larder. He found a packet of Hobnobs, and sitting down, opened the packet on the kitchen table. Iris made the tea, and put a cup in front of him, noticing the biscuit crumbs he’d scattered and reaching instinctively for a cloth.

'Watch out for the crockery,' she said, gesturing at her parents' old dinner service which she had stacked ready for hand washing. 'I need to wash all these before lunch. And my wretched elbow is playing up.'

Don glanced at the piles of plates, wondering why Iris always made such hard work out of easy tasks.

'Why don't you put them in the dishwasher?' he advised, 'That'll save you the effort.'

Iris said nothing, her irritation guttering like an exhausted candle. Don's tendency to provide glib answers needled her, however often she told herself it was just the way he was. She turned away, rewrapping the small plaster disc and pushing it to the back of a drawer. Don shook the biscuit packet, shaking crumbs on the table again as he sorted through the flyers and circulars.

'This one's not junk.'

He handed Iris a small white envelope with a handwritten address.

'One of your school chums?'

Iris kept a meticulous correspondence with friends going back to her school days, and she held out her hand with pleasurable anticipation. Glancing at the envelope, she gasped with sudden shock. She put the letter down on the counter and backed away to the sink.

'What on earth,' started Don, 'Iris, what on earth is the matter?'

Iris had visibly paled, her mouth moving as if she wanted to speak, but could not. Don picked up the letter.

'Who's it from?' he asked, 'Are you expecting bad news from someone?'

Iris shook her head, and then, straightening her back, spoke firmly.

'No, Don' she said, 'It's just that the handwriting on that envelope is Hope's.'

The envelope contained three sheets, folded unevenly.

Monday

Dear Iris,

If I tell you the truth, you will change it into something you can live with, something that fits into your world. You won't notice yourself doing it. You never do. So, if the doctors are right, I'm heading for dementia. Please don't think you can make decisions for me, though. I'm going to sort that out without you and Don deciding to institutionalise me. Even Birdie struggled with being in that Care Home, and her mind was still beautiful, I'd say poetic actually. Tom would agree.

You know the thing that really bothers me at the moment. It's those new Cedars at the end of your garden. The ones shaped into spirals, that you're so proud of. Okay, so Don has an eye for garden design. Everything always looks so well composed, and things flower just when they should. But those Cedars are artificial, Iris. They're not real. And yeah, I know you've got that Paradise Palm, sitting in absolute shade in your hallway for the last ten years. Well, that's obviously artificial because there's no light. But outside? Where there's all the air and sunshine and water to grow for real. It makes me feel totally distraught, Iris, it really does.

By the way. When you barged round to my house and started talking about Jeannie's father. You couldn't have been more wrong. But if I'd known about Joseph. Who knows what I would have done? Perhaps I would have written to him, perhaps not. But I would have decided for myself, and that makes all the difference.

The thing is - about beauty. We can't help having a false idea about it. It's to do with biology, I guess. That odd Christian writer. You know. The one who wrote a novel about prejudice in New York, when it was a new place. Can't remember his name. Well, we're living in these bodies, so we pay attention to the embodied world, and we call nature beautiful. But he says we're deluding ourselves because nature is full of hideous slime and putrescence as well as pretty flowers. He's wrong, though. Just because diseases and decay are part of nature too doesn't change the essential truth of beauty. It just means we don't have the right perspective to see it. Humans are bound, Iris. We're knotted into our bodies, and who we think we are, and it gets in the way. It's like, well, it's being a time-bound life form that makes us blind. But not desolate, like Don's fake trees. If you don't believe me, go and really look at them. Just because something looks real, doesn't mean you have to accept it.

I'll write again soon.

Love and Blisses, Hope

Iris felt her heart scudding. She looked again at the first page. No date. It was certainly Hope's style. All that stuff about beauty and time. But it was so lucid, she must have written this a long, long time ago.

'Well, are you going to tell me what it says?'

She looked up at Don, startled. She'd forgotten he was there.

Iris tightened her hold of the letter. 'It's nothing,' she said, 'just Mel sending some old notes she thought I'd like to have. She must have had them in an envelope already.'

It was enough, Don wasn't really interested. She tucked the letter into her pocket. Hope was right about those wretched trees though. She'd always disliked them.

Chapter 4

Alone the following morning, Iris sat down to deal with her emails, flicking the radio on as usual. Everything she had done for the past three months had been rooted in loss. Hope was the first person she thought about every day, and the subject of her dreams. She found herself holding imaginary conversations with her lost sister, and Tom's call had left her feeling even more troubled. She turned the radio off, abruptly, not in the mood for Radio Three. Instead, she opened Spotify, looking for something different to listen to. Should she be putting Hope's death behind her, by now? Don seemed to think so. But again and again, Iris found herself imagining herself back in 1970, the year everything had changed.

She tapped 1970 into Spotify, scrolling through the list of albums. Bridge of Troubled Water. It had been year she and Don had got engaged, as well as the year Hope had run away. That would do. She sighed, clicking on her inbox, deleting the junk mail and answering requests from this and that committee. But every now and then she flicked back to the Spotify tab, turning the volume higher and higher. Simon and Garfunkel's harmonies were impossibly fraught with love and tension. She felt tears welling up.

Until that last summer, before she left to go to university, she and Hope had been so close. They'd rowed, of course. Like sisters must, thought Iris, remembering their tempestuous arguments. But never, until then, had their rows meant anything. Even though Iris was two years older, she'd never minded when they'd been taken for twins. Hope made life sparkle, and having an irrepressible, unpredictable little sister had felt like owning the stars. It had been after her 'O' Levels that her parents had decided that Iris should start thinking like an adult. Was that when she'd started to lose Hope? Her parents had decided she should think about the future, become informed about the world. And somehow, they'd made it feel like an honour, a special privilege for her, the elder sister. She was encouraged to stay up and watch the late evening news with them on the BBC. It was when she had first been horrified by the precariousness of everything, the impassive faces of newsreaders made her anxious and afraid. It was as if it were yesterday, thought Iris, impulsively typing "Six Day War" into Google. Scrolling down, her memory snagged on a black and white photograph from the BBC archive. The picture showed two destroyed planes almost side by side on the ground. The fuselage of each plane had disintegrated into fragments and pools of oil that stained the concrete like spilled entrails and blood. The wings and tailfins remained, futile but intact. When she had first seen that image, sitting on her parent's sofa and staring in silence at the television, she had been horrified by the fragility of existence. The utter wreckage of the cockpits and cabins had looked like twin funeral pyres. Involuntarily, she had squinted her eyes to blur her vision, wanting, but not daring, to run from the room.

Now, Iris stared at her screen until tears obscured her gaze. She felt her every decision since then had been charged with a desperate, unnamed need to protect herself. How had she allowed herself to become so bunkered? Standing up abruptly, pacing to the window, she looked out to where Don's cypresses obscured the world beyond. Her eyes ached with grief and there was a giddy hollowness inside her that made her feel brittle, insubstantial, as if she had never lived. She brought her fingers to her face to push away the tears, almost surprised to feel her skin still there.

On Spotify, the music had changed. Iris let it play on while she stood at the window, paralysed by the conflict between grief for the life she had let go and regret for the one she had held tight. Unerringly, the guitar introduction to *Both Sides Now* began. Joni played with such confidence and strength until, almost indistinguishably, the guitar gave way to her tentative, tremulous voice,

'Rows and flows of angel hair and ice-cream castles in the air

And feather canyons everywhere, I've looked at clouds that way

But now they only block the sun, they rain and snow on everyone

So many things I would have done...'

Was Tom right, she wondered. If she agreed to the party, she'd have to confront Joseph. Would he ever forgive her for keeping Hope's death from him? How could he? A terrible grief cut through her like shards of glass, and Iris began to weep. How had she let her sister go?

PART TWO

Chapter 5

Hope sat curled in a fading wicker garden chair with her sketch pad propped up on her folded legs. Beside her, on a small patch of grass in full sun, Iris stretched out on a blanket, trying to find a comfortable position in which she could hold up the book she was reading and shield her eyes from the light, while doing her best to tan her fair, freckled skin. The afternoon air seemed to lie heavily across the garden, and sharp bands of light and shadow fell between the slats of the new fence that their parents had had put in that year. From the street outside, the occasional sound drifted into the garden, and from time to time, a car passed, changing gear as it tackled the hill.

'I swear this garden is smaller than it used to be.'

Hope let her sketch fall forward onto her lap. She'd been doing a pencil sketch of her mother's roses, but having no colours to use was too boring for words. In addition, the heat had made her lethargic, and she wanted to provoke Iris.

Iris lifted her head and squinted at Hope.

‘Hey you, let me have the chair now. You’ve had it for ages.’

‘I’m not moving,’ Hope retorted, ‘you can read anywhere. I’d have to start again if I sat in a different place.’

‘This book’s no good, anyway. What time will Mum and Dad be back?’

Iris turned over and pulled herself upright. She glanced at her sister’s sketch pad.

‘Wow, that’s quite good, you know.’

Hope didn’t answer, but picked up the pad again, frowning over her drawing.

‘What’s the book about then? Will I like it?’

‘Oh, it’s about this girl. As far as I can tell she’s obsessed with herself. Vain. Anyway, even though she’s completely dull, men keep falling in love with her because she’s so beautiful. She’s got three suitors. I bet I know which one she’ll marry. It’s too obvious.’

‘Sounds insipid.’

Iris nudged at the book with her toe. How slowly time passed. It was still two weeks before she left to go to university. Even her suitcase was half packed. For the first time she could remember, she had absolutely nothing to do.

'God, I'm looking forward to Aunt Jane coming. When'll she be here. Do you know?'

'Can't be soon enough,' said Hope, 'I wish she lived close by, not in dreary Wales.'

Iris frowned at Hope. Trust her to have an opinion about a place she'd never even visited.

'I can't imagine that anywhere Aunt Jane lives is dreary.'

The two girls caught each other's look, grinning briefly.

'Oh, this sketch isn't working.' Hope unfolded her legs and flung her pencil to the ground, 'Do you want some lemonade? I do. I'll get some. I need my crayons, anyway.'

'No, I'll get it. I'm already up. Are your crayons upstairs?' Hope nodded, folding herself back into the seat.

Iris returned with a glass of lemonade clinking in each hand, and a packet of ginger biscuits, which she'd tucked under her chin. She lifted her head, and the packet fell to the ground.

'Hey, they'll all break if you do that!' Hope picked up the packet and opened it carefully.

'That's ok, you can give the bits to your teddy.'

'Not fair, Iris, I was twelve last time I had a picnic with teddy. Anyway, I got extra biscuits. Mum thought I was cute'.

'Yeah, and your teddy is still wearing that crazy scarf you knitted him in the hottest summer ever. It's thin at one end, and the other end is about three times as wide.'

'You could have shown me how to do it properly, you know.'

'Still can. I've offered to show you how to knit so many times.'

'When have you ever?' retorted Hope, 'Oh I can't talk to you now, Hope, I have to revise my geography. No, I can't come cycling today, Hope, I need to write an essay. No, Hope, I don't want to play a game, it's too childish.'

Iris didn't want to argue, what was the point? It was too hot, and besides, now that the planning for York was done, she was feeling miserable. What would it be like, away from home, away from her sister?

'It's going to be lovely to have our bedroom just for me. Bet you'll miss me though.'

Hope was fidgety, provoking. She wanted something tangible from this soon-to-be-gone sister of hers. It wasn't university itself, but Iris's determination, her careful list-making and planning. It all felt like a catastrophe looming. She tried to ignore a half-formed feeling that she didn't belong, any more, in her sister's world.

'Miss you?' Iris tried to laugh the idea away, 'My annoying, know-it-all, tight-stealing sister. Oh yeah, naturally. I'll cry in my pillow every night.'

Iris's voice had a discordant sound, and Hope stared at her suspiciously.

'Look, I worked hard for my A levels.' Iris's voice was angrier than she'd meant.

'Not being the family genius, I mean.' She tried to soften her tone. What was up with Hope today? She wanted Hope to be fun, not miserable.

Iris leapt to her feet, startling her sister. She stretched out her hand, grinning at her.

'Come on, you.'

Hope got to her feet cautiously.

'Backsies with a dare. And I get to set the first dare.'

'You're on!' Hope jumped forwards, landing with her arms reaching out, one to the front and one behind her like a cartoon character. 'What'll we do?'

'Okay, okay. Let me think. I know, backsies with a biscuit in your mouth, humming the National Anthem. If the biscuit breaks, you lose.'

The two sisters turned to stand facing away from each other, touching back-to-back, and each put a biscuit between her lips. Using the mutual pressure between their backs, they slowly lowered themselves to a seating position on the ground, humming an erratic version of God Save the Queen as they tensed their leg muscles to lower their bodies. The rules of the game meant they weren't allowed to use their arms to support themselves as they sat down. Iris held her arms out to the sides, like an aeroplane's wings, while Hope used hers to conduct an imaginary brass band.

'Easy squeezy.' Hope called, triumphantly waving her unbroken biscuit in the air, and Iris giggled, holding hers up for inspection. 'Your turn then.'

Hope was ready for her. 'Backsies with drawing, best picture wins.' she declared.

Iris rolled her eyes but grabbed a sheet of paper and a pencil ready to play.

'OK, but I declare "down in ten"'. This was a rule the two of them had agreed some years earlier following one of their more spectacular arguments after Hope had frozen into position, holding them locked into place, hovering above the ground for so long that Iris had suddenly felt her legs gave way and crumpled to the ground.

'How about down in twenty?'

'Fifteen.'

'Done, but I get to count.'

A long, slow fifteen seconds later, the two of them simultaneously sat on the ground.

'Picture swap.'

Hope and Iris exchanged pictures, still sitting back-to-back. Hope had drawn the hollyhocks in front of her, outlining the tall, pale pink blooms with light strokes of her pencil, and she'd even sketched a couple of the flowers gone over, their petals dry and faded on tall stems. She looked at Iris's drawing. Her sister had drawn a cartoon teddy bear, with one paw in the air, as if it were waving. The teddy had the same embroidered nose and mouth as her own bear and was wearing a ludicrous scarf. On the teddy's cheek, Iris had added two mournful tears and something that looked like a tissue in one of the bear's paws.

Hope bent her neck backwards, so the crown of her head lightly rested on Iris's.

'When I go to university, teddy will come too.' she said.

Hope spoke firmly, wanting to imprint her words on this motionless summer afternoon, whose crystal, sparkling hours seemed suddenly weighted by the time to come.

Iris said nothing, thankful that seated like this, back-to-back, she didn't have to look at Hope. There was an aching lump in her throat, she had the strangest sensation that she was somehow already gone. She was going to York, she was starting a degree that would help shape her whole life, and even so, she wondered, sitting there, who she would be known as if not “Hope’s sister” or “the other Greenwood girl”.

Seconds glistened in the heat. All of time seemed to pass before Hope spoke again.

‘You know, I have no idea what I’m going to do at university. Dad’ll come down on me like a ton of bricks if I say I want to do Art.’

Iris moved away from her sister and stood up.

‘You know what, I am going to teach you to knit. Right now. You and me are going to make a pair of mittens. We’ll do them without fingers, so it’s not too complicated. Come on.’

After they’d disappeared in to the house, the kitchen door banging shut behind them, the garden seemed to contract into silence. insensible within its tall fences.

Within two weeks, the weather had changed, the hollyhocks had gone over, their colour faded. It was raining. Not heavily, but the drips rolled persistently down the window of the girls’ shared bedroom. Hope sat on her bed, tongue between her teeth as she concentrated on the final rows of a red mitten. Beside her lay the right-hand mitten that Iris had already completed, waiting for its more raggedy partner. Hope sighed and put down her knitting.

'You're going to have to show me how to cast off again.'

She moved to the window by Iris, who was staring at the rain.

'I wish Aunt Jane had come to stay for the Bank Holiday. I wonder why she didn't,' Iris said, 'she promised to visit before I went to uni. You'll get to see her at half term, I expect, but I won't see her until Christmas now.'

Hope contorted her body, pressing her cheek against the cold glass and looking out the window from the bottom up towards the sky.

'Somebody told me that if you look in a raindrop when a light is shining through it, you can see the world, but upside down?'

She sighed.

'Doesn't seem to work at the moment, though.'

Chapter 6

It is late October, and a steady rain is falling again. The roads and pavements are bleared and dark. Where a drain is blocked at the bottom of Milsom Street, a pool of water eddies in the road, and every time a bus groans into gear around the corner, spray flirts the legs of passing pedestrians, who mutter with tepid irritation. Most faces are concealed under dark umbrellas or coat hoods, and, obscuring the Georgian roofscapes that cradle the city centre, the low cloud has the effect of diminishing people, draining their separate identities.

Hope picks her way through the puddles. She's not bothered by the rain, and will linger in the city centre, wishing her weekends were more interesting. She doesn't want to go home yet, preferring the dreary wet streets to the subdued predictability of her home life, and so she slips into Duck, Son and Pinker, shaking the rain from her long hair; one slight teenager amongst many. Unlike Hope, most of the teenage girls in the music shop in pairs or threes, bonded by boredom, if not friendship. The boys coalesce in larger groups, finding courage only when safely held in their tiny tribes. Noone is there to buy anything, but simply to be somewhere. As usual on a Saturday, there is a restless queue of people waiting to use the sound booths. Two glass and metal cubicles with headphone sets. Customers cannot handle the LPs but must ask a member of staff for assistance. In the pop section, faces peer from the album covers as if staring into a mirror. Mostly, they are young men leaning towards the camera lens as if it would endorse them, approve their tentative rebellions. Who are they, Hope wonders, and who do they want to be. They look more interesting, anyway, than the idiotic packs of boys she has learnt to ignore.

Behind the long mahogany sales counter, the sales assistant, Chris, is flirting with the new Saturday girl. He flaunts his experience with idle indifference. He's wasted here, he knows, thinking, as he leans towards the new girl, that he has nothing left to learn. He's been here every Saturday for over six months, for God's sake. The record counter is beneath him, really. The managers should move him to one of the long rooms where musical instruments recline in polished rows. The stringed instruments would be best, though dealing with parents might be a drag. All those eleven-year-olds who are starting to learn the violin. God. They could move him to the piano room of course. Go into the piano room, and it's like going into an eighteenth-century drawing room. There's even a Gainsborough on the wall. Someone told him it was genuine. Chris can sell stuff. He knows how to get people interested, make them feel the need to own something. And he's played the piano since he was seven. His teacher told him he had sensitive hands. Girls like that. When he meets a girl, he knows how to make his eyes look soft and dreamy too. He smiles at the Saturday girl. What was her name again?

Hope is bent over a stack of LP's her head down, her damp hair a cascade over her shoulders. Chris has seen Hope in the shop before, and catching sight of her now, raindrops glistening on her dark coat, he abruptly turns away from the Saturday girl, leaving her with a galling sense of abandonment and neglect. Chris has that effect. Hope isn't looking in his direction. Has, in fact, never noticed him. She's holding an album in her hands, looking at the sleeve. Even from behind the counter, Chris can see that it is the debut album by Yes, with its striking pop art blue and red cover design. She really is something special, he thinks, wishing she would come over to the shop counter. Hope holds the album in front of her, tilting the front cover to different angles as her eyes explore the design. He is entranced. What is she doing? He's not meant to leave the counter, but the manager isn't to be seen, and he quickly lifts the wooden flap, slipping underneath.

‘I can put you on the list for the listening booth.’

He startles Hope.

‘I work here.’ His eyes are gentle, curious. He really wants Hope to notice him.

‘It’s simple. You choose a track, and I set it up so that you can listen to it. I’ve only heard their single. Could have been written for you, babe.’

He can feel her embarrassment. There’s a soft blush of colour on her cheeks. It’s a rush. She really is something else. The way she’s searching his face, looking at him. Wow. But she says nothing. This one is shy. He wishes he was wearing his purple shirt instead of the white shirt and plain tie that the shop insists on. He can feel his hair move though, where it brushes over his collar. He takes his charm for granted. He likes the way her shyness makes him feel.

‘Hey, come on babe. You need to listen to this in stereo, you know. Which track shall I play for you?’

A slight frown crosses Hope’s face.

‘I’m sorry. I’ve never heard this band. I just liked the cover.’

Hope holds out the album, and Chris takes it.

'Hey, you know. Why not choose a track? It's either that or the rain, you know.' He tilts his head towards the window, where the rain is falling in sheets. He doesn't want her to go, and there's something about his determination that catches at Hope. He smiles at her, and to his surprise, she smiles back.

'OK.' she says. She takes the LP from him and scans the track list.

'But I shouldn't.' she adds, looking at Chris with an earnest expression. 'it's not right. I can't buy it you know. I don't have enough money.'

Chris isn't often thrown like this.

'You think people listen to albums here and then buy them? Wow. Most kids in those booths just want muck around. Listen to a new track. Maybe something they caught once on the radio. Maybe something with a cool album cover.'

He grins at her. She is so solemn, so ordered. That air of self-containment she has; it piques him. Not like other girls. He wants to hold her attention, wrap her in his will. He holds the record out, this object they have in common, looking at her as if to mesmerise her.

‘You just wait over here. I’m going to play the single for you. It’s called “Sweetness”.’

He smiles again. Hope feels herself drawn towards him.

‘Wait till that guy has finished. Then I’ll put you in next. Just wait a couple of minutes. Stay here, ok?’

In the booth, the headphones are insecure, heavy on her head. She’s never worn headphones before, they feel too large, strange. She has seated herself on the rotating stool and the glass of the booth reflects her image on three sides. Twisting the circular stool, she turns towards the blank wall away from the reflections, away from the sensation of being at a window, watched.

And then. And then the sounds of guitar and voices began. The stereo sound is a revelation to her, and in the epoch of a second, the borders between her senses collapse. The sound is fluid, she can feel it in her brain, moving sinuously. The music seems to be somewhere in the middle of her skull, as if her individual consciousness had been displaced. Unconsciously, Hope closes her eyes more tightly, folding in on herself to contain the sensations. The sound is everywhere and no place. As the first voices float to the surface, the music divides and redivides and the layers of sound in each ear pull against each other and behind her eyelids she can almost see swirling, kaleidoscopic patterns, tumbling colours that move with the urgency of sound. Shape and formlessness are, she sees, two aspects of the same reality, and this sound-infused light is changing her world.

She barely acknowledges Chris when she emerges from the booth, slipping between the record stacks and out through the door. Outside, the tall Georgian buildings lengthen down into their mirrored selves on the smooth wet pavement. The dark shape of each illusory door and window is as perfect as the real thing. Where the originals touch the ground, their reflections are firmly formed, as if drawn with a heavy pencil. Those from upper storeys are lighter, less distinct, tremulous with possibility. The pavement canvas redefines grey into a kaleidoscope criss-crossed by the figures of water people, their umbrellas below their inverted forms. As couples and groups of friends move across this rain-glassed landscape, they release a cascade of motion, each droplet catching light from who knows where. Above her, Hope sees the raindrops are laughing in sheer joy. She leaves the shop, framed momentarily in the doorway as she drinks in the sky before setting off slantwise, finding new space between the worlds.

Behind her, trapped by the heavy mahogany shop counter, Chris watches her disappearing form, unable to distinguish between possession and loss.

Chapter 7

The cottage hat Jane shared with Birdie in South Wales was almost half a mile from the nearest village, sitting squarely as if to hold itself secure in a patchwork of fields that amble downhill to the Gower coast. The village itself was nothing more than a scattering of cottages, and their closest town was a 30-minute drive. When they'd moved to Flag Cottage, almost twenty years earlier, local opinion assumed that they were two single women, sharing a house for convenience and economy. For two decades now, they've said nothing, done nothing to correct that settled view. Both envying and keeping their distance from the interlocked generations of kin on the Gower, they were known those poor English spinsters, perfectly nice, but a bit stand-offish. In this way they'd found a welcome and acceptance, so profoundly they remained unknown.

The week after Jane had once again cancelled a visit to her brother and nieces because of her persistent exhaustion, Birdie had insisted that she see a doctor. Jane, finally accepting the anxiety in Birdie's eyes, agreed to go to. The doctor had been more thorough than she'd expected, arranging tests and X-Rays. Jane told Birdie he was an old fusspot, but she went along with his advice. Today, she'd been called back to get the X-Ray results. She had driven off that morning under a thin blue sky, their old blue Triumph Herald spluttering and lurching into action, audible for several seconds after vanishing down the long track that led to the lane.

From her open window, in the quiet of the late morning, Birdie could hear the insistent, repetitive keening of a cow who had been separated from her calf. She was in the broad-beamed stone barn at the side of their cottage, cutting mounts for a gallery in Swansea. The gallery was a regular customer and had ordered frames for a run of prints. It was simple, if repetitive, work. They didn't really need the money these days, but Birdie loved the steady precision of the work. Bent low over the thick cream mount, she checked the corner of the board before angling her blade. Her long dark hair was carefully tied back in a scarf, and her glasses, which were no use for such close work, lay on the table beside her. She'd taken off the thick leather gloves she wore for cutting glass and held the cutter in her left hand. The cow continued its insistent plaint. As she pressed the knife into the stiff board her grip slipped, and before she could jerk the blade away, she'd sliced cleanly into the top of her right thumb, spilling blood onto the mount.

The cut wasn't deep, and only hurt because of the unexpected shock, but the mount, of course, was ruined. Birdie shook her head angrily at herself. The accident, now that it had happened, should, she felt, have been foretold and avoided. Stupid tears welled from her eyes, and she flung her head back impatiently to stop them rolling down her cheeks. Squinting at her left hand, she watched as the thumb continued to bleed. Enough. It was impossible to concentrate anyway, knowing that Jane would be on her way home from the doctor's appointment. Knowing that Jane would have the results of her X-rays by now, would perhaps have had confirmed what Birdie herself still only feared.

Leaving the studio, Birdie crossed the garden and went into the small kitchen. She was there, washing potatoes, when Jane arrived home. The back door led straight into the kitchen, and facing west, the late sun framed Jane's silhouette in the doorway.

Coming into the kitchen, her face white and tired, she hugged Birdie close.

'Not like you to finish so early. Have you run out of pictures to frame?'

Birdie pulled free of her embrace and took Jane's hands. Jane reached forwards and stroked Birdie's face, feeling the contours of her cheekbones beneath her pellucid skin.

'You'd better sit down. It's bad news, I'm afraid.'

'Cancer?'

'Yes.'

Outside, a chatter of starlings wheeled noisily before emptying the sky. The world constricted and became silent. Only the rich golden sunlight hovered, angling awkwardly at the open doorway as if to offer hope where none could be taken.

There is such a void between the expectation and confirmation of fear. The space between the two occupies itself in a matter-of-fact way, with tests and investigations, knocking down the what-ifs and maybes tenanting the dark hallways of anxiety, turning intangible dread into the solid presence of fact. Birdie, knowing now that dark hours of brooding fear and anxiety had been, in fact, not imagination but reality, would, she realised, give anything to go back in time, when all she had to worry about was worry itself. If she hadn't insisted on the doctor, then Jane would not have to sit here, bouldered by such a word.

'Cancer. He's absolutely sure. I've probably had it for some time.'

Jane reached further into the darkness to draw out the words she had no choice but to share.

'It doesn't look like I'll make fifty. He says six months. A year if I'm lucky.'

Birdie felt physically winded, her lungs incapable of breathing in or letting go. Holding on to the kitchen sink to keep herself from falling, she gazed at Jane, not daring to cry. Tears would be a confirmation of grief, and grief without the possibility of reprieve was, suddenly, an impossibility for which she was not, could never be, prepared.

That night, holding Jane in the darkness, Birdie felt as if she were a stranger to herself, holding a stranger in her arms. It was as if every intricacy, every joy of their lives, every breath they had ever shared was nothing more than the reflection of an illusion. In the hiddenness of their life together, their imagined futures had always been threaded and layered in the stories they wove together, the fabric of their unassailable togetherness. Now, she felt an anguish so deep and dark that it seemed to erase not only their future, but their past and present. Inexplicably, Jane seemed to be fast asleep, and as she turned over, moving free of Birdie's arms, her dark hair caught under her shoulder. Releasing the long strands, Birdie gently pulled the cover over Jane's shoulder. For aeons, she felt, she lay still, void like an empty shell, waiting for the morning to explain how the world worked now.

It was only a few hours later when Jane, silent but wide awake, was startled by the sound of Birdie crying out.

'Oma, Oma. Wo bist du? Oma, Wo bist du ?

She shook Birdie gently.

'Wake up, wake up. It's a nightmare. It's ok. You're here now.'

Birdie sat bolt upright in bed, her heart pounding.

'It was my granny. I couldn't find her again. I was walking through the streets alone. I couldn't find her, but I knew she was there.'

The nightmare was always the same. Lost in the Dresden streets of her childhood home, Birdie's nightmares took her on an endless search for the grandmother she and her parents had left behind when they had fled to England two years before the war. In her dreams she was in a Dresden that no longer existed, for

Birdie had been just six when her parents had told her that they were leaving, moving to England to sidestep a war. Engrossed in arranging dance lessons for her dolls, she had been curious, not perturbed. “Will I go to the café for hot chocolate with Oma in England?” she’d wanted to know. Her parents must have reassured her, equivocated somehow, because Birdie had sat in the window of the new London flat, watched that first autumn thin out to winter, plump again into spring and summer and catch fire with autumn leaves again while she waited, waited to see her Oma trotting down the street.

When she was eight, and her grandmother had disappeared forever under the Armageddon of bombs that had destroyed her home city, her nightmares had started. Each time she woke, she had the feeling of having plummeted into some untenanted, echoing space behind her head. Birdie had tried to tell Jane what it felt like, explain her bitter sense of shame and the deep scars of guilt that were carved into her subconscious. She knew herself to be illogical, irrational, but had never shaken off her conviction that she ought to have known, could have saved her grandmother. Every time the nightmares came, Jane was calm, patient, knowing from experience that Birdie just needed time to journey back across the years.

It wasn't, she'd learnt, that Birdie didn't know where she was after she woke from her nightmares, but that the child within her was once again dislocated, set down in an unfamiliar place.

In the half-light, undecided between night and day, Jane and Birdie lay in each other's arms, as distant from each other as they had ever been.

Chapter 8

Mid-December, and Iris had arrived home at the end of her first term. She was in the kitchen with her parents, sharing all her news. Hope had retreated to their shared bedroom, having only briefly said hello to her sister. It wasn't that she didn't want to hear about York, but something inside of her kicked out. She felt fiercely defensive, bruised by the idea that anyone else, even her parents, should be witness to her ignorance of Iris's new life. It was unbearable to be so separate. She had always known exactly what Iris was thinking and feeling.

The bedroom was cold, and with a mixture of resentment and nostalgia Hope decided put on the fingerless mittens she and Iris had knitted together. The left one, Iris's, was perfect, red yarn looped in tidy rows, the pattern of stitch increases to the thumb gusset ordered, symmetric. In contrast, the glove on her right hand, the one that she had made, had lumps in it like floury woollen dumplings where she had created new stitches to replace those mysteriously lost in earlier rows. There was a sizeable hole in the thumb joint, through which Hope was twiddling the blunt end of her pencil, murmuring the words of a Thomas Wyatt poem for an essay she was writing for English.

'They flee from me, that sometime did me seek...
With naked foot stalking in my chamber
I have seen them, gentle, tame, and meek,
That now are wild, and do not remember
That sometime they put themselves in danger'

She was drawn to the plaintive loneliness of his voice, only to suddenly find herself on the outside again, wondering who 'they' were and whether the woman in the next stanza was one of 'them' or someone new. She pulled the counterpane around her shoulders and spoke the poem out loud, feeling its incantatory qualities. It was if Wyatt was trying to elicit sympathy through sound, but the words refused to settle, to describe some real situation. She read it again, trying a more prosaic tone in order to focus on the narrative, but this made the poem stumble and collapse. How on earth was she supposed to write an essay on poetic form with this?

Eventually, Hope heard Iris's step on the stairs to their attic room. Drawing her knees further under the counterpane, she picked up her pen and exercise book again, propping Wyatt on the pillow beside her. She stared blindly at the poems and at her notes in turn, adding a few words to her exercise book and underlining them firmly. She rubbed her nose and furrowed her forehead, flipping the pages of poetry forwards and backwards as she pretended not to wait for Iris to enter the room.

'Mum says dinner will be ready at seven.' Iris's words fell awkwardly, 'Return of the preferred daughter, so there's pudding as well.'

'Your suitcase is on the bed. I bought it up for you.'

'Yes, thanks. I would have brought it up, but Dad kept asking me questions.'

Iris noticed the red mittens, the memory of sitting together over them seemed like a piece of ancient history. Hope seemed distant, and Iris felt awkward, as if she and Hope were almost strangers. She cast about for a way to get her sister's attention. She folded her arms squarely in front of her, standing at the end of Hope's bed.

'"Now, young lady, I hope you're keeping up good study habits. Two hours every evening. That's the way to succeed." In other words – Iris, are you going to the pub every evening? Fat chance on a student grant.' She looked at Hope and was rewarded with a half-smile.

' "Tell me, have you joined any university societies yet? When I was in my first year, I joined the Debating Club and the Amateur Geologists Society. That's where

I met Duncan, and it was his father that found me my first job, you know."'

Hope smiled properly this time.

'Code for "Iris, for goodness' sake make some nice friends. Preferably people from the right kind of families."'

Hope kicked off the counterpane, and sat up, pointedly crossing her legs at the ankle with a display of mock modesty.

'"Well, young lady, I hope you have a good supply of nylons. Nylons and a good wool skirt will make a good impression. You need to look smart to show that you are worth taking seriously as a Law student." That means, dear sister, I hope you aren't wearing those dreadful bell bottoms like the shop girls do, they really aren't seemly.'

Iris giggled.

'Dad wouldn't talk about my tights. Too, too immodest. Mind you, if he did, I bet he'd call them nylons.'

'You know, we're finally going to see Auntie Jane next week.'

‘Yes, I know. She wrote to me about three weeks ago. She’ll be here for Christmas. It’ll be fab to see her.’

Iris jumped to her feet.

‘Tell you what, let’s see if she’ll come ice-skating again. She was so funny last Christmas.

‘I don’t think it’s that easy,’ Hope hesitated, ‘you know she seems to keep getting ill. Hasn’t Mum told you?’

‘No, she hasn’t. I knew she had the flu, but that was epochs ago. What’s up with her now?’

Hope looked at Iris. The way her question was held in the set of her mouth, the angle of her head. Iris had absolute confidence that Jane was, or would be, fine, back to the aunt they knew, energetic, alert and opinionated as ever.

Hope thought, and then said, ‘I think she’s got donttellitis’.

‘Dondelitis? What’s that? Are you having me on?’

‘No, listen. I’m being serious. ‘*Don’t – tell – itis’*. You know, like when there’s something mum and dad don’t approve of, or don’t want to believe, and they always clam up, and that’s it. Hey presto, the problem goes away. I bet Mum didn't mention me in her letter to you, did she?'

'I don't get it. What is wrong with Auntie Jane?'

'That's the trouble. Nobody will say anything.' Hope waved her hand dismissively. 'Oh God, Iris, just ignore me. It's probably nothing. I did miss you, even if you are the preferred daughter.'

It was as if Iris had the power to stop time passing, thought Hope. Something about her made change impossible, she was so neat, ordered, steady. And yet, she felt, it was as if Iris had returned after a long odyssey. Was it because of the changes in her own life? So much seemed to have shifted since Iris had left. Hope, alone, had started to feel the need for a whole new way of being, something different to make sense of life. She wasn't, anymore, the person that Iris thought she was looking at. The thought made her feel uncomfortable. And yet there were ways in which she envied her sister's sense of belonging in the world, the way in which she tackled the business of arranging her future with such composed certainty.

'So, what's the new news in Bath then?'

There was no real curiosity in Iris's voice. She assumed that the world at home had simply paused while she was absent and expected Hope to be the same. Hope didn't know what to say.

Iris glanced at Hope, sitting cross-legged on her bed. She was still wearing the red gloves and a pullover that had gone at the elbows. She had that semi-mutinous expression she'd had whenever she was told off as a kid, Iris thought. She looked again. There were shadows under Hope's eyes.

'Come on. Tell me. What did you mean just then?'

'What?'

'You said you bet Mum didn't mention you when she wrote to me. Have you been in trouble at school or something?'

'You are joking, aren't you? I work hard. You know, sometimes I wonder what would happen if I didn't. Dad would go nuclear.' Hope shifted uncomfortably, 'Well, if you must know, it's Mum. It's like. I dunno. Since you've been gone. Honestly Iris, you'd think we were living in the 1950's. She keeps getting at me. Why don't I use my allowance to buy some nice clothes. Have I thought about getting some nice cosmetics. She even said the other day that I should get a perm, you know.'

'And that's it? Honestly Hope,' Iris appraised her little sister, 'you really are going to have to grow up one day, you know.'

'Give me a chance, Iris. I'm not a kid. But I just might want to be myself, you know. She just won't leave me alone. It's as if there's only one way to grow up, and that's the way she did it. Come to that, it would be nice if I was allowed to express my own opinion from time to time. Have you ever noticed how boring it is here? I mean, really boring.'

'Oh, come on, you sound like you're about seven. What do you want? I mean, really. What is it that is so wrong with your life?'

Hope said nothing. She knew that whatever she said would seem sulky, ridiculous. But honestly, Iris had no idea.

'Well, at least they let me go out, I suppose. I go into town most Saturdays. Meet people who aren't from school.'

'Boys, you mean?'

Hope threw a pillow at Iris.

'Yeah, big sis. Boys,' Her mind flitted to Chris, whose easy charm and half-given promises unsettled her, 'but not like that.'

'Go on, where have you been meeting boys then?'

'Boy, Iris. Singular. And he's interested in music, that's all. He works in the music shop.'

'So, where do you meet him then?'

'God, Iris, I told you. Nothing like that. I talk to him in the shop, that's all.' Hope felt a flash of irritation. Iris had got it all wrong. 'He's lent me the new Grateful Dead album. I made him put it in the sleeve of Beethoven Symphony so I could smuggle it into the house. Not much point really though. I can't exactly put it on Dad's stereo, can I? And our Dansette's just useless for real music.'

Iris didn't respond, and Hope realised her sister had no idea who the Grateful Dead even were. She felt a flash of pity for Iris.

'Go on, tell me about York then, and don't tell me you've met a handsome well-connected geologist with a High Court Judge for a father. Don would never forgive you.'

'Don't be silly. You know,' the pale skin on Iris's neck flushed deep red, 'I know we agreed to be just friends, but I have really missed Don. We've been writing a lot.'

'No way. Didn't know dull Don could write letters.'

'Honestly, Hope. Can't you take anything seriously?'

Hope wanted to tease Iris about him but hesitated. Don had been around simply forever and was fair game as far as Hope was concerned, he was so boring. But Iris seemed on edge, almost defensive, and Hope didn't know what to say. She sat silently, looking at her chewed fingernails.

Iris was silent too. She wished she could tell Hope about York, how differently she felt about herself now she was a university student, making her own decisions. She gazed around the bedroom they'd shared all their lives. Their two beds had identical dark blue blankets and brushed cotton sheets for the winter. Each of them had a chest of drawers and a shelf. They shared the heavy dark oak wardrobe in one corner of the room. She liked how nothing had changed. Hope's half of the room was still untidy, the pile of books still heaped on the floor beside her bed were probably the same ones, that had been there in September, thought Iris, and of course none of Hope's drawers were shut properly. Her own side of the room was depleted of course, but there were still some school books on her little shelf, and a folder she didn't recognise. She jumped up.

'Hope. What's this heap of paper doing on my shelf?'

'It's not a heap. Give it here.'

Pulling the paper down from the high shelf, Iris saw that she was holding a pile of sketches. All of them of portraits.

'Hey, Did you draw these?'

'Yes, of course I did. Give them here, nosey.'

'But Hope, these are really good. Isn't this Paul McCartney?'

'If you must know, I've been practising portraits. Now give them here.'

Iris's attention was caught by the sketch of a teenage boy with shoulder-length blond hair. He stared out from the paper with the eyes of a hawk, seeking, hungry.

‘Who’s this then?’

‘No-one. Give them here, Iris.’

‘It says ‘Chris’ in the corner. Who is Chris, Hope? You have to tell me. Right now.’

‘If you must know, he’s the boy who works in the record shop.’ Hope was fidgety, ‘It’s not easy finding people who will sit still while you draw, you know. Give it here.’

‘He looks…’ Iris didn’t know what to say. She thought the boy in Hope’s sketch looked a bit rough somehow, but she didn’t dare say so. Mind you, she thought, that was the problem with a girls’ school. You didn’t get the chance to meet boys. Alright for her. Don was her best friend Ursula’s twin brother, and their families had been friends forever. She felt sorry for Hope, always so hopeless when it came to meeting people. But if she challenged Hope about this boy, she would just dig her heels in. Iris had a better idea. She would help her meet some decent boys.

‘Tell you what, though.’

Iris sat down beside Hope and nudged her with her shoulder.

‘Ursula and Don are having a party for New Year.’

‘So, what, they always have a party. I used to come, remember. Ursula and Don have to wear their best clothes and serve canapes. Their dad always tells the same stories every year and Mummy always pretends she’s hearing them for the first time.’

‘No, silly. This is a real party. Mr & Mrs Fellowes are going out for the evening. It’s a sort of reunion for all of us, now we’re away at uni. There’ll be lots of boys from Kingswood, and all the girls from my class. Why don’t we ask Mummy if you can come too?’

‘Really?’ Hope was open-mouthed. ‘Would you really? That would be fab. Are Mr & Mrs Fellowes really going out. Wow. That sounds really cool.’

Iris was unpacking her case now, carefully putting her clothes away, arranging her things exactly as they had been before she went to university.

‘That’s ok. I’m sure Mummy will say yes, it isn’t as if you’re really a kid anymore.’ Iris paused, a neatly folded blouse in her hands.

‘Mummy told me you’ve joined an Art Appreciation Society in town. How did you convince her to let you go?’

‘I make sure I get A’s in all my homework.’

Iris giggled.

'No, really.' Hope sighed, 'It's my only ticket out of here. And they can't keep me in if I'm always top of the class, can they?'

Hope flopped back on her bed, dangling her legs over the side and propping her chin up in one hand.

'What do you do then, visit galleries and art exhibitions?'

'Yeah, well, not exactly. I mean, we do talk about art, and every month someone shows a collection of their paintings. But it's probably not exactly what Mum and Dad think it is.'

'So, what is it really then?'

'It's just a group of people who want to use art to change the way people think. They're very anti-gallery. Anyway, Mum has agreed that I can go to Bristol with them in January. Someone's knows a guy who's going to put together an installation in his studio. All new stuff. Mum thinks it's at Bristol Museum.'

'Wow. Since when did you get to be so good at telling lies?'

Iris's voice was light and jokey, but only just.

‘Not fair.’ Hope’s eyes blazed, ‘I haven’t told a single lie.’

Iris raised an eyebrow.

‘Ok, ok, yeah, I may have left out some details. But you should see the stuff they produce, what they’re doing, I mean.’

Iris looked doubtful.

‘Hey, come on sis. I’m not a baby. And I’m not stupid either. Now shut up with the heavy stuff and I’ll do you a lovely portrait. You can give it to darling Don.’

Chapter 9

The kitchen window at Flag Cottage was set deep into the thick wall. Outside, the darkness was relieved only by a quiet yellow square of light from the small window they'd had put into the north side of the barn. Jane was still out there, and Birdie could just see the back of her shoulder where she was busy at her easel. Since the doctor had confirmed the cancer, she had been out there for hours every day, working simultaneously on three large canvasses. Her hands were cracked and dry from constant cleaning with turps, and the cuffs on all her clothes were permanently stained with daubs of paint. Birdie felt helpless, as if all she could do was worry about her. This surge of creativity was so frantic. Jane's summer exhibition had sold within weeks, and already she seemed to have enough new paintings to mount another. Collectors hovered, Birdie thought, like vultures waiting to devour everything she produced.

Fame had been a painful acquisition, and now Birdie resented its intrusion into their lives. Jane should be resting, they should be spending time together, pouring an eternity of love into whatever time they had left. In the kitchen that mid-December evening, Birdie had made an unwieldy pastry that crumbled awkwardly as she rolled it. She glanced out of the window again, willing Jane to return to the cottage. She couldn't see her shoulder now. Had something happened to her? Fear had acquired a whole new repertoire in Birdie's heart, and she watched every insignificant shift in their days as if it were an announcement of disaster. She wanted to rush out to the studio. Perhaps Jane was lying, collapsed on the stone floor, she imagined, knowing in the same breath that she was being ridiculous, knew how Jane would frown, the small crease between her eyes deepening if she saw, like a shadow, Birdie come hurtling across the internal landscapes of paint, texture and colour that filled her head.

Forcing herself to remain in the kitchen, Birdie filled a pan with cold water and set it on the stove for the carrots. Washing them under the cold tap, her gaze flickered again and again to the studio window. There was no movement. If I don't see a movement after I've done these, I'll just pop out, Birdie told herself, cutting the vegetables into heavy chunks. She felt a spiral of anxiety in her stomach, and shook her head, as if to dislodge it. Maybe she should lay the table first and then check for movement again. Birdie ridiculed the talismanic superstition of her actions; how idiotic she was, bargaining her fear against these inconsequential tasks. Jane liked mustard with her meat pie, so she shook the mustard powder loose from the tin, grinding it into a liquid paste with the back of a teaspoon. She looked at her watch. The pie wouldn't be cooked for 30 minutes yet. She should leave Jane until dinner was ready. Really, there was nothing to worry about. She went to the back door, where she could see light from the far side of the barn spilling onto the vegetable patch, casting irregular shadows where the last of the winter veg still stood. Birdie decided she would just pop into the garden, lift a few leeks. They would go well with the carrots. Easy to dig in the dark, and she'd be able to see Jane in the studio as she passed.

Pulling her wellies on, Birdie slipped from the back door into the December evening. She had to cross a patch of shadow on the blind side of the barn. For a moment, blackness, tangible, almost animal in nature, lumbered around her; a hostile force between the two buildings. She had the sensation that the space between the house and the barn was somehow barred, stymied in darkness and as impenetrable as a medieval forest. Telling herself to be practical, she stumbled forward, following the barn wall round to the window on the far side. Jane was standing immobile beside her easel, her back towards the cold glass. Relieved and guilty, Birdie quickly lifted two fat leeks and stood for a long moment under the dark sky.

Stillness, like silence, has many qualities. Birdie might have been a deer, sensing the air for danger, there was something transient about her form, even when motionless. Above the land, where deep cloud shrouded the night, the stillness of the sky had a muffled quality, as if it were a heavy quilt subduing, at least for a while, their restive world. And to the south, pellucid above the Atlantic Ocean, a sempiternal presence held the stars while they formed and shone and then burnt out. Holding the leeks loosely at her side, Birdie stood a moment longer, feeling the night-time air breathe into her, filling her lungs with whisps of antiquity.

Over dinner, Jane was exuberant, she talked enthusiastically, vibrating with colour. She devoured the meal, all the time waving her fork in the air to demonstrate the paint she had been using, how it lay on the canvas like warm butter, resonating with energy and meaning.

'These leeks are divine. From the garden?'

Not waiting for a response, Jane took another hungry mouthful, suddenly intent on the way her taste buds responded to the stimuli of her meal. She felt as if she had never before tasted with such intensity, the sensation of flavour was almost overwhelming. Impetuously, Jane reached across the table, grasping Birdie's hand.

'Come and have a look, will you, after dinner? I need to see the painting through your eyes.'

'Of course.'

Birdie's response sounded tight, as if pulled unwillingly from her. But Jane needed Birdie to share her mood of giddy joy.

'And it's so beautiful tonight, outside. All the cloud was beginning to clear as I came in. A meadow of stars, as they say, you know. But there'll be good frost in the morning, I promise.'

How lucky she was, thought Jane, to have Birdie. How lucky they had both been, to find each other. Every day was a gift, and they should live exuberantly. There was such energy in her painting now. She couldn't wait to show her the thoughts she'd sketched out that evening.

With the remains of their meal on the table between them, Birdie watched Jane. She wished she knew how to share Jane's exhilaration. She adored the way that a painting, a tune, or some small sign of new life on a dull day unlocked such joy in Jane, propelled her into a mood of boundless energy. She thought, regretfully, of how they seemed to have lost their shared sense of the ridiculous. Since her cancer diagnosis, Jane had been acting as if nothing had changed, as if she didn't care that she might use her straitened allowance of life too intensely, too fast. Birdie felt that she alone was hampered by the burden of caution and care. If only Jane would slow down and rest more. She should conserve her energy. That way, she might delay the cancer. She turned to Jane.

'Are you definitely going to Bath next week?'

Jane's mood plummeted like a shot pheasant. That "definitely" hung in the air, full of judgement and prudence. "should you," it meant, "a sick woman, a dying woman, risk a journey of a hundred miles. Should you not stay indoors, avoid winter bugs as if your life depends on it?" Jane felt herself beaten down by the way Birdie seemed to see her, a fragile and vulnerable thing. Birdie's fearful caution that was diminishing them both, she thought, and the unceasing restless concern made Jane feel panicky, as if her anxious care would foreshorten their time together. It was different for Birdie. After all, thought Jane, hating herself as she thought it, Birdie would have time enough to come to terms with all this after she herself was dead. A tight clutch of grief gripped her heart. Was that the way it had to be? Did having a fatal illness have to mean that you were like a wild bird caged, even by those who loved you, even before the end?

'Jane?'

'Nothing's changed, my darling. I'll go down on Christmas Eve and stay for three nights. David and Elizabeth will be expecting me, you know.'

They fell silent. Jane was determined not to let her nieces down again. Her brother was a dear, of course, and she'd grown fond of Elizabeth. But the girls. They were glorious. As 'Auntie Jane' she possessed a kind of magic. How sad it was that the girls had never met Birdie. How sad now, that they never would. They'd have to grieve separately, too. For Birdie that would be so hard. If only things had been different, more honest.

'Oh, Birdie, How I wish you could have met Iris and Hope. Hope especially.'

Birdie flinched as if she'd been struck.

'Don't say that. Please Jane, don't.'

Jane realised what she'd said even as Birdie's eyes filled with tears.

'Darling. I didn't mean to say it like that. Honestly, I didn't. I mean I wish you could meet them. And I have been feeling so well. Who knows? Doctors make mistakes, happens all the time.'

Birdie nodded, her head buzzing as if she was about to faint and scrambling for an excuse as she bolted from the room.

'Cup of tea? I'll put that kettle on. I won't be a minute.'

Jane wondered again what had happened to them. This brittle distance appalled her. There were so many things she hesitated to say, for fear of misinterpretation. How could she tell Birdie she was happy? The day she had heard the doctor confirming his diagnosis, that day, she had felt she was driving home to die. She had lain awake that night, pretending sleep, and each gasp of air had felt mechanical, her lungs a bellow she had to monitor, or else they would stop. But so quickly that she could hardly believe it, the fear had fallen away, and she had been overwhelmed by a new way of being. A gentleness and oneness. She didn't clamour for time, or more world to experience, and neither did she feel cheated. Body and breath, she had started telling herself. Body and breath. Gifts to enjoy, not possessions to defend. Her sadness was… how could she describe it? It felt wholesome. She wished Birdie could relax too. There would always be more things to do than time to do them in. So what?

Her glance drifted to three samples of wallpaper that had been casually taped to the wall facing the window for several months. They had planned to redecorate and hadn't yet decided which paper to choose. On the shelf to the left, there was a broken cup, waiting for one of them to reattach the handle. It had been there several weeks. And yet. As it was, broken on the shelf, the cup looked just right. The patterns cascading across the wallpaper samples were a perfect medley whose soft colours were caught in timeless perfection. Looking at her hands, resting on the table, one with daubs of orange paint on the thumb, it was as if they were not just hers. They also belonged to a category of objects that existed even when she did not. She had been thinking about Dürer's intense search for the representation, not of a particular hand, but for the universal essence of flesh and fingers, the elemental potential of creativity. How could she tell Birdie that her cancer was a trivial thing? No more a calamity than dying in one's sleep at eighty or ninety.

She lifted herself from her chair and made her way to the kitchen. She wrapped her arms around Birdie. They should do something. Go out somewhere. A picnic, maybe. At the weekend. The weather was glorious, elemental and ragged with powerful grey skies. They'd go down to Sandy Cove. Have the place to themselves. There, they could talk.

Chapter 10

Iris closed the door to the bedroom. Hope had gone out and, finally, she had some time to herself. She'd been home for nearly two weeks, and there were two weeks more before the next term started. Two whole weeks. She wished she hadn't invited Hope to Ursula's party. What on earth had possessed her?

Iris had fetched a clean towel from the airing cupboard. She sat down and laid it across her knees. She unbuttoned the cuffs of her blouse and folded them up, turning the sleeves into neat bands until they were almost to her elbows. Sharing a room with Hope was like living in a jumble sale. Hope hadn't even made her bed properly. Her Candlewick bedcover was quite uneven. From where she sat, Iris could see right under the bed, which meant that the cover must be dragging on the floor on the other side.

Iris smoothed the towel over her lap and started to shape her nails with an emery board. It was difficult to do the nails on the right hand, and she stuck her tongue out between her teeth with the effort of concentration. Hope hadn't let her see the portrait she was doing yet. She'd made Iris sit for two hours and then tucked the sheet of paper away in the drawer of her bedside cabinet. Bossy, that was it. And so opinionated. Iris ran the tip of her thumb over the tops of her nails to make sure they were smooth. Carefully folding the towel in on itself, she took it to the bathroom and shook it into the sink.

Next, taking the lid from the glass jar of hand cream, cool, and comfortingly solid, Iris applied a thick layer of cream to each of her nails. She really needed some of that new cuticle cream, but this would have to do. With a blunt wooden stick, she pressed her cuticles firmly, pushing them as far down as she could until it hurt. Iris could see a heap of books under Hope's bed, plus what looked like a copy of Melody Maker. Best not let their parents find that. With the satisfied sense of a job well done, Iris scooped a small amount of pale, lightly scented cream onto the back of one hand, and turning the back of the other hand to face it and massaged her hands with a practised circular motion. She held her hands out in front of her, spreading her fingers, pleased with the result. She had nice fingers, she thought, twisting and turning both hands to see how they tapered elegantly. Should she put some pearl varnish on? Best to leave it. She'd do it tomorrow just before she changed. Her parents had bought her a pale pink cardigan for Christmas. It would be perfect over her blue dress. Goodness knows what Hope would wear. She didn't seem to care about making herself look good. As if it was beneath her, somehow.

Their shared bedroom looked out over the street. She could hear a bus grinding its way up the hill. Would Hope be on it? Iris went to look out of the window. Standing next to Hope's bed, she could just see the top of the bus going past the fence. The stop was a short distance further up the hill, but the bus didn't stop. Hope was probably in the record shop talking to that boy. Ghastly Chris, Iris called him to herself. Maybe it was a good thing she was taking Hope to the party. She glanced down at Hope's bedside cabinet. The drawer wasn't closed properly. Perhaps she could just have a quick peek at the picture, make sure Hope hadn't made her eyebrows look too bushy. They were her worst feature, she knew. Anyway, it wasn't as if she would be doing anything she shouldn't. It was her picture, after all.

Opening the drawer, Iris saw the large green satin diary that Auntie Jane had given Hope for Christmas, but the picture wasn't there. That diary had been a bad idea. Now, Hope scribbled away every night before they went to sleep. Iris had to lie in bed and pretend to read a book. If only Auntie Jane knew how secretive Hope could be. That was the word for her, Iris thought. She felt excluded from Hope's world, and how it hurt, being left alone, when she'd so looked forward to coming home, assuming that they would be just as they'd always been. Secretive. If no-one took her in hand with her soon, she'd start to believe she could get away with anything. Iris would talk to her parents herself, but what could say? Younger sisters always got things their own way.

Perhaps she should just have a quick look in Hope's diary. Make sure there was nothing too awful. She wouldn't read it all, just skim through. It was only because Hope had stopped confiding in her. She opened the drawer wider, shifting the diary so she could look inside without actually taking it out of the cabinet.

"Dear Diary" she read *"Did you know that VG was only 37 when he died? Can you imagine that. Packing a WHOLE LIFE into 37 years. But PP is still alive. He's nearly 90 now. Thing is, diary, I don't want to write about boring things... Got up, had a boiled egg and then did my household chores. Or, went to school and managed to get out of swimming because I have the curse this week. I mean, how DULL is that."*

Iris shifted awkwardly. She would get a crick in her neck, reading at this angle. She moved the diary a little, careful not to scuff it.

"So, I've decided, diary. I won't write things every day. I might need to change the dates at the top of your pages. If I write loads one day and then nothing the next, I mean. But you won't mind, will you? Be a free spirit, diary. VG didn't know he was going to die, well obviously he did at the end, but before that. But look at what he did. EVERY DAY must have been more interesting than a WHOLE YEAR of some people's lives. I've just got to get through my A levels, then I'll be free. In the meantime, I'm going to write about things that are INTERESTING and ALIVE. OK??"

Iris was baffled. She had no idea who or what Hope was writing about. She flicked forward and started reading the latest entry.

"Today isn't worth writing about. Spent the day doing boring stuff. I'm going into town tomorrow. Perhaps something interesting will happen. Not likely though. I wish Iris would come with me. But she won't. These days she doesn't seem to notice me at all..."

Iris shut the book, recoiling with shame and loss. What had she been thinking? She wished she could unread Hope's words. And yet, Iris thought, everything was changing. A new decade was coming; they would probably both be married and settled by the end of it. She sighed. Maybe going to the party together wasn't such a bad idea, after all. She would lend Hope her pink flowery blouse with the princess sleeves. It was really pretty, just putting it on made her feel girlish, and it had just a touch of sophistication. It would suit Hope, she decided. Iris caressed her cheek with the smooth tips of her nails. Imagine, she thought again, a new decade was about to begin. Anticipation fluttered in her heart.

Chapter 11

Iris and Hope had been at the party for over an hour, arriving earlier than anyone else. But now, the house was crowded and noisy. The sisters had been talking to each other, and when Iris darted off to join the queue for the bathroom, Hope was left standing alone in the kitchen, twirling a glass of Mateus Rose. It tasted awful, she thought, unused to wine. Around her, girls talked to each other with exaggerated gestures, one eye on their conversations, the other on the boys who passed through the medley of colourful dresses and perfume-laden chatter to refill their glasses and grab platefuls of snacks. Hope knew she looked odd, but she didn't care. She was relieved that she didn't look like these girls, wasn't wearing Iris's ghastly blouse. She took a nervous gulp of her wine, wondering what to do. In the living room, the volume on the stereo rose suddenly, and someone turned off the overhead light. Hope slipped through into the relative darkness, finding a spot away from the door, where she might be able to stand unobserved, without the burden of looking as if she had no-one to talk to.

Across the room, Don & Ursula's cousin, Joseph, was wishing he was back home in Manchester. He and his family had come for Christmas, and his aunt had said that it would be so nice for him to stay on for the party. It had meant borrowing a shirt and tie from his cousin, and he felt ridiculous. Around him, the party seemed to be full of clones – all the boys dressed in smart jackets, and the girls… even worse, despite all the different colours of their dresses they still all looked the same, anyway. As if being a human was based on what other people saw when they looked at you. It made him want to run away. He frowned at his feet, wondering why he just didn't walk right on out, go and breathe the night air. Would Don even notice? Just then, his attention was caught by a slight girl in a black skinny rib pullover and black bellbottom trousers. She had a circular pin badge pinned to her jumper, but he couldn't see it clearly. She looked like a tiny dark sprite, and she was balancing on one leg, frowning to herself.

Hope had found a spot by the stereo where she could pretend to be looking at the records. After a few minutes, she relaxed. Nobody was paying her any attention. She decided to stand on one leg, balancing her uplifted foot on the calf of her standing leg, just to see how long she could stand still without wobbling. Across the room, Joseph watched her curiously. Was she for real? After about ten minutes, she carefully lowered her foot to the ground, looking around her as if deciding what she might do next. Joseph thought she might leave, suddenly, disappear and never be seen by mortal folk again. If she was a sprite, then he needed to be quick. Hurriedly, he crossed the room until he was beside her. He had no idea what he was going to say.

'Um, excuse me for asking, but are you a ballerina?' he blurted, immediately regretting his words. Oh hell, he thought. What a stupid thing to say.

Hope could see he was talking to her but didn't hear his words above the music. She shook her head, leaning forward and cupping her ear in her hand. Thank God for that. Joseph thought, relieved.

'I'm Joseph.' JOSEPH, he mouthed, pointing at himself. 'I'm Don's cousin.'

Hope nodded at him, 'Joseph?' she repeated, queryingly.

'Yes,' he said, 'Don's cousin. I live in Manchester. Down here for the holidays.'

Hope looked intently at him trying to hear what he said. John's cousin, did he say? She didn't know John, but then she didn't know any of the boys here really.

'Hope' she offered, holding out her hand. 'I'm here with my sister. Did you say you came with your cousin? John?'

Joseph nodded emphatically.

His long fair hair reminded her of Chris, but his face was quite different. He's got eyes like Ringo's, she thought. Full of a sort of dreaminess, and a bit sad. He looked out of place amongst Don and his friends. Joseph looked at her. She was extraordinary, but he didn't know how, or why. What could he say to her? She was even more like a sprite, close up. He felt sure she was from another world, one where they had a million things to say to each other, if only they could start talking. The music was too loud, though. He rubbed the tip of his nose with his thumb, looking embarrassed and uncertain. Then he noticed the badge on her jumper, a small tin thing with a picture of Sweep, the puppet dog from the Sooty Show. As he recognised it, his expression transformed from abstracted embarrassment to gleeful exuberance. Bending his elbows and pressing his arms to his sides, Hope watched him as he lifted his hands to the side of his mouth as if they were paws and make a sound like a tiny trumpet. He mimicked Sweep to perfection, and as Hope started to laugh, he waved his hands and twisted his head and shoulders from side to side. Within seconds, she was copying him, both of them soon helpless with giggles.

***

In the relative calm of the dining room Iris sat, waiting for Don to return. It was quiet here, away from the stereo and the frantic noise of the kitchen. Don had been to fetch her another drink, and as he came back into the room, she felt her world was secure, and perfect. Ursula sometimes grumbled about her brother, said he was like a middle-aged man, but Iris loved him for his quiet determination. And he treated her like a flower. She could see a perfect future with him and quietly assumed they would become engaged once they both left university. As he sat down beside her at the table, she remembered that she hadn't seen Hope for some time.

'Perhaps I should go and look for her. I promised Mum…'

'Don't worry,' Don assured her, 'Ursula saw Hope a few minutes ago. She's talking to Joseph.'

Iris inclined her neck, waiting for more detail.

'Joseph. He's our cousin. He's alright. Well, a bit of an idiot, actually. But sound enough. I like him. He's never hit it off with Ursula, though.'

‘Where are they? In the kitchen?’

‘No, apparently, they’ve been sitting on the front doorstep. He’s probably telling her how to communicate with the spirit world. He’s a bit odd like that.’ Don held his hand over hers, ‘Look, why don’t you just stop worrying about your sister for once. I’m sure she will find all his nonsense right up her street.’

Iris was persuaded. The party was perfect. Don was perfect. Her life was going to be perfect, too. She couldn’t wait for the 1970’s to arrive.

Not yet a single tangible event, the party was beginning to shape itself into different objects for each person there, becoming more concrete for each as the evening went on; an assimilation of impressions and feelings that could, in future days and weeks, be shared, chewed over: The party would become a thing, an event that could be defined. But as the evening shaped itself around them, the futures to which this party would lead were still tenuous, uncertain.

Outside, sitting with her back against the front door, Hope felt the warmth of Joseph’s arm where he leant against her. He was drawing numbers in the gravel drive with his foot.

'Only two hours more,' he said, 'and we'll have known each other in two decades.'

'Feels like longer.' she answered, 'No, shorter. Actually, both together.' It was impossible to know.

'I'm not sure about time, anyway,' Joseph went on, 'Even Einstein says it's an illusion.'

'So, what's real then?' Her voice came from the stars, she thought. Or maybe from deep in her belly.

'Well,' he spoke slowly, 'I think we have this amazing ability to tune into another plane. Like we have this spiritual sixth sense. Maybe that's what real is, the things we can't get at with our five senses.'

'Like God?'

'I was thinking of love. Divine love, I mean. Not Marvin Gaye songs. You know, in the universe.'

Hope was silent for a moment, her heart on fire with new sensations. Only in books and music had she heard ideas like this, and somehow words and songs didn't count. Here was a complete stranger, talking about reality and illusion as if he had lived a thousand years already. Hope felt the blunt force of revelation waking her as if from a dream. Joseph's words made it possible for her to know, absolutely, that her entire existence was a fragment, a joyful fragment of a universal oneness that danced, free of time and space. She held her chin in her hands, leaning forward, wanting him to say more.

'It's more than that,' she gestured at the darkness beyond the houses, 'The universe is all divine energy. Being a human, or a star, or a tree, that's the illusion, the temporary thing. We aren't special or different from everything else. Being clever is just another illusion. Trees and rocks and all the rest of it…' she paused, unable to find words to hold her feeling, Well, that's what real is, it's that everything is just manifestations of cosmic energy.'

Hope waited, slightly anxious, for Joseph to reply. Perhaps he would he think she was crazy, after all.

In thc distance, St Stephen's chimed ten times.

'Imagine being a bell,' Joseph said, 'Feeling all that sound shuddering through you.'

'And it's the 1970's in Russia already.' said Hope, her heart leaping.

Half an hour later, back in the warmth of the party, Hope sat on the staircase, waiting for Joseph to return with a drink. She was still shivering slightly from the sharp cold air they had just left. Closing her eyes, she hugged her knees lightly to her chest, feeling the insubstantiality of her body and wondering if this was what it was like, falling in love. She'd had no idea. Her thoughts were sunlight and stardust. She encircled the night sky, held the slow motion of stars and the unfolding of a leaf in spring. She was a fragment of the cosmos, the silences shimmering beneath a Sonata in G Minor. Love had punctured time. She was a tree, a breeze, a new, impossible thing.

Hope decided not to wait. She would go and find Joseph. Maybe they could dance together. Passing the living room, she saw the figure of a young man with shoulder length blond hair bent over the stereo. Uncertain in the patched and tattered light, Hope made her way over to him. But as he turned towards her, she found she was looking at Chris.

'Wow. A beautiful coincidence. Hey babe.' He smiled.

As if for the first time, she felt, Hope looked at Chris, really looked at him. And it seemed to her, suddenly, that his poise, his careful attentiveness, the way he talked were all somehow falsehoods, things he did to help him take what he wanted from the world. Chris in the record shop was at ease, assured. Here, he seemed almost predatory. She felt his eyes on her and backed away. Muttering about a friend, she fled towards the kitchen.

'No sweat, babe, I'll find you later.' His words clung to her retreating back.

***

In the kitchen, a smiling boy was holding a tray of chocolate brownies. Hope took two, suddenly starving. She didn't want to stay in the crowded house; she wanted to be held amongst the stars again. Joseph would find her, wherever she was. Almost unnoticed, she slipped outside.

By a quarter to twelve, the party had changed. A general air of anticipation filled the house. Even the music seemed to be poised, waiting and watching the minute hand heave its way up towards twelve.

'Iris? Has anyone seen Iris?'

Sarah, usually a calm and easy-going girl, appeared at the kitchen door looking agitated and flushed. She saw Ursula by the sink and fought her way through a press of people, all clutching cans, bottles and glasses, talking more loudly than ever.

'Ursula. Where's Iris? She needs to come now. It's Hope.'

Sarah's face was white and pinched and her eyes were scanning the room feverishly. She grabbed hold of Ursula's arm.

'Where is she? She really needs to come and get Hope.'

Ursula realised that the conversation around them was thinning out in response to Sarah's insistent agitation.

'Sarah. Calm down. What's the problem? Iris is here. I mean, she's just gone to the loo, but she's here. What's the matter with Hope?'

Sarah shook her head mutely. She looks as if she's about to cry, Ursula realised, suddenly completely sober. At that moment, Iris reappeared in the doorway. Deftly, firmly, Ursula put her arm around Sarah and led her out.

'We need your help.' she muttered to Iris.

In the hallway, Sarah, unable to speak coherently, pulled Ursula and Iris towards the stairs.

'What's going on, Sarah?' asked Iris. Sarah shook her head, her eyes fixed on the floor.

‘Dunno. It’s something to do with Hope,’ responded Ursula, ‘Sarah thinks there’s something wrong.’

Sarah put her hand on Iris’s arm, gripping tightly.

‘She’s upstairs. In the bedroom with all the coats. I went to get my camera. I wanted to take some photos at midnight.’ Her voice was choked.

Iris shook Sarah’s hand away and dashed up the stairs. At first, she could scarcely see her sister for the pile of coats that were spread-eagled on the bed. Then she saw her long hair, cascading around her sleeping face like a disarranged chestnut halo. Hope was breathing deeply, if slowly. The coats around and over her concealed her form. She looked so young, a child still, in the soft line of her jaw where she lay, her head on one side. For a moment she looked as if she had fallen asleep in the middle of a game of dressing up, wearing her mum’s cast-off clothes and a swirl of silk scarves from Aunty Jane. Iris crouched over her sister’s face, stroking her cheek to get her to wake up. Hope pulled her face away from the tickle of Iris’s fingers and mumbled in her sleep. Her voice was low and compliant, her words indecipherable.

‘Oh god, Hope. What have you done? You promised me you wouldn’t drink anything. Dad’ll be mad with me. Wake up, Hope, hey sis, wake up, won’t you?’

‘It’s worse.’ Sarah spoke in a low voice, ‘There was a boy in here. He ran out when I opened the door.’

Sarah gestured at the heaped coats and jackets. Pulling them to one side, Iris saw that her sister’s clothes were half pulled off, her trousers down to her knees.

‘I covered her up,’ Sarah was really weeping now, ‘but I didn’t know what to do. Is she drunk? Shall we call an ambulance?’

As if she were dressing a doll, Iris leant over her sister and fastened her clothes, gently pulling up her trousers. Hope seemed to be conscious, but somehow absent, and her eyes were closed. Iris sat heavily on the bed next to her sister.

‘This isn’t alcohol.’ Ursula surprised Iris with her firm assertion, ‘I don’t think we need an ambulance, but she needs air, fresh air and perhaps a glass of water. Will you get some, Sarah, but for god’s sake don’t tell anyone what’s going on.’

‘As if.’ muttered Sarah, turning towards the door.

'And if there are any of those brownies left, bring them up here. All of them.'

Sarah nodded, relieved to have something to do. She was back almost instantly, clutching a glass of water and the tray of brownies.

''What do you want me to do with these?'

'Nothing, thanks. Who was the boy, Sarah?' Ursula's voice was harsh, demanding.

'I don't know.' said Sarah, 'Medium height, longish hair, almost down to his shoulders. Fair haired, I'd say.'

'Blond hair?'

'Yeah, I guess so. I'm sorry, I just didn't take him in. Hope…' Sarah's voice broke again.

With appalled certainty, Ursula looked at Iris. Iris held her gaze for a moment and then nodded.

'Look, Sarah', she said, 'You've done everything you can. I'm okay to look after my sister now, though, if Ursula will just stay with us for a while.'

'Yes,' Ursula added, 'I know you won't say anything about this, will you. You're not that sort. I'll sit with Iris and Hope for a while; you go back to your friends. You know my brother, don't you?' she added.

'I think so.' said Sarah. 'He's your boyfriend, isn't he, Iris?'

'Well look, if for any reason he wants to know where we are, then just say you haven't seen us. He doesn't need to know anything about this. It's just girls' stuff. Okay?'

'Ok,' said Sarah, her voice full of doubt. She looked at Iris and Ursula, who stood like implacable sentries, determined to close her out. 'Right. Don't worry. I really won't say anything.'

Ursula shut the door behind Sarah. Alone with Iris and Hope, she floundered briefly.

'OK, brownies first.' She picked one up and delicately sniffed at it.

'I thought so, these are hash brownies. Someone thinks they're being clever. I saw Hope stuffing her face with these earlier. She was sitting on the stairs waiting for…'

'Waiting for Joseph, your cousin with the shoulder-length blond hair.' interrupted Iris.

‘Oh Iris.’ Ursula’s voice cracked.

‘I can’t believe Hope would be so stupid. I know she had a couple of drinks, but marijuana. She’s mad.’

‘Do you think she didn’t know? After all, she’s a bit of an innocent, isn’t she?’

‘God knows.’

Iris was frightened. Hope looked alright, just sunk in a deep sleep. But she couldn’t rouse her.

Ursula spoke slowly.

‘There is another boy here with the same kind of hair, you know. He looks like Joseph from the back. He’s one of Jake’s friends. Jake said he offered to bring lots of records for the party, so he invited him to the party. Could have been him, do you think?’

‘Ursula, your cousin has been with Hope all evening. We both know that. God, even Don saw them together.’

Ursula’s shoulders sagged.

‘You’re right. God, what a mess. What are we going to do?’

The two girls stared at each other in silence, Hope lay unmoving on the bed, her dark hair strewn across her face.

Iris spoke, slow and determined.

'This… whatever it is. It never happened, right. Nothing. Hope won't remember anything. Look at the state of her.' Iris's voice sounded calm.

'You need to tell your cousin that Hope is… oh, I don't know. Tell him you don't know her. Or that she's only fifteen or something. Anything so that he doesn't try and see her again. I'll stay here with Hope. We can,' she paused, 'we can manage this. Make it all go away.'

Ursula was silent for a moment. The shrill of panic in her head started to recede. Iris was right, she thought. She could deal with Joseph, she'd talk to him first thing tomorrow, before he had the chance to say anything to Don. Those brownies could go straight in the dustbin. She'd do that now. She looked at Hope's form, empty as a shadow. The girl did look as if she was just asleep. She'd probably wake up, none the wiser. Even if she did remember, she could never be certain, not with her being so out of it.

Ursula put her hand on Iris's arm.

‘I won’t say anything. And I can deal with Joseph. He won’t be calling for Hope, trust me.’

Shivering with the release of tension, Iris nodded silently and watched as Ursula left the room. A few minutes later, she heard the muted sounds of cheers, followed by Auld Lang Syne. Outside, there were church bells ringing in the New Year. Her eyes swam with bitter disappointment. She should be with Don.

‘Happy New Nothing, Hope.’ she muttered.

Chapter 12

January 5th. I never thought I'd be glad to see Iris go back. Feels really ... I don't know – sad, maybe - saying that. She seems different, somehow. Or maybe it's me. Little sister stuff. I used to look up to her and all that? Sounds a bit predictable, doesn't it. Anyway, she's gone. She had a go at me about the party, said I ruined it for her. Well, I didn't mean to. How can it be my fault that someone drugged me with cake. I mean. It does make sense now. I was sensible about the booze, but everything did go really weird after those brownies. I know I fell asleep, but I can't remember why I was upstairs in the first place.

Look, diary, important stuff. I know I keep you hidden, but you must swear to secrecy about Joseph. I've met my soulmate. He is funny, and clever and wise. And quite good-looking, in a sort of poetic way. Which is good, because he's nuts about poetry. There's this quote by William Blake. He wrote it down on a piece of paper for me.

He who binds to himself a joy
Does the winged life destroy
He who kisses the joy as it flies
Lives in eternity's sunrise.

So amazing! It's like the feeling I got when I listen to, oh, I don't know. Maybe that guitarist in Fleetwood Mac? Anyway, there was something about him. Joseph. I just like writing his name. Joseph, Joseph. It's like the way we looked at each other was like two old souls meeting. Or two parts of an old soul that had got separated and just met again for the first time in hundreds of years. That's the best way to say it. Even though it sounds crazy. He's into mythology and was telling me about the time when people used to see fairies. In fact, apparently there are these photos of actual fairies that were taken by two girls a long time ago. The girls are old women now, but they still talk about it. I guess it does make sense, but at the same time it was a weird conversation to have with a boy. It made me like him more, though. He's studying the same A levels as me, and he's going to do English at uni. He kept going on about Blake. He says Blake has this idea about how we can't see into infinity because we imprison ourselves. Something like that. So that's why we can't see fairies.

That was after I'd eaten the brownies and everything already started to feel really intense, like Joseph's words were actually dancing in the air, making shapes. I don't know. At some point my eyes went really weird. Like the party was a kaleidoscope. The lights were jumping about, and Joseph's face. The best way I can describe it is like looking at pebbles at the bottom of a clear river. Lots of ripples? Does that even make sense.

Hope paused, flicking her hand to shake out the tension in her fingers. She hadn't been frightened, exactly. If she wrote about the feeling of time being bunched up, then bits missing, that would be scary. She'd been talking to Joseph. All good. Then she was arguing with Chris, but where had Joseph gone? She remembered feeling as if her body was transparent. No, not transparent, just that her body was part of everything else. That was a nice bit, wasn't it? Part of the universe? Everything seemed completely distant at one second, and then really intense. Had time passed?

Hope shook her head. She wanted to remember the experience. But even when she concentrated, nothing would go into sentences. She tried again.

The thing is, I really felt like I could see the real world, for the first time ever. I'm not sure about the fairies (sorry J!) but there was something. Like we're all sleep-walking most of the time. Like there was a really dull painting of some people. All greys and browns. And then you rub it off, and you can see this amazing portrait underneath. That's the real nature of the people. Like JL was saying on the TV when he was talking about him and Yoko? Universal love. That's the ***whole point****, isn't it???*

So, I guess I really felt love for Joseph, real love. Doesn't matter that we didn't know each other. He has beautiful eyes. I'm trying to be honest here, and I can remember I was talking to Joseph, and he was really listening. We started snogging. I remember that. It was so beautiful. But then time jumped, and I have these crazy images of Chris. Chris isn't hip. He just wants people to think he is. I have this horrible dream of him snogging me too. Stroking my body. Like he was trying to shag me. That's ridiculous. I don't even like him. Not like that. That bit must just be a nightmare. I had this sensation of jumping from reality to dreams and back again. I don't think I felt frightened, though it feels scary now, looking back. The thing is, Chris is irrelevant. He's just a lost boy. Meeting Joseph though. Well, EVERYTHING is different now.

Hope stopped writing, leaning back on her pillows. Supposing she had had sex, she wondered. What would it mean? It did happen to girls, she'd read somewhere, even if they didn't really want to do it. She shrugged the idea away. It didn't happen to real people like her, that was for sure. And anyway, she wanted to remember that sense of bliss. That was real.

She wrapped the diary in a piece of plain paper and pushed it underneath her mattress. Outside, darkness wrapped her street and made it seem detached from the world, its empty pavements punctuated only by the thin light of a few streetlamps. All the houses had the same character, Hope decided, huddled together, myopic and uninterested in the prospect of another new decade.

Flexing the fingers in her right hand, Hope thought how incredible it was that this small object of flesh and bone could create paintings and music. Iris wouldn't understand. Didn't know what painting was really like, the way it made everything stop. Painting made her feel as if her whole being was channelled through her hand and into her paints. There was something in that stillness that made her feel she'd dissolved, like she was in a state of oneness with every atom in the universe. She would do anything, she thought, to hold on to that sense of bliss. She wished she could tell Joseph.

Hope stood up and stretched. He would find her, she was certain. She would get a letter any day now. And then, if Iris was in a better mood when she came back from uni, she could always ask her to help. John's cousin.

He'd said he was in Bath with his cousin. Even though Iris had said she didn't know who he was, surely one of her friends must know. It was her boyfriend's party, after all.

Chapter 13

Two months later, on a cold February afternoon, Hope was held in the grip of lethargy. She stared out of the window, an open copy of Macbeth face down in front of her. The remnants of daylight had disappeared behind a solid barrier of rain. Sunday afternoon, and she had tons of homework to do. It had been impossible to talk to Iris. She pushed the book, her notebook and pen to the edge of the small desk that they had shared since Hope was 11, putting her elbows on the wooden surface and leaning her chin on her upturned hands. How did Blake used to sit, when he was sketching, Hope wondered and tilted her head, so it rested on her left hand only. She held her right arm out, as if embracing an imaginary sketchbook, the heel of her hand raised from the surface so that nothing could be smudged.

'Oh, what's the point.'

Hope shifted restlessly, raising both hands to her head. She'd tried asking Iris about Joseph, but Iris said he must have been a gate crasher. Claimed that even Don didn't know him. Hope was bored with herself, bored with her life. She picked up the copy of Macbeth and read through the list of names and dates on the flyleaf, each written in regulation blue school ink, first initial, last name and form. So, what are you doing now, J Forther, VI-B, 1960? Hope wondered. Probably married, she decided. Bet J Forther stopped thinking about Shakespeare years ago and is saving up for a washing machine.

Outside, the dull, damp February darkness had turned her window into a mirror. All Hope could see was her own reflection, and the rain-splattered image looked blurred, indistinct. She sighed and pulled her notebook towards her. With reluctance, she started writing her essay on Macbeth, which had to be completed before double English, the following afternoon.

It was still raining when she woke the following morning. She must have slept through her alarm, because her mum was at the bedroom door.

'Wake up, Hope. You're going to be late if you don't get a move on. Hope. Come on. Get up now, will you.'

Hope sat up abruptly, picked up her alarm clock and shook it.

'Do you want a boiled egg? There's just time, if you hurry down.'

Hope made a face.

‘Just toast.’

‘Look at the state of this room. Oh Hope, you haven’t even put your books in your bag.’ Elizabeth started across the room towards the desk. Hope swung her legs out of bed and stood in between her mum and the desk.

‘Don’t, Mum. You don’t know what I need.’

‘I don’t know what’s got into you, Hope. You’d better be downstairs in five minutes. Understood?’

The door closed. Hope stood in the middle of the room, caught between irritation and guilt. Sometimes, she felt like she was still a kid. Why did her mum have such a nothing life, anyway? What was the point? Her whole life was so boring, so predictable. Perhaps after university she would be free. A level study seemed to be designed to suck the joy out of existence. Maybe it would be different if she didn’t feel so exhausted all the time. All she wanted to do was sleep. But Monday morning was insistent, and she had to get up.

Murmuring, ‘Oh what’s the point?’ she clambered out of bed, scooped her English books into her bag, grabbed her uniform from the wardrobe and trailed down the stairs and into the kitchen, her satchel pulling on her shoulder.

'Hair, Hope!'

Hope ran her fingers through her hair, reached into her blazer pocket for her hairgrips, and then sat down for her breakfast. This term, and then just one more.

Chapter 14

Finally, after two last minute changes of date, Hope was going to Bristol with the friends she'd met at the Art Collective. Well, not friends, really, she told herself. But at least they were different. At home, Hope still referred to them as the Art Appreciation Society and had grown careless about whether or not she was deceiving her parents. Walking towards the bus station, she was relieved to see Clive and Toria were already there. Toria, tightly belted in a cream trench raincoat, was wearing sleek leather boots, a pink and yellow Liberty print scarf and gold-framed sunglasses, even though the day was grey. She was the tall, willowy sort, and Clive liked to describe her as having feline insouciance. Sometimes he seemed to adore her, other times he made vicious comments about her wealthy family background. As far as Hope could tell, Toria didn't care which he did.

'Hope, darling,' said Toria as if making an announcement, 'you've arrived.'

She offered Hope a fleeting kiss on the cheek, carried on wafts of expensive scent. Toria was probably ten years older than Hope but seemed genuinely fond of her. Hope warmed to her attention.

‘Cool coat, Toria.’ Hope said, ‘Hi Clive. I can’t believe we’re finally going at last.’

Clive looked at her, a flicker of hello in his eyes. He was a student at Bath University, Hope knew, studying something to do with engineering. She’d tried asking him about it once, before she had realised that Clive responded to any conversation about himself with a shoulder shrug and small jerk of his head that made his heavy brown fringe fall across his eyes.

‘You seen Kristian?’ he asked her, ‘the bus’ll leave soon.’

‘Uh, no.’ Hope glanced at her watch. They still had five minutes.

‘Bloody Kristian,’ drawled Toria, ‘I mean, is it a Norwegian thing, do you think? The man is always late.’

Toria always described Kristian, who had lived in the UK since he was 12, as a foreigner. It gave her the sense of having collected something interesting, unusual. She lifted both hands to her face and delicately adjusted her sunglasses.

‘Well, we can’t go without him this time,’ said Clive, ‘he’s the only one who knows where the exhibition is.’

They were going to see the work of three artists who shared a studio in an old warehouse, somewhere in Bedminster. One of the artists had been at art college with Kristian, but had dropped out, or been pushed out. Hope wasn't sure which.

'Isn't Spud one of our beautiful people today?' asked Toria.

'Could be.' Clive didn't care one way or the other.

Hope shoved her hands deep into the pockets of her coat. The day would be ruined if Spud was there. With her dark, unreadable eyes, Spud had a look that made Hope feel half-formed, childish, even though they were probably almost the same age. She had very straight dark hair, cut in a long bob with fringe that covered her eyebrows, under which her narrow face always wore a thin-lipped, sardonic expression.

Toria peered along the row of waiting busses as a couple of drivers emerged from their staffroom at the end of the concourse. One of these sauntered up to the Bristol bus, pressing the button to release the doors, and jumping in.

'Oh hell. He's going to leave.' Toria turned to Clive. 'Can't you tell him to wait?'

Clive shrugged.

'Tell him yourself.'

Toria bit her lower lip and said nothing. The three of them stood and watched as the bus reversed out of its bay and swung forward. A blast of diesel fumes filled the air. Hope's attention was caught by a figure hurrying towards them. It was Kristian.

'No way,' he said, 'why didn't you stop the bus?'

'That's not how busses work in this country,' said Toria, with an acid tone.

'So, we catch the next one. Let's do greasy spoon.' Kristian jerked his head towards the bus station café. 'Come on, people. What's time, anyway?'

Hope calculated how much later home she might be, having told her parents she would be back before dark. Oh well, if she had to, she could always call, say the bus had been delayed. She didn't want Toria to think she was a child.

The four of them sat at a red Formica table in the café. The café was uncared for and cold, the door constantly swinging open. All the tables were fixed to the floor, and the whole place echoed with a harsh, tinny sound. Chairs scraped with a loud screech back and forth on the linoleum floor, competing with the clatter behind the counter. Hope looked through the long window at the line of busses. They had an hour to wait. At least it didn't look like Spud was coming. She played with her Styrofoam cup of tea. It tasted foul. After what seemed like hours, they got up and made their way out to join the small huddle of people that were standing by the terminal for Bristol. Ten minutes later, a long queue had formed behind them. As their driver climbed into the bus and opened the doors, Spud materialised, as if out of nowhere. She fell in beside Kristian.

'Excuse me, love,' said a woman behind them, 'you can't just push in, you know. You should go to the back of the queue, you should.'

Spud sniggered to herself and whispered something to Kristian, who turned away, ignoring her. As the queue shuffled forward, the woman behind her complained loudly to those around her, but Spud took no notice.

Bristol was encumbered by heavy grey skies that wrapped the buildings in misery. Passers-by looked drab and grey, their coats as muted as the pavement slabs. In contrast, Toria looked like an exotic bird, escaped from captivity. Kristian led them towards Southmead, confidently at first, and then once they'd cross the river, with increasing hesitancy. Spud gave a caustic commentary as they trudged along until Kristian snapped at her.

'Cut it, Spud. I don't need to listen to your misery, right.'

Spud shrugged, looking as if she couldn't care less, but she didn't speak again for about half a mile.

'Yeah. Here we are.'

There was a note of relief in Kristian's voice as they turned into a down-at-heel street. There were a few houses, one boarded up, further down, there were three industrial buildings, all looked disused. He stopped at the second one and then turned.

'Oh, shit. Forgot to say. Brought us some Sunshine. Everybody in?'

Hope didn't immediately understand, then she saw Toria's mouth break into a wide grin beneath her dark glasses. Clive nodded, flicking his hair out of his eyes, which Hope saw were a dull blue, as pallid as his face. Standing there in the grimy street, Hope realised how little she knew about the people she was with. She was out of her depth and desperately wanted to find a way to avoid taking the acid. The others hustled closer. Even

Toria had a weird intensity to her as she hovered over Kristian, waiting impatiently while he eased a small plastic bag from inside the waistband of his jeans, glancing carefully down the empty street.

'I've got four, anyway.' he said. Hope was giddy with relief. It was obvious that all the others would want the tabs.

'Cool,' said Spud, 'one each.' she gave a brief, dismissive look at Hope, 'She's not the type, let's face it.'

Hope flamed with shame and anger. She turned away while Clive, Kristian, Spud and Toria huddled together, and then, awkward and bitterly furious, she hammered hard on the door of the warehouse.

Chapter 15

When Hope had handed in her Macbeth essay, she had felt a tinge of guilt mixed with a giddy sense of rebellion. Banquo, she had decided, was just as responsible as Macbeth for the violence because he too believed that the world was a battlefield, where success was measured by gaining wealth or power rather than being a good or bad character. At the end of her essay, she'd compared Macbeth and Macduff to LBJ and Richard Nixon.

Her English teacher, Mrs Salt, moved up and down the rows of desks as she spoke to the class. The pile of marked essays sat on her desk while the lesson passed slowly. As usual, the girls had to wait until the end of the lesson before Mrs Salt handed them their marked homework.

'Hope Greenwood.'

Hope rose from her seat.

'Hope, I want you to come and see me at the end of school today. Here's your essay.'

'Yes Miss.'

Hope took her notebook and flicked to the last page of writing. Mrs Salt hadn't marked it. No double ticks or question marks in the margins. No red underlining. Hope found it hard to concentrate for the rest of the day. What had she done? She knew that she hadn't exactly answered the essay question, but she'd written from the heart. She'd really meant everything she'd said. She was counting on getting an A in English.

At four-thirty Hope knocked on the door of the teachers' common room. Mrs Salt opened the door and directed Hope to the Head's office next door. The Head wasn't there, Hope was relieved to see.

'Sit down. Do you know why you are here, Hope?'

Hope lifted her head.

'Is it my essay, Miss?'

Mrs Salt looked at her speculatively, as if Hope were a battered library book, spine and pages coming adrift.

'Not entirely. Hope, I hope you agree that you've not been yourself for most of this term. I know the Lent term can be difficult, it's the end of winter, it's still cold and dark, and nobody feels very enthusiastic. There's something very lowering about February, isn't there?'

Mrs Salt tried to hold Hope's gaze, but she wouldn't meet her eye. Why had the girl become so withdrawn? She'd been such a high achiever in the Lower Sixth. Mrs Salt wondered if she might be ill. The parents hadn't said anything. She looked out of the window as she spoke.

'Hope, as I have told the class many times, it's your work and your attitude of mind in this last full term that will make all the difference to your A level results. Now. I want to see the old Hope back. You've got a good brain and you're a hard worker, aren't you. Let's give it a couple of weeks, and we'll see what you can do.'

'What about my essay, Miss?'

Mrs Salt frowned.

'You will have to rewrite your last essay. What you submitted was not at all suitable. I'll give you an extra week, but I expect to see a new essay addressing the topic on my desk by next Monday.'

Feeling aggrieved and inadequate, Hope's eyes filled with hot tears.

'Yes, Miss,' she muttered, holding her schoolbag tight to her body and turning to the door.

Mrs Salt looked at the girl's dark shadowed face. She had no sympathy for teenagers who moped like this, and when she spoke, the frustration in her voice was clear.

'Hope,' she said, 'I mean what I say, you have an excellent mind, and there is no reason you shouldn't do very well in your exams. If I'd marked that English essay, I would have had to give you a C minus. You just didn't pay enough attention to the play. Start again. Rewrite the essay, and I will disregard the one you've already submitted.'

Hope fled, gripping her schoolbag even tighter as if it could encompass the sense of injustice, the tears, the feelings of futility and the embarrassment that stormed her.

Friday 6th March

March 6th. Art was good today. We looked at skies in paintings by J.M.W. Turner and Constable. Mr T showed us the painting by Constable first. It's an oil painting showing the sky over Hampstead Heath. Although the sun is out of sight, the shadow of a cow in the middle ground shows where it must be, on the left. The clouds on this side are lighter, more whites as well as more layers of colour. On the right, Constable has a group of darker clouds, as if there might be a shower, but the ground is all quite bright, so it's not quite clear where the rain would fall. I could see how the darker clouds give structure to the painting, how they work with the dark area of trees at the back of the foreground. Ditto the light clouds on the left mirror the brightness of the water in a pond on the bottom right.

Mrs S was awful to me again in English before lunch. I was already in real trouble about my essay on Macbeth, and I've got to do it again. She's not going to say anything to my parents (so she says, anyway). I guess I'd better get on with it though. AND she's set another essay. Wish I didn't feel so tired. My curse is late. I know what that means. It means next month I'll have double the cramps and have a REALLY bad month. I walk down the street sometimes, looking at all the women. Odds are, every fifth one is in the middle of her period. Do we all have to feel like death, every month?

Me again. It's no good. I can't sleep. I wish I could find a way to talk to Joseph. I know he came from Manchester; he told me he was here for Christmas with his cousin and just stayed on for the party. But of course I don't know who his cousin is. And Iris was no help. I wonder if he tried to find me. Perhaps he's given up, but no. I can't think that.

Oh, P.S. Diary, I managed to borrow a book by William Blake from the library. He was a painter as well. I did not know that. I might try and read some of his poems in break tomorrow. Nothing else to do. Then, if I ever do see Joseph again. Well, you know.

And P.P.S. Aunty Jane is FINALLY coming to stay. I'm so looking forward to seeing her.

Chapter 16

Easter was only a week away, and Elizabeth was looking forward to having Iris home. She'd gone back to York so abruptly after the New Year, making excuses about university work, although Elizabeth had felt certain there was more to it. And then, she wasn't convinced Hope was doing as much work as she should. It would be good for Hope to spend time with her sister. The plan was for David to go and meet the train alone. Elizabeth would take Hope to do some shopping. Her clothes were looking rather scruffy. If she looked smarter it might help her grow up a bit, get back on track with her schoolwork. Heaven knew she needed to buckle down and get some work done.

Elizabeth hadn't told her husband, but she had made up her mind to go and see Hope's form tutor, Mrs Salt. There might be something she could suggest to encourage her daughter to start working properly again. She had made an appointment for the following Thursday. David was in the process of qualifying to be a magistrate and was out until late on Thursdays. Elizabeth had decided she wouldn't tell Hope either. It was just a bit of behind-the-scenes encouragement. A girl didn't need to know everything her parents did to help her get on in life. She had calculated that when she got to the school gates her daughter would be at the bus stop, waiting for her usual bus. Even so, she parked on a side street, hurrying to the main entrance with her head down.

That day though, Hope hadn't caught her usual bus but had decided to stay on late in the Art Room. A long low building behind the playing field, it was separate from the main school buildings and looked out across the lower field, beyond which was the school boundary. The Art Room itself was generally kept locked unless there was a class, but 6th form art A level students were allowed to go in when the room was not being used. It wasn't that Hope had a particular piece she was working on, but she knew that there she wouldn't be bothered by anyone. The main window of the Art Room faced west, and it was still light at five o'clock. The sun was too low to be seen and there were deep banks of clouds above the tree line, which thinned to a smear of grey closer by. Drawing clouds had proved to be much more difficult that Hope had imagined. One on its own was fine, she could draw a single cloud entirely to her own satisfaction. But what Hope wanted was to draw a cloudy sky, where the different heights, densities and positions of the clouds had a sense of energy, a dialogue with each other. In Constable's painting she'd been struck by the way his clouds created, collectively, something far more alive than the single item, cloud. She sat down at one of the long desks and picked up her pencil. After twenty minutes or so, she pushed her chair back and stood up. She couldn't work out how to reconcile the distances and intensities of the cloud patterns in front of her. Besides, the light would soon be gone.

Reluctant to leave the Art Room, Hope remained at the desk. Her long hair falling around her shoulders made her look as if she was deliberately cloaking herself. On an impulse she flicked off the overhead lights and sat in the gloom. There were lines of wire looping across the ceiling, on which were pegged various paintings, pieces of work in progress by fifth formers. Like snapshots of time, they were suspended at uneven intervals on the thin wire. Hope angled her chair so that she could see the line of pictures stretching across the room. The light was too poor to see the detail or even the way that colour had been applied. If today were a picture, she thought, it would be a smudged drawing. A nothing day. And here she was, sitting amongst the remnants of it. When had it started, this bunching up of time into short moments during which she felt her life had meaning, and the brutal, unforgiving weeks of ennui with nothing much about them? Was it to do with Joseph? Today was the March

12th and still she'd heard nothing. She used her thumb to count the number of weeks. Ten whole weeks. Actually, seventy-one days. Her conviction that he would contact her had faded to a dream.

In those weeks, she'd drawn his face over and over, and now couldn't tell which was the most like him. She'd folded and refolded her impressions of him like pages in a book, fingered and smoother so often that the originals were irretrievably altered. He'd talked enthusiastically about William Blake, but now she had her own experience of reading Blake which, instead of refreshing her memory of their conversation, had all but erased it. She held imagined dialogues with Joseph to try and make him stay real, but found instead that they had the opposite effect, crowding out her recollections of what they had actually said to each other. She remembered his smile as a movement only, the way he pulled his lips to one side. And most of all, she wanted to hold on to his intense idealism, the way every word he spoke seemed to pull on his inner thoughts. In truth, her real sadness was that through him, she had glimpsed and then lost sight of a part of her self. She wanted nothing more than to find him again, as if he alone allowed her to open up her vision of who she wanted to be.

The uneven labour of cars climbing the hill towards Lansdown seemed to grow louder as the colours of the late afternoon diminished. If Hope had been able to, she would have sat there until it was dark. But as the late afternoon closed in, the fear that boiled in her belly like a street fight was harder to ignore. She still hadn't had her period. Every time she tried to remember what had happened at the party, after Joseph had left her sitting on the stairs, all she could recall were a twisted heap of images. Chris's face, his intense gaze on her. The way the room had swooped and shuddered as the effect of the hash brownies overwhelmed her. Joseph's face, looking tender, or was it unhappy. If anything had happened to her though, Iris would have known. She remembered Iris and Ursula bringing her a glass of water. Iris would have said something. Hope's thoughts paced in stubborn circles, like prison guards, each circuit of conjecture and impossibility making the next more difficult to ignore. She jumped from her stool. She realised she was getting cold, besides which, the janitor would be making his rounds soon. He would want to lock the doors and switch off all the lights. She shuffled her cloud drawings into her satchel and headed back to the main school building, just in time to see her mother leaving by the side door.

Chapter 17

Jane should be on the train home by now, Birdie thought for the millionth time. She'd been to Bath to see her nieces, at long last. Birdie had been sitting alone in the kitchen, listening to the clock ticking. She was trying to read but not really concentrating. Every few minutes she glanced at the time. Jane's train didn't get in until three-thirty; she had hours before she needed to set off for the station, but still, she couldn't help herself tracking the clock, as if that would hurry the time along. She stood up restlessly, looking round the kitchen for something to do, anything really, that required her attention. The previous day, she'd scrubbed the flagstones and washed the windows, outside and in. She'd tidied the kitchen cupboards and repaired a broken mug that had been sitting for months on the windowsill. It was one of Jane's favourites and Birdie wanted to surprise her with it.

Outside, her garden was still sluggish under late frosts. The morning had been foggy, and an empty quietness still lingered outside, hovering between the still dormant trees and bare earth. Before Jane had left, Birdie had felt disorientated, leaning sideways as if the world was out of kilter. In the silence of the remote cottage, there was a sort of static stutter which came from her anxious thoughts, a constant alarm crackling like an insistent radio signal. She wished she had been more positive about Jane's trip. Too late to undo that. She took up the mended cup and examined it closely. It was just possible to see a hairline mark where she'd glued the broken pieces together. She set it down on the windowsill and looked at it from a distance of several feet. It looked perfect.

Perhaps she could make a start on the vegetables? It was still only twenty past twelve. If she made a casserole, then she could leave it simmering while she ran down to the station. Segmenting the heavy hours into tasks, Birdie wrapped herself in a large cook's apron. She cut and sliced the ingredients with deliberation, at one point running out to the garden to get kale. Because Jane wasn't there she shouted, 'thank you garden!' as loudly as she could, opening her lungs to the damp air as if to throw the planets out of orbit and change the course of the future with her yell.

That evening, tired, but glad to be home, Jane was silent. She knew Birdie wouldn't mind. David had been impossible to talk to. She'd wanted to tell him about the cancer, as she'd planned. But she just couldn't. She felt like a curio in his house, an antique oddity that could be described with a concise, uninformative summary. She was his clever little sister who lived alone in a ramshackle cottage and painted. If she'd told him about her illness, there would have been questions. He would have sliced her life into segments and offered solutions. David would want to talk practicalities. And that would have meant telling him about Birdie. Not Birdie, her gallery assistant and friend, but Birdie, the centre of her world and love of her life.

David had such narrow views. The whole "clever painter" thing he did when he introduced her to people. It was as if he needed to make jokes about her life, its whimsical implausibility. He wasn't interested in her art. In any art, in fact. She knew how surprised he would be if he knew how much her paintings fetched. And so, she left after a pleasant stay. All very civilised. Hope had seemed subdued, which worried her, although Elizabeth had reassured her that there was nothing wrong, just the pressure of exams. Should she have paid her niece a bit more attention? But what, after all, could she do, if there was a problem? She'd write to Hope, send her some sketches. See if she could get her to open up that way.

After their meal, Jane sat in front of their open fire, watching Birdie as she jumped up from time to time to poke the burning logs, or add new ones. The Troubles in Northern Ireland were on the evening news again. Callaghan was talking about his recent visit, and the presenter was providing an explanation of how the split in Sinn Fein was making things worse, not better. Jane was lost in thought and almost jumped when Birdie asked her a question.

'Shall I turn it off? It's all a bit depressing, isn't it.'

Jane nodded. Birdie stood up again and went to switch off the set. She stood there watching as the picture shrank unevenly to a small bead of light and vanished. Jane had a closed, thoughtful expression. Birdie thought she recognised it. It was the look she often wore when she was putting together ideas and colours in her mind for a new canvas.

'We could sit in the studio if you like. I've left my book there. I don't mind the cold if you don't.'

Jane shook her head. There were things she and Birdie needed to talk about. She didn't want to put it off any longer.

'No, darling, it's not that. Actually, it's something else. I don't know where to start though. I want us to talk about my brother and my nieces. My head is just spinning with everything that's happened over the last few days. It's as if. Oh, I don't know, this cancer makes everything so strange. Do you think you can bear it if I just talk?'

Birdie moved to sit on the arm of Jane's chair, but Jane shook her away.

'No, darling. I'm absolutely fine. Sit somewhere where we can see each other properly.'

'How about the hearthrug?' Birdie stretched out on the rug in front of the fire, pulling a couple of cushions under her arms so that she could prop her head up.

'There, I'm all yours.'

'And you get to hog the fire.'

They smiled at each other. Familiar banter, arguing over who was closest to the fire in their cold cottage. Birdie always claimed she felt the cold more intensely, and this time, it made Jane smile. There was something so precious about their mundane, everyday lives. Boring lives, Hope might say, if only she knew. She pulled her legs into the armchair and wrapped her arms around her knees.

'This is me, doing Hope.'

Jane hugged her knees tight and hunched her shoulders. Birdie bent her head sideways in question.

'It's how she sits now. Withdrawn. You wouldn't believe the change in her. If I'm well this summer, I'd love her to visit us. I think she'd be fine. With us, I mean. But that's not what I want to talk about. Well, not exactly.'

Jane paused, nervous of Birdie's response to what she wanted to say.

'It's ok, darling. I've been thinking too. I understand how awful I've been.'

'I wouldn't call it awful, exactly.'

Jane managed a half-smile. Birdie shook her head.

'No, I think I have been awful. To you, I mean. Dashing out of the room every time you wanted to talk. I'm sorry.' Birdie paused, 'Not just awful to you, either. I've pretty much hated myself. Anyway, what I'm saying is… you really don't have to keep worrying about my reaction to everything. We can always talk things out, can't we?'

Jane took a deep breath.

'The thing is, Birdie. We don't have wills, either of us. And the way things are, that doesn't make any sense. I want to make a will, and I think you should too.'

Birdie lifted her head to speak.

'No, don't stop me now. Let me say it all. When I was with David and Elizabeth, I felt terrible. I couldn't tell them about the cancer because, well, if I had told them about that, but still kept secret the most important parts of my life. Us. You. All we have done together over the years. Well, I'd have felt like a fraud. I'd have been a fraud.'

Jane thought about her conversations with David. He took it for granted that everyone lived like him, or would do, if they could. He fretted about property values, the impact of rising taxes and how long the Labour government would stay in power.

'The thing is, Birdie, you can walk up and down his street and see the same comfortable, unthinking lives being lived in every house. Hope said something similar to me, and she's right.'

'Okay. But this isn't what's on your mind, is it? That's not all you want to say, that your brother has a shallow life and deep pockets?'

Jane grimaced.

'Sorry. No. The thing is... Well, you know what my paintings sell for. I own this house. Even the framing business is in my name. I have a ridiculously large bank balance. When I make my will, I'm going to leave everything to you.'

Birdie was startled.

'Jane, you can't. That's never going…'

'Don't say anything yet. I haven't finished.'

Jane could feel her breath coming in shallow bursts. She knew what she was about to say was right, but she felt more scared than ever in her life before.

'I can see all sorts of problems. Obviously, I won't be around to insist, and it's not fair to put you in such a horrible position. My brother can be…'

Jane trailed off. She couldn't see David understanding or accepting her decision. When had he ever? Who knows what she would say. She shook herself. For heaven's sake, why couldn't she just speak up. Was it so hard to tell Birdie what she now knew she had to do.

'So. Here's what I know. What I need to do. I think I have to tell David and Elizabeth the truth about you and me. It's the only way they'll understand why I'm leaving you everything. And accept it, with luck. If I don't say something, it would be… well, I just can't bear to think of leaving you without having sorted David out first.'

The air was silent with pain.

Chapter 18

One day, Hope promised herself, she'd tell her mum exactly what was wrong with her and her square ideas about life. Just because Iris was studying law didn't mean that Hope intended to copy her. Hope wished she could tell her mum about the trip to Bristol, that would show her there was nothing to worry about. That so-called exhibition had turned out to be one graffiti-ed wall, and Hope had ended up baby-sitting the others while they were off their heads, trying to keep them out of trouble. They'd walked down the river to a park, where Toria had laughed for about three hours without stopping, and Spud had tried to climb a tree. Without her to look after them, they'd have been arrested for sure, or run over. And then there was Chris. She'd avoided him ever since the party, which meant she'd not been to the record shop for months. Her mum had no idea. The only things she knew were what she and her boring friends read in The Daily Telegraph. God.

She looked at her watch. Her parents were out. They'd both gone to meet Iris's train in Bristol and wouldn't be back until nearly six o'clock. The promised shopping trip had been cancelled, of course. Small mercies. She had a pile of revision on her small desk, and she'd worked late the previous evening. Levels weren't exactly challenging, but she hated her art work. Everything was wrong. It wasn't just that she couldn't draw a cloudy sky, nothing she drew made any sense. Her portraits looked like people, okay, but they didn't look like people that ever felt anything. And landscapes. Dull. Even the colours somehow sat separately. Like obedient children in a row of desks, but not connected. None of her stuff was any good. She pushed her chair back abruptly. It was ages since she'd been into town. Why shouldn't she? She didn't owe anyone anything. And anyway, she hadn't specifically promised that she'd stay at home and revise all day.

Milsom Street was expansive in the spring sunshine, and Hope felt lighter, more optimistic just by being in town again. She walked down towards Pulteney Bridge, her open coat swinging as she marched along. She didn't even care if she saw Chris. If he thought that she'd visit the shop especially to see him, that was his mistake. Who cared what he thought. Even if he was still working there. She'd go in and flip through the records. Maybe even listen to something. Pushing the door open, she saw him straight away behind the counter. She didn't even bother to look away, so she was looking directly at him when he noticed her, and for a moment, caught her eyes. The next second, it was as if he'd been caught in an enemy searchlight. He simply stopped talking to his customer and bolted from behind the counter.

Hope stared at the empty space he'd left, oddly exultant, and at the same time almost doubting that seeing her had caused him to run like that. His expression though. That was startling, it was imprinted on her mind so clearly that if she closed her eyes, she could see every detail. Turning, she almost ran out of the shop. Quickly, she found a bench and pulled out her sketchpad and pencils, shutting her eyes every couple of minutes to where the image of his expression bounced off the back of her eyes. When she'd finished, she started to breathe again. She held the sketchpad away from her for a few seconds before turning it to look at what she had drawn. There it was. The look of horror and guilt on his face. As clear as anything. This was what she wanted her drawings to do. Never mind that it was only Chris. She looked away from the picture, staring into the river which flowed strongly from Pultney Bridge. A litter of broken branches had been caught in the weir and the silvered water hurried over them, intent on its progress. After a moment or two she looked back at her sketchbook. She wanted to catch the portrait by surprise, to see it again as it were for the first time, to see if the knotted pencil lines had more to say. Something intangible in the pencil strokes held together an odd collocation of being and flight, the moment of Chris's shocked expression and his abrupt retreat. She felt extraordinary.

There was nothing to stay in town for. All the everyday complications of life, all her exhaustion and defensiveness had dissolved, and simply being was effortless, sublime. Gazing about her, the edges of her field of vision seemed broader, and sound interleaved itself with sight, creating a kind of harmony, a transcendent melody of all her senses.

The sound of the bus rattling her home was less like noise than pure motion, ecstatic and full of energy. Hope saw that everything, the bus, the people, the street outside, was flickering joyously, dancing in a vibrant array colour and light.

Letting herself in and walking into the house she had left just two hours earlier, Hope no longer cared about the argument with her parents, could barely believe she'd wasted so much energy on such trivial anger. It felt like someone else's history. She felt invincible, possessing and possessed by a transcendent reality, as if her body, her sense of self and her thoughts were unfettered, freed from time and place. This must be how enlightenment feels, she thought, closing her eyes. The knowledge of flight of a soaring eagle, or the rolling waters of a sun-filled stream.

Hours later, Hope was surprised when she heard her parents downstairs. She felt as if only a few minutes had passed. So, they were back, with Iris. Unfolding her legs from beneath her, she danced down the stairs, gloriously alive with her newly found love for the universe and everything in it.

'Hey, Mum. You're back so soon. See you've brought the student home with you.'

Elizabeth looked sharply at Hope. She had a look of gleeful speculation, the teasing expression that she'd always had when she was cooking up some new mischief with her sister. Elizabeth relaxed, cautiously. Perhaps Hope had simply been missing Iris, she certainly looked delighted to see her. Thank Heavens for that. Hope grinned at everyone.

'Suppose you'd all like a cup of tea?'

Elizabeth watched Hope as she swirled around the kitchen, asking questions about the journey to Bristol, teasing Iris about student life, all the time dancing around like a seven-year-old. Perhaps that was all there was to it. Hope simply missed Iris. Elizabeth's heart contracted.

Hope marvelled at herself. Was it this simple? She felt like she'd discovered something extraordinary, this chatter, this ease. Her parents, she saw, were just figures. Made of plasticine, even. All she had to do was bring joyful colours, and they would love her. Should she tell them about the drawing? No, her mum would want to know who she'd drawn. And Iris might recognise him. Had she even seen him though? Hadn't he been just a fleeting presence passing her and Joseph at that party, so briefly that they hadn't even turned. Maybe she'd show the picture to Iris, later. Hope's smile was like the falling shards of light in a kaleidoscope. Everything would be fine.

After supper, they all sat together in the living room. A small table lamp shone dimly in a corner of the room, the light from which fell on Elizabeth's hands, where they were lightly folded in her lap, and on the side of Hope's head, seeming to shimmer down her loose hair. David was a mere shadowy presence, undefined. Iris lay on the sofa, her feet resting on Hope's right leg. Because the lamp was behind her, it cast distorting shadows running from her hairline to her chin. Her eyes pooled into defensive darkness, in contrast to the openness of her brow and cheeks. She was looking at Hope, but the way the light fell unevenly on her face concealed her expression.

As the evening drifted by, Hope began to feel tired and petulant. Her great gift, her generous abundance of joy, was being neglected, misunderstood. They were still watching her, she thought, catching her mother's glance, hovering in the background as if she was watching a fractious child. Suddenly Hope realised she had been fooling herself. Her parents didn't know who she really was, and neither did Iris. They were looking at a version of Hope that no longer existed. A wave of fury went through Hope, she hated her family, their smug beliefs that they already knew everything there was to know about her. Hope's dark eyes were hooded now, she was bored of pretending and angry that her charade had worked so easily.

Chapter 19

The following morning, Iris was awake first. All the previous evening she had been cradling a secret, and waking up, she felt so alive, so tremulous. It was a novel experience for her, and she felt she might almost burst. She, Iris Greenwood, was going to be married. The Hilary term at Oxford had finished five days earlier than her term in York, and Don had arranged to visit her in York before they both travelled south. He'd arrived on Thursday, and for the last one hundred and sixteen hours they had been engaged. Just the word, engaged, made Iris feel that she was a real person, more tangible in the world. She turned over in her bed, watching Hope sleep, and hugging herself in secret delight. She and Don had agreed not to tell their parents just yet. But Iris had to tell someone, she'd insisted. Don hadn't been keen on the idea of letting Hope in on the secret, and she'd had to persuade him. He didn't know Hope like she did, she'd argued, pushing away her memories of New Year's Eve. All that, she'd now decided, had just been a ghastly mistake. Hope had been too young to go to the party, too immature to keep herself safe. Besides, nothing serious could have happened, the boy was Ursula and Don's cousin, after all. The pact of silence she and Ursula had agreed meant that she couldn't, wouldn't raise the subject with Hope either. But now, needing Hope as a confidant, Iris had decided to put all that out of her mind for good.

Watching her sister sleep, Iris tried to think of the best way to wake her and share her amazing news. Should she make it a guessing game? No, that wouldn't do. Hope would guess all kinds of wild and improbable things. Maybe she should say "Don has asked me to marry him" or "I'm engaged to be married". No, and again no. Iris's heart was beating loud and fast, it seemed impossible that Hope slept on. She felt under her pillow, where she'd hidden the small blue velvet box containing a delicate gold ring with a single diamond. She pulled it under the bed covers, turning on her side to look at the reality of the ring again. She took it from the box, kissing it gently, and slipped it snugly onto her third finger.

'Hey, rabbit, are you lost in your burrow?'

Iris's heart thudded even more loudly. Hope was awake. Had she been watching her? She turned over, allowing just the top of her head to show above the counterpane. Could she just leave the ring on? Well, why not? She pushed the empty box back under her pillow, trying to prevent Hope from seeing the velvet box.

'What are you up to, sis? Have you got chocolate in there? Share!'

'No, stupid.'

She'd made a mistake. She couldn't tell Hope. Beneath the covers she pulled at the ring, trying to take it from her finger.

'Huh. My beautiful sister comes back from university, and she calls me stupid. Oh woe, oh unfrabjous day.'

Hope perched on her bed, adopting a ridiculous pose with her arms outstretched and her head twisted to one side.

'This is how the Mock Turtle looked, when it was called stupid. Oh woe, woe and double woe.'

Iris laughed. It would be alright. Hope was alright. She had so missed her so much.

'Well, listen, Mock Turtle, here's something to make you happy again.'

She sat up triumphantly and held out her left hand.

'Look! I'm engaged.'

Hope looked at her, eyes dark and sharp. She hunched up under the blankets, tucking her knees under her chin and clasping them with her arms.

‘Say something. Say something. I’m going to get married.’

‘Um. Who to?’

Iris withdrew her hand, the small ring sitting uncertainly on her third finger. She reassured it gently with the fingers of her right hand.

‘To Don, of course.’

The world was a house of cards, falling. Hope stared. Married? Iris must be making it up. Couldn’t be. Iris didn’t make jokes. Don had been around for years. But really? The whole of the rest of their lives together. How bored Iris would be. And what about her? It was impossible. But Iris was sitting on the edge of her bed, her face suffused with red, her eyes shining.

‘Do Mum and Dad know?’

‘Of course they don’t. You mustn’t say anything. Promise you won’t. Don’t breathe a word or else.’

Iris’s face changed shape as she spoke. Her broad, calm features were narrowing. Hope had never noticed before how mean and defensive her expression could be. Her eyes had no warmth, just flickered coolly in judgement over everything. Iris clearly didn’t care about her. She looked at the ring her sister was cradling.

Iris caught her gaze and flung it back, shaking her head defiantly. She resisted the urge to wrench it off and hide it again in the velvet box. Hope was going to have to deal with this. She needed to grow up. Realise that there were other people in the world.

'God, Hope. If you had half a brain, you'd know I wanted to marry Don one day. I've known since I was 15 that we'd spend our lives together.'

Hope leant forward, but Iris carried on. If Hope spoke now, she'd say something awful.

'Look, when I've got my degree, I want to settle down. I want a family, and I don't want to land myself with the problems that Mummy had.'

'What problems? What do you mean, problems? Mum is just fine.'

Iris rolled her eyes.

'Have you ever stopped to wonder about Mummy and Daddy? No, probably not. You just take them for granted. No, actually, you probably pity them for living such ordinary lives, don't you. Do you really know anything about what it was like before we were born?'

Hope creased her brow.

'Well, you know they got married when they were 23. They wanted kids, but then decided to wait, because of the war.'

'Yes,' Hope was still puzzled, 'but you weren't born until 1950. That's ages after the war finished.'

'Exactly.' Iris lifted her chin, 'I don't know about you, but I have very irregular periods. Like Mummy. She told me once that it took her five years to get pregnant. I don't intend for that to happen to me. I want to get married, and I want to have a normal family.'

Hope felt like she had been split into two. There were two of her, just happening to be in the same place. One of the Hopes was thinking about her parents. It was true, she'd never really wondered why they were so much older. Mum had never talked to her about having periods. One day, she'd given her a package of towels, told her that she would need them for the curse. She'd shown her how to hook the towel to a ghastly nylon belt, and that had been it. The second Hope was hot and grinning, flushed with relief that the fear she had been so resolutely ignoring for the last few weeks really was just a ridiculous nightmare. She knew she was alright. Nobody had shagged her. It had just been part of the whole weird hash brownie thing. She hadn't had her period because, well, it was obviously a family thing. Quite silly, really. She'd known she couldn't be pregnant. Really, she had. In fact, she felt very tender, down there. She wouldn't be surprised if her curse came tomorrow. Everyone knew being anxious could have an effect on a girl's monthlies. She started trembling with relief. In the same moment, Hope felt a rush of generosity towards Iris. She grinned broadly at her. Like a skylark, she could fly now, high above other people's notions of her. So, Iris wanted to marry Don. They'd have a dull life, of course. But Iris didn't care about being happy. All Iris wanted was to be like everyone else. She wanted a pretty birdcage with sprays of millet and a cute mirror. She looked at her sister. How typical of her to worry about what life would be like when she was fifty. As if today wasn't glorious enough. How she wanted her sister to see through her eyes, live in the moment. Be happy. Inside her head, a voice was yodelling 'I'm not pregnant. I'm not pregnant' over and over again. Iris, sitting opposite her, with her small hands and thin fingers, was no more than a doll. She grinned broadly at life.

Iris moved her left hand, hiding it in the folds of her eiderdown and she looked Hope cautiously. Even if Hope didn't like Don much, she must surely see what a good decision this was. Iris knew she was growing up and felt a little sad that Hope was still such a child. She watched as Hope twisted around, and jumped out of bed, letting the bedcovers fall on the carpet. What was she doing? Iris tensed. She wouldn't be able to bear it if Hope laughed. She saw she really had made a mistake. Hope was just a silly kid who jibed and laughed at everything. The eighteen months between them might as well be eighteen years.

'Aren't you going to say anything?'

'Well. Wow. Obviously. And congratulations. I think being in love is amazing. Wow.'

'Oh, you're impossible Hope, I don't know why you think it's so funny. I wish I hadn't told you. And if you dare breathe a word.'

Now what was wrong? Hope recoiled.

'God Iris. Can't you accept my congratulations. Just believe me for once. I mean it. I'm very pleased for you and Don. I hope you'll be very happy together.'

Hope wanted to run outside, feel the wide sky above her head and fill her body with early morning air. But Iris was still waiting. Did she really think she would be in trouble with Mum and Dad for agreeing to marry Don? Don, for goodness' sake. Hope's face tightened.

‘And no, of course I won’t tell Mum and Dad, if that’s what you’re thinking. There’s no need to make me out to be some horrible person.’

Just yesterday, Iris had really believed that Hope’s eyes would light up in genuine delight when she heard the news. How Hope would be excited for her. How could she have been so stupid? Her eyes started to prickle, but she didn’t want to be the one who cried. She was in the right; she had every reason to feel angry with Hope.

‘Well, that’s something then. I suppose that’s all I can expect from someone like you.’

Iris hated her sister.

‘Someone like me.’ Hope whipped round, ‘What does that even mean?’

In her pale cotton nighty, Hope leant over Iris’s bed. She was framed by a halo of light from the window, and furiously, she waved her arms at Iris.

‘Look at me. Do I look like a doll? Someone like me. Do you think I’m made from Identikit? Have I got a factory fitted personality or something? There’s just no talking to you.’

Hope span round, reaching for her dressing gown and wrapping it around her shoulders. Without looking back at Iris, she stormed out of the bedroom.

Chapter 20

Over the next few days, Hope made sure she was busy. Iris was mean and she didn't ever want to talk to her again. Avoiding conversation and spending as much time as possible alone, she pretended that she was busy revising. She always had a couple of text books and a sketch pad, which she carried around the house in a shoulder bag woven from thick wool with a plaited strap in the same dark brown and cream colours. Iris thought it an ugly thing. The weave was so loose that pencils sometimes protruded through the bag, so it wasn't even practical. In the evenings, Hope sat curled up in an armchair, the bag on her knee. She looked as if she was permanently on the point of leaving, thought Iris, wishing herself back in York.

When Friday arrived, Iris was relieved. She could get away from the house at last. She was meeting Don in their favourite café at twelve o'clock, he was buying her lunch. She couldn't wait to see him. She sometimes wished Don hadn't been so determined to go to Oxford, where his father had studied.

'Who knows what the future holds,' Don had said in the heavy tones that made him sound so grown up, 'we owe it to ourselves to get the best education we can. We'll still have the holidays, and we can write every week.'

At the time, Iris had agreed. He was probably right. She loved the way Don always knew the best thing to do. She spent the morning with her father and then caught the bus into town. As the bus creaked and squealed down the hill, she wondered what she should say to Don about the argument with Hope. She hoped he wouldn't hold her responsible for Hope's horrible behaviour. Perhaps it would be best just to say nothing, just say she'd told Hope, and leave it at that.

'Strangest thing,' said Don, after standing up and kissing her on the cheek when she entered the café, 'I bumped into your sister, heading towards Walcot Street. She seemed pleased to see me. I take it you've told her about our plans?'

'Hope?' Iris was surprised, guarded, 'Sorry I'm late. The bus. I didn't know Hope was in town today.'

Don was holding a chair back for her, and she sat down, feeling a rich satisfaction in being looked after.

'Yes, she said she was pleased for us. She can be quite sweet really, can't she? She even remembered what I'm studying and asked me about Oxford.'

Iris said nothing. Hope had now apparently convinced Don, as well as her parents, that she should be admired for working hard and praised for growing into a sweet young woman. It was too much. Iris was used to people describing Hope as 'the clever one', but she didn't mind that, it was true, and anyway, Iris knew that she was so much more reliable and good-natured than the hot-headed Hope. But now, everyone seemed to be fooled by her sister. Was Hope doing it on purpose?

After they'd eaten, Don walked Iris to her bus stop and waited with her. A couple of minutes before the bus was due, Hope appeared. She seemed excited and somehow pleased with herself. She greeted Iris and Don as if nothing was wrong.

'Hey, big sister and future Bill, twice in one day, eh, future Bill?'

Don looked puzzled. Hope smiled brightly at him.

'You don't mind, do you? You're going to be my brother-in-law, so I thought I'd call you Bill. You know B.I.L. - brother-in-law.'

Iris pretended to read a poster on the bus shelter, holding back while Don and Hope chatted lightly. Finally, the bus swung round into the bay at the back of the Abbey, and the two girls boarded. Hope looked solemnly at her sister.

'Look. I'm sorry Sis. Really. I wasn't laughing at you. Really, I promise. It's just like, engaged, wow. I can't imagine settling down, husband, babies. All that sort of thing. There's so much I want to do before all that. But hey, why not, if it makes you feel happy.'

Iris nodded reluctantly.

'Come on. I really mean it. Friends?'

'You know I'm only here until Sunday week, don't you?'

'Yeah. Like I said, I'm sorry. I don't want to fall out. Um, you know how it is. Time of the month and all that. I was just feeling crampy.'

They looked at each other in silence for a moment, and then Hope's serious expression melted into an affectionate grin.

'So go on then. Tell me all the details. Did he go down on one knee?'

Iris smiled, her pale blue eyes shining.

That week, the two girls spent hours together, revising, or talking and giggling about anything under the sun. Elizabeth watched them. Huddled together, their long dark hair made them look almost identical, although Iris was slightly taller and tended to move with an air of restraint, while Hope appeared to be in constant motion, never speaking without a lindy hop exuberance of gesticulations. Relieved that her daughters were getting on so well again, Elizabeth hovered in the background, looking for opportunities to keep them close. She wanted to do something to show them how happy they made her, these two lovely girls becoming young women. Before Iris left, she said, they should go to the hairdresser.

'Look at you both. You need a trim, the pair of you. I'll make you an appointment for Saturday.'

'Don't forget my Art Appreciation Group is on Saturday afternoon.' said Hope.

'No matter, I'll make the appointment for late morning, you can have lunch in Sally Lunn's. My treat. Then you will have the afternoon for your Art Group. How's that? In fact, why you could take Iris with you. I'm sure she'd enjoy meeting the group.'

Hope looked down, not wanting to provoke questions by saying Iris couldn't go.

‘Oh, thank you, Mummy,’ Iris said, ‘I do want a cut, but do you think I could spend a bit more money this time, have my hair cut and styled? I feel like a schoolgirl with this long straight hair.’

She ran her fingers through her hair, which like Hope’s, hung in loose tresses over her shoulders.

‘That would be so cool, Mum. Let’s do it, oh please say yes.’ Hope looked enthusiastic.

A flicker of sadness ran through Elizabeth, even as she smiled at her girls and nodded.

‘Good idea,’ she agreed, ‘I’ll book you both for a restyle.’

‘I don’t suppose you’d like me to come with you?’ she added.

A look flew between Iris and Hope.

‘No, I didn’t imagine you would.’

Elizabeth disappeared into the hallway to call the salon.

Chapter 21

The following Saturday, on their way to the hairdresser, the two girls cut through Abbey Churchyard. They could hear a girl's voice singing over the sound of a guitar, and as they got closer Hope recognised the song. It was Donovan's *Hurdy-Gurdy Man*. The singer's voice was compelling; she wove the tune into the air as if creating a magical illusion. Hope wanted to listen properly and moved towards the busker. But when she saw that the girl with the guitar was Spud, she grabbed Iris's arm and steered her behind the benches, away from Spud's line of sight. Iris let herself be led away, but once they were round the corner, she shook herself free of Hope's grasp.

Later, in Sally Lunn's, Iris dabbed carefully at her mouth with the damask serviette. Her lips felt greasy with butter.

'That girl had a nerve, I think.'

'Um. What girl?'

'The one who was busking, earlier. You must have seen her.'

'Er, no. Not really.'

Hope looked down at her plate, alarmed. Clearly Iris had seen Spud. Damn. Nobody could say the two girls looked alike now. Iris had asked the salon to cut her hair in a feathered bob, and the stylist had curled the ends of her hair under. It looked like a roll of carpet, thought Hope. What would they think of Iris at the Art Collective, looking like that? Even worse, what would Iris say if she recognised Spud. Hope bent forward, her new heavy fringe falling forward as she circled the plate with her finger, picking up crumbs.

'Hope.' Iris was sharp, embarrassed, 'Honestly. You can't be that hungry.'

'So, what do you want to do this afternoon?'

Hope ran her finger around the plate again and looked up at her sister.

'I thought we were going to your Art Group.' said Iris.

'Well, yeah, but. I mean, do you really want to?'

Iris ran the palm of her land over her new sleek haircut.

'I don't understand.'

Hope tucked her foot onto the edge of her chair. It was so awkward, seeing Spud like that. The way she sang had sent shivers down her spine. Her voice was just so amazing, like the sensation of watching water glistening in sunlight. Real, that was the word for it. Hope looked around the small upstairs room of the café, god, look at them all, all fooled into paying extra for a currant bun with a bit of history on the side. She pushed her chair back, dramatically.

'Oh, God, Iris. What are we even doing here?'

Iris smiled, wary of Hope's edginess, but not wanting to start an argument.

'Well, I'm thinking about having another Sally Lunn. I don't know about you.'

Hope's eyes had darkened; she shook her head impatiently.

'No, I mean really. Look at us. Two girls from a nice school eating fancy buns.' She was silent for a moment, 'I mean, do you ever stop and think about school?'

'In what way?'

'Well, for a start, it's crammed with girls who come from families just like ours.'

‘Actually, most of them are much better off than us.’ interjected Iris.

‘That’s not my point. It’s like we’re being brainwashed. There are people out there doing amazing things. They don’t see the point in A Levels, careers, and all that.’ she paused, ‘I mean, look at John Lennon. He didn’t do A Levels.’

Iris started to object, but Hope interrupted her.

‘OK, bad choice. What about Van Gogh, or Shakespeare?’

‘What is your point, exactly. I think we’re very lucky.

‘It’s like being in a fishbowl.’ Hope sighed, ‘How is school going to help me find out what I want to do with my life. I don’t want to study Law, or History, or read literature written by people who have been dead for hundreds of years. But those are the choices I’ve got. Because we live in a fishbowl. We’ve all agreed that it’s a nice fishbowl, and it’s full of nice people, and all the nice people go to university and buy houses and... and stuff.’

Hope just managed to stop herself before saying “get married and settle down’”.

‘But honestly? What if that makes you feel dead inside? Half the time, I just feel like I’m pretending.’

‘Oh, don’t be so dramatic, Hope. You act like there’s something wrong with going to university. It’s a jolly sight better than just being a secretary. Or a nurse.’

‘That girl with the guitar…’ Hope started.

Iris interrupted.

‘Exactly. Look at her sitting on the pavement, quite filthy. Asking people for money because she’s playing the guitar. Where’s she heading, do you think?’

Iris ran her fingers over the contours of her hair. The salon had sprayed the curls to keep them in place. She should buy a hairspray for herself, she thought. Perhaps when she returned to York... That girl, though. The fact that she had been busking, the way her eyes had darted from face to face as strangers passed by, the heavy men’s jacket she wore, worn at the cuffs. Clearly one of life’s failures. Her skin, Iris thought, had been unnaturally pale, adding poverty and the likelihood of a broken home to her description. In her mind, the things she could see by looking at the girl so surely predicated the things she imagined she knew, that no room was left for doubt.

‘I thought you said you hardly noticed her. She’s just the sort of girl that will get into trouble, if she isn’t already. Did you see the state of her shoes?’

‘You can’t mean that? Did you actually listen to her, Iris. Come on, you must have heard. She has a fabulous voice. Better than Donovan, that’s for sure.’

Iris shrugged.

‘I’m right though. She looked like a drug addict to me.’

Mute resentment flamed through Hope, together with the uncomfortable realisation that Iris might have a point.

‘Well, for your information, that girl is in the Art Group. She’s called Spud. I know her. I didn’t know she could sing like that, but her paintings are amazing.’

‘Oh, Hope. What are you doing with a person like her? Honestly. I despair sometimes.’ Iris picked up her serviette again, wiping imagined crumbs from her lips.

Hope took a deep breath, trying to steady the emotions boiling inside her.

‘You don’t have to come with me this afternoon. You wouldn’t enjoy it, anyway. Why don’t you just go home?’

‘Well, I can’t, can I. Mummy would start asking questions. Do you want me to tell her your so-called Art Group is full of drug addicts and criminals?’

‘Oh, for God’s sake, don’t. Please, Iris. Let’s not argue again. Honestly, I don’t think you should come. It’s just not your sort of thing.’

‘And it is yours? I suppose.’

Even the thought of trying to explain made Hope feel exhausted. In her heart, she knew she was right, and knew, too, the complete impossibility of getting her sister to understand. Iris was so opinionated, these days. But she wouldn’t give in. Iris and she were just growing up to be different. That was all there was to say. She softened her voice.

‘Well, yes,’ Hope said, ‘it sort of is. At least, it’s the best I’ve got at the moment. Come on, big sis. Tell you what, why don’t you go to the cinema. I’ll meet you at the bus station later. They’re still showing *Paint Your Wagon*, I think.’

Suspicious, and wishing she knew how to make Hope see things more clearly, Iris gave in. She nodded and watched as her sister left the café alone.

Chapter 22

Making her way back to the bus station from the Art Collective meeting in Walcot Street, Hope promised herself she would be nice to Iris. She should feel sorry for Iris, really. She would probably never understand how to be alive, not really alive. Iris only saw the surface of things. That was sad, wasn't it? Hope sat with her head almost pressed against the glass, listening to the sounds as the bus changed gear, climbing Bloomfield Road and grumbling its way past the Victorian houses whose honey cream stone had long been swathed by heavy black crusts of urban pollution. The houses looked sad, thought Hope, like a long line of mourners. She turned to Iris.

'Look at those houses. It's like they've got black lungs on the outside. And they're all the same. All with the same families living in them. All trying to lead the same lives. Ours is the same. Doesn't it make you feel sad?'

Iris shifted awkwardly on the hard leather seat. Surely Hope could let it drop, this constant carping about perfectly decent people.

'Don't be silly, Hope. What's wrong with being like everyone else? I like these houses.'

‘Oh Iris.’

Hope really was a pain in the neck, thought Iris. She’d done her a huge favour, sitting through a long boring film on her own. She was tired. The film had been utterly idiotic. No-one would throw away all that security and wealth just to ride off into the sunset. It was plain daft. And now Hope was being ridiculous. She sat upright, holding onto the back of the seat in front of her.

‘I mean it. One day you’ll realise how fortunate we are. Just because you’re younger than me doesn’t mean you can avoid taking responsibility for yourself you know.’

‘Good god, Iris. You sound like Dad.’

Iris said nothing but gripped the bus seat more firmly. Her lips were pressed together. She wouldn’t be provoked. She wouldn’t.

Hope could see Iris’s reflection in the grimy window. Her mouth was pursed and tight, like a school teacher, Hope thought. Well, she wasn’t going to let Iris ignore her all afternoon. She glared at her image in the glass. Iris still didn’t say anything. Hope wanted to poke her.

‘No, actually you sound like Don. That’s just the sort of thing he says.’

Iris turned to her and snapped back.

‘Well, Don thinks you are spoilt and irresponsible. He says you need to grow up.’

‘Oh, that’s rich. I suppose you and Don have cosy chats about how much better than me you are. How sensible you are. Planning your future. I can imagine the tales you tell him about me.’

Hope was impossible to talk to. All her friendly behaviour over the past couple of weeks had been just a sham. In reality, Iris thought, knowing she was right, Hope had no self-control at all. And without self-control, how would she ever grow up. She observed Hope’s flashing eyes with cool objectivity. She had, she felt, a duty to be blunt.

‘You’re being ridiculous. In fact, I do everything I can to protect you from other people’s opinions. You don’t know what I’ve had to do to stop people saying things about you.’

Hope turned away again to stare through the window. This was not enough. Iris needed Hope to understand. All these weeks, she’d not said anything about that awful party. She'd tried to suppress her feeling, tried to imagine that really, nothing had happened. She'd tried to cast doubt on what she'd seen, what she'd imagined. But Hope didn't care how much pain she caused. Iris couldn't bear it.

'I have, you know.'

Hope still refused to turn around.

'I won't even let Ursula and Sarah talk about you, and they know exactly what you are capable of. They were there, remember.'

Hope started drawing shapes on the window with her finger. It was like being with a toddler, Iris thought. The tension in her head was at breaking point.

'Maybe it's nothing to you, but none of my friends would go to bed with a boy like that. You didn't even know him.'

Hope spun round then, her eyes wild and furious in her face.

'Do what? What are you talking about.'

Iris drew her hands together on her lap. It wasn't fair that she had had to carry this secret for so many months. Hope needed to take some responsibility for herself. She hissed at Hope, thankful only that the bus was almost empty.

'We found you in that bedroom, your clothes half off you. I was so ashamed.'

'You're crazy. I passed out at that party because of those horrible brownies that your friends were handing out. I don't remember what happened, but I think I'd remember that.'

Hope fought bitterly, waves of fear and anxiety overwhelming her again. Life was impossible. Iris was a bare-faced liar. But she still hadn't had her period.

'Anyway, how do you think Mum and Dad would react if they knew you'd taken me to a party where there were drugs?'

Iris ached with the sheer wrongness of everything. If their parents found out, Iris knew she would be blamed.

The following morning, to Hope's relief, Iris announced that she would return to York that afternoon. She would take the coach. It was all arranged, she had some important reading to do, she said. Needed to be on campus so she could go to the library.

Following Iris's departure, Elizabeth realised that Hope seemed to have become uncommunicative again.

She busied herself in the kitchen, watching her daughter who was almost slumped at the kitchen table.

'So, she went back to York very suddenly, didn't she. I hope she's not working too hard. You'll miss her, I expect.'

The two girls had had such a wonderful time together, Elizabeth thought. It had been so good to see them laughing and talking. They had brought out the best in each other. Being alone with Hope made Elizabeth feel inadequate.

'How is your revision schedule going, darling?' I can help you go over it if you like. I've got plenty of time today. Your father is out all evening again.'

Hope sat hunched and silent. She had a book propped up in front of her, but it was only camouflage. Never in her life had she been so frightened.

'Hope, are you listening to me? I do wish you wouldn't read at the table.'

Elizabeth peered into the larder, knots of tension cramping in her shoulders. There was half a box of All Bran on the shelf. Iris's favourite, though no-one else in the family liked it much. It would go soft before Iris was back home again. She picked it up, indecisively.

‘I don’t imagine you’d like to help me finish of Iris’s All Bran?’ she smiled, ‘It would be a shame to let it go to waste.’

Hope glanced up. Her mother. A blue lambswool cardigan. Grey slacks. Slender gold chain glinting in the morning light. Same light, glancing off her mother’s wedding ring. The chain had a small cross on it, an anniversary present she and Iris had bought for their parents’ thirtieth wedding anniversary. The burnish on the gold reflected the light. Hope had tears in her eyes, and the gold cross appeared to have fingers of flame. It seemed more real than Elizabeth herself. Her mother’s features were blurred, the pastel colours of her clothes melting at the edges, seeping into the fabric of the kitchen, the magnolia walls and light oak cupboards. The gold ring sent out long beams of light, cutting diagonally across the room. Hope jerked her head sideways to dislodge her tears.

‘God, no,’ she muttered, ‘I don’t see why I should suffer just because Iris has such lousy taste.’

The fog of colours that was her mother vibrated.

‘Language, dear.’

Hope was unsteady.

‘What?’

‘Pardon, Hope.’

Hope imagined herself as a black canker. A patch of mottled damp under the window. The smell of something unseen, decomposing beneath the sink. She tried to make herself smaller. It concentrated her misery into an acute pain. At least pain was real. Better than the awful storms of doubt in her mind. Why wouldn’t her curse start? She was being ridiculous. It had only been a bad dream. Surely, she would have known. If that had happened. Had she known? She could remember talking to Joseph, looking at the stars together. She’d felt her whole being vibrate. More alive than she’d ever felt. Even though she had been, probably, a little bit drunk, when she was with Joseph the whole world had been so sharp and clear. Then… she remembered sitting on the stairs. Hope was exhausted. A thousand times she’d tried to piece together her memories. Hash brownies, unfamiliar alcohol, fog. Time had started to lurch, and the sounds of music and chatter had seemed to bunch up and crash like waves on a stony shore. Her body felt alone, as if her spirit had left it unguarded. She couldn’t remember when she was with Joseph, and whether Chris had been pawing at her. She hated herself.

'Darling?'

Her mum had clearly been saying something. Was she talking to her? Must be. The kettle started to scream on the hob. Elizabeth put down the box of All Bran and picked up a cloth.

'Sorry, Mum?'

'I was just saying. Look, Hope. Whatever it is, don't worry yourself so. You'll be fine. Just a few more weeks, and A levels will be over. You've always been so good at exams. I don't like to see you getting in such a stew. Cup of tea?'

A Levels? Hope barely even registered the idea that she would be taking exams in 9 weeks' time. Nine more weeks. She must have her period before then. She must. And her mum thought she needed a cup of tea. Hope stood up abruptly, the chair scraping on the floor.

'I'm going up to my room.'

Hope stood for a moment, vacant, before picking up her book. It hung in her hand with the pages splayed and spine bent back, as if it were a small, frightened animal.

'But your breakfast?'

'No thanks, Mum. Not hungry.'

Ellizabeth stared at the empty doorway, frowning to herself.

Chapter 23

Jane had woken with a headache. Most of it she'd chased away with her early morning walk, but she felt a sense of compressed sadness, a heaviness between her eyes that lingered. The previous evening, she and Birdie had talked themselves out. She knew she had to go to Bath while she still could. David must be told, and then she would be able to make her will. She knew Birdie was uncertain, that she didn't want Jane to fall out with her family. Besides, Jane thought, Birdie was still refusing to think about what would happen to her when Jane died, so she wasn't being practical. Jane grimaced on the word 'when'. In their conversation last night Birdie had continued to talk about what would happen if she died, if David was awkward, if any will was contested. In part, Jane envied Birdie's ability to cling to uncertainty, the way that she defended herself by refusing to confront reality. But the deeper part of Jane knew this pretence was a false luxury, one she feared Birdie would one day regret.

She would make David promise not to contest the will. Her brother had never been interested in her as a girl. Didn't trouble himself with who she was as an adult, either. He knew she shared a house with Birdie, but he'd never met her. All the things people don't tell each other. Was it really better to go through life in hiding than risk upsetting other people? Was it really acceptable to avoid the pain of honesty and divide one's life into small boxes? Irritated with herself, she flicked through the calendar on the wall by the front door. She'd suggest the Whitsun weekend, when Iris might be home as well.

Their letterbox clattered, making her jump. Amidst the sheaf of catalogues and official looking letters that thumped to the floor was a small white envelope.

She picked it up with the rest of the post and went into the studio. Birdie's head was bent low over her work, and she didn't look up. Jane gazed at her for a few seconds, and then, more quietly, turned and went back to the kitchen. Finding a sharp knife, she opened the envelope with care. Inside, unexpectedly, was a short letter from Elizabeth.

Dear Jane,

It was good to see you in March and looking so well. Glad to hear that you've shaken off that unpleasant illness. It went on too long. Did the doctors ever decide what caused it?

We're hoping that you'll come over again for Whitsun. Iris will be home, and Hope will be on half-term. Of course, there's very little for her to do at school now. It seems the teachers just supervise revision. She is finding it rather unsettling, I think, not having the routine. I'm sure she'll get her head down soon, though.

Well, do let us know if you're able to visit. Could you come on Friday, stay until the Monday? We thought it might be nice to take the girls out somewhere. Blow away the cobwebs.

With fondest love,

Elizabeth

p.s. David says to apologise for not writing. This business of becoming a magistrate is consuming so much of his time. But then, you know what David is like, once he makes his mind up.

Jane glanced up at the clock. Eleven-thirty. Would Elizabeth be at home? Possibly not. She looked at the phone indecisively and then lifted the receiver. Elizabeth answered on the second ring.

The day before Jane was due to leave for Bath unfurled in gentle sunshine. Birdie was working in her vegetable patch, muttering over the notes in the tattered and slightly muddy notebook with her planting notes from the previous year. She trusted Jane, she told herself again, and David was her family, after all. The notebook contained information about sowing dates, transplanting, varieties of seed. But what would Jane do if David reacted badly. Supposing he upset her, made her ill again? She tutted over her scrawled handwriting. She knew she'd planted a couple of rows of something at the weekend. But had forgotten to write it down. She rifled through her box of seed packets, hoping for a clue.

Jane was also outside. There was something about the way the light shifted in spring, and it was one of those days where the unfurling day seemed to contain both change and serenity. She sat on their old wrought iron bench, her easel beside her, looking over the garden. Birdie was bent over a rake, creating a fine tilth for the carrots that she wanted to sow. She'd already planted onions, and left broad avenues between the rows in order, as she explained to Jane every year, to protect the carrots from carrot fly.

There was such balance and anticipation in the spring. For Jane, it had always meant the start of a collection that might go on sale in the winter months, and for Birdie, the persistent coaxing of vegetables from muck. Birdie stood up, easing her back. Their soil was great for root vegetables, thick loam, slightly given to clay, but it was hard work making it friable enough for the tiny black carrot seeds. Finally satisfied, she tore open the packet, sprinkling the contents into her left hand. She manipulated her thumb joint, watching the seeds roll around in her hand. Some got stuck in the long deep life line that curved boldly across her palm, and she pushed at them with her right index finger.

She resisted the urge to show Jane, ask her to marvel yet again that something so tiny was packed with the magic it took to produce long orange roots. She felt she could almost taste the sweet earthy bite of early autumn. On days like today, the present and the future were entwined as one. Being itself was enough, with its tremulous light and beauty. Birdie knew with utter certainty that she and Jane would be together forever. Their lives were made real with canvas and soil, paint and seedlings; the world of doctors and diagnoses could be nothing more than the memory of a nightmare that one might have had.

Each absorbed in their thoughts, they heard the phone ring from the house, but with a brief shake of their heads, they silently agreed to ignore it. When the ringing eventually stopped, the ensuing silence had a sharp metallic edge to it. Birdie felt annoyed. Even unanswered, the phone had changed their morning. She bent over the tilth and whispered to the falling seed.

Within minutes, the phone rang again. This time it sounded louder, hectoring them both. Birdie held her empty hands up, waving them at Jane to indicate that she would go and answer the beast. Jane watched her as she kicked off her wellies. She could see Birdie's back through the open window as she picked up the receiver but was too far away to hear her voice. After a few seconds, Birdie's posture changed abruptly; her shoulders rigid and her body creased forwards. Something like alarm flickered through Jane. Was it bad news?

Birdie put down the receiver and hurried out.

'Your brother is on the phone. He needs to talk to you. Something's up.'

Jane nodded. Birdie wanted to follow her into the house, but sat instead on the bench, staring unseeingly at Jane's canvas. In the kitchen, Jane picked up the handset.

'David. It's Jane.'

Birdie could hear the sound of David's voice, speaking rapidly, but she couldn't hear his words.

'David. Slow down.'

Jane turned to face the open kitchen door, moving as close to it as she could. She held Birdie's gaze while she spoke to her brother.

'You're talking too fast, David. What's the matter?'

'Missing? Since when?'

'Just last night. Are you sure she hasn't just gone to a friend's house?'

Birdie watched as Jane gripped the handset, plucking at the coiled wire with her other hand with rising agitation.

'No. I see.'

'Oh David.'

Yes, I thought she was ok. A bit on edge perhaps. Worried about her exams, do you think?'

'Not revising. No, I didn't know that. Do you think that's connected?'

'No, of course you don't. Sorry. Silly question.'

‘David.’

‘David, listen a minute. David. You need to tell the police.’

‘You really must. You do know that.’

‘OK, you do that. Keep me informed. Anything I can do. Call straightaway.’

‘Yes, I expect so. It’s very out of character.’

Ok, David. Good bye for now.’

Birdie came to the back door as Jane put the receiver down and took her hand.

‘I guess you got all that?’

‘I think so, yes. Hope has run away?’

‘Well, she’s certainly gone missing. Poor, poor Hope. I told you she was very withdrawn at Easter, didn’t I? David says her schoolwork has been terrible. She’s meant to be revising, but apparently Elizabeth doesn’t think she’s done anything much. Just been hiding away in her room. Oh, I knew she was troubled. I should have talked to her, somehow. What should I do, do you think?’

Knowing this wasn’t really a question, Birdie hugged Jane silently. After a few minutes, she held her head away. Strands of Jane’s hair, long thick grey tresses knotted roughly into a bun, was falling across her face and into her eyes. Birdie lifted the wisps away from her face. Jane sighed.

'I can't do anything right now, can I? I'll just have to wait. My visit is cancelled. I guess that's for the best. But what if she needs someone to talk to and I seem to be staying away. That's not going to help.'

Birdie swallowed an impulse to offer reassurance, what use were words of hollow comfort? She put her hand gently on Jane's forearm.

'Let's stay inside for an hour or so. That way, you'll be ready for the phone. You could make a start on this month's ledger. You're better at the figures than I am. I'll get on with writing out the labels for those prints I framed last week. That's got to be done, too.'

The phone remained silent, and by mid-afternoon the sky had clouded over. Jane, finally, was snoozing in an armchair, so Birdie tiptoed out of the room. She wanted to rescue Jane's canvas and tidy away her gardening tools before the air got damp. She lifted the large canvas awkwardly, and with it propped on her hip, opened the door to the studio. As she did, she glimpsed a figure approaching. She paused in the open doorway to watch. A few seconds later she let out a breath of surprise.

The girl saw her. She lifted her head and stared at Birdie. Birdie looked back.

'You're Hope.'

The girl nodded reluctantly. The contours of Jane's face were clearly traced on Hope's face, below which, like a falling tide in a narrow harbour, emotions eddied and swirled. The girl's skin seemed too delicate, too thin to contain so much tumult and the sight of her made Birdie feel helpless, exposed. She spoke without thinking.

'How did you get here? Jane's been frantic with worry. She's worn herself out.'

Her voice sounded harsh, as if too long unused. She shook her head, raising her hands with a rapid conciliatory gesture.

'Gosh, Hope. I'm so sorry. What on earth must you think of me. Please, come in, Jane's inside. She'll be so relieved to see you.'

Hope flinched. She looked uncertain, fearful, and her expression was guarded.

Birdie wanted to tug Hope's hand, draw her in, reassure her and make her stay. She held herself motionless, willing herself not to frighten this wild spirit.

‘Your aunt is inside,’ she repeated, ‘she’s having a snooze. Would you like me to tell her you’re here? Or do you want to sit down.’ she gestured at the garden, ‘You can stay out here if you prefer.’

Following Birdie’s gesture, Hope looked around the garden. She saw a wooden table and bench under the window, both cluttered with pots and compost and packets of seed. A wheelbarrow leant against a metal garden chair, upended against the risk of rain. Two more chairs were stacked next to a pile of seasoned logs, and the garden itself had only the tiniest of lawn areas, everything else being divided into variously sized vegetable and flower beds. A long thin rope with a wooden clothes-line prop looped from a tall metal post to the side of the house. Jane’s stool and empty easel sat apart, as if observing the scene. Birdie couldn’t help herself, not knowing what to do with this silent girl. She moved towards the easel, needing to do something.

‘I must just put a few things away. When I looked out of the window just now, I thought it was going to rain.’

Birdie pushed into the open door of the studio, carefully putting the canvas down and returning to the garden. Hope was still standing on the edge of the path.

Birdie was relieved. She had had a sudden terror that the girl might have vanished.

Hope looked so much like Jane. But so young. She was the same age, Birdie knew, that she herself had been when her family threw her out. But of course, this girl wasn't Jane, nor was she some revenant of Birdie's own past. What must the girl be thinking of her? She must look like a mad woman. Here she was, trying to be busy again, exactly as she had in those first weeks after Jane's diagnosis. She paused with Jane's palette in her hand. Hope had still said nothing. The rain was closer now, and Birdie could feel the light changing, flattening everything. Somehow, the purpling afternoon brought time into one absolute moment, unencumbered. Birdie took a deep breath and tried to relax.

'I don't suppose you could help me with the easel, could you? I always get into such a muddle when I try to fold it away.'

The first fat raindrops had already fallen by the time they went into the cottage. Birdie stood alone in the kitchen, Hope and Jane were in the living room, their voices muffled by the long passageway leading to the kitchen. Birdie had offered to make tea. She stood in the larder for several minutes, pretending to search for a packet of chocolate biscuits. Eventually, Birdie retreated back first from the narrow larder. As she emerged, she heard Jane's footsteps coming towards her., Jane looked tired. Her voice was distracted, irritated even.

'You are coming in, aren't you? There's no heart-to-heart going on in there. I honestly don't know why she's come, what's on her mind. And every time I mention her father, she just snaps shut. Honestly, David needs to know she's here. He is her father.'

Birdie was startled. It was unlike Jane to sound so brusque. She half nodded, pausing deeply, and when she spoke, her voice was firm.

'Of course, he needs to know. But that may not be possible at the moment. Hope needs to know that she's done the right thing, coming here.' Birdie lifted her chin, 'And she didn't come here for you to act as a messenger service straight back to her family.'

For a moment or two Jane was shocked by this unexpected bluntness. But almost instantly, she saw the honesty of Birdie's words. Her face softened.

'Oh darling, whatever this is, I think we both need you. You are coming in, aren't you? Hope may not know it, but you're her family too, you know. I'll take those biscuits, if you can bring the tea through.'

Family. Was that right? That astonishing recognition she'd experienced when she'd first seen Hope. The sensation of meeting an ancient connection. It was like, she thought, meeting a long-lost relative for the first time. Birdie realised she hadn't even told Hope her name, let alone why she was there, in her aunt's house. All that would have to wait. She hefted the tray and straightened her back. Right now, the tea was what mattered.

Chapter 24

By ten o'clock that night, the house was quiet. Hope sat on the bed in the little boxroom at the top of the house. Once upon a time, it had been the attic and still had the pinched feel of a room that doesn't quite belong. Shelves along one side of the room were cluttered with various objects. At one end was a heavy cardboard box, open at the top. It contained empty Kilner jars, some of which bore old labels with indecipherable handwriting. Next to that, three rolls of unused sugar paper, each held by a brittle rubber band. Folded neatly in a pile were two pairs of worn curtains and some old sheets, marked with paint stains, clearly used for decorating. Under the pointed eaves at the narrow end of the room was a small wooden table, on which sat a pile of encyclopaedias in dark green covers. There were part rolls of wallpaper underneath the table, and beside them, a small mouse trap, empty of bait.

The whole room was in waiting. As if it and its contents might have some as yet unknown reason for being. The thought made Hope feel oddly reassured. She undressed, putting on the long cotton nightie that Birdie had found for her, and lay down in the narrow bed under a heavy eiderdown. She stared into the blackness of the room until it gave way to shades of darkness. The night was overcast, and her window faced open fields. She watched as slowly, the framed night turned acquired a distinct form, not grey exactly, but a weaker version of the blackness in the high eaves of the attic room.

Hope couldn't tell how slowly or quickly time was passing. What would her parents be thinking? They would still be worried, even though she had eventually agreed that Jane should phone them, just to say that she was safe and well.

Since Easter, Hope's anxiety about her period had intensified, becoming obsessive. Every day, repeatedly, she decided that nothing had happened to her at the party, that she wasn't menstruating because she had an irregular cycle, because she was anxious, not eating proper meals. Every day, in quick succession, fear drowned her thoughts, and she was exhausted from the sheer effort of searching for an explanation of what had happened, the certainty that she craved that everything was alright.

Earlier that morning though, all her attempts at rationalising her fears had crashed. Her dad had offered to drop her off at school so that she didn't have to catch the bus. She was late, disorganised, eating a piece of toast in the kitchen, still wearing her dressing gown. She could hear her father moving about. He liked to get the car out of the garage before finally leaving the house, and she heard the front door close as he came back inside. She had looked up, still chewing a mouthful of toast when he put his head round the kitchen door. 'Come on, tubby,' he'd said, 'we need to leave in 10 minutes.' He disappeared outside again.

With that one word, her limbs had turned to liquid. She was pregnant. The impossible, guarded against and fought so relentlessly for so many weeks, had become the only truth. And the only thing possible in response was flight.

In the dark, her eyes filled in helpless self-pity. The unfamiliar bed and the different quality of silence here, so deep in the countryside, gave Hope the odd feeling that she had slipped realities. Her everyday life had not so much disappeared as become an intangible, dreamlike state. And still, time passed. Without her noticing the shift, the square shape of the window lightened again, and grey light crept into the room. Nothing seemed entirely real; the shapes and forms in the room had indeterminate edges that shifted as she looked at them. She got out of bed, sitting in the thin pre-dawn light as waves of desolation crashed around her. She hadn't even told Jane she was pregnant.

Sobs of fear and certainty racked her. The walls and sloped ceiling seemed to be leaning in, and she felt oppressed, trapped, as if there was no oxygen in the small room. She started breathing erratically, anxious that her lungs would stop working if she didn't concentrate. The ends of her fingers buzzed and tingled alarmingly, and her ears were full of storm. Of all eternity, the only second that existed was this one, and it was trembling with terror. She couldn't trust her body to keep going without her utmost attention, and every breath she took made the feelings of panic worse. Trembling, giddy with fear, she was certain that if she didn't get a glass of water she would die. Her legs uncooperative, her teeth chattering and heart falling in her chest like an avalanche, Hope stumbled downstairs to the kitchen.

Birdie swung round as Hope burst into the kitchen. In once glance she took in Hope's panic, her face was pale, and her breathing sounded forced, fluttery and unnatural.

'Sit down. Hope. My dear girl. What is the matter? Sit down. You look dreadful.'

Birdie held a cool hand to the girl's forehead, quickly establishing that she didn't have a fever. Hope began shaking, and great sobs ballooned from her, followed by aching tears. Birdie led her to a chair and sat her down without speaking. She took a woollen jacket from behind the kitchen door and laid it across her knees. Hope sat, rocking forward and backwards on the chair. She wasn't sure if her fingers and toes were numb or whether they were tingling with a panicky coldness. Birdie left her for a moment, retrieving the cup of tea she had just made and offering it to Hope.

'Here you are. I haven't touched it. Let me just add some sugar and more milk for you.'

Birdie added several spoonfuls of sugar and enough milk to cool the tea.

'Drink this. It'll help, I promise.'

She sat down next to Hope, and held her hand over Hope's, steadying the cup as the girl lifted it.

'There. Well done.'

Birdie looked at Hope, who looked like a fledgling fallen from a nest too early. She wanted to get Jane but didn't dare leave Hope alone while she was so distraught.

After a few minutes, she saw with relief that Hope's breathing was beginning to slow down.

'Do you want to tell me what's wrong? she asked tentatively, 'I can call a doctor for you if think you need one.'

Hope shook her head, not able to look up. After a few minutes more of silence Birdie added, 'I could give him a ring quite easily. He lives in the village. Even if you don't think you are ill, it might be a good idea for the doctor to have a look at you, check you over.'

Hope buried her face in her hands and mumbled something incomprehensible in a harsh voice.

'Can you say that again, Hope. I'm sorry, but I didn't quite hear you.'

Hope lifted her head to look at Birdie through her fingers. Birdie, of whom she had known nothing until yesterday, seemed so real. So… so ordinary and calm. Hope closed her eyes for a brief moment, trying to slow her breathing.

'I'm not ill. I'm pregnant. Or at least, I think I must be.'

Birdie could see that the sobs were about to drown Hope again. She reached out her hand, touching Hope's shoulder.

'Steady yourself, my dear. Cry, by all means, but keep breathing, if you can.'

Birdie sat next to Hope, who cried quietly. Her head was full of useless, foolish questions that wouldn't help Hope in the slightest, she knew. What difference would it make if she asked how, and when, and who knew? The answer to the last of these was clearly 'no-one', and the other two, for now at least, were irrelevant. She sat in a silence shaped by Hope's grief, around the edges of which hovered her own memories of being seventeen, of feeling that her life was over.

'Birdie.'

Birdie jumped back to the present. Hope looked calmer now.

'Will you tell Jane?'

'Is that what you want?'

'Well, yes. No. I don't know. How do I find out if I'm really pregnant?' She pulled her fingers through her fringe, 'No. Don't wake Jane up. I will tell her though, I promise. Oh, god, what shall I do.'

Chapter 25

When Jane woke to the unfamiliarity of the guest room the sun was shining in from the wrong direction. Sleepily, she wondered why had the window moved. Of course, she remembered, Hope was in the house. What time was it? She twisted blearily to pick up her watch and found that she had slept later than usual. Lifting her head to listen more clearly, she heard the sound of a voice rising from the kitchen. Was that somebody crying? Was Hope alone down there, she wondered. She hadn't wanted to push the girl, the evening before, knowing only too well how being asked questions could feel intrusive. She rose quickly, pushing her arms into her old, checked dressing gown and opening the door. At the top of the stairs, she was astonished to realise that it wasn't crying at all, but gales of laughter. She heard, indistinctly, Birdie's voice break through the giggles, and then again, the howling sounds of laughter from Hope. The sound was infectious, joyful, and even before she reached the kitchen, Jane's face was split in a broad smile.

Birdie was standing by the back door, arms outstretched. In one hand she held a wooden spoon, in the other, the bread knife. She was waving the knife at the door mat, which she'd somehow propped up on a chair.

'Cripes, no. Demmit! My muse has deserted me and I em ze most tragic of souls!'

Birdie's expression was woeful, but catching Jane's eye she almost gave way to giggles.

'No, no!' Birdie tried again 'Em I not a paintah? Em I not the man with ze zeitgeist. See here, this humble jobbing dauber who comes to gaze on my mastahpieces!' Birdie waved the wooden spoon at Jane.

Hope whirled and saw Jane in the doorway.

'Morning Aunty Jane, here you are. Look at Birdie. She's so funny. She's been telling me about the students you teach.'

'Well?' Birdie demanded stridently, gesturing at the door mat, 'Ken you not discern who I em? Just gaze on my creation. So richly drawn! So distinctive! Hev you ever seen such brush strokes before?'

'Why Johannes Smythe, as I live and breathe,' Jane held Birdie's eyes with a questioning smile, 'and to what do we owe the pleasure of this early morning apparition?'

She walked over to her niece, enfolding her in a warm hug.

'He's actually just John Smith,' she murmured into Hope's hair, 'but don't tell him I told you.'

She held Hope close for a moment. When she was about to let go Hope sensed her movement and clung to her.

'Oh. Aunty Jane.' Jane felt Hope's laughter dissolving into tears.

'Oh pet, whatever is it? You can tell me anything, you know.' She looked over the top of Hope's head towards Birdie, who nodded, putting down the knife and spoon before tiptoeing from the room.

Chapter 26

When Hope had returned home from Wales, she hadn't said much. Jane had already phoned ahead, explaining about the pregnancy, how distraught Hope was and how she'd asked Jane to break the news. Hope was upstairs in her room now, and Elizabeth had just phoned the university Law Department, leaving a message for Iris to contact her as soon as possible. She'd had a hard time persuading David, but eventually he accepted that Iris would have to know. Elizabeth replaced the phone and sat down heavily, staring out the window. Hope hadn't even got a boyfriend. Well, not as far as she knew. She could see the tulips nodding brightly in the garden. They seemed fantastical. And when had it all happened? She stared at the phone. It could be hours before the message got through to Iris. What would Iris think, though – getting a message to ring home like that.

Elizabeth stood decisively. She'd go for a walk. Her head was so full of fog. She needed the air. Fetching her shoes from the hall cupboard she stopped in her tracks. How could she be so idiotic! Of course she couldn't go out. What if Iris called? She was a jumbled muddle of loose ends. David could act the outraged father if he must, but she still had to hold the family together.

The telephone pealed loudly. Twenty minutes. The university must have pulled Iris out of a tutorial. Elizabeth wasn't ready. She answered the phone as if it might explode in her hands.

'Mummy?'

Iris's voice was low. She sounded distant, wary. Elizabeth felt as if her limbs were dissolving.

'Oh, Iris, it's you. Thank goodness.'

And Elizabeth found, suddenly, that she couldn't speak. She held her hand to her throat in alarm.

'What's happened, Mummy? What is it. Has there been an accident?'

Iris's voice was rapid, high. Elizabeth stared at the back of the front door, willing herself to be calm.

'I'm sorry, dear. It's just. Well, it's Hope.' She spoke quickly, 'She's fine. I mean, she's not ill or anything.'

Elizabeth pressed her fingers into her closed eyes.

'The thing is, she disappeared from home, and then we had a call from Aunty Jane. She told us that Hope seems to be pregnant. She's home now. Hope is, I mean. She's not saying anything much. But your father…'

Elizabeth stopped.

'Iris?'

'Yes, I'm here. Mummy? What is she going to do? I mean, it's too late for an abortion, I suppose.'

Elizabeth felt she could breathe again. Iris always was so sensible. She wished she wasn't so far away. The house felt steadier when her elder daughter was at home.

'The plan is, she'll just go into school for exams. We can make sure nobody finds out, I think. Then she'll go back to Wales. She'll stay with your Aunt Jane until... Well, the baby will go for adoption, of course.'

There was a silence at the other end of the phone. Then Elizabeth heard her daughter sigh.

'Are you alright, dear?'

'Of course I'm alright, Mummy. It's not my fault this happened. I wasn't to know, was I?' There was an odd defensiveness to Iris's voice, but she hurried on. 'It's good of Aunty Jane to help. I hope it doesn't make her ill again.'

Elizabeth wanted to tell someone how awful it was, pinioned between David's brusque unspoken judgement and the pale wordlessness of Hope. How, this morning,

Hope had been slumped over her breakfast, her father lowering outside the house like a vengeful thunder cloud. She'd been on edge; David might have come into the kitchen at any moment. He might not have known Hope was there. Worse, he might have known and decided to come in and rage at Hope. Elizabeth felt ashamed, guilty, bitten by regret. Perhaps David had known Hope was in the kitchen. Anyway, he had disappeared into the garage and driven off to work without saying goodbye.

'Mummy?'

'Sorry dear, yes, I'm still here.' Of course, she couldn't tell Iris. Why, she was just a child, herself. 'I know, your Aunt Jane is a godsend. I don't know what I'd do else.'

'Look Mummy, I should go. I have a tutor group at twelve.'

Putting the phone down, Elizabeth was restless and dissatisfied. Iris hadn't even seemed shocked. Why had she made that comment about it not being her fault? What a strange thing to say. The whole conversation though, the thought, worrying at it like a terrier, had had an air of unreality. She'd heard herself, as if from another room, talking about Hope, and as her words fell from her, they became insubstantial, unreal, as if the things she was saying couldn't be part of any possible reality.

The phone rang again. Elizabeth lifted the handset, cautiously saying hello.

'Mummy?'

'Oh Iris. It's you. What is it, love?'

'Look, Mummy,' Iris began, 'it's just occurred to me. This will be kept secret, won't it?'

'Well, yes of course. I sincerely hope so. We won't tell school. And then she'll be away, so no-one outside the family need find out. It's not as if she has many close friends at school. She always had you, I suppose. Sorry, dear. Why do you ask?'

Iris drew breath.

'It's just. Well, I don't want to tell Don, alright. He mustn't know.'

Elizabeth's frown relaxed. Don was such a lovely lad. So polite. She'd worried when he'd gone to Oxford, so far from York. But clearly, he and Iris were still fond of each other.

‘That’s up to you, darling, but I think it’s best. I can promise that we won’t mention anything to his family, of course.’

‘Yes, Mummy, but you need to make sure that Hope doesn’t say anything either. You must tell her. You must. Don would be so shocked. I know he would. I don’t want her to ruin my life.’

‘Well…’

‘You must, Mummy. If you and Daddy talk to her, perhaps she’ll listen. She was rotten about Don when I came home, and I just don’t trust her. Look, I really have to go. Just talk to her for me, ok?’

Elizabeth stood in the hall after Iris ended the call, anxiously twisting the gold chain around her neck. She had no idea what she should do next.

Chapter 27

Three months passed. Jane was in her studio finishing off a painting. She wanted to get it done before Hope arrived the next day. She and Elizabeth had talked and talked, Elizabeth apprehensive, with a fresh set of worries and potential difficulties each time she rang. In contrast, the agreement she and Birdie had come to, that they would offer Hope their home once her A level exams were finished, had been simple, heartfelt.

And now the July sunshine was streaming through the open window. It was too bright, Jane decided. It distorted the colours, making her lines seem lighter, more garish than they really were. For the last few years, she'd been using clean, bright hues for her landscapes. She'd been aiming to create a compelling voice for the countryside she painted and had used saturated colours to force the viewer's attention. Now, though, she wanted to paint differently. Bright colours created distance and separation, she thought. She hated the way people looked at paintings as if they were simply objects and couldn't bear the idea that her art had colluded in this division. This separation, these divisions between observed and observer were fragmenting the world, and Jane wanted her painting to show harmony and togetherness. It was exhausting, trying to do things differently, and these days she didn't have as much energy as she needed. She stood back from her canvas, eyeing it critically.

Birdie, at the other end of the barn, was bent over the work table. She wore glasses most of the time, but when, as now, looking at close detail, they were shoved onto the top of her head, tangled in her curly hair.

'I'm stopping for a while,' Jane said, 'the sunlight's just too strong, and I can't see what I'm doing.'

Birdie didn't look up. She had a sharp knife in her hand and was carefully cutting through thick cardboard to make a mount.

'OK. Put the kettle on, then. I just need to do this.'

Jane stood still, watching Birdie. There really wasn't enough space for all the framing work they were taking on. Perhaps she could make her studio space smaller, give Birdie more room. And they really should get around to putting up some better shelves. That had been on the list for months. Jane wondered if it might be a good idea to get Hope to help. She'd need to do something while she was staying with them, for heaven's sake.

Birdie looked up.

‘Ten fingers still in place and intact.’ She grinned at Jane, waggling her fingers at her.

It was an old joke. Jane had lost the tip of a finger some years ago, helping Birdie cut wood down to size for a frame. But today, Jane didn’t respond.

‘Hey darling. Where are you?’

‘Hmm. Sorry. I was wondering if Hope could help us put up some shelves.’

Jane gestured at the wall, where piles of bricks supported old planks, making an unstable stack of shelving already over full with framing timber, pots of varnish, brushes and other paraphernalia.

‘No, really. I mean where are you. You’ve been miles away for days. I don’t think it’s just the painting, is it?’

Outside the window, a bee explored a clematis flower meticulously, working its way deep into the calyx before crawling out, its flanks heavy with yellow gold. Rising to the air, it seemed to pause and think, before diving into the next bloom. There was a hum in the air; other, more distant bees, each bent on saturating its light body with pollen. Beyond the boundaries of their garden, out of sight, there were swallows wheeling the air, feeding, finding sustenance. They soared above the wheat field sloping south, where even the faintest hues of green had been transmuted to gold in each ripened ear.

'Is there something you're not telling me?'

Some days, Birdie was sure that Jane was hiding her pain, even though Jane was usually so completely herself that she seemed entirely healthy. Somehow this intensified Birdie's anxiety, making her brittle and unsettled. Jane had promised again and again not to keep anything secret, and wanted Birdie to find, as she herself had, a way of living with the cancer as if it were a distant inconvenience, a matter of minor adjustments and cancelled plans on her rare bad days. Jane painted with her customary energy, Birdie's garden was glorious; a red, yellow and green riot of summer fruits and vegetables. Now, with Hope about to change their lives, Birdie was aware of uncomfortable resentment, as if Hope would steal their precious time together.

'Jane?' Birdie repeated.

Jane shook her head. How could she explain how she felt, angry that the next two months were going to be all about Hope, when what she dearly wanted was time alone with Birdie. She wanted to hoard time for them both, as well as for her painting. With Hope there, how would they live? She felt cheated, and that made her feel mean. She turned towards the door.

'Oh, it's nothing. I'll make that tea.'

A band of intense sunshine infused Jane's figure as she stepped through the doorway onto the path leading back to the house. In the shimmering air her form seemed insubstantial, as if her existence were just a trick of the light.

That evening, their last alone before Hope, was even worse. Birdie was annoyed with herself, feeling that her resentment about Hope's arrival was mean-spirited and unsupportive, but Jane was ready to be generous, and so Birdie had said nothing. Flicking heedlessly through a newspaper, Jane didn't feel able to tell Birdie how little she wanted her niece to arrive, not after Birdie had been so generous and opened her heart to the girl. And so, separated by silence, they'd gone to bed, each locked in self-recrimination and out of sorts with the other. Two hours before dawn, in the utter darkness, Birdie's familiar nightmare had woken her, her heart pounding as the cold steel shafts of adrenaline disabled her limbs. Jane had slept on. Birdie, listening to her steady breath in the darkness, had slowly relaxed, eventually falling into a deep sleep at dawn. When she finally awoke, Jane was sitting on the side of the bed, cradling two cups of coffee.

'Peace offering?'

Birdie nodded silently.

'I'm sorry,' Jane said, 'I just couldn't find the right words last night. I feel so mean.'

'You feel mean? But you are being so wonderful about everything.'

'But I'm not. Not really,' Jane said, 'the thing is... how do you really feel about Hope's stay? I know what you said when David threatened to throw her out. It's just that it's all about to become very real. Are we going to be ok?'

Birdie shuffled herself up in bed, propping the pillows behind her back. Seeing Jane's tight, worried face, Birdie suddenly realised that the cause of the distance between them was not Hope's visit, but the way she and Jane hadn't told each other what they been thinking. She smiled gently.

'Actually, I think we are. It's not just that she reminds me of you, you know. It's... oh, I don't know. I mean, I don't get the whole adoption idea. You know I don't. To give away your own child. But goodness, Jane, she's just been abandoned herself, and we both know how that feels. She needs you. You're here for her. It might be as simple as that.'

Jane looked thoughtful for a moment.

'I think you're going to find that she needs you too.'

'Maybe. I'm not family, I suppose. That might be helpful.'

'Well, actually you are, even if you both have to get acquainted.' Jane smiled, 'But it's not just that, anyway. You're persistent. You never cut me any slack, and I have a feeling you might help her be a bit more truthful, to herself, at least. Anyway, it might sound insane, but I'm more concerned about us. Play-acting we're just friends out there is one thing. But in our own home? For two months. Eight weeks.'

The thought of summer passing into autumn hung in the air between them. Already, the leaf tips on the chestnut tree had a dry, papery look, presaging winter.

'One bear at a time.'

Jane looked surprised.

'What? What was that? What on earth do you mean?'

‘Ein Bär und dann der nächste. One bear and then the next one. It’s what my Oma said. Wrote. My parents used to read AA Milne’s poems to me when we moved to London. You know, the one about the bears in London. Something like “I always take care on a London street. There are bears on all of the squares.” No, that’s not it. Anyway, in the poem Christopher Robin is worried that there are fierce bears in London. I suppose I must have taken it to heart. I remember being frightened that there really were bears. And dad would have told Oma. He’d have thought it would amuse her, I expect. Anyway, in one of her letters she told me to take them one at a time. She said it was the best way to deal with bears. One bear and then the next. I can’t believe I’ve never told you before.’

‘One bear at a time,’ she smiled, ‘Well, I think you and I can probably pull that off. Not so sure about Hope though. I think she’s more likely to bring a troupe of dancing bears.’

‘The thing is,’ Birdie said, ‘there is one bear that really needs dealing with. I don’t think it can wait.’

‘What is it, darling?’

‘Your will.’

Silence trailed after the word. It was a topic they'd barely talked about since Jane had decided, all the way back in March, that she was going to leave everything to Birdie. If Jane had made that planned visit to David, if she had told him the reality of her life with Birdie, if Hope hadn't catapulted into the foreground. Well. They couldn't change that. Yet here they were, nearly five months on.

'The thing is, I have a suggestion for you. Just listen, ok, and don't say anything. We can talk about it again at lunchtime, when you've had a chance to think. I just want to say my piece before Hope gets here.'

Jane nodded.

I don't want you to leave me your money.' She held up her hand, 'You know that already, but listen. Please. This is what I want to say. I think we should put the framing business, including the studio, in our joint names. Make sure that no-one can sell the business from under me, if… when you're not around. I don't want to go anywhere else, and if you do that for me, then I'll have everything I really need. The rest of it, Flag Cottage, your paintings, your bank balance. Well, I can see why you don't want to leave it to David, but why not leave it to Hope and her sister? That way, if Hope changes her mind, well then… at some point, she'll be secure. I mean, she's secure now, I know. She can stay here as long as she wants to, even if she does keep the baby. But I mean…'

'After I've gone.' Jane finished for her.

Birdie could feel the bones in Jane's shoulders as she pulled her into a tight hug. She was astonished by how strong Jane was. She couldn't break free, even if she'd wanted to.

'Birdie.' Jane's voice was muffled on her shoulder.

'No, darling, don't argue with me straight away. Please, just think about it.'

Jane held Birdie tightly for a moment longer and then released her gently.

'You must think I'm an obstinate sort of person.' Jane looked serious and then laughed out loud.

'Ok, I am obstinate. In fact, I'm bloody awkward. I've still got no idea why you tolerate me, darling. But Birdie. The truth is, I've been thinking along the same lines. I've been meaning to say something, but it seemed unfair. After all you've had to put up with. I do want to do something for Hope, and Iris of course. Who knows what's ahead of them, even without a teenage pregnancy in the mix. I'd like to know they could choose to be independent, whatever that looks like, I suppose.'

'Thank goodness, I was…'

Jane stopped her. 'If we sort out the best arrangements for you through the business, including the studio as well, then in my will I can simply say that my estate is to be divided equally between David's direct living descendants, including any dependent children.'

Birdie looked at Jane.

'So, if Hope has the baby adopted, she and Iris will get half each… And if Hope has twins and keeps them, then Iris would get twenty-five per cent.'

'Gracious! Yes, I suppose she would. Seriously though, they're both fair-minded, and they've always been very close. I'm confident they'll understand and respect my wishes for them. Good heavens, they must know I love them both.'

'You are just wonderful.' Birdie paused, 'I know it's selfish, but I do wonder sometimes. You know, if Oma would have been there for me. When my parents kicked me out. I was seventeen, too, you know. Having someone on your side, whatever happens. And I'm going to do everything I can for Hope.'

She and Jane sat together in silence, drinking their coffee and feeling the sheer glory of simply being together. After a few minutes Jane took the mugs away, climbing back under the covers with Birdie. The day need not begin yet, not when they had such aeons of love and desire to share first.

It seemed as if the universe was as perfect as it ever could be when Birdie sat up again.

'Look at the time! She'll be here soon. Her bus gets into Swansea at quarter to eleven, doesn't it.'

'No, darling, quarter past eleven. Don't panic, I'll be there in plenty of time.'

'Should I come with you, do you think? Will you be ok to drive?'

'Hey, Birdie. Slow down. One bear at a time, yes? Of course I'm fine to drive. How many times do I have to tell you. I'm fine. Really fine. But please, you mustn't treat me like an invalid in front of Hope. We're not going to tell her about that, right? I still haven't told David, remember.'

Birdie closed her eyes and nodded. She had agreed, and she would stick to her word. For the next eight weeks they would be two spinsters sharing a house and business, they had no relationship, and neither of them was ill. It would be ok, she told herself. It wasn't really a deception. The important thing was their shared support for Hope. Jane was relying on her. Birdie flinched. Could she do it?

'Birdie.'

Birdie looked up.

'I can see what you're thinking. And I know. Part of me agrees with you. It's just… This is all too much. Us. Cancer. Pregnancy. It's not just Hope I'm worried about, dealing with all that. It's me, too.'

'Don't worry, darling.' Birdie held out her hands, 'I've promised. One bear at a time. I get it. I really do. Go on, off with you. I'll make a start on the paperwork while you're gone.'

***

That night, back in the little box room, Hope sat on the edge of the bed, taking in the silence. The outlines of objects were familiar this time, though their contents were still mysterious. She'd had to insist that she didn't want Jane and Birdie to move anything for her. She'd tried to explain that the flotsam and jetsam of the room was oddly comforting, and Jane had pretended to understand. The various boxes and stacked shelves made it feel like being in a railway station waiting room, she thought. Jane had suggested she might like a mirror in the room, but Hope had refused that vehemently. The last thing she wanted was to see the reflection of her body. She'd taken to wearing wrap around skirts. Over these she wore baggy shirts which hung in folds from her narrow shoulders obscuring her pregnant belly.

Whenever the baby turned inside her, Hope did her best to distract herself. She'd get up and walk around, or listen intently to the radio, or stare at the pages of a book, any book, with fierce determination. When it was still, Hope could think about what she would do afterwards. After the adoption. She had agreed to read English at Exeter. If she was going to be a teacher, her mum had said, it was absolutely essential that nobody found out that she'd been pregnant. That was fine by her, she thought, once the baby had been adopted, once she had left home for good, then she would be fine. The worst thing was how much she missed Iris. She hadn't seen her since February and had guessed that her parents had kept them apart on purpose. Did Iris even know? Surely, she must. Hope felt the baby lurch inside her belly just as the first sharp calls from the blackbird cut the air outside. She tried to focus on the autumn ahead, when her real life would start again.

Chapter 28

Some weeks later Birdie and Hope were sitting on the wide stone steps on Swansea Beach. In front of them, the sand lay like scalloped lace, edging the departure of the last high tide. There were dark, shadowed furrows, scuffed and indented by the hundreds of feet that had crossed the beach that day. Fragments of bright shell and small pebbles freckled the beach, their shapes casting short dark shadows in the strong sunlight. Further off, the sand seemed to have an impossible and inexhaustible flatness stretching east and west as if without end. Ahead of them, where the shore met the small motions of a retreating tide, it looked as though a blue-grey satin cloth had merely been carelessly laid on its surface. Hope had the sense that the sand continued unchanged under the sea, until rising to the surface on the next shore in France. Or maybe Spain. She was uncertain. Where the sea was nearest, small points of light lay scattered on the surface, and in the far distance the utter stillness of the sea was abruptly delineated by a sharp dark line which firmly divided water from air. To their right, The Mumbles, low and dark in the distance, looked like an afterthought, an interruption to the absolute timelessness of the sky-rimmed sea. Birdie interrupted her daydream.

‘If we had binoculars, you’d be able to see the lighthouse.’

Jane was at the solicitor in town, finalising her will and the transfer of the business into Birdie’s name. Jane had suggested that Birdie and Hope could visit the sea front while, as she explained to her niece, she dealt with various boring legal matters. Birdie felt unreal, picnicking with Hope, paddling along the water’s edge and watching families enjoying the summer sunshine while Jane dealt, alone, with the practicalities of her still unimaginable death.

She looked towards the sea, flat and blue in front of her. She felt herself drawn in by the flow of mutability and permanence; the mysterious way that each droplet was as old as the universe, and as fresh as a new-born drop of dew.

Even today, with Jane dealing with the wretched paperwork in the office of a stranger, Birdie found herself tranquil and at peace. The brevity of her life, Jane’s life, even the life of Hope’s unborn child, was somehow held in the sense of timelessness where the land met the sea. Of course, she knew that the coastline changed like everything else, but it didn’t feel that way. It felt solid, permanent, real.

Hope, beside her, was sitting motionless, her bare toes curling in a small drift of sand on the warm stone steps. She was looking down the beach. Two figures had caught her eye: One, a young woman, whose long hair fell over her face as she bent forward, was digging in the wet sand with a small red spade. The other, a small boy who couldn't have been much more than a year old, was holding a thick rubber bucket in his free hand. She could be looking at herself, Birdie thought, but in a different universe. The woman had the same dark hair, slight frame and narrow face. The sand around the two figures glinted where the light reflected from small pools left by the retreating tide.

Hope shifted uneasily and Birdie sensed a brittle tension in her. She turned towards her and saw that she was staring fixedly, hot tears welling in her eyes. Birdie put her arm around Hope, who began sobbing violently, leaning into Birdie, her whole body shaking. It was the first time, since that first night, that Birdie had seen Hope cry. Impulsively, she wrapped her arms around Hope, smoothing her hair, but almost immediately, Hope shook her off.

'Don't. Please. I'm fine really.'

She sat up straight, but the tears ran quickly down her face, and she didn't try to brush them away. Her grief just needs space, Birdie thought, knowing how unendurably lonely a person could feel if pain and anguish were pushed away too soon. She sat still, trying to hold a sense of sanctuary and quiet acceptance for Hope. It was about time she cried properly. For weeks now, Birdie had watched her determinedly ignoring her pregnancy, flinching with suppressed anger every time Hope talked about the future, without even seeming to consider the Mother and Baby Home into which she was booked, or the experiences of childbirth and adoption which lay ahead of her. Birdie knew herself caught between sympathy for the way Hope had found herself rejected by her family, and despair at her refusal to question the plan to give her child to strangers. Hope, thought Birdie, gave the impression that childbirth and adoption were nothing more than a tedious interruption to real life, no more than a trip to the dentist.

Birdie was almost glad that Hope was crying, as if the tears somehow justified the deep affection she had for this oddly self-contained girl. In the same breath, she was ashamed of herself, surely, she didn't need evidence that the girl was suffering, however indifferent she might seem to be. Birdie tried to push away her own thoughts:

She wanted to surround Hope with a sense of peace, and she couldn't do that while listening to the chatter of her own judging mind. She breathed deeply and slowly, reaching for the eternal presence of the landscape and drawing it into her heart.

After a few minutes, Hope turned towards her. Her face was calm again, though the glistening of tears lingered on her cheeks.

'How do you do that?'

Birdie tilted her head, questioning.

'Do what?'

'I don't know. You have a way of making me feel safe. It's like you are some sort of Buddha. At least, that's what I imagine a Buddha does. You can just bring peace into being. I wish I could do that.'

Birdie smiled.

'I'm not sure your aunt would agree with you. She says I should stop and think before I speak. And she says I'm too noisy. When I'm framing and she's painting… I feel like a piglet that's somehow barged into Evensong.'

Hope giggled and then frowned again. Birdie needed to answer her question.

‘No, come on, tell me. How come you have this way of being at peace? I wish I could do it.’

‘I’m sorry, Hope. I do know what you mean. The thing is,’ she paused, searching for words, ‘Well, the way I see it is that every person, every action, thought or feeling we have, well, we’re just a part of the whole universe. Look at the sea. Today there are sparkles kissing the tops of small waves, and the colour. Well, it’s a beautiful lazy blue. I come down here in the winter, when the sea is the colour of steel. Then the waves are topped with a spray so brutal that it looks like it could break concrete. And then other times, the waves sound petulant, like they’re bored of striking the shore, again and again.’

‘You mean everything changes, so there’s no point in getting upset about anything?’

‘No.’ Birdie was vehement.

‘No, I mean absolutely the opposite. We have to care. This quiet, gentle sea is the same sea that pounds the shore, throws up cascades of spume, wrecks boats. It isn’t one thing or the other, it’s both, and both matter. Okay, so we’re humans, and we experience reality as a sequence of moments. And yes, on a cosmic scale that means we get distressed by things that may be just a flicker in the universe. But it all matters. Even if – no, especially if we know it is temporary. And we do have an unhelpful tendency to think joy is to do with having nice stuff or doing nice things.'

Birdie felt her voice catching in her throat. She closed her eyes, searching for the words she needed.

'But it doesn't mean we shouldn't care about anything, Hope. Laugh and cry with real passion, and don't ignore what's going on for you, or you'll find, one day, that you've never really lived at all.'

Birdie stopped, her mind suddenly crowded with thoughts of Jane; her intensity over the last few months, the way she'd pushed herself to carry on painting, the new stacks of canvasses in the studio. Real passion. The realisation winded her. What made her think she could give advice to Hope, she thought, seeing how blindly she had been begging Jane to stop and rest, to live cautiously, to be an invalid.

'Look, Hope,' she started. She needed to tell Hope what she really thought about this baby. Hope needed to hear the truth. About what hiding from reality was doing to her. If only Hope would look inside herself, make her own decisions. Letting the child go should be accompanied by a sense of trembling enormity, thought

Birdie. Her own heart ached for the child, who might never understand his mother's decision. She wanted Hope to feel like the ocean in winter, to pound the shore with shivering sighs as water hurtled and fell on the coast. She and Jane would tell Hope that she had choices, they must. Once Jane had signed the new will, Hope would have no reason to give up her baby. She would persuade Jane to tell Hope everything, she must. Birdie reached out her hand, brushing her fingers lightly on Hope's shoulder.

'The thing is,' Birdie started, 'there are always more choices than we imagine...'

Hope stood up quickly, interrupting Birdie.

'I know what you're trying to say. I really do. I've promised to go to university and all that. Even though I don' think it's a good idea. But I'm okay about this… I'm okay about this baby. You're right, he's got a whole life to look forward to. I'm just, like, I guess I'm just a bus or something. Taking him to the first destination on his journey. He belongs to the universe, not to me.'

Hope looked away, her gaze fixed on the blue sea, still glinting in the afternoon sun. She wouldn't think about the baby now. This whole thing was just a random accident, and she had to go through with it because the accident had happened to her. It could have been anyone. And really, the baby needed to be free too, just as she did.

'It's the only way I'll be able to be myself. You don't know what it's like, Birdie. At home, everybody is exactly the same. And when they decide something, they do whatever the neighbours do. I need to find my world, like you say, embrace every moment. But I'm really fine, honestly, I am. It was just a random emotion drifting by.'

Hope stood up, carrying her sandals in her hand.

'Ice cream? Go on Birdie, let's have an ice cream before we meet Auntie Jane.'

Birdie was shocked. Clearly, her compassion had been misplaced. She was overwhelmed by anger again. How could Hope be so stupidly thoughtless? The rest of the world might as well be a figment of somebody else's imagination to her. Universal love. All that meant to her was a selfish determination to ignore or reject the things she didn't like about life.

'Jane should be finished about now. Don't you think we should wait for her before we buy ice-cream. She's the one who's having a tough day.'

'I thought she was doing boring paperwork for the business?'

'Yes. Yes, she is. That's what I meant. It's tough doing things you don't like. You'll discover that too, one day.'

The thing about Birdie, Hope was learning, was that she could swing from serenity to storminess in a moment. She wondered what had made her angry this time. In a way, she liked Birdie better for her impulsive moods. Birdie wasn't boring, and she never, ever treated her like a child. Even Jane still did that, especially when she was tired.

'You're right. Let's go and find Auntie Jane. She'll definitely need an ice cream.'

The two of them walked away from the beach together in silence. When they reached the solicitor's, there was no sign of Jane, so they sat together on a bench, overcast by the shadows of tall buildings.

'Birdie,' Hope started tentatively. The tone of her voice caught Birdie, whose anger had already passed.

'I'm sorry, Hope. Ignore what I said on the beach, Jane's always telling me I get too involved in other people's lives. You must make your own decisions.'

'No. It's not that. I really need to ask you something. Before Aunty Jane comes back.'

Birdie stilled herself, wondering if she was ready for whatever Hope was going to throw at her next.

'Okay. I'm listening.'

'It's what you were saying about love.'

Birdie remained guarded. She was prepared to listen. But she wasn't going to be complicit in lies and secrets. Jane would just have to forgive her, she decided, because if she needed to, she would knock the walls of silence into rubble. She nodded slowly and looked at Hope.

'It's just, there this… Well, there was this, I mean. Well, I was talking to one of Iris's friends at a party, and he's studying English at university.'

Birdie tilted her head.

'You know how everybody goes on about hippies, you know, cosmic love and dropping out and all of that.'

Seeing Birdie's wary look. Hope shook her head, energetically.

'No, I'm not about to join a commune. I'm not that stupid, It's just, well. It's all of that universal consciousness stuff that people talk about. Like Maharishi, I mean. Anyway, this guy. This friend of

Iris's, I mean. He was talking about a poet called William Blake. You've heard of him, right?'

'Yes, of course,' Birdie wondered was going through Hope's mind now, 'quite the visionary of his time.'

Hope ploughed on.

'Well, what you were saying about caring too much. Did you know Blake said it too? Listen. I wrote it down and memorised it. Will you listen?'

'Of course.'

Hope closed her eyes.

'"He who binds to himself a joy

Does the winged life destroy

He who kisses the joy as it flies

Lives in eternity's sunrise"

Isn't that just so fabulous. That is what you were saying, isn't it?'

'Yes. I suppose it is.'

Birdie looked up at the first-floor window, where the name of the solicitor had been painted in large black letters.

‘But the thing is,’ she added slowly, ‘it’s not always obvious what our joys are… the kind of life you seem to fear so much may be over keen in telling you how to bind yourself, but if you just shut out those voices and look the other way it can still be difficult to find the real joys - the ones you should love and kiss as long for as you can.’

Beside her, Hope thought of Joseph and sighed.

‘Oh yes. If only we could live our lives like that. Really live, I mean.’

Chapter 29

Finally, September had arrived. That afternoon, Birdie had set off with Hope for the Mother and Baby Home in Bristol where she would spend the next six weeks. She would stay in a small hotel overnight and return the following day. Left alone, Jane had wandered aimlessly in and out of her studio, and now, in the early evening, she stood at the end of the garden, where their boundary gave way to a riot of brambles. The blackberries were late this year, and the only ripe fruits were right in the corner, just beyond her reach. Just there, beyond the overhang of the oak tree, the evening sunshine lingered. She felt empty. She poked about for a stick to try and pull the ripe berries towards her. A few would be nice this evening. With the cool evening air on her face, Jane felt a sense of peace. She hadn't realised how much she had longed to be alone. Although, she reflected, she was never really alone now, the cancer had become her a constant companion, interrupting her thoughts and daydreams with its way of barging into her life with its insistent interruptions to her daydreams. Sometimes, she thought, it was hard to know what of her physical self was hers in truth, and what belonged to the cancer.

Now that Hope was gone, she wondered if Birdie had been right all along about Hope. It was useless, she thought. Since those initial tears back in April, Hope had never once told Jane how she felt about the baby, her situation, the future plans she had agreed with Elizabeth. Jane sighed. Perhaps it would have been better to have been completely honest with her. The cancer, the will, Birdie. The time, though, had never been right. And there'd been the unresolved issue of David. How could she tell seventeen-year-old girl things she couldn't even say to her own brother. And so, as the weeks had slipped by, and she'd stayed silent. Birdie had been angry. Upset to, and once or twice they'd come close to rowing about the situation. Even that was difficult, with Hope constantly in earshot.

Jane gave up her search for a stick. If she fell in the brambles, she'd be stuck there all night. Better wait until Birdie got back in the morning. She turned back to the house. Some trick of the sunlight, no doubt, but the house seemed to be gazing at her. The two rear upstairs windows looked like eyes, and an irregularity in the stone below could almost be contoured like the planes of cheekbones, certain angles picked out in relief by the evening sky. Jane, still some thirty feet from the house, knelt on the path to see if a different angle enhanced the illusion. The result was disconcerting. She felt dizzy again and paused before trying to stand again. As she crouched there, she could smell the compact, musty scent of the soil, and it seemed to her to have a gnarled quality, like the roots of an oak, or her painter's hands.

As is so often the case in late summer, the light slipped from the sky, not in imperceptible degrees, but in sudden jumps. Around her, the brambles, hedges and trees turned from intricate greens to dark silhouettes. The slate roof came into its element, black and funereal against the darkening sky. Her sense of self seemed to be disappearing into the gloom as the garden darkened, as if she was a nothing more than a shadow, vanishing with the daylight.

Here I am, she thought, just a creature, knocked into nothingness by the disappearance of light. Fear drenched her to the centre of her being. She wanted to howl with the enormity of her emptiness. Once again, she had the sensation that her mind was unravelling into filmy memories, old photos from forgotten places. She hated the way this happened with increasing frequency. However few the number of weeks she had left, she wanted to inhabit them fully, live each moment. But she found her days were being claimed by memories and regrets. Her time was being stolen from her by her own past. She should cry out, like a fox in the night. Why couldn't she yell? No-one would hear her. She willed breath into her lungs, the scent of loamy earth overpowering her. As she rose to her feet, she became certain that her death was close, much closer than she'd believed. She doubted if she would see her niece again.

The following morning, she rose early, full of a gritty determination to seize the morning. Birdie couldn't hope to be home much before midday. Working rapidly, she had quickly primed a canvas, and her paint brush was hovering indecisively over a palette of burnt ochre and phthalo green when she heard the car crunch along the track. Birdie, home already.

'What a journey.' Birdie jabbed a spoon into the jar of coffee, flinging the granules into two mugs. When the kettle whistled, she picked it up, gesticulating at Jane as she did so, and spilling boiling water on the floor.

'It's a long way, isn't it. Even with the new bridge.'

'It's not that. It's Hope. Can you honestly tell me that this is really what she wants? She's got this ridiculous barricade separating her actions from her feelings. Oh, it makes me so cross.'

Jane said nothing, quietly wiping the spilt coffee from the kitchen table and rinsing the cloth under the cold tap.

'And when she talks about her future. Oh Jane, why does it hurt so much? I can hardly bear to listen to her.'

Birdie blew on her coffee to cool it before taking a gulp but scalded her mouth anyway.

Jane wanted Birdie to stop thinking about Hope. There was nothing she could say now that would make any difference. Hope had made her decision and was gone. The Mother and Baby Home would take over now and see to all the details of the adoption. But Birdie was still agitated, so wrapped in fury and distress that Jane couldn't reach her.

'Why don't I add some more cold milk for you?'

'Don't worry, I'll do it. My fault for being in a hurry. Ouch. That's going to blister.'

Birdie poked at the top of her mouth with her finger. It was hot and sore. She sat heavily, her shoulders and back crumpling as she leant forward.

'Oh Jane, it was awful. We spent most of the journey like strangers on a bus who've fallen into conversation. Remarking on the views, talking about the road. That sort of thing. I dropped her off at the Mother and Baby Home. I didn't go in with her. I just couldn't. I watched from the roadside as she rang the bell. A woman came to the door and seemed to be asking her questions before she finally let her in. God, Jane, there's an unctuous cat-got-the-cream air of sanctimonious do-goodery about the whole thing. Looking after the girls. Giving the babies the best chance in life. What gives them the right? For heaven's sake, Jane, it's 1970.'

'Hope has to make her own decisions.'

Couldn't Birdie stop, thought Jane. She wanted to tell her about the previous evening, her experience in the garden. How could she grab every moment of her life if Birdie wasn't even paying attention.

'Birdie, listen.'

'I heard you. How could you say that? Hope hasn't made a decision; she's been herded like some kind of farm animal. And we could have done more. So much more.'

Birdie's anger was exhausting. It was awful, Jane felt, the way her energy deserted her so quickly, leaving her drained and irritable on the turn of a thought.

'We did what we could.'

‘Not good enough,’ Birdie picked up her cup and threw the contents into the sink, ‘and anyway, I need to get on. I wasted the whole day yesterday.’

Chapter 30

Hope had insisted that Birdie didn't come to the door with her. As she stood outside the tired Victorian building, she had been assailed by a sense of unreality. Behind her, she knew Birdie still sat in the car, unwilling to leave. The building in front of her seemed utterly uninterested in her presence, as if her existence was of no importance. Eventually, the door was opened by a tall woman. Her stooped back and cricked hip betrayed years of trying to appear shorter, less conspicuous, and her hair, a mix of chestnut and grey, lay heavy on the back of her head in a tight bun. The tired lines around her mouth gave her an air of disappointed resignation. She hadn't seemed to be expecting Hope and quizzed her for several minutes before opening the door wide enough to allow her to enter the building.

'Stay there, Miss Greenwood. Someone will fetch you presently.'

Hope stood in the uncared-for vestibule with her suitcase beside her. The walls had been painted in an institutional green colour which was ill-matched with the patterned tiled floor. In a couple of places, where tiles had cracked or broken, the gaps had been inexpertly filled. There was a window to the north, but whatever view there might have been was obscured by heavy net curtains. The etched glass on the front door admitted the only other source of light, which slumped heavily onto the floor, illuminating nothing. Heavy brown wooden doors presumably led to the kitchen, a living room and other rooms. They were all closed, and Hope didn't dare open them. There was a notice board at the bottom of the staircase, which held a notice outlining the days and times of Church Services, a rota of household tasks on which different hands had scrawled their names, and a small black and white poster advertising a lecture on home hygiene, the date of which had already passed.

Ten minutes ticked by. Hope glanced at her wristwatch. Was it really still only a quarter past four? There were distant sounds coming from other parts of the building, but she could hear nothing clearly. Had she been forgotten? There was nowhere to sit, and she started pacing around the vestibule, angling her head to peer up the stairs, the bare walls guarded in the same dull green paint. She wandered over to the window and lifted the net curtain to see what lay outside.

'Ooh, you better not do that!'

The voice made her jump. Turning, she saw a heavily pregnant woman in her early twenties coming down the stairs.

'Sorry,' said Hope, letting the net drop. Was this the person sent to collect her, she wondered.

'Them curtains is there for a reason,' the woman continued, 'so as the neighbours doesn't have to see us sinful girls. My name's Mel, by the way.'

'Oh. Hello. I'm Hope.'

Hope held out her hand.

'Well, it's Pamela, actually, but I don't like that. Think my mum must have run out of names by the time she got to me. I've got five sisters. So, it's Hope, is it?' she gave Hope a broad smile, 'When're you due?'

'Um. Oh, you mean the baby. Beginning of October. That's what they told me.'

'Course I mean the baby. So, you're a week after me then. What happened to you then? Me, I got a bit merry at Christmas, if you know what I mean. My boyfriend had been on at me for ages. So, we had ourselves an early Christmas present. We was careful and everything, but then we did it again on Boxing Day. I think that's what done for me. He scarpered of course.'

she grinned at Hope, her face a mix of friendliness and bravado.

'They're all the same, if you ask me. Anyway, what are you doing down here in the hallway, apart from showing your sinful self to the neighbours?'

'Someone let me in and then told me to stay here. I've been waiting for ages.'

'Tall, was she? With the face of someone chewing lemons?'

Hope nodded, almost smiling at the accuracy of the girl's description.

'Mrs Cox. She's in charge here. I tell you now, so you know it. She can see round corners, not a word of a lie. And as for rules. We reckon she makes up a new batch every morning. You want to watch her. She thinks we should all be wailing and ashamed and as rotten as hell. Anything she can do to help us along the way. Well, don't say I haven't warned you.'

Hope looked at Mel, baffled. Why on earth would Mrs Cox be so unpleasant? Wasn't the Home going to look after her? She looked at Mel, her eyes dark with anxiety.

'Oh, don't look so worried. You look like you've seen a ghost. Don't fret. We still have a bit of fun, you know. She does go out, sometimes. You come with me, now. I'll show you around the palace.'

'But' Hope stalled, 'shouldn't I wait here? Won't Mrs Cox wonder where I am?'

'Don't be daft. She'll of told one of the girls to come and get you, but they obviously couldn't be bothered. You come with me. You can tell me all about yourself.'

Mel guided Hope up two flights of stairs, talking as they climbed.

'So, what's your story then. Boyfriend?'

Hope shook her head. All these months, and no one had asked her questions like these.

'Somebody else's boyfriend, then?' continued Mel.

Hope shook her head again. She had no words to explain, not even to herself.

'Oh gawd. Well, you don't look like one of those what sleeps with every good-looking boy.'

Mel grinned again, her brown eyes looking doubtfully at Hope.

'We don't have secrets from each other in this place, you know. After all, we're in the same boat.' She paused on the stairs, with a sudden air of concern and sympathy.

'You aint one of those with a family problem, are you?'

Hope couldn't think what Mel meant. She looked questioningly at her.

'Blimey. Are you innocent, or what? You know what I mean. Lecherous uncles and brothers. There were a girl here last month. Elspeth. She was got up the duff by her own dad, they said. She's gone now. Had a little girl. I never met her, of course.'

Suddenly, it was as if the air had collapsed. Hope's sight became fuzzy, and she thought she would faint. There was a window on the landing, covered, like all the others, with a thick net curtain, but Hope didn't care. She needed to breathe. Struggling with the window catch, she opened it wide and took in several lungfuls of air, oblivious to Mel's warnings to leave the window well alone.

Within moments, there was the sound of a door banging, and Mrs Cox was beside them.

‘Miss Greenwood. You will close that window immediately.’

‘Oh, excuse me, but I felt giddy. There’s no fresh air in here.’

Mrs Cox widened her eyes, looking coldly at Hope’s pregnant body.

‘Pamela, you will add Miss Greenwood’s name to the rota for additional duties, if you please.’

Mrs Cox tightened her mouth, as if judging Hope to be a trouble-maker and nodded dismissively before descending the stairs.

Mel whistled.

‘That’s you up at six to scrub the floors then. Sorry love, but don’t say I never warned you.’

Hope looked unsteady, as if she might fall over. It was too much. Just a few hours ago she had been with Jane and Birdie, loved and held, without question. And now, she had no idea who she was, or why she was here. The sickly green walls seemed malevolent and cruel. Mel looked at her.

‘Whoa, girl. Why don’t you hang on to me. Only a few more stairs to the recreation room. You can meet the rest of us. Cuddle time is over, but I don't expect anyone's gone out yet.'

'Gone out?' echoed Hope, faintly.

'Come on. It's not that bad here. Mrs Cox will keep you at it, but there's plenty of free time. You can go out whenever you want, after lunch of course. You can go to the park. Catch a bus into town if you want to. We're not prisoners, even if Mrs C thinks we should be.'

'Are we allowed to write letters, then?'

'Course you are. Some of the girls write to their boyfriends every day. Not that they all get a reply. Living in fairy tales, half of them. But you go right ahead.'

The following day, Mel sought her out after lunch.

'Better today?' she asked. 'Sorry about the extra cleaning. Mrs C, you know.'

'Oh, I don't mind. It's not as if I'll be here long.'

'If you say so. But the days don't exactly fly past in here. Best bit of the day now though. We all go to the recreation room at two o'clock. I'll take you up, come on.'

Hope nodded listlessly. She had spent months intent on ignoring her condition, building defences to block out the changes in her body. And now, she felt utterly trapped. Last night, she had found she was to share a dormitory with five others, and that morning she had been doing housework with three more of the residents. If only she could run away, be alone somewhere, away from everyone. The open way the others talked about their pregnancies intimidated her, and she hated looking at them. The casual way they heaved their swollen bellies around oppressed her, made her dizzy with horror. There was nothing about this place that made sense.

'You coming, or what?'

'Sorry.'

Why was Mel so friendly, she wondered. As if Hope could possibly mean anything to her. There really was no point. But she followed Mel into the recreation room anyway, at least it gave her something to do. The room had just one tall window facing south and light streamed through it, suffusing the cream nets draped over the glass and falling on a group of young women, one sitting in a shabby brown armchair, the others crouching close by. The seated figure held a bundle of blankets, her face illuminated, joyful. What was she holding? Hope stopped in the doorway. She reached forward and tugged at Mel's sleeve. Mel turned, her face wide with delight.

‘It’s cuddle time. There’s five babies at the moment, and we all get to share cuddles with them.’

Hope felt a heavy drumming in her head. Dizzy, she grasped at the door frame for support. The sunlight disturbed her vision, everything was blurred. Skin cold, feet bound in lead. She couldn’t. She couldn’t. Breathe. Speak. Stand.

Chapter 31

The slight cold Jane had complained of when Birdie returned from Bristol had developed into a horrible rasping cough and temperature. Wednesday was market day in Carmarthen, and Jane was not well enough to go. Birdie didn't want to leave her, but there was business to be done. She pulled up in the car park and leant over into the back seat to grab her shopping bags. The town was already busy. In the past, they had loved market day; it gave the town a sense of purpose and good-natured enjoyment. Next to the livestock market there was a smaller auction room where anyone could sell their surplus vegetables and eggs. They had often sold produce their themselves and always revelled in the sight of the boxes and bunches of homegrown vegetables on display. Today, though, Birdie walked straight past the auction room, heading for the chemist. There was a knot of people by the clock tower, mostly women, some with large prams which they rocked back and forward as they talked. Pedestrians slowed to get past. The women irritated her unreasonably. Why did people get in the way so? She wanted to get to Boots, go to the butcher, pick up some pictures for framing from the gallery and get home.

Birdie blamed herself for Jane's illness. Four days ago, when she had returned from Bristol, they had both been out irritable and bad-tempered, their divisions over Hope seeming sharper than ever. And so, they'd decided to go to the pier to stare at the ocean and endless sky. They'd arrived at the pier mid-afternoon, pleased to find they had it to themselves. With the air blowing through their hair and the gulls circling, laughing overhead, Birdie had felt the knots fall from her shoulders. Jane had encouraged her to fool around, had laughed at her antics and egged her on. The way they were with each other, able to drop into exuberant silliness and laugh until their sides hurt. They had stayed out for too long, though. Relishing every second of their reconciliation. It had been nearly dusk when they packed up their picnic and headed home. And now Jane was ill.

Birdie pushed through the crowded street, not caring if she seemed rude. There was a queue in the chemist, and she jittered anxiously from foot to foot, willing the pharmacist to serve people more quickly. Finally, she finished her shopping and headed to the gallery to meet Simon. He owned the business and was one of her regular customers.

‘Birdie. How good to see you. Now, you’ve chosen quite the best moment to call in. And I’ve got something most interesting for you. A couple of extra canvases, you know. Originals. Quite distinctive, actually. I’ve met the chap. Londoner. Like me. A retired Naval Captain though, would you believe. Moved here four and a half years ago. Taken up oils. Very well-spoken. And I don’t have to tell you how rare it is to get something really good from a local painter. I suppose we can call him a local, wouldn’t you say?’

Birdie nodded abstractedly, thinking about how long she’d already been away from Jane.

‘Just wait there, I’ve got everything ready for you in the back room.’

Simon disappeared. Birdie sighed, putting her bags down by the counter and flexing her hands, feeling the sore marks where the handles had reddened her flesh. She could hear the gallery owner moving about. What on earth was he doing. Finally, he returned with the canvases.

‘Now, those three we’ve already talked about.’

Simon indicated three prints by Constable. Bread and butter for the gallery, just needing dark stained pine frames to finish them off.

'And here are the captain's canvasses. Let me show you.'

He smiled wryly and picked up a sharp knife to cut through the brown string holding the wrapping, but Birdie stopped him.

'Look Simon, I'll get them home and have a look, shall I. I can give you a call to discuss the options. I'm sorry. I really must get back.'

Simon was disappointed, but Birdie took the bundle under her arm and almost ran out of the shop and back to the car park. She loaded the paintings into the boot, wrapping them in the extra blankets she kept there for that purpose. As she closed the boot, she suddenly realised that she didn't have her shopping bags. She must have left them in the gallery. It was only a five-minute walk, but Birdie felt suddenly useless; how could she be so careless. She was hot with fury at herself. Could she do nothing right? Even something so basic. And when Jane most needed her. If it weren't for the medicine in the bags, she might have abandoned it all, but she forced herself to return to the gallery, where she quickly picked up her shopping, lifting the bags to show Simon and shaking her head without speaking as she dashed out the door.

Jane heard the car arrive with relief. She felt hot and shivery at the same time. She'd drunk the glass of water Birdie had left her but didn't trust herself on the stairs to get more from the kitchen. Birdie hurtled up the stairs, dropping a kiss on her forehead.

'Sorry darling. I didn't mean to be so long. How are you feeling? You don't look any better.'

Jane put her hand on Birdie's arm; she didn't trust her voice.

'You're hot. Way too hot. Have you had some more aspirin? Let me get you some. Shall I call the doctor?'

'No need, darling,' Jane croaked slowly, 'aspirin though. And a cup of tea would be nice.'

When Birdie returned with the tea, she had to wake Jane to give her the aspirin.

'That'll do the job.' Jane reached forward to take the tea, 'I'll drink this and have a little doze. Right as rain this afternoon. Promise.'

By lunchtime, Birdie was exhausted. She'd spent a useless hour in the studio, darting back to the house every few minutes to listen at the bottom of the stairs. Now, she had soup and bread on a tray ready for Jane, but couldn't decide whether to go up, or wait for her to call. Hovering in the hall, she noticed the post still lay on the floor. There were several letters, mostly with typed envelopes. A small envelope with the stamp stuck crookedly in the corner caught her eye. The handwriting was Hope's. She took it, with the tray, and climbed the stairs. To her relief, Jane was propped up in bed, looking slightly better.

'I've made you some soup.'

She proffered the tray in Jane's direction.

'And there's a letter for you, I think it's from Hope.'

Jane took the tray and propped it on her knees.

'Thank you darling, just what I need. Smells delicious. If I tuck in, will you read the letter? Let's see if she's settled in.'

Jane patted the side of the bed and Birdie sat.

'"*Dear Auntie Jane,*

I felt really sad when I left your house yesterday. You have been so kind to me, really opened my eyes to life. For one thing, it's been amazing to be talked to like an adult. Everyone else treats me like a kid. You tell it straight.

You'll never guess what, but Birdie took the wrong road. We were halfway to Abergavenny before we realised. I think she'd forgotten about the Severn Bridge. Like, it's only been open FOUR years. It didn't matter though, we had all the time in the world, and the countryside is so beautiful. You can really sense the ancient ways, like the spirits of Welsh bards are still moving across the hills. Maybe I'll move to Wales after university. I'd be closer to you then.

After, well, you know. The thing is, I feel it's really important that I make decisions about my OWN life. I'm fed up with doing what's expected of me. This whole year has made me feel like I'm trembling on the edge of who I will be. Birdie has been awesome and kind. She's not prejudiced about things, and she's so wise. The thing is, what she says about everything being connected is just so true. Sometimes I get that feeling when I'm drawing. You know, like the whole universe is on my side. It makes me realise that I just have to be free.

But you know Dad. He's going to insist that I go to university. If I don't, I'll be going against everything. Like there would be no road back. It makes me feel like I am about 100 years old and only a kid, both at the same time.

Anyway, I really wanted to say thank you, thank you, thank you. You're an amazing aunt.

And next time I see you you'll have got rid of that horrible cough. I'm sure you will.

With all my love, Hope.

p.s. please write to me if you have time. Everyone here is really unfriendly.

Birdie put down the letter. She hardly dared look at Jane. How could Hope write such a letter. It told them nothing. Was she never going to talk about the baby, its future. Did she honestly think that her pregnancy would disappear entirely if she never mentioned it? Caught between anger and grief, she glanced at Jane, who had her eyes closed and looked as if she might cry. After a few seconds she looked sadly at Birdie and shook her head.

'I'm sorry, my darling,' she said, 'You were right. I should have told her about the will, everything. How could I have been so stupid?'

She lifted her hand, pulling her fingers against the skin on her neck in agitation.

'I've made a terrible mistake. Sometimes I'm as stupid as my brother, aren't I?' She pushed the tray away. 'I can't eat this now. I'm sorry, I'll eat it later.' She picked up the letter and skimmed the paragraphs, her jaw clenched. Birdie laid a hand on her forearm, but Jane shook it away. There was a fierce determination in her face as she spoke.

'I am going to write to her. Will you bring the writing paper for me? I'll do it as soon as I've had a little sleep. Oh Birdie, you've been more right about this all along. She's not facing up to things, and the dreadful thing is, I've helped her do it. It's as if she thinks that real life will simply reappear once this whole sorry episode is over. How can I have been so stupid.'

Throughout the afternoon Jane's symptoms worsened. She complained that her head hurt, and Birdie couldn't bring her enough blankets to keep her from shivering. By nine o'clock, she was clearly running a high temperature, her breathing was laboured, and she thought she might have flu. When the doctor arrived, he quickly decided it was pneumonia, and that Jane needed to be taken straight to hospital. Within half an hour, Birdie was left alone in the empty house, watching the tail-lights of the ambulance disappear in the darkness. The unused pad of notepaper lay on the bedside table.

Chapter 32

'Oy, Hope. 'Nother letter for you. From your Welsh boyfriend again.'

Mel lifted the envelope to her face and sniffed loudly.

'He don't use no aftershave then?'

Hope laughed.

'Yeah right. You never give up, do you Mel? The only person who writes to me is my aunt. She lives in Wales. Last month, she was in hospital, but she seems to be better now.'

Hope put the envelope in her pocket.

'Seriously, though. Your aunt. Why's she write so often then?'

'It's complicated,' Hope sighed, 'when I realised I was pregnant I went to stay with her. My parents didn't want me at home. She lives with Birdie on The Gower. Well, her real name is Birgitte. They've got a cottage.'

'Oh yeah. Lezzies, are they?'

'No. Of course not. They run a business together. They've converted a barn into a studio, so everything is in one place. They're both single, so it makes sense.'

‘Hmmm. If you say so. What’s the studio for then?’

‘Is there anything about anybody you don’t want to know?’ Hope teased.

She could hardly believe how quickly things had changed. Four weeks ago, she’d been so wary of Mel. Now, they seemed like old friends.

‘If you must ask, well, Birdie runs the picture framing business and my aunt’s a painter.’

Mel stared at Hope as if she had never really seen her before.

‘Wait on. Your surname is Greenwood, isn’t it?’

‘And?’

You’re not telling me that you’re related to Jane Greenwood. Strewth.’

‘You’ve heard of my aunt?’

‘Well, yeah. She is quite famous, you know.’

‘I know, but, I mean.’

Hope shook her head, hunting for words.

‘Yes, I know she’s like, well thought of by other artists. But.’

‘But what?’

'Well, I suppose I didn't think ordinary people would've heard of her.'

Mel froze momentarily, and then flushed a furious red.

'Oh, go to hell, high and mighty Hope. God knows why I bother with you. Ordinary people. You mean people from secondary modern schools. Thickos. Me, for example.'

Hope was horrified. How could Mel misunderstand her like this. She wanted to run away. Mel's anger was sudden, intense, like a volcano. She felt helpless in its force. She could do nothing. She stared at Mel in shock.

'Thing about you, Hope, is you're not interested in anybody except your own self. If you showed half the interest in me that you should, you'd know I was studying Art at Evening Classes before I ended up here. I bloody love painting.'

Mel turned her back and began walking away. As she reached the door she turned.

'Your precious aunt came and gave a lecture at our college last year. She was amazing. Bloody brilliant, in fact.'

Mel glared at Hope.

‘And she was really interested in us ordinary people, too.’

Left alone, Hope sat, inert, on the side of her bed. She tried to shut out Mel’s sudden, furious anger, the way she’d looked so wounded, but she couldn’t. She felt the hot shame of her stupid, stupid clumsiness. She thought they had liked each other. Perhaps she’d been wrong. Perhaps Mel had thought of her as stuck-up, all this time. Hope couldn’t believe how quickly Mel had flared up. She hadn’t meant any such thing when she said… What were the words she had used? “Ordinary people”. Was that so awful? She picked up a book, trying to read herself into forgetfulness, but after turning a few pages, she gave up and threw the book on the floor. Perhaps Mel had just felt sorry for her. The others thought she was a snob, so why not Mel?

She lay on her back on top of her eiderdown, her eyes wide open, staring at the ceiling. Avoiding each other at mealtimes wouldn’t be too difficult, she decided, and Mel always went to cuddle time in the afternoons. In the evenings, they often watched television together, but Hope thought she could stay in the dormitory. But they were on the cleaning rota together most mornings. Should she talk to Mrs Cox, ask her to change the rota?

Mel's baby was due in two weeks. It wasn't long. Surely, they could avoid each other? Or perhaps she should pretend to be unwell. Would that work? Still lying on the bed, her limbs torpid and her head pulsating, Hope felt the baby move deeply and firmly within her, flexing and turning as if exploring the confines in which it lived, awaiting a life as yet unknown. Hope picked up her book again and frowned at the pages.

The morning after their argument, Hope was late down to breakfast. When she arrived at the dining room, Mel was sitting at the end of the table, grinning widely. In front of her were several birthday cards, which she had propped up between the cereals and bowls. She was busy unwrapping a small present, which looked like it must be a single.

'Desmond Dekker!'

The other girls crowded round, looking envious.

'Who's it from, Mel?' asked the girl at her left.

'Dunno. Hang on, let me get at the card.'

Mel tore open the envelope, which she dropped on the floor beside her. When she opened the card, her face paled suddenly, and then turned bright red.

‘Oh gawd. Mike. It’s from me fella. Bloody Hell. What’s he want after all this time?’

The card contained a folded letter, which Mel pushed rapidly into her pocket. Looking up, she saw Hope framed in the doorway.

‘Morning Hope. It’s me birthday.’

‘I, I can see,’ stuttered Hope. ‘I’m sorry, I didn’t know.’

‘Yeah well, that’s just you, aint it?’

Hope flushed deeply.

‘Well, Happy Birthday, anyway.’

‘Look, Hope. You got a minute after breakfast? I just want to have a word. Quiet, like.’

Hope flushed even deeper red. She nodded and sat down to eat. The other women were clustered around Mel, and Hope didn’t have to speak to anyone.

She was cleaning her teeth when Mel tapped her on the shoulder.

‘Look, I want to say sorry. Flying off the handle like that. I didn’t mean what I said. Well, I did mean some of it, but not in an angry way. I don’t suppose you can help how you are. Distant and all that.’

'It was a party.' Hope said.

'Come again?'

'A New Year's Eve party. There was a plate of chocolate cake, and I ate loads. Turned out it was hash brownies. Anyway. I was out of it. There was this bloke. Afterwards I couldn't remember what happened.'

'You mean?'

Hope nodded. She'd thought she would feel weak and helpless if she told anyone what had happened to her, but instead she felt defiant.

'The dirty bastard. Did you tell…'

Hope shook her head, interrupting Mel's question.

She looked warily at Mel, not trusting her to speak.

'New Year's party, was it? I suppose the stupid bastard was drunk. Or stoned himself. Stupid men and their stupid sex drives. They don't even know what they're doing, half the time. You were unlucky to fall pregnant. Poor you.'

There was a silence.

'Mel?'

Mel looked up.

‘Can I ask you something?’

‘Break the habit of a lifetime,’ Mel giggled, ‘yeah, of course you can. I’m not the only one who’s allowed to be nosy.’

‘Oh. Sorry. It’s none of my business. Sorry Mel.’

Mel gave Hope an odd look.

‘It’s just a word, girl. I didn’t mean nosy. Curious, is better. That’s how you make friends you know. And anyway, how can you find out what you’re like if you don’t know anything about other people? Go on, ask away.’

‘Last night I heard you muttering to yourself. Whispering maybe. I’ve heard you before. Who are you talking to? Is it Mike?’

Mel took a deep breath.

‘Mike? God no. Until this morning, I thought as I’d never see him again, but in his card he says he can’t live without me. He even wants me to marry him. Got a job and everything. Well, I need to have a good talk with him before I agree. But no, I weren’t speaking to Mike.’

She paused.

‘I talk to my baby. Done it ever since Mike scarpered. I just figured that if I was going to have to give him away, I wanted to tell him everything I knew about life before he went. Just so as he’d know a few things to keep him going, you know.’

‘You mean, like he was a real person?’

There was a fierce note in Mel’s voice as she replied.

‘Oh, I got a proper baby here. And I’m a proper mum too. For however long it lasts. Could be weeks, could be the rest of my life. Don’t make no difference to it being real,’ for a moment Mel’s eyes were sharp as daggers, ‘whatever all the Mrs Coxes in this world want to believe.’

Hope looked down and ran her hand over her belly. The sensation was really strange. She held her hand still as she looked carefully at Mel.

‘My dad has dontellitus. Me and Iris always laughed about it. Before, I mean. Anything he doesn’t like, he doesn’t talk about it. Pretends it doesn’t exist. We used to try and wind him up. But look at me.’

Mel waited for Hope to continue.

'Don't – tell – itus… you see, like it was a real disease. Sometimes I think I hate him.'

'What did he say about you when you got pregnant then?'

Shadows crowded Hope's expression.

'He's never even mentioned it.'

Mel opened her mouth as if to speak, but said nothing.

Lying in bed that night, listening to Mel's soft tones on the far side of the dormitory, Hope put a tentative hand on her belly. In her mind, she cast about for something to say.

'Hello, baby. Sorry if I've been ignoring you. It's just. I mean. I never felt you were really…'

She felt like a fool, worse, she felt ashamed. Abruptly she pulled her hand away and tugged the eiderdown over her head.

She woke suddenly in the half-light. It felt like minutes later but must have been hours. Silhouetted against the faint grey window was a figure. It was Mel.

Hope slipped out of bed and padded over.

‘What’s the matter?’ she whispered, ‘Can’t you sleep? Are you ok?’

Mel drew breath sharply.

‘It’s coming,’ she whispered back, ‘I’m going into labour.’

She clamped her mouth shut as the bands of pain tightened around her belly. She felt as if her spine had been crushed to liquid.

‘Do me a favour?’ she gasped as soon as she was able.

‘Of course. Shall I get someone for you?’

‘No. No, I’ll be fine. This’ll take hours. I want you to call Mike. When it’s daytime, I mean. You’ll need to call him before eight, ‘cos he leaves for work then. Can you sneak out before breakfast. I want him to know.’

Hope flinched at the idea of calling this stranger to tell him such news. What could she say to him?

‘Wouldn’t you prefer to call him yourself?’

‘No time. I can’t go out like this, can I? And he needs to know now, before the baby is born. I want him to know what’s happening now, not afterwards.’

Hope looked uncertain.

'Please, Hope. If you get into trouble with Mrs C I'll tell her it was my fault. Honest I will.'

'I don't care about Mrs C.'

Hope suddenly realised she that Mrs Cox didn't matter. Nor did what other people would think. She would talk to Mike, tell him that his baby was arriving. A real baby, like Mel said.

''Give me his number, I'll go as soon as it's light.'

'You're a mate.'

Rummaging in her bedside drawer, Mel thrust a small diary into Hope's hands.

'Mike. Mike Okeke. His number's in the back. You just need to add 01 for London. Just ask for Mike. God, Hope, you're an angel.'

Mel's voice rose as the contractions gripped her again.

'Oooh. God, too quick. I need to get meself to the midwife. See you later.'

With a grin stretched tight between excitement and pain, Mel left the room, moving as quietly as she could while the other girls slept on.

Chapter 33

Jane had been discharged from hospital nearly four weeks ago, but the sensations from that evening alone in early September rarely left her now. Death, she thought was like an off-stage character, invisible, but with an immense influence. She felt its presence more and more, but wasn't sure when, or rather how soon, it would take centre stage. Since coming home, she'd taken to having her breakfast in bed, after which Birdie would help her downstairs, where she spent most of the day simply relishing the sense of being alive.

The spontaneous and regular sensations of delight were a revelation. When the doctor had handed her a death sentence, almost a year ago now, she'd returned home feeling as if her legs would collapse beneath her at any moment. She had felt flimsy and insubstantial, barely trusting her body to stay alive. But only very briefly did she find herself overwhelmed by dread. At first, she had resented the cancer as if it was the only thing that stood between her and immortality, but those thoughts were distant and somehow irrelevant. What had changed, she thought, was that she no longer resented her body for its frailty. It was simply doing what any living thing must do. She had outlived the doctor's prediction and learnt to live with a grace and joy she had never imagined possible.

Sitting in the garden as it folded itself into late autumn, she could see Birdie, head bent over frames, the door of the studio open. The smell of glue eased its way out, curling itself into her nostrils where it mingled with the deep scents from the garden. The leaves on their horse chestnut had already faded, drying and crumpling to an ethereal brown. On the windowsill in the studio Jane knew there was a small pile of last year's conkers, kept for the purpose of repelling spiders. Half-closing her eyes in a gentle squint, Jane could imagine that the bare branches, sticky buds like toffee apples, candelabra fit for the ballet, the shy green leaves of May and the viridescent spiky green baubles were simultaneously present, that all the myriad forms and colours of this one tree danced together in a world beyond time. She smiled. Her thoughts were interrupted by the postman's van.

'Just one from Hope,' said Birdie, handing her a thick envelope, 'fatter than usual.'

Jane started to read aloud.

'Dear Auntie J,

Thank you so, so much for your letter. Your story about Birdie's carrots made me laugh! I didn't know badgers liked eating carrots. But I need to write you a proper letter. The thing is, I feel really bad. I can't believe how you let me get away with being so awful. It's like I turned up at your house with all my melodrama and ruined your summer. And you never even asked me to explain. I'm really grateful, don't get me wrong. I love you and I wish I was as wise as you and Birdie.'

Birdie crouched down beside her, tense. The letter Jane had planned to write to Hope before she was ill was still unwritten, both of them aware of the prevarication, but neither of them understanding quite why they had yet to tell Hope about their plans for her future.

'The thing is, well, this woman Mel had to go to hospital yesterday because she went into labour. You know, I told you about her, how annoying she was? Except she's really not. She told me I'm selfish and don't care about other people. And you know what, she's right. Not normally, I mean. But since I found out I was pregnant. I've been a real cow, haven't I? Anyway, the day before was Mel's birthday, and her ex-fiancé sent her a single. It's called "You can get it if you really want" and he wants her to have the baby and then get married.

She says she's thinking about it. Typical Mel. Sorry, I'm rambling, aren't I. We had a bit of a row. She was right and I was wrong. It doesn't matter, but I told her about what happened to me. First person I've told. Even Iris never knew, though she thought she did.

It was like the world suddenly switched on again. I'm jealous of Mel, 'cos she's gonna have her baby and get married (she'll say yes, I bet) and although she never meant to get pregnant, she and Mike (that's her fiancé's name) are in love. I spoke to him on the phone. He has this amazing deep voice. Mel says that's because it's full of African sun. And then I'm so glad for Mel too, she deserves a happy ending. And then I feel really sad for me, because my baby doesn't have a father, just some stupid, stupid boy who took advantage of me when I couldn't stop him. I've actually been crying a lot about that this week, and I never cried before.

Even before Mike got in touch, Mel was talking to her baby. She said she wanted to tell her baby everything she knew about life, in case he had to grow up without her. Made me realise how childish I've been. Pretending nothing was happening. Why is it easier to ignore things when they aren't right?'

Jane stumbled over Hope's words, unable to continue. Birdie put her arms around her and held her tight for a long moment, both feeling the weight of too many silences.

'Let's finish the letter. There's not much more to go.

Anyway, I've been grounded this week because I got caught making a call in the phone box down the street when I should have been cleaning. I can't see Mel because she's still in hospital with her new baby. So, I've had lots of time to think. I don't want to grow up to be the sort of person who keeps secrets and pretends things aren't true when they are. That's what Dad does, you know. If he doesn't like something. It's not exactly trusting the universe, is it. Sorry. Feeble joke there.

If I write any more, I don't think I'll be brave enough to post this letter, so I'll just tell you (again) that I love you. I love my baby too, and I hope he has a good life. I'm going to try and talk to him as much as I can until, well you know. Until he's adopted.

Can I come and see you when this is over? Please say yes. You and Birdie are the only people I can talk to. I'm going to stop now and rush out to the post box before I lose my nerve.

ALL my LOVE, H xxxxx'

A small drop of concentrated ink, dropped into a jar of water, begins with whorls and loops to unfold itself into the clear liquid. Sometimes it will appear to pause, uncertain perhaps, before the hues mix and blend. Eventually one can see that this quality the ink had, this notion of colour, was only a fleeting identity. If this, then not that; if not that, then this. And yet, words could change everything. Jane closed her eyes. The secrets she thought would protect her for the rest of her life now felt like jagged rocks, haphazard and dangerous. Hope's honesty floored her; the words she had written arcing across the gaps between silence and truth.

Her gaze was caught by a leaf that had loosened and surrendered the tree. In the still air it eddied to and fro as it swirled to the ground.

'You see those leaves, just beginning to fade?'

Birdie shook the tears from her own eyes and looked up at the chestnut tree.

'They're going to nourish next year's leaves. And the year after, and the year after that.'

Birdie watched as other leaves swirled to the ground, catching the low sunlight as they performed eloquent arabesques. It wasn't that Jane didn't want Hope to know about the will, she realised, it was just that she couldn't put it in a letter. Honey-yellow hues of autumn light slanted across their garden.

'I'll go and see her,' said Birdie quietly, 'tell her everything, shall I?'

In answer, Jane lifted Birdie's hand in her own, tracing the blue lines that journeyed visible under the skin, continuing to run her finger beyond where she could see the veins to where she imagined they must go, until she reached the tips of Birdie's fingers.

Chapter 34

The air in the Bristol Maternity Hospital smelt of antiseptic, and in the ward, there were metal screens covered in drab cotton to separate the beds. Hope darted along the rows of women, looking for Mel.

'Well, I never did. It's Hope Greenwood, as I live and breathe. Thought you'd forgotten all about me.'

Mel was sitting up in bed wearing a nylon nightie and a pale pink bed jacket. Hope smiled at her.

'Likely story. They've only just let me out.'

'Huh? What do you mean?'

'Phone call? Remember that? Only got caught by Mrs C, didn't I. She grounded me for a week. Old bat.'

'What a trout. I'm sorry. So, you've heard all about my drama then?'

Hope nodded.

'You're alright now though, aren't you?'

'You're joking, right? I've got stitches all across my belly, I've hardly slept, and I'm treated like an unmentionable by most of the people here. As for the rest of me. Well, let's say I'll never look at a dairy cow again without pity in my heart. God's honour.'

Hope grinned.

'And Mike? Did he get in touch? I spoke to him alright. Once his mum had given me the third degree. She's a talker, isn't she? Mike seemed a bit shocked though.'

She looked at Mel. It was alright, wasn't it. It had to be. She relied on Mel to make everything work out.

'It is alright, isn't it? I've been thinking about you all week.'

'You are a strange one, Hope Greenwood. 'S that true then? You've actually been thinking about me. Next thing, you'll be wanting to see George.'

'George. Is that what you've called him? Course I want to see him. You don't think I caught a bus all this way just to see you, do you?'

'Mike's dad.'

'Mike's dad what?'

That's his name. George. I mean, Mike's dad is called George.'

Hope sat down beside Mel.

'So, it is alright then, you and Mike?'

Mel started giggling. The ripples of her laughter encircled Hope who couldn't help giggling too, and within seconds the two of them were hooting with laughter.

A nurse appeared at the end of Mel's bed, frowning.

'Nurse, oh nurse. Can you fetch little George from the nursery for me. Only I'm not allowed up yet, on account of the stitches.'

The nurse started to shake her head. She was too busy. She would try later. She couldn't make any promises.

'Oh, I'll get him. That's alright, isn't it nurse? I can fetch George if you show me where to go.'

'Don't bring the wrong baby!' Mel giggled as Hope was directed towards the end of the ward.

'Not very likely, is it!' Hope flashed a deep smile at her.

Mel sat back in the narrow iron bed. Who'd of thought it. Hope, of all people, making her feel special. She and Mike, they'd be alright.

Hope looked furious when she returned from the nursery.

'Bloody hell,' she said, 'poor lamb was all by himself. The nursery's ok, just a large room, but George's crib was pushed away from all the others, under a window.'

'You know what, Hope. Me and George don't care, and we're not going to care, ever. Some dumb nurse thinks browniness is catching, well, I feel sorry for her.'

Mel took the bundle of blankets and baby from the crib.

'Stop looking so cross, Hope. You going to cuddle this baby, or not?'

***

When Hope finally returned to the Mother and Baby Home, Mrs Cox was waiting. She opened the door sharply.

'You're very late, Miss Greenwood. I do hope you are not going to give me cause to ground you again?'

Hope looked at Mrs Cox, who was made of dark shapes and hard edges.

'Sorry Mrs Cox,' she began 'the bus…'

‘Never mind that now. You have a visitor. Not family. Most irregular. Apparently, the matter is urgent, so I have put the lady in my office to wait.’

Mrs Cox opened the door to her office. It had shelves and shelves of dark brown folders; her desk was a dull, unloved oak oblong which appeared to be squatting on an olive patterned carpet. There were no pictures on the walls, and the single bar electric fire had a faded appearance. Birdie stood directly beneath the bright overhead light, wearing a pale green wool coat with her favourite fuchsia beret. She had been examining the callouses on her fingers but raised her head sharply as the door opened.

She seemed to Hope like a tulip in November.

***

By the time Birdie had driven back from Bristol, it was nearly midnight. She turned off the car engine, feeling a mixture of exhaustion and elation. Hope was coming home. Home to Jane and Birdie. She would stay in Bristol until the baby was born, and then the four of them would live together. Birdie couldn’t wait to tell Jane. The world felt larger, more generous. And Jane would have the joy and anticipation of a new life in the house. It would do her so much good. Hope had given her a sketch she'd done of her friend Mel. It was a beautiful drawing, Mel looking over the head of her gorgeous baby and grinning at Hope as if she'd won the Pools. Birdie picked up her bag and the sketch, hurrying towards the house with so much joy to share.

There was a light on in the kitchen. That was so typical of Jane, Birdie thought. She'd forget to eat if Birdie wasn't there to remind her. She pushed open the door, immediately seeing that there was a note on the table, written in unfamiliar handwriting.

"Miss Greenwood has been admitted to Swansea General Hospital. Please call Swansea 7934 when you return home."

The telephone was answered after an eternity of rings.

'Miss Greenwood? One second. Let me check the record. Um yes, I have it here.' The voice paused, 'Yes. Miss Greenwood was admitted by ambulance at ten-thirty this evening. The doctor gave her oxygen, but I'm afraid she didn't regain consciousness. I am sorry, but I believe it was expected. I have a note here saying her next of kin were informed of her passing at eleven-fifteen.'

Ancient atoms stirred. If they could, they would pierce the canopy of time and counsel grief, not guilt.

PART THREE

Chapter 35

Since the beginning of the year, Iris has been marking a small calendar with the date her period starts. She hasn't told Don. When they married three years earlier, right out of university, she'd taken a secretarial job. They'd both wanted to start a family straightaway, so her income wouldn't be important, Don had assured her. Just pin money. And now they have this lovely house. Three bedrooms. Separate garage. Her inheritance had been a godsend, of course. Poor Auntie Jane.

It is August now, and Iris is sitting at the dining table, rifling through the Galloping Gourmet cookery book that her mother gave her as an engagement present. She doesn't know if Don is planning to take her out this weekend. Three years married on Saturday. She'll plan a special meal, just in case. Once she's written her list, she goes upstairs to change out of her blouse and skirt. She sits down at her new dressing table to wipe off her make-up. They've had the room done recently, bought G-Plan wardrobes and cupboards. Their new bed fits into a wall-length array of drawer units in the same pale cream colour with polished teak surfaces and drawer handles. It all looks so smart, and Iris loves the tiny shelves for ornaments that stretch above the headboard.

She pauses, a cotton wool ball in her hand, looking at her reflection in the mirror. She thinks she can see worry lines developing on her brow. She opens her eyes wide, trying to relax her face and make the creases disappear. Perhaps it is her new haircut. Don hasn't really commented on the new style. Perhaps it doesn't suit her after all. From nowhere, Hope is in her mind again. That time they went to the hairdresser back in 1970. Hope so secretive about herself. Does she still have the same long hair? And that awful fringe she'd had. Gosh, she'd almost forgotten that.

For no particular reason, Iris gets up and goes into the small back bedroom. She has inherited one of Jane's canvasses, which hangs there, almost filling an entire wall. She looks at it with her eyes half-closed. Such a shame the colours are so bright; it really would have been nice to display it in the living room, or even the dining room. Not everyone has such a famous artist in the family. Don was right though, it was rather loud.

Going back to their bedroom, Iris pours some liquid cleanser onto the pastel blue cotton wool ball and carefully wipes her lips and cheeks. Once finished, she stretches her lips wide, checking for dryness, and then smiles at her reflection. She opens one of the drawers and tidies everything away, carrying the used cotton wool ball to the bathroom to dispose of in the lined bin. Pausing before going downstairs, Iris goes back into the bedroom, closing the door behind her. Opening the bottom drawer of the unit on her side of the bed, she pulls out the calendar. It is 48 days since her last period now, and she feels not hope but dread. This has happened too many times before. If she allows herself to feel excited, the late, low cramps, dark pain and sense of failure will only be worse. She puts the calendar away, turning about for some other thing to think about...

Staring at herself in the mirror, she decides she will write to Hope. She really will, this time. She won't apologise about her wedding, not in the first letter. Hope must surely know that inviting her would have been impossible. Their father had made it quite clear, when he heard that Hope had decided to keep the baby, that he never wanted to see her again. Such a dreadful time. And he'd stuck to his guns. Even so. By the time she and Don got married, Jeannie would have been almost two. She'd have made such a sweet bridesmaid. Iris snaps the drawer shut. Ridiculous daydreaming. Of course, she'd needed her father there. To walk her down the aisle.

She wonders what Jeannie looks like. She asked her mother once, if she'd ever seen a photograph. Poor little mite. Not knowing her grandparents. No family at all, really. She and Ursula have kept their promise to each other, and Don still doesn't know that Jeannie is his cousin's child. Five years though. Strange how she missed Jeannie, even though they'd never met. She would love to be a proper aunt. Perhaps it wasn't too late. Jeannie must be starting school soon. In Wales, she supposes. But even if they have moved, she can write to Flag Cottage. Surely letters will be forwarded. She wonders, again, what Hope looks like now.

Chapter 36

Birdie and Jeannie stand waving by the gate to the road. Hope is going to Bristol, making last minute arrangements for her new home. Jeannie will start school in September, and Hope is going to go back to college to become a teacher. This is her last trip before they move for good. She will probably stay for a couple of nights, sign the contract for the new house, even start thinking about furniture. Birdie knows that Hope will stay with her boyfriend, Blue, whom Birdie has yet to meet. She wonders why Hope is so secretive about him. It's daft, she thinks, the way Hope acts like a teenage girl, sneaking around as if Birdie was a disapproving adult, she can't see the point in it.

The late summer shadows are lengthening earlier each day, and Birdie has decided she will take Jeannie to the beach, build sandcastles and listen to the sound of the sea folding onto the shore. If Jeannie can stay awake late enough, she will let her watch for the flash of tawny owls. There's a special treat lined up too. Birdie has convinced Hope that Jeannie is old enough to look after a rabbit. She will take her to the pet shop and let her choose for herself. It will be good for the child.

Two days pass, and Hope returns, turning her car into the driveway at Flag Cottage on Sunday evening. It is almost dark. Jeannie has been sitting in Birdie's bedroom, her eyes glued on the lane, waiting for her mum.

'She's here!' shrieks Jeannie, 'Aunty Birdie, Mummy's here. Come on.'

Hope is hardly out of the car, tired, feeling irritated by the way she and Blue had said good-bye, when Jeannie hurtles out of the gloom.

'Mummy, come on. Come with me, please. You've got to come now.'

Hope frowns.

'Well hello to you too. Can't you wait five minutes, baby. I'm desperate for a cup of tea.'

'But Mummy…' Jeannie's voice starts to rise.

'Hang on Jeannie. Take this bag for me, why don't you? Then we'll have a hug, and you can show me anything you like. Have you and Aunty Birdie been making something?'

Hope has completely forgotten about the rabbit purchase.

'No but,' she watches as her mum heaves a rucksack onto her back and heads into the cottage.

'Don't linger,' Hope calls, 'you'll get cold out there.'

'And you need to give me that rucksack and listen to your daughter.' Birdie's voice is firm, 'She's been waiting for hours, sitting upstairs, staring out the window.'

'What on earth for?' Hope can only feel how tired she is, how offhand Blue had been when they'd said goodbye.'

'Come on Hope. You must remember. Jeannie has something new to show you.'

Hope looks blank. Jeannie is listening, and Birdie doesn't want to spoil her big moment.

'Das Kaninchen. No. Um. Oh Heavens, Hope. Just go with her.'

Hope follows Jeannie out into the gloom. It isn't until she sees the hutch that she remembers. Of course, the rabbit. How could she have forgotten.

'Wowee, little egg. Who's this, then?'

‘This is my rabbit. All mine. Auntie Birdie bought it for me. He wants to live in Bristol with us.’

Jeannie looks up at her mum, searching her face for attention.

‘I don’t know what to call him, though.’

This is Hope’s super-power, and she bends over the cage, murmuring to the sleek brown ears and darker rump, all she can see beneath a haze of straw.

‘Oh wow,’ she says, ‘that’s amazing!’

‘What is it, Mummy, what did he say?’

Hope flings out her arm.

‘Miss Jeannie Greenwood, may I present Buddha Bunny?’ She turns to the cage, ‘Buddha Bunny, I think you’ve already met my little blue egg, Miss Jeannie Greenwood.’

Jeannie’s eyes are wide as seashells.

‘Wowee, Mummee.’

At the back door, Birdie stands in silhouette.

‘Oh Jane,’ she murmurs to the listening dusk, ‘must I really let go, again?’

Chapter 37

Jeannie, Hope and Buddha Bunny have been living in Totterdown for three months. Their mid-terrace house in Firfield Street, where the houses huddle and gossip on the hill like a crowd at a carnival, has wide views across the city. Totterdown, rebellious but alive, is still reeling from the demolition of hundreds of homes pulled down in readiness for vast road scheme that was then scrapped. Between Firfield Street and the rest of the city is a wasteland of rubble and scars. At night they can see a huge patch of darkness in the foreground, beyond which the lights of the city blur from individual scoops of yellowish light in Arnos Vale to form a low-hanging orange fog lying over the far side of the city centre. Hope says it is a haven for low slung night foxes and a playground for spiralling wheels of seagulls, but Jeannie wonders where all the people have gone. She likes looking at the city though and listening to the sound of trains as they shriek their way out of Temple Meads. One of the first things Hope bought for their new home was a second-hand wooden stool on which she and Jeannie have propped Teddy, so he has a fine view of the city. Jeannie promises him that one day, very soon, Auntie Birdie will visit on a big whooshing train.

The week before Christmas, Birdie arrives at Temple Meads. Jeannie hops up and down on the platform. As well as her battered travelling bag Birdie has bought a large suitcase with her, which Hope carries through the front door.

'Now, Jeannie, while your mum makes me a lovely cup of tea, are you going to show me around your new house?'

Jeannie pulls at Birdie's hand.

'Do you want me to carry that suitcase up for you?' asks Hope, 'It's very heavy.'

'No, I think it can stay there for now.'

Birdie twinkles her eyes at Jeannie and allows herself to be led away.

In the kitchen, busying herself with the kettle, Hope listens to Jeannie's shrill voice and Birdie's calm tones as talking to Buddha Bunny in his garden hutch. She desperately wants Birdie to love the house. Eventually, the two come downstairs, and Birdie smiles at Hope. A genuine, warm smile.

'Lovely,' she says, 'just lovely, Hope. You can tell that this house is enjoying having you living in it. Now, let me see.'

Birdie drags the large suitcase into the kitchen.

'Well, what do you think we've got in here?' she asks Jeannie, drumming her fingers like batons on the hard leather case. She shows Jeannie how to flip the metal clips to release the lid, which she flings open with a flourish, revealing odd-shaped bundles, wrapped in torn sheets from the South Wales Evening Post.

Jeannie looks at Birdie, who nods.

'Go on', she smiles.

'Parsnips!' Hope starts giggling as Jeannie unwraps an earthy parcel.

'Oh, wow Birdie, home-grown parsnips for Christmas. That's so cool.'

'And potatoes, look Mummy, look what I've found.'

'And leeks, and onions. Oh Birdie, that's fab. What else can you find, Little Egg?'

Jeannie tugs at a large bag, and peeps inside. Her voice is awed.

'Mummy, look. Our Christmas decorations. Look, the paper chains that I made for Auntie Birdie are here.'

‘And the angel for the tree. Oh, Birdie. This is amazing. It’s like you’ve bought the whole Flag cottage Christmas to Bristol. Wowee, Jeannie. It’s like magic.’

***

But by the day after Boxing Day, Birdie is exhausted and disappointed. Her visit has been such hard work. Something is wrong with Hope, that much is clear. But she’s so evasive, and Birdie has wanted her visit to be fun, if only for Jeannie’s sake. They have chatted together, and cooked, and played games with Jeannie, and spent hours inventing imaginary conversations with Buddha Bunny. What Birdie really wants to do is sit Hope down and ask her what’s bothering her. Even after Jeannie has been tucked up for the night, this has somehow been impossible. Birdie is worn out by the sense of constant play-acting.

On the final day of her visit, they take down the cards and decorations. As always, Birdie gathers up the cards, cutting the fronts off to save the pictures for next year’s present tags. She pauses over one, reading the message inside. Looking up sharply, she is about to speak, but then, with an effort of will unnoticed by Hope, she presses her lips together tightly and slips the uncut card deep into her pocket. Jeannie wraps up the baubles and the tree angel, breathing heavily with the effort of laying them carefully in the box, and Hope curls the tree lights around an old piece of cardboard. When Jeannie leaves the room to check on Buddha Bunny. Birdie puts down the scissors.

'I'm sorry I didn't get to meet Blue.'

'Yeah. Me too.' Hope has her head bent over the decorations, 'He just got this amazing chance to go to Poona. Like, the universe was nudging him, he said.'

'And Poona is important because?'

'It's kind of a spiritual place, Auntie B. One day, I'm going to take Jeannie out there. There's an ashram, you know.'

'And Blue is a disciple?'

'Well no. Blue, well, he says he's a seeker without a home. But he knows people everywhere.'

'And yet. he doesn't make you happy, does he?'

'Of course he does. Don't be silly, Auntie B. He's a free spirit. That's what I love about him.'

Birdie pauses, trying to organise her thoughts. Is it just Blue, she wonders, that has Hope so brittle? She's about to speak when a loud wail came from outside the window.

'Jeannie.'

Hope jumps up and ran into the garden to find Jeannie standing by an empty hutch, the door swinging open. The rabbit has gone.

It is Birdie who organises the search. They spend hours looking around the garden, the street, and even the derelict site below Firfield Street where all the houses were demolished. All they find are pieces of coloured tiles and broken terracotta chimney pots, smashed remnants of lost houses. Jeannie wants to search forever, holding out a large cabbage leaf, as she walks up and down, calling for her pet. But guilt and sorrow cannot undo loss, and Buddha Bunny will never return. Under a winter sky, every small dark mound of earth and rabbit-shaped shadow only shows Jeannie that the universe is unjust. This knowledge is new, and she will bury it as quickly as she can. Even so, the unmarked wound will scar and shape her.

Chapter 38

Two weeks later, Jeannie is back at school. If she is still sad, she is learning to hide it well. Today is Thursday, which means, Jeannie knows, it is hot chocolate day. She loves whisking up the milk, the way the bubbles jostle to the surface and settle there, laced in brown powder. Jeannie is tall for her age and has a square settled face. As she grows, it seems to Hope the shadows of all her ancestors take turns to occupy her face. At birth, she had looked just like her grandfather. Then one day at the beach, when she'd turned to laugh over a silly game, Hope had seen her sister's face. But now, Hope thinks how self-contained Jeannie looks. The angle of her cheekbones, the set of her eyes and determined chin, once seeming only borrowed, have become her own.

'Mum' Jeannie tugs at her, 'Bear sent me a message today.'

'Now how did he do that, I wonder?'

'Don't be silly, Mummy. He just did.'

'And what was so important that he had to interrupt you at school?' asks Hope.

Jeannie sighs and let go of her mum's hand.

'He's missing Buddha Bunny, mum. When will he come home?'

'Well, I just don't know, Jeannie. But he does send you lovely letters about all his adventures.'

'I know.' Jeannie feels Hope's answer isn't, somehow, quite enough.

'He's missing Auntie Birdie as well. He says she can come and live with us.'

'Oh, if only she could, little egg. I'd love that, but it's just impossible.'

Hope doesn't understand how her honesty perplexes Jeannie. Too young to reconcile adult super powers with the inability to choose exactly what you wanted to do; Jeannie feels at sea when her mum says she is sad as a result of things she herself has decided. Why had they left Wales if it made everyone sad? But, as is becoming her habit, she comforts herself with more practical matters.

'Is it still hot chocolate day?'

'Sure is, my little blue egg. Come on, let's go and tell Bear what we've been doing today.'

Jeannie sits at the tiny Formica table in their kitchen. She is kneeling on a chair so that she could reach the table properly.

'Mrs Oswald says we have a very exciting project this week.' Jeannie is talking to Bear while she carefully stirs the hot chocolate powered into the warm milk. She waves the spoon in his direction.

'It's a special picture called a family tree, Bear, and Mrs Oswald says we can show our pictures at assembly, if we are really good.'

She puts the spoon in her mouth, using her tongue to check its contours for any lingering drops of hot chocolate.

'Can I draw Auntie Birdie's tree, mummy? Cos we don't really have any trees here, do we?'

'Oh, egg! A family tree is a picture which shows all the people in your family. It's not a tree in the garden.'

'But I want to draw a tree. I like trees.'

Jeannie pushes the mug of hot chocolate away from her, and some of it spills onto the table. She pretends not to notice.

‘Well, let’s do both. Why not draw a huge picture of a tree, and then you can draw all the people in the tree, like Christmas decorations. We’ll get a nice big sheet of paper and do the tree part together, and then you can take it into school to show Mrs Oswald. Do you think she’d like that?’

Jeannie loves Hope like a mermaid loves the sea. She jumps down from her chair to push her small head into her mother’s side.

‘The hot chocolate has had an “oopsie, oh dear!”’ she announces, and pulls on a tea towel to wipe the damp table.

The following afternoon though, on the walk home from school, Jeannie is shut tight like a sardine tin without a key. When Hope unlocks the front door, she drops her coat and gloves on the floor and marches up the narrow stairs into her bedroom. Bear, as usual, is gazing serenely across the darkening Bristol skyline. Roughly, she pulls him from his seat and shoves him under her bed. Standing on tiptoe, she presses her face against the cold glass, looking out at the black wasteland beyond their street. She can hear the radio in the kitchen. She presses her forehead harder against the glass until the coldness hurts.

In the kitchen, preparing beans on toast for Jeannie's tea, Hope is standing with her eyes closed, listening intently to the elegiac regret in Freddie Mercury's voice singing "nothing really matters… anyone can see… nothing really matters… to me". Even after eight weeks at number one, Hope loves listening to Bohemian Rhapsody. She waits for the piano and guitar to describe the shape of infinity, before the final, almost inaudible line of voices seeps out from beneath them. It conceals a kind of wisdom, Hope thinks, like a mantra. She lifts her right arm, ready to conduct the closing cadences. But as the piano took over from Freddie's solo voice the volume fades suddenly, and the end of record is drowned by the DJ. His voice has a clashing, chirrupy resonance that seems to destroy all the possible universes that the music has invited into being.

'Jeannie. Teatime.'

Hope's voice is sharper than she intended. She walks into the hallway, picking up the abandoned coat and gloves. When she tucks Jeannie's gloves into a pocket, she finds it stuffed with torn pieces of paper. It is the picture of the tree they laboured over the previous evening.

'Jeannie?'

Hope sighs and climbs the stairs to Jeannie's room. She pauses in the doorway for a moment, gazing at the back of her daughter's head, then she moves forwards, putting her hands on her daughter's shoulders. All of a sudden Jeannie turns, folding her tense and furious body into her mother's arms.

'Mrs Oswald said my tree picture was all wrong. And all the boys laughed at me. They said I was a stupid girl. Mrs Oswald didn't even stop them. She just kept asking me stupid questions.'

'Like what, sweetheart?'

'I hate school, and I hate living here. I want to go home to Auntie Birdie.'

Hope tries to hold Jeannie close, but she will not be soothed. Prickly with shame and fury, Jeannie knows that her mother has failed her. Mrs Oswald had been kind to her, in that way grown-ups have, Jeannie thought, when they feel sorry for you.

'Poor little egg. And silly Mrs Oswald. She should know that not everyone has a big family. I bet some of the other children didn't have grannies and grandads to draw.'

'They did so. And they had lots of aunties, and brothers and sisters and daddies. Real ones. I want a family tree like that.'

Since before she can remember, Hope has escaped the skewed, unjust, and hurtful ways of the world by retreating into her imagination. She is gripped by ideas, compared with which facts are pale and featureless. For her, the world is a pale shadow of what she has come to recognise as the divine; the universal energy that breathes form into and out of being. She has no idea that Jeannie is different. She strokes her daughter's head, searching for tales and notions to dispel the sadness.

'Sweet pea, having Mrs Oswald's kind of family tree doesn't really matter you know. You and me, we're children of the whole big universe.'

Jeannie's face is still troubled. She detaches herself from Hope's hug and sits on her bed. For the first time in her life Jeannie understands that Hope doesn't know everything. What use is it to offer her the universe when all she wants is to have a real family? She stares out through the uncurtained window at the darkening void on the landscape where the abandoned and demolished streets descend the hill like ghosts.

Hope gazes at the bruised angel in front of her.

'Hey, come on, I can't have my favourite cosmic star all upset about a rotten old family tree. Let's drive up to The Downs later, shall we? See how many stars are out there tonight. That'd be fun, huh? Don't let school make you sad, Little Blue Egg. It really doesn't matter.'

But still Jeannie won't speak. Hope puts her hand under Jeannie's chin, half-caressing, half-pulling at her face to get the child to turn towards her. Jeannie shakes her head, pulling away. Abruptly, and with all the force of a wrecking ball, Hope is overwhelmed by angry despair. All her palaces of magic and dreams are reduced to so much rubble. Damn Mrs Oswald, insisting on ruled lines to connect names and dates where there should be sparkling turrets and glistening boughs.

Chapter 39

'Hang on a minute, I don't get it. You're pissed off with Jeannie's teacher because she got the kids to do a family tree?'

Mel takes the kettle off the gas while Hope leans against the work surface next to the cooker.

'Sorry Hope, just need to squeeze past you a moment.'

Hope flattens herself so that Mel can get to the cupboard where she keeps her mugs.

'Well, I get that she didn't do it on purpose, but it's kind of limiting you know, I don't think kids should only think of the nuclear family and all that when it comes to, well, deciding who's in your family.'

'Pass me the milk, can you?' says Mel, 'I'll do some for the kids as well. Yeah, I kind of get you, Hope, but since you got that Christmas card from your sister. I mean, Jeannie has got real family as well. Can't she have both?'

Hope's face tightens.

'I wish I hadn't told you about that card. Iris hasn't spoken to me for six years. And now, because she's tracked me down and sent me a card with angels blowing trumpets on the front, I'm meant to forgive her.'

Mel laughs.

'I'm sorry, Hope. I don't mean to laugh, it's just… you know, angels blowing their trumpets. You do fix on the weirdest shit sometimes.'

Hope tries to smile back.

'Thing is, you don't hate your sister. You're just pissed off because you think she abandoned you.'

'Well? She did.'

'And now you're going to sit in judgement on her for the rest of your lives.'

'Oh, change the record, Mel, for God's sake. I just don't see why everyone makes such a big deal out of blood family. There are real connections that go back centuries from our previous lives you know. I'm just saying those are sometimes more important, okay?'

Mel sighs. Why does Hope have to make the world so complicated. She doesn't get it. Mel doesn't think about Mike, or George and Moira, as cosmic souls. They are her family, that's all. Knitted together in ordinary, everyday love, with their fair share of mutinous moments thrown in. Who needs to think about the universe when you have a life to live?

'Hope, it's your shit, right. I only care because I care about you and Jeannie. We're family, right?

'Of course.' Hope can tell there is more. Mel's kind of love was as honest as a boulder and could be as bruising as a rockfall.

'So, sister to sister, I think that your karma might just be staring you in the face.'

Hope trails off. Mel chews her thumb nail intently.

'Thing is, Hope. All this isn't going to go away. This thing about family, I mean. You know. As she gets older. Jeannie will want to... Well, you know you can't pretend she hasn't got relatives forever.'

'She's got Birdie.'

'Yes,' said Mel, gently, 'and she's got an aunt and uncle in Keynsham, and grandparents, wherever they live. Thing is,' Mel is determined, 'you can't do anything about one half of her family. I guess you couldn't find that bastard now even if you wanted to. But your sister. Can't you let it go?'

'She's pregnant.'

‘What? Who is?’

‘Iris.’

‘Wow. Well… I mean. How do you know?’

‘It was in the Christmas card. Apparently, she’s enormous and they’re sending her for a scan.’

Hope looks towards Mel, everything in the room seemed fuzzy and she can’t focus properly. Somehow, her eyes have filled with tears again.

‘Oh, wow. Hey… come on, Hope.’

Hope’s body is brittle and rigid, her face a frozen mask as hot tears run down her cheeks. Mel reaches forward and gently pulls her to her feet. She looks at George and Jeannie, who are watching Jackanory.

‘George. You’re in charge. Me and Auntie Hope are going to the kitchen to cook your tea. Look after your sister for me.’

Neither George nor Jeannie turn their heads away from the television, and Mel leads Hope quietly back into the kitchen. Through the window, Hope can see an elderly man in the next-door garden, filling a coal scuttle before returning to his house.

‘What if they don’t like her?’

The question floors Mel. Jeannie is adorable. She creases her eyes, shaking her head.

'And what if they do?' she counters.

'I guess I just don't want anyone to lay stuff on Jeannie. Make her feel that she's not good enough unless she goes to a nice school and behaves in a certain way. You know, wears the right clothes and stuff.'

'Way too much worrying, Hope.'

'Huh. No. I mean, yes. But no. I'm wrong.' Hope's face is hot and agitated.

'You're not making much sense, hon.'

'No, listen. I think I get it now.' Hope runs her fingers through her hair, twisting her body to one side as if to release a trapped demon.

'Hey. Wow. Finally.' She breathes deeply and looks at Mel, 'What I just said. Nice school. Being judged. That's what happened to me. But Jeannie has me. She won't ever need to feel abandoned. I don't know why it was my karma, but. God, how stupid I've been. It doesn't have to be in hers. It won't be. I can see to that.'

Hope's face is fierce, as if she has slain dragons.

‘So, um, now you, er, get it. Is that good? I mean, do you know what you’re gonna do? You know, just ask, won’t you, if I can help.’ Mel feels her confusion must be obvious. ‘Um, what does Birdie say?’

‘She thinks I should reply to Iris. She wrote to me after she went back to Wales.’

‘Well, maybe if you really mean it, about her being family, then. Maybe you should listen to her. You know.’

Later in the evening, Mel is sitting at the kitchen table, finishing a sketch of the kids she is going to send to Mike’s mum for her birthday. If Hope hadn’t been so jumpy, she would have shown her the picture, but Hope had left quite suddenly. She shouldn’t have asked so many questions about Iris, Mel tells herself as she tilts the sketch from side to side. She almost jumps when the phone rings.

‘Mel. Listen, it’s Hope. Jeannie’s just gone to sleep. Look. I never answered your question this afternoon. I just needed a bit more time.’

Hope is silent, and after a few seconds Mel asks her if she was still there.

‘Yeah, I’m here. You know what I said?’

‘Um, yeah.’ Mel wonders exactly which part of their conversation Hope is referring to.

‘Well, it seems obvious to me now. My karma is mine, not Jeannie’s. So, I’ve decided. I’m going to go and see Iris. I can’t write her a letter; I need to actually see her. Thing is,’ Hope rushes on, speaking firmly, ‘the thing is, I don’t want to take Jeannie with me. Will you look after her for me for the day? I mean at the weekend. It’s like you said. I should listen to Birdie more. She still speaks to Jane, you know.’

At the end of the phone, Mel rolls her eyes and smiles.

‘Saturday suit you?’ she asks.

Chapter 40

Leaving Bristol on Saturday morning, Hope has a photo of Jeannie tucked into an envelope. She will give it to Iris. She hugged Jeannie extra hard before leaving her with Mel and is now making her way to Keynsham. She grips the large black steering wheel of her Hillman Imp and wills it up the hill, out of the city. Where the car seems to falter on the steep street, she finds herself rocking forward and backwards, urging it to keep going. The engine is sluggish and uncertain in the damp chill of a February morning, and she worries it will stall before it warms through. She isn't thinking what it will be like, seeing Iris again.

There are more people driving into the city than out, and Hope has that disconcerting feeling that she is travelling the wrong way, as if the rest of the world has a common purpose, knows something important, of which she alone is ignorant. Above her, the skies are a uniform, soggy grey, and every now and then she has to flip the windscreen wipers on to clear a light drizzle away. The road flattens out and the car engine settles into a steady, unassuming roar. Hope hasn't let Iris know that she's decided to visit, so can't be sure that she will even be at home. She has Iris's address, and the envelope containing the photo is in her pocket. In front of her is a Ford Capri, nudging impatiently at an old blue Rover that leads them slowly like a convoy. Or a pilgrimage, she thinks, liking the image better.

The A4 shakes off the last vestiges of the city, and there are stables in the fields to her right, a landscape of browns and greys. On the left, there is a long slow-moving field, enclosed by post and rail fencing. It is dotted with what looks like hundreds of crows, all standing idly or making small hops. They are like miniature black sheep, grazing aimlessly, accepting the fence as a boundary to their wanderings. Hope smiles at the very idea of a crow-field and then feels curiously saddened. How forlorn they look, penned in as if they have forgotten how to fly.

Immediately in front of her now, the Rover is moving even more slowly, as if in pain. In her rear-view mirror, she can see a new line of cars growling along behind her. She becomes suddenly, acutely aware that the driver is really struggling to keep her car going, and a minute later the Rover coughs out a few desperate black smoke rings before coming to a stop. Hope stops too; she is apprehensive at the way the road dips away in front of her and doesn't have the confidence to pull round the stalled vehicle. She is the only one who worries about this though, and sits there as other cars change gear, speed up and swerve past. She must get out of the car, she thinks. Offer to help in some way. Her journey is broken now, and she wonders if this means that she and Iris will not meet, that somehow, it is impossible for them to talk again. She sees the driver has opened her door and is stepping out. Hope winds down her window, waiting for the woman to approach.

'It's so good of you to stop.'

Hope feels awkward, she cannot explain now that it was nervousness, not compassion, which made her stop. The driver is a woman in her sixties, much taller than Hope. Her hair is knotted into a bun, and she is wearing a dark woollen coat over a midi skirt and long brown boots. She smiles faintly at Hope.

'I don't suppose you know anything about cars, do you?'

Hope shakes her head.

'No, me neither,' the woman continues, 'mind you, even if I did, I think this poor old girl has had it.'

Hope likes this tall stranger. She is so completely calm, as if breaking down at the side of the road was nothing, not even a minor irritation.

'Have you come from Bristol?' Hope asks.

'Yes. I was on my way to Bath. There's a rugby match this afternoon.' Annoyance, briefly, shimmers in her eyes. 'My grandson is in the squad, you see. I always go if I can.'

The skies are still sodden, heavy, unyielding. But it feels to Hope as if there is a sudden shift in light, the disturbance of something she couldn't, until that moment, have named. Of course she will see Iris. Iris is her destination, but now she sees that she must be open to change. She sees that all the effort and strain she has exerted this morning was a delusion. It is enough that she has decided to take the picture to Iris. The route, she suddenly understands, must find itself, and she has only to be attentive. She gestures at the passenger seat.

'Well, I can give you a lift, if you like? I'm headed that way.'

She has made a commitment now, and the stranger looks at her with cool grey eyes. Hope feels her statement, perhaps her existence, is being evaluated.

‘Really,’ she urges, ‘I’m on my way to see my sister. It’d be no trouble. My name’s Hope, by the way.’

‘Stephens. Judy Stephens. And thank you, I accept. If you’re absolutely sure?’

Hope nods carelessly, as if travelling to Bath is an everyday event, though in fact she hasn’t been back to the city since her mother drove her away, in almost complete silence, the day after her final A Level exam. She is convinced that she can feel the enormous, extraordinary rightness of going back to her home town before seeing Iris. She will invoke the past, revisit those first few months of 1970, and experience, again, the places where, somehow, she had lost her sister. First, she will go to the music shop. It is the place she last saw Chris. Then to Sally Lunn’s. On the way back to Keynsham she will drive past their old family home. This decision feels as obvious to her now as a revelation; impossible to foretell, but inevitable once known.

Judy Stephens talks intermittently about rugby, the weather, her abandoned car. After a few miles, she realises that Hope doesn’t require conversation and relaxes into a comfortable silence. Driving, Hope becomes aware that there is a liminality between the road and the verges, the fields and the sky, a resonance that diminishes difference of form. She is part of an eternal energy flow in comparison with which, the forms of people and things are fictions, delusions of temporary convenience. She can see, hear and sense with deep acuity, almost feeling the way a crow has just creaked into flight ahead of her. It isn't that her senses are jumbled, but that all the millions of small acts of perception share a quality more fundamental than the categories of smell, or sight, or sound.

These sensations displace time and, feeling like an unfamiliar version of herself, Hope parks the car, says goodbye to her passenger, and starts walking towards the Abbey. The same vibrant energy, the ethereal sense of bliss is present in every stone, every building. This must be how a planet feels in its orbit, this certainty of direction. There's something about her being in time and place, she feels, a sense of isness that leaves no room for small human fear or doubt. She heads towards Duck, Son and Pinker, and opens the same heavy door, steps into the same dark interior. She is thinking about Chris, thinking about the New Year's Eve party, and is filled with a gentle sadness for the million ways in which she has lost Joseph.

Her version of the party that left her pregnant has long since ossified into a narrative that she calls true, but from time to time she acknowledges how much it is cradled in uncertainty: It is still only a story that she has herself constructed and has the comforting feel of a factual narrative that cannot really hurt her. Standing in the shop, Hope is meeting her own ghost as well, and mistaking courage for strength, she approaches the shop assistant with a smile. The woman is bubbly, out-going. She has been joking with the customers, and she looks friendly, comforting.

'Can I help you?'

'Um. Yes. Silly request really, but I'm trying to track down an old friend. I used to live here, you see. And when I moved away, well, you know,' the woman looks curious, but puzzled, 'I mean. Well, he used to work here. Would have been about five years ago. He's tall. Almost six-foot, blond hair. I mean, I don't expect you have any information, but as I was passing…' Hope feels her skin turning red, is it so hard to mention Chris by name?

'Oh wow, that sounds intriguing. But no, I've no idea. My husband might know. Chris, he's the deputy manager here, I only do a few hours at the weekend. A bit of extra money before my little stranger arrives.'

She doesn't notice Hope recoiling at the name but smiles again and touches the gentle curve of her belly.

'So,' she leans forward conspiratorially, 'on the hunt for an old boyfriend, are you? What's his name?'

'No, honestly. Just a friend. We used to hang out together.'

Hope's voice sounds as if it is coming from somewhere in the distance, and she is worrying away at the vast improbability that this woman's husband is the same Chris. She had not thought for one moment that she would meet him in person; she only wanted to encounter her own memories.

There are too many possible worlds both present and past. Each seems to hover above her, and Hope doesn't want any of them to crash into reality. She can hear a clock ticking. It is too loud. The seconds seem to waver, uncertain of the direction of time. The woman looks at her again. She is concerned now.

'Are you alright love? You look awfully peaky all of a sudden. Don't you go fainting on me, will you.'

She glances across the shop floor. A small, dark-haired man is approaching them.

‘Oh Chris. This girl’s feeling a bit faint. Can you get her a glass of water?’

Hope’s body is on fire. Not Chris. Thank God. For a few seconds, her head hums and hisses with static. And then, abruptly, falling as if into an abyss, she loses consciousness. Unnoticed, the clock resumes its certain beat.

Chapter 41

The afternoon sky is clear when Hope turns into the street where Iris lives. It's later than she'd planned, the daylight is fading, and the afternoon air is sharp with cold. The road curves to the west, and she squints, trying to read the numbers on the pairs of semi-detached houses as she drives slowly along. She'd been so glad to get back to the car after leaving the record shop and had sat for about half an hour before starting the engine, exhausted, fragile and with a depth of confusion that she couldn't overcome. The utter certainty of her morning, the profound sense she'd had of being in tune with the universe, had taken her to seek out her past. So, what had happened? Why had she fainted like that? Surely that deep, deep sense of universal harmony, when she knew that everything was part of the divine, then only bliss should result. Instead, it had been like finding a shattered mirror, and she'd felt as if her existence was in fact a kind of non-existence; that everything she felt most deeply was based on nothing but the uncertain illusions of a lost girl.

There are lights on in some of the houses in Iris's street; large square windows separated like framed prints on an endless wall. Iris lives at number seventy-one, and

Hope can see light spilling onto the drive in front of her house. She stops the car, not quite opposite Iris's, and sits indecisively. Through the window she can see a tall display cabinet, a standard lamp and a door to the side of the room, which is ajar. The top of the sofa is visible, and there are wall lights that match the overhead light. No pictures. Hope is assailed by a longing for her sister. Six years. She remembers late summer days, that last long holiday together after Iris's A levels. The sense of August heat, shimmering over the games they played, the warp and weft of their frequent disagreements, and the long slow way they fell apart, even before Iris had left for university. She doesn't want to knock on the door like a waif, so she sits a few minutes longer, stilling her breathing and hoping for calm. Further down the street, the lights come on in another two houses. The repeated pattern of the buildings, as they dwindle into the late afternoon gloom, has a poetry that Hope didn't expect, and its compelling rhythmic quality draws her in. All the houses align in matching pairs, repeated along the street in a regular pattern; in harmony with the everyday world they stand for and contain. She wishes now that she'd written to tell Iris she was coming.

Stepping from her car, Hope can see the faint glimmer of Venus, the Evening Star, as it is slowly revealed by the encroaching darkness of a February evening. It peers down on her as she shivers in the cold, pulling her hat down over her ears and wrapping a scarf around her neck. She is the only person to be seen outside, but a silent fox has just vaulted a fence behind the houses on the opposite side of the street, and a late blackbird appears briefly and then vanishes again. The air has a thinness to it, carrying sound with preternatural sharpness and defining the shadows in a palette of purples and greys. Ten years earlier, there were fields here, yet now the street settles into the evening as it always does, as if it always has. Above, the sky pays attention to mantling the day in darkness. Venus watches carefully as Hope rings the bell. Inside, Iris rises awkwardly from a chair, her pregnant body cumbersome now. As she opens the door, Iris is framed by the lights in her house, and Hope's face is lit by the light spilling forward. The universe changes course, once again, and the two women search each other's faces to see who they have become.

PART FOUR

Chapter 42

When her grandson, Tom, had started university in autumn 2019, Hope had already been living in Bath for five years. Birdie, by then in her mid-eighties, had finally decided to leave Flag Cottage at the same time as Hope was retiring from teaching, and the two of them had decided to buy something together. Until two months ago, when Birdie had been hospitalised by a broken hip, the arrangement had suited them both, each of them independent but happy to be close again, sharing laughter and old stories.

The soft Bath stone Victorian house couldn't have been more perfect; already converted into two flats, it had a level access and flat garden. The views were astounding, and from her first-floor windows, Hope could look right across the city to Tom's university campus at Claverton Down.

Tom was on her mind as she walked home from the Meditation Centre. He was in his second term now and was, Hope worried, somehow absent from himself. Striding up the hill, she felt how glorious it was to walk, buffeted by the cold March morning air. She and Tom had played tennis the previous week, but there'd been no fun in it. She might as well have been playing with a stranger, there was no, she struggled for the word, there was no *is-ness* in him. She hadn't thought it a good idea, him going to university, no matter how clever he had been at school. After qualifying as a teacher when Jeannie was nine, Hope felt she had sleep-walked through thirty-five years of work. She had forgotten most of her students the moment they left her class. Such a long time, she thought, to spend being pulled about by the demands and opinions of others.

It was different for Iris, always had been. And, to her surprise, for Jeannie too. Her daughter took after Iris, she knew. They both had the same cautious, settled temperament. A preference for a well-ordered, predictable life. Hope rolled her eyes at the thought. But Tom was like her. He even looked like her, the same dark unsettled eyes and narrow face. Retiring had been the best thing, she thought. Being in one's sixties was just so different; having her own way with time again, really, sometimes her sense of excitement and joy was like being a kid again. Every day, she felt so alive. Like her being was brimming with possibilities and magic. Tom, she thought again, should never have agreed to go to university. It was all wrong.

Opening her front door, aware of the lonely emptiness of Birdie's flat, Hope was met by a wall of heat. Her glasses steamed up rapidly. She must have forgotten to turn the heating down. She shook her head in self-reproach before dropping her bag onto the floor beneath the coat rack and dashing into the kitchen. Her mobile phone was ringing loudly where she'd left charging on the table.

'Hello.'

'It's me.'

'Jeannie, darling girl. I know it's you. Your name is on the screen, remember?'

Jeannie felt the familiar irritation of being corrected by her mother.

'Where've you been? I've been trying to call you for half an hour.'

'Hey, you know where I've been. The Meditation Centre. Morning meditation. Awesome breathing practice this morning, really, just awesome. I left my phone here. No battery.

Jeannie hated her mother using words like "awesome".

‘You shouldn’t be going to those classes now, Mum. I did tell you last week. God, you’d think they’d cancel anything where you all breathe over each other, for heaven’s sake.’

Hope sighed. Poor Jeannie, so worried about this Coronavirus that had suddenly become the news. Jeannie didn’t realise how much worse things seemed to be with this habit of fretting and worrying about everything. Hope breathed slowly, holding the deep sensation of wholeness and calm she had found in her morning class, the divine beauty of seeing the world with a recognition of non-attachment and gratitude for what is. How hard it was for Jeannie, she thought, the way she was given to sifting things into categories of good or bad, safe or scary.

‘I do understand darling. You must feel awful, watching all the bad news. Don’t forget though how worry is toxic too. Meditation is how we stay healthy, you know, it’s not a cause of ill health.’

Jeannie pushed her fingers deep into her hair, almost scratching her scalp. The previous day, she’d had an odd conversation with her aunt, who’d seemed to think she would be able to go ahead with plans for Uncle Don’s 70th, and now her mum thought worrying about the coronavirus was worse than catching it.

‘Look, Mum, I didn’t call to talk about that anyway. I’m worried about Tom.’

Hope pressed the loudspeaker button so she could put the phone back down on work surface. She stood tall, stretching her neck to release the small curls of tension and easing into position for Standing Mountain pose. She breathed slowly, willing herself to really listen to her daughter.

‘Are you still there, Mum? Tom. Have you heard from him? It’s just that I texted him several times at the weekend, and he hasn’t replied. I tried calling him this morning, but no answer.’

‘Jeannie, darling. Slow down. He’ll be fine. He’s eighteen, he’s left home is all. Why do you worry so?’

Jeannie felt her stress level rising. Any minute now, Hope would be reminding her of how she’d had to let go of Jeannie when she had left home.

‘He had a flare up just after Christmas, remember. And I don’t think he’s truly over it yet.’

Hope and Jeannie would never agree about the treatment of Tom’s arthritis. When he’d been diagnosed, the year he took his GCSE’s, Jeannie had been pleased that the consultant had put him straight on steroids. At the time, and often since, Hope had wondered if her grandson's arthritis was how his body was trying to alert him, make him pay attention to deeper, spiritual parts of his being.

'My darling girl, he's adjusting to a new way of life. It's no wonder his body reacted. But honestly, Jeannie, trust the universe on this one. Mind and body, you know?'

Jeannie clenched her mobile. Oh, what was the point. Hope would never agree that having your child leave home into a world when some weird virus was laying waste to people was a good reason for being just a little uptight about the situation.

'How about you, little blue egg? I know what it's like, when your child leaves home. Perhaps you don't remember, but I went through what you're experiencing now. It's a tough gig, being a mum. Anyway, I saw him on Friday. He was fine then. Said he was going to have a detox weekend. I expect he's turned his phone off.'

Jeannie was thrown again. Talking to Hope was like talking to some kind of AI guru. She gave information in such a disconnected way. Did she do it on purpose?

‘What do you mean “a detox weekend”? Does that mean he’s only eating rice again?’

‘I don’t know, darling,’ Hope spoke more gently, ‘I think he’s just turned the internet off, doing a digital detox, you know. Can’t be for long, he must have lectures soon.’

‘Mum, if he gets in touch, you will let me know, won’t you? I’ve asked Peter to call me if he hears from him, and he’s agreed.’

Hope tensed. Why couldn’t Jeannie let Tom be? Did she have to try and run his life for him, still?

‘Jeannie. You know that I won’t do that. You call his father, or Iris, or anyone else. Get them to act as messengers if you like, but I can’t, I won’t. Tom has the right to keep himself to himself when he wants to.’

She sounded sharper than she’d meant, caught in a knot of irritation and guilt. Her daughter had defences like spring-loaded doors which snapped shut at the first sign of danger. Then there was no getting through to her that a person had the right to be alone. It was a constant friction, particularly over Tom. Hope cherished the idea that her grandson was one of those rare, ancient and long-known souls that one meets perhaps once in many hundreds of years. For Jeannie, he seemed only to be a problem she needed to manage.

'Jeannie, I'm sorry. I get that you're anxious, but this really isn't only about Tom, is it? I'm sure he'll be in touch soon. It's just not in his nature to be thoughtless, you know that.'

Hope could almost feel Jeannie's frustration on the phone as her daughter ended the call with hollow assurances that yes, Tom could be relied on to be thoughtful, and yes, it was quite out of character for him to hide anything that really mattered.

Their conversation left Hope feeling unsettled. As a small child Jeannie had always seemed square and substantial in a way that Hope had found fascinating but also unfathomable. That solidity was hewn in her character too, and Hope had watched, baffled, as Jeannie obdurately rejected her mother's vision a universe that trembled in joy behind the world of things, unbound by form or convention. She stood for several minutes, remaining in Mountain Pose. The spring light outside had created a palette of soft blues and fresh greens, interspersed with tones from yellow to ochre that played on the buildings near and far. Hope wanted to be at one with the gentle energy of the world, not to shut Jeannie out, but to give herself the stillness in which she could calm her thoughts. She guided her inner gaze to rest in different parts of her body, releasing the tension in her shoulders and sending healing warmth to the old ache in her left hip.

She would make a Buddha Bowl for lunch, she thought. Hummus and salad. At this time of year her salads were a mixture of nuts, seeds and grated carrot, it was too early for salad leaves from the garden. She toasted a handful of seeds and nuts in a pan, setting them aside to cool while she focused her attention on blending the ingredients for her hummus.

Dancing around her kitchen, Hope lined up the ingredients she needed. Instead of fine ground salt, she decided to use coarse rock salt, gazing for a moment at its grey crystalline opaqueness and sensing the millennia that had passed since it was formed in arid basins from which the sea had long since evaporated. For a moment she held herself still, as if she were the unmoving centre of the universe that danced. The early morning sensation of deep calm was still there, a peace so dispersed that it was impossible to tell whether it rested inside her body or in the atmosphere around her. Silence embraced her, or she embraced it, it was hard to tell which.

Her chick peas had been grown in Egypt. Such a long journey, she thought, wondering how she had never really noticed before the irregular planes of their shapes, or the small point at the top, from which a root would emerge if the peas were soaked for several days. They weren't really round at all, but polyhedric shapes. As she drained the aquafaba into a cup, her thoughts travelled to the unknown workers who had cultivated them, to the long days of sun and heat during which the plants would have matured, hanging beneath their small pinnate leaves that so resembled vetch.

The garlic she was using was homegrown, planted twelve months ago by Birdie. She unpicked its tissued skin, white and fragile, beneath which thin streaks of dark pink could be seen. It would be the last ever crop of garlic planted by Birdie, and every clove felt precious, succulent with memories that curled into their aroma as she crushed two cloves with the back of a wooden spoon. Usually, Hope tipped the chick peas and garlic into her blender with all the other ingredients, but today she reached instead for her pestle and mortar, once owned by Jane. The vibrant yellow of the Spanish lemon was almost too much, and she carefully squeezed the juice into the mixture, her nostrils jostled by the acidic notes it released. Turning the pestle again and again made her wrist ache, and she had to keep changing hands, waiting for the last few peas to relinquish their forms into the soft paste. Finally, it was done, and she transferred the hummus into her favourite bowl before adding a swirl of thick olive oil that was almost green in hue, and a final dusting of deep red Hungarian paprika.

Hope stared at the small bowl containing so many centuries, spanning so many continents and holding the work of so many, many hands, known and unknown. She looked at her own hands, which had brought together this palette of colours, flavours and textures. There was something about the way the essence of each ingredient had its own energy, its own character, she decided, each finite, but representing an eternal moment, just the same. She felt it must be what that poet had described. She murmured the lines to herself, an odd sadness filling her eyes with tears.

"To see a World in a Grain of Sand,
And Heaven in a Wild Flower,
Hold Infinity in the palm of your hand,
And Eternity in an hour."

She knew the words like she knew how to dance, but inexplicably, with an uncomfortable jarring feeling, she couldn't find the name of the poet, even though she sensed that it should, really, be as familiar as her own. The gap disturbed her; it was becoming a habit. Not forgetting things as such, she thought, but this odd sense it gave of, of there being empty spaces and dark lacunae, as if there were holes in which nothing existed at all.

Chapter 43

That evening, Hope stood in the attic bedroom, gazing at the final chiffon threads of pink and blue that ribboned the sky before dissolving into atonal darkness. She wanted to send, with the departing sun, all those thoughts and feelings that should die with the day. She decided to call Tom. The phone rang several times. Hope wondered if he could still be in a lecture. It seemed a bit late in the day. She was just about to give up when Tom answered.

'Hey, Nan. You ok?'

'Pretty good, I just had a feeling to call you.'

'You're a mind-reader. You must have known that I wanted to talk to you.'

'Uh huh.'

'Thing is,' Tom hesitated, 'Mum's been trying to call me all weekend, and I haven't picked up, because I need to know what I think before she, you know, before she tells me what to do.'

'Okay, I'm listening.'

'You know everyone is going to have to quarantine, don't you? Doesn't matter what Johnson says, he'll have to do it soon. Uni are sending us all stuff about how to do remote learning, and we've already started on-line seminars. Thing is, I don't want to stay here. You've seen my room. I'd go mad in a week. But I'm not stupid, I know that people like me have a higher risk. So, my head is telling me I should go home. I can't stay with Dad, his internet is too flaky, but if the government makes us stay at home for weeks on end…'

Tom trailed off.

'You think it would be bad for you and Jeannie.'

'That's about it.'

'Not an easy one, huh?' Hope paused, 'have you spoken to your Dad? He might have a view.'

'Not possible. He's on Eigg at the moment.'

'You know your mum and Aunt Iris are still planning to have a party for Don, don't you? Are you sure about this lockdown? It's not just media frenzy?'

Tom knew from Hope's tone of voice that she wasn't really asking him questions. He said nothing. There was a long pause.

'So, here's what I know. Both your options are going to be difficult, and which ever you end up doing, you'll probably think you've made the wrong choice. The thing is, darling boy, I don't think you can ask me to decide for you.'

A lump came into Tom's throat. If Nan wouldn't help him.

'Hey, Nan. You always have the answers.' He tried to keep his voice light, hide the rising panic he felt, 'You don't think that I would blame you if I start going crazy on my own or if I couldn't keep the peace with Mum?'

'Well, actually, yes. That's how humans work. But more importantly, you need to make your own decisions. Especially scary ones, where you have lots of strong feelings.'

Hope stopped talking, listening to the silence at the other end of the call.

Fear rose through Tom's body like a corrosion of self. Everything was so uncertain. His limbs seemed to lose their form, as if he were falling through acidic clouds of cold grey. He didn't wasn't to feel like this again, not now. He couldn't tell Hope how frightened he was, how he kept feeling like he was falling back, backwards into a dark abyss that was located somewhere behind his head.

'Are you still there?'

‘Sorry, Nan. Yeah. Still here.’

‘Hmmm. I can hear pain, you know.’

Tom felt tears well up.

‘OK. Here’s what you’re going to do, darling boy. Come and see me.’

‘What, now?’

‘Is that a problem? Why don’t you walk over. It’ll only take you an hour. I’ll drop you back at your halls later this evening. Promise.’

Tom felt curiously lightened. It was as if all he had needed was this simple sense of purpose.

‘You’re on, Magic Nan. I’m on my way.’

Hope smiled. It was what he had called her when he was a little boy.

‘One other thing, Tom. Just walk, ok. No phone, no music. Just walk here with open eyes and let your mind do what it will.’

‘Yeah, ok, Nan. You’re a star.’

Well, we’re all ancient atoms and star dust, Hope murmured to herself, as she ended the call.

Chapter 44

The following Sunday, Iris felt a little under the weather. A slight toothache, that was all. Nothing to worry about, but she'd told Don that she would forego church that morning. She'd already listened to Sunday Worship. The sermons on the radio were shorter, which she liked. Their vicar did have rather a tendency to go on, and she was sometimes a bit neglectful of the gospels, Iris thought. Last week, her whole sermon had been about the Coronavirus. As if they hadn't all heard enough about that on the news. For weeks, it seemed, she and Don had had to watch news reports of the illness spreading across China, Australia and the U.S. And now all the BBC coverage was about an outbreak in Italy. It was too much.

She finished loading the dishwasher and sprayed the splashback behind the hob to remove the greasy splatters from Don's fried breakfast. Glancing at the clock, she saw that The Archers would be starting in a few minutes. Don wouldn't be back until gone eleven. And he did have an annoying habit of talking over the radio if he wasn't interested in the broadcast. Removing the rubber glove on her right hand, she turned on the radio before returning to her task. Her tooth was actually quite painful, she thought. So, she shouldn't feel guilty. The oven was due a clean, and the utility room needed some attention too. She could do those while she caught up with The Archers. She was about to rinse her cloth when the pips came on, heralding the ten o'clock news bulletin. She pulled off her glove again, hurrying to the radio to turn down the volume so she didn't have to listen to any more statistics about people falling ill, dying.

She didn't have to stay in the house, she thought. She could go into the garden, tie up the rose that had come loose during the stormy weather. But no, Don would comment on that. If she were well enough to be in the garden, then she was well enough to go to church. Feeling helpless, she stood in the kitchen, wondering what to do. She could, she supposed, start writing the invitations for Don and Ursula's 70th birthday party. Seventy in June. It still seemed impossible. At least he'd promised to retire, finally. The Health Service always needed Finance Managers, of course, but over the last few years Iris had come to realise that Don needed the NHS far more than it needed him. And he was always so smug when people professed amazement that he was in his 60's, let alone pushing 70.

She checked the food caddy to see if the bag needed changing. Recycling food waste was all very well, but it was such a messy thing to keep in the house. Don had spilt coffee grounds again. Why couldn't he be more careful? Iris sighed, picked up the melamine tray on which the caddy sat so that she could rinse it off in the sink. At the front of the house, the letter box clapped open, and she could hear the weight of the Sunday papers being heaved through the letter box. She replaced the cleaned tray and stood for a few moments, irresolute. She'd forgotten that the papers would come. Well, she didn't really have a choice, she couldn't leave them on the doormat for Don to trip over when he got back. She marched resolutely into the hall and picked up the bundle, trying to fold everything together so that the headlines were on the inside. She carried the papers to Don's study and dropped them, face down, on his desk. It was no good though. She'd seen that the headline was loud and black, more coverage of coronavirus. Why on earth had it been allowed to get into the UK?

There must be other jobs to be done, she decided. She would ring Jeannie. They had so much to discuss about the party. The twins knew she was planning a surprise do for Don, but they didn't appreciate how much planning was involved. Jeannie was a godsend.

Chapter 45

Hope sat back on her heels on the hard floor at the kitchen end of Birdie's long living room. Everything had been so simple. She'd spoken to Birdie, who'd said that if there was a lockdown, then she clearly wouldn't be able to come home until it was over. So, Tom could use her maisonette. Easy for him to move back to the university when the restriction orders ended. No hassle with Jeannie.

He'd arrived that morning with his stuff, which had taken all of twenty minutes to unpack. And now the two of them were locked in deadly combat over a game of tiddlywinks. Everything was perfect. Hope had a large green tiddlywink in her left hand, which she span between her fingers as she rolled her shoulders while considering her next move.

'God, get me a pillow from the bedroom can you, Tom. This is killing my knees.'

'Can I trust you?' Tom scrutinised Hope, scrunching up his eyes, and tilting his head to one side in a parody of suspicion. She laughed.

'Boy. Pillow. Ancient Nan. Now, if you please. Or I swear I'll tip your winks into the waste paper basket.'

'Who has a waste paper basket, these days?'

'Well, clearly Birdie does. Now go on, get me something for my knees, lovely boy.'

She grimaced as Tom returned with the pillow. God, how her knees hurt.

'We could play on the carpet, if you like?'

'Don't be soft. Can't tiddle the winks on a carpet. They might go anywhere.'

She took the pillow.

'Thank you, sweetie.'

She watched him as he squatted down on the floor, eyeing up the tiddlywinks.

'Can I ask you about uni?'

Tom nodded, his head still bent over the game.

'I just wondered why you decided to go?'

Tom looked at her sharply and laughed.

'God Nan. You have to go to uni, it's just a thing. Everybody wants graduates. And you know. All those amazing exam results of mine. The big deal. Kinda made it inevitable, don't you think?'

‘You sound angry.’ Hope’s voice was firm, but her face was questioning. Tom shook his head as if to dismiss her question.

‘I really don’t have a choice, you know.’

‘Hmm.’

‘Can you imagine what Mum would have said?’

‘I guess so.’

‘Come on. Let’s see if you can beat me.’

Both of them knew that the game was ruined. After twenty minutes. Tom sighed and stood up.

‘How come you always win?’

‘Mind over matter, darling boy. I just refuse to think about what might go wrong. The tiddlywinks respect that.’

She was trying to provoke him. He shook his head slowly. It was good to be here. Even if. He stopped himself; time to let go of his sense of unease. He and Nan could make this fun. He waved his hand in the air, raising an eyebrow as he spoke.

‘Oh yeah. Object Oriented Ontology. Of course.’

‘Explain!’

‘God. I’ll try. Well, it’s this new philosophy. A student at uni was talking about it. Something about objects experiencing their own existence. In ways we can’t understand, I mean. So that the whole thing about the world being based on human perception is wrong. The tiddlywinks are choosing to let you win, is all.’

‘Yeah, that makes sense. Sounds like something Krishnamurthi might have said, though. And he died before you were even born. Cup of tea?’

Hope rose to her feet.

Tom smiled at Hope. Trust Nan to come up with Krishnamurthi. She always did. He bent over the tiddlywinks to gather them up. Hope snorted with laughter.

‘Actually, It was Birdie. She taught me. We used to play tiddlywinks all the time. Before your mum was born. Afterwards, too. When we lived in Wales.’

‘What about Mum? Did she get a look in?’

Hope shook her head, her laugh fading.

‘Your mum had her bear. Seems now she spent years and years just talking to that bear. Just think, when I was your age, I had a toddler, and Birdie, and the cottage in Wales. Did I tell you about the first time I met Birdie?’

‘When you ran away from home? Yeah. I know.’

‘Sorry. I think about her a lot at the moment. I expect it’s because she’s not here.’

Hope shook her head, her long silver hair falling like a mist over her shoulders.

‘Hey, boy. Tell me something I don’t know.’

‘Like what?’

‘Oh, I don’t know. Um, tell me something about uni. How about the food? No? Ok, tell me something about the people you’ve been living with up there. Will you miss any of them?’

‘Er Nan, heard of WhatsApp? Insta? And all the rest of it. You think I’m going to miss them now I don’t have to wade through the mess they leave in the kitchen?’

‘Sharp?’

‘Yeah.’ Tom paused, ‘Yeah, maybe I am angry about uni, Nan. It’s all a load of crap. The only real person I’ve met is someone called Jeb. They’re studying theology. Hey, tell you what Nan, have you come across Matthieu Ricard?’

‘I have. So, this Jeb…’

‘Well, they’re a Buddhist, and they lent me a book by Matthieu Ricard. I’ve left it at uni though.’

‘What’s the book called?’

‘“Altruism”. You’d like it, Nan. I should’ve brought it with me.’

Hope rolled her eyes.

‘Books I can do. You can borrow my copy. Hang on. I’ll get it for you. Before I forget.’

Hope returned in a few minutes, the book in her outstretched hand.

‘There you go. When you text Jeb, you can ask them if they’d like to borrow any others. I’ve got nearly all Ricard’s books.’ She paused, ‘and one other thing. Even if I have told you before, I’m going to say it again. When I left the Mother & Baby Home, when I realised that having a baby was going to be ok. More than ok. Well, that was all thanks to Birdie.’

Hope’s mind flew back, Birdie, arriving at the Mother & Baby Home after she’d been to visit Mel in hospital, She’d been so full of energy, her bright green coat and black eyes.

‘And?’

'Sorry. Well, she told me that fitting in was optional, but following your own truth was not. Or shouldn't be. She and Jane did that, you know. Believed in themselves. Can't have been straightforward, they got together in the nineteen-fifties, after all.'

Through the window Hope could see a few early tulips murmuring in the breeze. She stood up, ruffling Tom's hair as she moved away.

'But you know, because of Birdie, I reckon Jane's atoms are still joyous in the universe, somehow.'

Chapter 46

'Iris. What a lovely surprise.'

Birdie was sitting in her wheelchair in the communal living room. The large space had been designed to appear cosy, with low ceilings and soft lights that were left on all day. Furthest from the window was a large dining table with a small arrangement of dried grasses that had been dyed to contrast the pale cream chair backs with a note of bright colour. The rest of the room had small tables in the same dark wood, arranged with clusters of three or four chairs. The room was L-shaped, and every wall had a large painting, illuminated with subtle lighting. Birdie felt that she was living in a furniture showroom.

'You've bought me daffs. How very kind you are.'

She had never understood why cut flowers were offered as gifts. It was like giving someone a corpse, she thought. But she smiled, taking the cellophane-wrapped bunch, putting it on her lap while she leant forward so that Iris could kiss her cheek. Iris asked how she was feeling, and Birdie offered her a suitable evasion in reply. This habit of lying, she thought. But here's Iris, who clearly wants to hear me say how well I feel. And I do feel wonderful, but not in a way that she would ever understand.

She leant back in her chair while Iris disappeared to find a vase for the daffodils. She watched her arrange them in their watery grave, like Rosetti arranging Ophelia's hair, thought Birdie, and then thrust them forward again for inspection.

'There, very spring-like, don't you think. Now, would you like me to put them in your room?'

Birdie couldn't bear the idea. The daffodils would scream in the night, she thought. One's own journey to death was unexpectedly beautiful, but watching the young fresh blooms wither and die would be quite another thing.

'Why don't you put them over there, under the window? Then everyone can see them.'

Iris hesitated.

'Not everyone here gets visitors.' Birdie added.

Iris nodded, and placed the daffodils carefully on the window sill, standing back to make sure the flowerheads were fanned out in an even semi-circle. She stepped forward to remove a leaf, which she screwed up and threw away.

She had bought biscuits, and a flask of tea, which made Birdie soften in gratitude. It was the sort of thing that Iris was good at, remembering that last time she'd visited the tea had been stewed and tepid, and Birdie had commented on how unpleasant it was. This tea was delicious, and she said so while Iris offered news and snippets from her life, mostly about her children, whom Birdie had barely seen in twenty years. Greg sounded like a replica of Don, she thought, as Iris worried out loud about his chances of promotion to Brigadier, and the way his wife made so many demands on him around the house, even though her salary couldn't possibly be anything close to his. As for Sam, his twin brother, Iris reshaped his future every time she mentioned him. Even if he was now in his early 40's, it meant nothing. He would, when the time was right, meet the right woman and fall in love. She had a feeling. Perhaps there might even be grandchildren, one day. One never knew, after all.

Birdie felt a sense of relief as Iris stopped talking for a few seconds to eat her biscuit, cupping one hand under her chin as there was no plate for her to use.

'Hope popped in yesterday. I'm so glad she's going to help Tom out. It'll be easier for everyone, especially now that the university is definitely going to be closed for a while.'

Iris lowered her cupped hand carefully, in case there were crumbs.

'Closed? I didn't know that. Jeannie didn't say anything when I saw her yesterday.'

Iris was puzzled. What could Birdie mean? And then she realised. Poor Birdie, Iris thought, smiling gently at her. She'd been so sharp, but at ninety, well, it had to be expected. Perhaps she thought it was Easter already. More easily confused since her accident, perhaps. And then, one only had to look at the people she was surrounded by now. And Birdie was prone to saying the oddest things. Always had been.

Iris felt herself scrutinised by Birdie's dark eyes. Did she have a crumb on her face? She reached into her pocket for a clean tissue and dabbed at her mouth.

'It was the main headline on the news this morning, Iris. Not just Bath, all the universities. And the schools, too.'

Iris felt herself crumble. What had happened now? She'd stopped listening to Radio 4 altogether and was busy filling her days with things to do. Of course, Don always had the evening news after dinner, but she had decided to make a start on redecorating the guest room, which occupied her evenings. During the day, she made sure she was busy with something in the kitchen or out in the garden whenever he switched on the television.

'Ah,' she stumbled, 'I must have missed the news this morning. Silly me. Hope is going to help Tom, you say?'

Birdie wanted to reach forward to Iris, touch her fingers on her forearm to soften the fear in her blank face. But Iris sat like a fragile figurine, and Birdie didn't dare.

'Tom is going to borrow my maisonette for a while. It makes sense. He'll still be in Bath, but he won't be alone. You know, we'll all be told to stay at home soon and it would be dreadful to be shut in that little room he has at the university.' She paused, watching Iris.

'Far better than going back to Jeannie's, too. And of course, his dad is still at that Scottish Wildlife place. Eigg. So that's not an option.'

Iris nodded uncertainly.

'Well, if you don't mind. It's your home, after all.'

It all sounded highly unnecessary, Iris thought. What if Tom had to stay in his room for a few days? Or even for a week or two? The boy had no common-sense. Just like his grandmother. He was over-reacting, as usual. Poor Jeannie.

Watching Iris, Birdie thought how terrified she looked. Like a doll with an unalterable expression, distant and pallid. She felt sorry for her.

'Well, that husband of yours is finally retiring then. Only a few weeks now.'

Iris accepted the topic gratefully, pushing all thoughts of the new virus to the back of her mind.

'Third time lucky, Birdie. This time he'll go. No economic crash on the horizon and Brexit is good and done.' She allowed herself a complicit smile, 'I think even he's realised he's not indispensable to the NHS now.'

Birdie nodded, suppressing her opinion of Don.

'And then, of course, he's seventy in June. He and Ursula…'

Awkwardly, she stopped, remembering the conversation she and Jeannie had had. They'd discussed who to invite to Don's party and Birdie wasn't on the list. It wasn't that she wouldn't like to invite Birdie, only Don would be bound to say something, he always did. And now Birdie was so incapacitated. How would she even manage the steps? So, she and Jeannie had agreed it was far more sensible not to mention the party at all.

'Well, anyway. There are so many things we'll be able to do. We're going on a cruise in the autumn. Let me show you.'

Iris flicked through the large screen on her smart phone, showing Birdie pictures of the cruise ship and itinerary. She would eat out every night for three weeks. There would be classes and lectures, and she might even persuade Don to learn ballroom dancing.

'And the best thing is, the boys are going to fly out to Cadiz, we've got a two day stop there at the end of the second week. We'll have a proper family holiday, the four of us together.'

'What about Greg's wife? Carole, isn't it? Won't she be there?'

'Oh yes, of course, Carole as well. Goodness. I mustn't forget Carole.'

The habitual small frown deepened on her forehead.

'I suppose it's difficult to think of her as one of us, even now. Don always said she wasn't really wife material, and I think he was right. She should have buckled down and had children straight away. I don't know how often I told Greg so. She's left it too late now, I'm afraid. It's not a proper marriage is it though? Not without children.'

This habit Iris had, of seeking confirmation that others should, or would if they were only able, live lives like hers threaded her conversation as much as her unspoken thoughts. She looked at Birdie, waiting for her to agree. Iris needed the world to be predictable, and for that, she needed it to think like her. Birdie knew this, but it irritated her regardless. On the windowsill, the daffodils looked at her accusingly.

'You know I'm not sure I agree,' Birdie spoke resolutely, 'it's the acts of seeing that make us who we are. When I look around me,' she gesticulated at the room, 'I need to see beyond these ghastly chairs. I need to see someone making a choice. Someone thinking. However different to mine their views might be.'

Birdie felt Jane beside her, chuckling in sympathy. She could hear her voice, whispering mischievously to her.

'Glad to see there's still some fire in you, then, my dear. You tell her. Look at this room. It's bland to the point of muteness. Those clusters of matching chairs, my poor darling. And the paintings! Dreadful.'

Birdie shook her head softly, closing her eyes to hear Jane's voice more clearly:

'We were always real, my darling, darling Birdie. Hope is right about ancient ties connecting us with eternal bonds, you know. Do you remember when I came into the kitchen that morning, the first morning after she landed on our doorstep? You were imitating that awful student of mine with a wooden spoon and, what was it, a bread knife? You held that poor girl gently poised between laughter and tears, and it was exactly where she needed to be. You and Hope. Me and you. Your Oma. And then little Jeannie. And now Tom. Real family, my darling, made of love and memory.'

Birdie, her eyes still closed, was overtaken by giggles that might be tears too. She ached with a longing to detach herself from her worn frame, to leave her body, despite all its memories of love and longing, to sink into a deeper way of being, beyond the limits of life in this world. If only she could float free on the joy that caressed her like an ocean. Her head sank forward, and she drifted.

Chapter 47

'Iris. Was I expecting you?'

Hope opened her front door, dishevelled and with muddy hands. Iris never called unexpectedly, and Hope felt a sudden pull of fear. Had she forgotten an arrangement?

'Where were you?' Iris demanded, 'I was about to give up.'

'I was just in the garden. Sorry. Well, come in, anyway.'

So, there hadn't been an arrangement. Thank heavens. Her sister followed her into the living room. Something had clearly upset her, but it couldn't be a crisis, Hope reasoned, or Iris would simply have rung.

'I'm sorry,' Iris said, 'I had to come. I've just had the most awful experience. I went to see Birdie, you see.'

Hope gestured to Iris, wanting her to sit down.

'She's alright, is she?'

'Well, yes.' Iris paused. 'But no, it was dreadful. I thought she was dying in front of me. We were just talking, when suddenly she said something very odd, then closed her eyes and appeared to go into a trance. Or something very like it, anyway.'

Iris didn't know why she'd come to see Hope. It all seemed a bit foolish, now she was here. But then Birdie had definitely had a funny turn, and for quite some minutes. Then when she had opened her eyes again, she had been so very peculiar.

'Iris. Why don't you just tell me what happened. Is Birdie alright now?'

'I think so, yes. Well, she said she was, but she didn't seem to know what year it was. She said that Jane had just been talking to her, and someone called Oma, whoever that is.'

'Oma was her grandmother, Iris. She was killed in the Dresden bombings. Birdie has always held her close.'

'Dresden. How peculiar. What on earth was her grandmother doing in Dresden during the war?'

Hope opened her mouth to explain and then changed her mind.

'More importantly,' she said, 'what's so dreadful about the fact that Birdie is still talking to Jane? Or to her grandmother, for that matter?'

Hope stood up and started to fill the kettle. Iris was irritated. Hope was in one of her awkward moods. Why did her sister always wilfully misunderstand what she was trying to say.

'No, Hope. You've got it wrong. Birdie said that Jane was talking to her. Now. This afternoon. It's all very well to talk to loved ones who've died, but they can't reply, you know.'

Even as she spoke, Iris regretted it. Hope would say it was perfectly normal to have a conversation with someone dead, and probably start one of her rambling explanations about the spirit of the universe, or talking about reincarnation, or something equally annoying.

Hope had her back to Iris, busying herself with a teapot and some cups. She seemed to be taking a long time. She spoke to Iris, her back still turned.

'Chamomile alright for you? I don't have any black tea. Or, um.'

Hope shook her head as if to dislodge a blockage. To herself, she mimed the act of pouring milk into a cup.

'Milk. I haven't got any cow's milk.'

Iris glanced at the back of her sister's head. How odd that they'd once looked so alike; Iris's hair had become wiry, a mix of white and iron grey which she kept in a short bob. In contrast, Hope's hair, which she wore long, was soft and white, it could almost be taken for ash blonde in some lights. Tendrils were caught on the collar of her red shirt, and the rest fell forward, brushing her shoulders and face. It looked like a river of silk, moving with every gesture that Hope made. It stirred now, like the movement of ruffled water. Iris wondered why Hope still had her back turned when she realised that Hope was crying softly to herself. Iris sat at the table, uncertain whether to speak or pretend she hadn't noticed. She felt a pang of pity for her sister.

Eventually, without wiping the traces of tears from her cheeks, Hope turned and sat opposite Iris.

'Birdie was only a kid when her grandmother died you know, but she loved her. She was her childhood magic. Birdie's been talking to Oma for over 70 years. I don't think they're done yet.

'I didn't know.' Iris said, 'I'm sorry, I know how fond you are of Birdie. I'm sure she's alright. I didn't mean to upset you.'

Hope shook her head, quickly, fiercely.

'No, it's not that. I know Birdie is fine, I only saw her yesterday myself. She's completely fine. Old body, is all.'

Hope had that same odd sense of loss and darkness. So far, she'd hidden it well from Tom, but it was there in the room with Iris and would not be ignored. Outside her window, the trees waited, expectant and still. Even in the kitchen, she felt as if time had paused, demanding that she find words to explain how lost she felt, how out of kilter with her own self. Must she tell Iris, though?

The light in the kitchen shifted as outside, a cloud obscured the afternoon sun.

'It's me. I'm lost, aren't I?' Hope looked at Iris, 'No matter what I say, I've never really connected. Not to other people, anyway. And these days…' she tailed off.

'What do you mean? Are you talking about being alone? You've always been so independent. I thought that was what you wanted. You could have married Derek, couldn't you. Although being married doesn't solve everything.' Iris fell silent.

The secret of Iris's engagement; the way Iris had told her early one morning; the shock of seeing a small diamond ring on her girlish finger. Hope felt it as if it had been that very morning, as if their parents were in the next room. She rubbed her hand over her eyes.

'God no. Not marriage. But I did find my soulmate. Long time ago. I met the most beautiful soul in the universe. And then I couldn't ever find him again. Another lifetime, maybe.'

'Was that…' Iris hesitated, 'Was that the man who went to India? When Jeannie was little?'

'Blue? No, although perhaps, if he'd hung around, we could have been good together.'

'You sound like a teenager. "Good together". Honestly Hope. Well, at least you have us, family.'

'Family. Well, there's a thing.'

Hope put her elbows on the table and rested her chin in both hands. She hated the sense of bitterness, but she felt she had no choice. Perhaps it was just old memories that had so destabilised her of late. She took a deep breath.

'The last time I saw David was when I was seventeen.'

'David?'

‘The man who used to be my father. Until he refused.’

‘Why do you call him David?’

Do you think he would answer, if I called him Dad?’

Iris was silent.

‘I saw Mum once, you know. Did she tell you?’

Iris shook her head.

‘When?’

‘She came to the hospital, two days after Jeannie was born. Couldn’t bear not to meet her grandchild, she said. But only the once. David again, you see.’

‘It was such a horrible time,’ Iris offered, ‘what with Auntie Jane dying unexpectedly like that.’

Hope looked at Iris, surprised into anger.

‘Have we really never talked about that? Jane’s death wasn’t unexpected. She’d had cancer for simply ages. She didn’t tell David because he would have interfered. She was trying to protect Birdie.’

Nodding slowly, Iris agreed.

‘Oh, I can see how that would have been. How awful. Did you know she was ill then? You were staying with them after all.’

Hope stood up, irresolutely, and then sat down again.

‘No, she hid it from me, too. David’s refusal to allow any version of the world he didn’t like meant that I lost my mum, Jeannie lost her grandmother, and I didn’t get to say goodbye to Auntie Jane.’

Hope glared out of the window, fighting deep buried anger and trying to breathe.

‘Dad was worried about you though. I know he was. He thought you were going off the rails. Don’t you remember how you virtually stopped studying at school?’

Ghosts flickered in the room.

‘For heaven’s sake.’ Hope’s voice was harsh, ‘I was a kid, trying to grow up. When I looked around me, the house we lived in, all those expectations from parents and school, the relentless pursuit of exams and prizes. I just couldn’t see myself. Oh, and all the other girls at school. I didn’t understand how they could be so… so, like they were. I wasn’t a bad girl, just lost, and yeah, more than a bit arrogant. But I so desperately wanted a better world, one that meant something.'

'Dad he only wanted to protect us. He was a good dad, really.'

Hope shook her head. There was a raw, strident buzzing sound in her brain.

'I didn't choose to be difficult, you know. I just couldn't bear feeling like a shadow. It was as if everyone else's version of me was more important than who I might really be. And then there was you.'

'What about me?'

'You? Oh Iris, don't you remember? Didn't you ever , not even once, that we had no choice? We were who we were told to be, labelled clearly so we knew we were two distinct people… "Iris is good at sewing, but Hope can draw. Hope can draw, so Iris is no good at it." It's like they always defined us by the boundaries that separated us, not the things we had in common.'

Iris leant forward on her chair, wanting to reach out and take hold of the teenage Hope, so palpable, so nearly real in front of her. They had been so close, in those days. How had it all slipped away?

‘But I envied you so much. I was always so worried about being told off, being judged. It never seemed to bother you.’

Hadn’t she always adored her sister’s free spirit, Iris thought; the way Hope had always done things her own way. Iris could see her still, aged six, breathing with concentration over a game of Ludo. Hope’s small frame electric with anticipation.

Hope looked up. The gulf between them, she saw, wasn’t just that they were so different, it was more; she struggled for the thought. It was the way Iris wanted to hold on to everything, as if existence was a collection of things, certainties, routines. Even memories, she thought. For Iris, memories were like old photographs, unchanging and unchangeable. Did things really seem more real when they were defined, predictable and familiar? A deep sense of envy possessed her. Her own life had been so exhausting, all that constant searching, and for what? She was an indeterminate beam of light, unable to hold on to anything. Iris, leaning forward across the table, seemed to be at a great distance from her.

‘Well, I don’t remember that. You, envying me? You had it all, didn’t you? I only ever wanted you to understand me. I wanted you to see the world like I did.

But… you never did. That was just in my imagination. And you were preoccupied, weren't you? Law school, Don, getting married. Having a home. Honestly, Iris. I thought you'd decided you were done with having anything to do with me.'

Hope sipped from her cup, wondering why Iris felt so far away.

'It was Birdie who told me that I should get in touch you know, back when you were expecting the boys.'

'Thak goodness she did.'

Would Hope ever have got in touch, Iris wondered, if it hadn't been for Birdie?

'I'd written to you four times, you know. I had no idea you'd moved to Bristol. And then, being pregnant with the boys made me realise how much I'd missed. Not being a proper aunt, I mean. I guess I really missed you too. I couldn't even invite you to my wedding, remember.'

Iris sat back, enjoying the sensation of sitting in Hope's odd little kitchen. She smiled to herself. She and Hope never talked properly, not really. Well, they talked about their everyday lives, but the past… almost never. And yet, after all, who knew Hope better than she did?

‘This is rather lovely,’ Iris said impulsively, ‘we should do this more often. Why do we only really see each other for family things these days? We should do things together. Just the two of us.’

Hope, startled, wondered what they could possibly find to do together. All she knew of her sister’s life was a constant round of shopping trips and lunches with friends. That and her endless committee work.

‘You know,’ Iris said, ‘it would be nice to have someone to go for walks with. Proper walks, I mean. Not trotting round Victoria Park on the paths.’

‘Really?’ asked Hope, ‘That doesn’t seem very,’ she paused, ‘well, very you, somehow.’

Iris looked at her, smiling at the old Hope, the one who was always so provocative. She understood her now.

‘Now who’s trying to create boundaries? It’s only that few of my friends really like walking, and Don certainly wouldn’t go with me. You know, it’s funny how I am surrounded by people who aren’t exactly like me. I don’t know how it’s happened, but it has.’

Hope saw that Iris really meant it. She could see Iris more clearly now, and for a moment it seemed as if it was the boundaries between them that had been an illusion.

'You've got me there. Sorry.'

Had she, she wondered, been busy defining her sister as her opposite in every way. Good, bad; light, dark; open and closed. Like Urizen and Los, she thought.

'Blake!'

Hope's voice was loud, exasperated. She put her cup down heavily on the bare wooden table.

'Sorry. It's been niggling me. William Blake. Songs of Innocence. I couldn't remember his name. I was making hummus the other day, you see.'

Hope was embarrassed. She forced a laugh.

'Oh, it really doesn't matter. But I've always loved his writing, and then I just couldn't remember his name. Holes in the brain, do you think?'

Iris smiled at the old family expression. She'd had no idea that she and Hope were this close after so much, how should she put it, after so much water under the bridge. And here they were, as close as ever. She wanted to seize the moment. Hope always to spoke openly, and the heavens didn't fall.

Iris smiled contentedly before plunging into the long-silent past.

'And we both know why that is, don't we?'

Hope looked curious, her eyes wary and probing. Iris smiled, confident that this moment, this was the perfect way to bring them closer together. They would be like they always used to be, sharing all their secrets and dreams.

'You know…' Iris smiled, a tremor of excitement warming her heart, 'Joseph.'

It was the first time she had dared mention that New Year's Eve, that party, the secret she and Ursula had kept for fifty years. It had always been seemed dangerous, taboo, even. And now, suddenly, all those years of silence seemed ridiculous. Look at them now. Good heavens, she thought, they were both pensioners. And she felt so comfortable with Hope, talking as they had when they were young. Inside, they were still girls, just pretending to have grown up. Iris looked straight into Hope's eyes.

'Oh, yes, I knew about Joseph. I found you, you know. Well, me and Ursula. It was pretty clear what had been going on at that party. And after that evening it was "Blake this, Blake that", as if you'd become some sort of religious convert.'

Iris paused. Hope's expression hadn't changed. If anything, a look of doubt seemed to flicker in her eyes.

'Of course, I didn't know about the connection with Blake until later. You know, when Joseph started his PhD. That's when I realised. I guessed he must be important somehow. Of course, by then…'

Iris trailed off, feeling she had somehow lost her way, said something wrong. Why was it so hard to just say what was on her mind?

Like a dark screech of wheeling birds, New Year's Eve fell from 1969 into Hope's afternoon without warning. She'd forgotten that it had been Joseph who had first quoted Blake to her. That meeting with Joseph and the way they had instantly known each other. Ancient souls entwined. For a moment Hope felt that she was a stone hurtling through the black void of lost time. After a few seconds, the shock dissolved into a shudder of energy, coursing through her body, tossing thoughts and feelings to the shore like flotsam. She had fallen in love in an instant. She'd felt every edge of her being melt into a glorious fusion with love, opening her heart and soul so absolutely that she felt she had known Joseph, as if for millennia. She stared at Iris, unable to speak.

Iris shifted on the hard wooden chair. Why was Hope silent. Did she think Iris really cared about that bit of silliness, all those years ago. Did she think Iris would judge her, still? She cleared her throat.

'Really, Hope. I have always known what you and Joseph did at that party. We don't need to talk to anyone else, but between us it's different.' She hesitated a moment before saying, 'Jeannie was conceived that night, wasn't she?'

Iris had never questioned her version of what happened that night. Burying her secret deep in the ground, the long years of silence had preserved it, rendering it ever more resistant to doubt. But for Hope, the long weeks of doubt and confusion after the party had never resolved into a single truth. Oh, she knew what she'd told Mel. It was the only truth she could imagine at the time, and then years later, she'd given Birdie the same brief summary, carefully avoiding any risk of compassion. Even to herself, her version of events had always felt more invention than truth.

Outside the window, the city paused. The sky itself seemed unstable. Time stumbled, unable to hold conflicting versions of the past.

Hope spoke slowly, forcing words through deserts of sand and glass in her throat.

'You think Joseph is Jeannie's father? How do you even know his name?'

'Of course I do. Joseph is Don's cousin, you must have known that. He was down from Manchester to spend Christmas with the family. He talked endlessly about William Blake too. I seem to remember he quoted Blake in his best man's speech at our wedding. He was a poet then, and he's a poet now. He's done well for himself, though. Quite the academic. You must have seen that biography of Blake he wrote, it was years ago?'

'You know Joseph? You mean, you actually know him?'

To Hope it seemed Iris was growing larger and larger, taking up all the space in her kitchen. Hope felt herself shrinking to a pinprick of light. Joseph. Don's cousin. His best man. It was if all the forests of the world were suddenly no more than sawdust on dry ground.

'Look, Hope. It wasn't until you ran away to Auntie Jane that I even knew you were pregnant. I thought you'd just been mucking about with Joseph. I didn't really think you'd actually let him, you know… Anyway, I didn't talk to anyone about it. Nobody knows. Especially not Don.'

Hope was staring at her now, her expression bruised and livid, as intense as an oncoming storm. Iris felt suffocated, panicky. She smoothed the fabric of her skirt with the palms of her hands and stood up.

'I really don't know how we got started on this. Let's leave the past in the past, shall we. I only really wanted to tell you about Birdie. I'll get going now.'

'Iris, you can't.'

Hope sounded as if she were alone on a stage, in a dark empty theatre. Her voice echoed in her own head. She was troubled by an eerie feeling of disintegration. It was as if she didn't, couldn't, somehow, hold the shape of her own existence in one piece.

'I can't take it in. Look, Iris, I never knew. That Joseph was Don's cousin, I mean. I had no way of getting in touch with him. I wanted to. So much. He changed my life that evening. We talked for hours. Could have been centuries. And all the time you knew who he was. Oh Iris, what have you done?'

Joseph still existed. He was a real person. Old threads of thought resurfaced, still a tangled weave of doubt. Before Hope had realised she was pregnant, she had thought those recurrent images of Chris, his face too close to hers, his hands on her skin, the weight of his body on hers, were all just snatches of a nightmare. When, exactly, had she decided that they were real? But Iris's version of the truth was unimaginable too. Impossible that Joseph would have done that to her.

The predisposition of the world to lurch between realities was familiar to Hope; she felt safer with uncertainties and possibilities, which kept her safe from the unendurable suffocation of being defined by others. But in that moment, her past splintering, she felt as one lost on a moonless night, she wanted to howl for light. She opened her mouth, uncertain what to say.

'Did you tell Mum?'

'Of course not.'

Everything was wrong, and it was her fault. Iris couldn't imagine what had come over her. The room felt cold; edgy and uncomfortable. The fact that Hope didn't know, had never known, that Joseph was her brother-in-law's cousin was obvious now. She was appalled. If only she had stayed silent. How could she have been so stupid?

Hope had her eyes closed. Every filament of her being was sitting with Joseph on the doorstep of Don's parents' house. The sounds of the party behind them and the still quiet of the garden, night air bathing them under stars whose light was already from aeons past. The sheer, utter rightness of sitting together, talking, laughing, breathing as one. A single tear ran down her cheek, acknowledging that, however she tried, time had her in its grip, bruising her with loss and sorrow. She hated the way Iris was hovering there, like a guilty child wanting forgiveness.

'Go away, can't you. I just need some peace and quiet here. I have to write some letters.'

Iris rose to her feet, uncertainly. She wanted to caution Hope, she was worried about Don, about Jeannie. But she saw she could say nothing. Hope and her meteoric moods. As bad now as when she was a teenager. Must she always be so unreasonable.

Hope hustled her sister to the front door and watched her leave without a word. She was quite herself. She wouldn't allow Iris to destroy her, although she knew Iris thought her unhinged.

Letter-writing had, in recent years, become a ritual with Hope. She'd started writing them after her parents died. She now had a folder full of these letters, which she kept under her bed. Her letters were her way of understanding parts of the self that were hidden, even from herself. She'd got the idea from Byron Katie, and they had become way of untangling her own sense of existence from others, especially those whose voices drowned her own in the darkness of night. Writing them, she was able to tell people the things she desperately wanted them to know, but because she never sent them, she didn't have to confront the vulnerability of exposure. She had things to say to her mother, and she wanted to write them now, before the thoughts slipped from her grasp.

Elizabeth,

Well, first of all, I knew you got in touch with Jeannie the month before David died. She didn't tell me, of course, but I saw how it threw her, him going so quickly. And then she only had two years to get to know you. Two years, watching you disappear, your mind unravelling. I've no idea what that must have been like. She's never spoken about that, either. ~~*Sometimes I wonder if that's what is happening to*~~

I wish you had lived longer, Mum. I wish you had had time to get free of David, and all his rules about how things should be.

You won't know this, but my old English teacher once refused to mark my homework because I hadn't followed the rules for writing an essay. The thing is, even then I knew that rules were things that stop us finding our true selves, finding our own dance of body and breath in the universe. I remember, even now. I felt angry, but excited. I'd done something different, deliberately, and I knew it was important, even if it did land me in trouble.

But you. You blamed me for being pregnant. And you decided that I must have done it on purpose. And you allowed that thought to change everything you thought about me. Just writing it down, it brings it all back.

I don't think I'm angry about it though. I never felt angry, just lonely. Mel used to tell me that anger gets stuck when it's repressed. That never made any sense to me. Energy attracts more of what we pay attention to. Makes me wonder how our family might have been different - if you'd stopped for one moment and questioned the things you and David thought you knew about me.

Iris thinks Don's cousin is Jeannie's father. Seems to be really important to her, god knows why. Jeannie has made it quite clear she doesn't want to talk about it, ever. Anyway, I think Iris is wrong, but then I never knew what really happened, Mum, and I still don't. You know, all that stuff about genes, or nationality, your age or the colour of your skin. It's a total distraction from the divine. We're here to dance, mum, and weave our filaments of cosmic energy into joy. Family is the people who fill your life with joy, and that's it. We could have had that, if it hadn't been for David, couldn't we?

Oh god, Mum, I hope you got to dance before you went, even if it was in secret.

Love and blisses, Hope

Hope put down her pen and smoothed the paper as if it were a child's head. She reached under her bed for the box in which she stored her unsent letters, diaries and other fragments of thought, and folded her words in with the rest.

Chapter 48

Three weeks later, as the world went online, Birdie sat at her tablet. With Tom's support, she had installed Skype. She wasn't sure how she felt about using it. The screen seemed to drain the vivacity from people's faces. The first time she'd Skyped Hope, she'd been astonished by just how old she looked. Even Tom had looked worn and absent.

'Well, Jane,' she murmured quietly, 'at least you and I don't need any technological gadgets to keep in touch.'

She was sitting in her room, her tablet propped on the small table, waiting for Hope to call her. It was hard to get her wheelchair close enough to the screen, and her back already hurt from the strain. It was fifteen minutes later than the time they'd agreed, and Birdie was about to send a text when Skype started its plaintive tone. That was another thing she didn't like, she decided. The ringing tone on Skype sounded like the repetitive moan of a tired child. Ghastly. Quickly, she pressed the connect button, and Hope's face.

'Hope, at last. I was beginning to think you'd forgotten me.'

'Sorry, Birdie. Long wait at the supermarket. They've reduced the number of people allowed in at one time. I had to stand outside for ages.'

'Poor you. I'm sorry. I didn't mean to snap.'

'It's tough in there, right?'

Birdie grimaced and shook her head.

'Yeah, I know. It was bad enough before. Wish you were home, Birdie.'

Birdie shrugged. 'How are you?'

'Desperate. How long is this going to go on, do you think? And I've got this horrible pain in my back.'

'Gardening, I expect.'

'Don't think so, Tom's been out there, but not me. Feels like kidneys.'

'Make sure Tom keeps an eye on you. That could get nasty. How is he? Bored too?'

'Maybe. A bit spaced out, anyway. He's studying hard, I think. Now, there was something I wanted to ask you, um… Forgotten. Damn it.'

Hope pushed her fingers across the side of her head, tilting it to one side as if trying to dislodge water from her ear. Birdie peered at the screen. It really was impossible. Like watching t.v.

'It'll come back.' Birdie said, with a reassurance she didn't feel, 'It's very difficult, isn't it. I think all of us are getting scrambled by lockdown.'

Seeing her own face on the screen, Birdie smiled carefully.

'It's easier for me,' she said, 'I just think about the glorious life I've had. You know, I was thinking about Flag Cottage in September this morning. Jane's favourite month. She always laughed at me you know, in the autumn. Harvesting my cabbages, making pickles that neither of us really liked.'

Birdie paused, her mind's eye alive with images of Jane and herself. Their garden, their life, together, hidden in the world. She sighed.

'I'm glad she went in September. It was the best month for her to choose. If she had to go at all…' Birdie sat up straight, tucking a loose wisp of hair behind her ear, 'Those five years after Jeannie arrived. Grief is like a landslide you know, changes the world for ever. But I couldn't mourn, not really. Jane wouldn't have approved.'

Birdie focused on the image of Hope on her screen. What was it about her? A sort of absence. Wretched computers.

'How is she now?' Hope asked.

'How is who?' Birdie was puzzled.

'Auntie Jane. I will write to her, you know. You must give her my love when you see her.'

Birdie drew breath. 'Hope, darling. Are you alright dear?'

'Well, yes, I should think so. Are you? And what about the garden, by the way. You didn't tell me.'

Birdie knew at once that this was much worse than usual. Iris had been trying to say that Hope was off balance when she'd called the previous evening. But this wasn't like Hope's usual meandering thought. It was as if she had somehow drifted into a different decade. What should she do? She couldn't bring herself to be brutal with the truth, but she couldn't let it pass, either.

'Ah that lovely garden. Do you miss it too? I still think of Jeannie, playing on the lawn when she was only a scrap. Do you remember when she was five? Her last summer in Wales. When you and she danced across the field. Weren't you collecting blackberries? I remember watching you both, so full of life.'

Birdie paused, wanting the right words to direct Hope, but without upsetting her.

'You know, that year, before you moved to Bristol. Five years after Jane died.'

Birdie looked at Hope to see if she was following her words. Hope was nodding, which reassured her. But Hope wouldn't remember, Birdie knew, how joy had been flattened like a bombed city after Jane's death. Hope had returned from that awful place in Bristol two weeks after Jane had died, looking pale but resolute. And then Jeannie had been born three days later. All in the chasm of Birdie's grief. Hope had insisted on naming her baby Jane, but it was too much, far too much, and she'd had to persuade her to soften it to Jeannie.

'Hope?'

Hope put her head on one side, stretching the muscles in her neck. She looked uncomfortable.

'I don't remember any funeral.'

'You weren't there, pet. And neither was I.'

Birdie caught a movement behind Hope.

‘Is that Tom? Tom,’ she raised her voice as if calling across a real room, ‘I’ve got a question for you about this Skype. Do you have a moment?’

Tom’s form reappeared on the screen, and he leant over his Nan’s shoulder.

‘Hey Birdie. How’s the kitchen disco at your place?’ He smiled, trying to look upbeat.

‘No need to keep my spirits up, Tom. I’m absolutely fine. What is it you like to say, Hope? I’m channelling my inner daffodil, that’s what I’m doing.’

‘Scuse me, Birdie. Talk to Tom. Bladder issues. Back in a mo.’

‘I heard all that.’ Tom spoke rapidly as Hope left the room.

‘What’s going on, Tom? She seems very confused, all of a sudden. Is there a problem?’

Tom couldn’t think what to say. The adults in his life all did this, talked to him as if he were just as old as them, as if he could handle stuff. It probably beat being treated like a kid, but sometimes, it was way too much.

‘She’s been fine, Birdie. Well, mostly. She repeats herself a lot, you know. Flag Cottage. How you guys changed her life. I suppose she's said some odd stuff too. But hey, that's Nan.'

Tom could tell Birdie wasn't satisfied.

'Sorry, Birdie. Yeah, you're right. The last couple of days have been a bit, um, well, kind of weird, even for Nan. Look, can I text you if any more weird stuff happens? That ok? Only I'd rather tell you than Mum. Or Auntie Iris. I'd tell them if there was a proper accident, but, you know?'

Birdie nodded. Tom thought he heard Hope returning and changed the subject.

'Nan's lent me this amazing book. Have you come across Mathieu Ricard. He's a Buddhist monk.'

'Your great aunt should have known you.'

Birdie loved and couldn't bear how like Jane Tom sometimes appeared. She saw the threads of thought and spirit that looped and bound souls together. Jane, Hope, Tom. The best kind of joy, always with a twist of grief.

'Of course, Mathieu Ricard. He's living in France now, isn't he. Taking care of his mum. She's got ten years on me, near enough. Mind you, I can't think of a more beautiful way to exit this life than in the care of someone like him. Oh, Hope. There you are. Is something wrong. You look worried?'

Tom felt his mind flex and grasp like the reaching hand of a climber. Something important. He wanted to stop for a moment, get a firm hold on an almost unseen thought. But the chance was lost, Hope was next to him again, now wearing a coat. He stared at her.

'Birdie?'

Hope sounded uncertain. She was picking at the sleeves of her shirt, worrying a loose thread. 'I'm just going to the, um. You know, the er, the place for yoga. It's my class today, and I don't want to miss it.'

'But Nan, you can't go out,' said Tom, 'we have to stay at home, remember?'

'Tom,' Birdie spoke quickly, authoritatively, 'from where I'm sitting, your Nan is definitely unwell. I hate to ask this, but you're going to have to take over for a bit. Ring a doctor, would you. And be insistent, there's a dear.'

Chapter 49

It was a clear Wednesday in June, and waiting for the supermarket delivery, Iris stood aimlessly looking out at the empty street. Beside her, sitting on a low table, was the brochure for their autumn cruise, cancelled now, until Lord knows when. Tucked inside the brochure was a piece of paper in Don's meticulous handwriting, detailing every call with the company, even though most of their interactions were by email, and she knew he had these too, stored carefully. She'd used to enjoy flicking through the brochure, but its promises were like fake news now. Just catching sight of the thing made her feel she'd been deceived.

Later, after the supermarket van had left, Iris put on a pair of long rubber gloves so she could wash all the packaging before putting the week's groceries away. Then she walked to the front gate, roughly scrubbing at the gate catch. She didn't care if other people judged her. You couldn't take too many precautions. Going back into the kitchen, she washed all the handles and taps, and then her hands, twice. It was nearly eleven am. She decided to save her permitted walk until the afternoon. In his study, Don's voice was loud. He sounded almost cheerful, she thought.

Standing in her kitchen, wondering what to do, she noticed that the bird feeder was almost empty. She might as well take it down and give it a good clean. And while she was in the garden, she could think about the plans that Don kept talking about. Once they had their deposit back from the cruise, he'd told her, they would use the money to redesign the garden. Get rid of the tired old rose beds. Don wanted something contemporary, stylish, but easy to maintain. For the last week and a half, he'd been trying to convince her that a row of cedar trees would create an eye-catching boundary. That hadn't sounded very low maintenance to her, but it turned out he intended to use artificial trees, promising her they were indistinguishable from the real thing. Iris found she didn't have the strength to oppose him. She wondered idly why making objections felt like too much effort these days.

In her pocket, her phone buzzed. She pulled it out with alacrity. A text, from Jeannie.

Hi Iris, Are you well. Not a crisis here, exactly, but can we Skype? I need to talk to you. X'

Iris wondered what was wrong. Tom probably. Poor Jeannie. It had been a bad move, him going to stay with Hope. She returned to the house to text back.

All well here thank you. I'd love to Skype, but now is a bit difficult, Can we arrange a time this evening?

Of course, she wasn't really doing anything, but Don didn't like her using Skype when he was at work. He told her that there wasn't enough bandwidth for everyone to be using the internet willy-nilly, not during working hours, at least. Her phone buzzed again.

You can't be busy, surely. It's a bit confidential, about Mum, and it's probably better if we talk alone.

What should she do? Jeannie was right, Don rarely missed an opportunity to criticise Hope. It would be easier to talk if he wasn't listening in. And if there was something really wrong.

Alright, Jeannie. I'll see what I can do. Wait for me to call you, though.

She would take her tablet up into the front bedroom, Skype Jeannie quickly, just to find out what the issue was.

On the screen, Jeannie's face was white and tired. She looked accusingly at Iris, speaking as soon as the audio connected.

'Is there something wrong with Mum? Something nobody's telling me about?'

'What a peculiar question. Why, do you think there is? Have you spoken to her?'

'No, I haven't. And even if I did, she wouldn't tell me the truth. It's something Birdie let slip.'

'Birdie? Could you be a bit clearer, dear. I don't know what you mean.'

Jeannie abruptly realised that Iris wasn't hiding anything. Her face relaxed and she looked properly at Iris.

'Sorry, Iris. Look, I know Birdie can be really difficult to follow sometimes, but she said something about Mum being much better now, and what a scare we'd all had. Of course, that made it blindingly obvious that I didn't know what she was talking about. So she clammed up. Said that people should be allowed to decide what they talk about and what they keep secret. Honestly, I get the same from Mum. You'd think it was a crime, wanting to look after your own family.'

'But honestly, Jeannie. I haven't heard anything. If I had, I would have told you.'

'I realise that now, I'm sorry. I didn't mean to take it out on you. But it's just one thing after another, isn't it. Only yesterday I had a long call with Peter. He's worried too. Says Tom seems to have lost focus on his course. And I didn't know anything about that, either.'

'Let's stick to Hope for a minute. I can't Skype for very long. Now, I'm talking to Birdie on Friday. We have a regular chat in the evening now, so let me see what I can find out. What about you? When are you speaking to your Mum and Tom?'

'Tomorrow. Perhaps I can get them separately for a change. It's a nightmare otherwise.'

'Don't worry, Jeannie. We'll find out. It's probably nothing. Birdie does come out with the strangest things sometimes. It makes me wonder if she's quite as sharp as she thinks.'

Jeannie nodded. Iris looked at her carefully. She was calmer now, she thought. And at any moment, Don might come thundering up the stairs.

'Look, I must go,' Iris said, 'but keep in touch. We'll get to the bottom of this, whatever it is. I'll talk to Birdie.'

Chapter 50

The following morning, Tom was doing a literature search when he heard a door slam heavily in Hope's part of the house. Then silence. Disturbed, he got up to see what had happened. In the kitchen, Iris glowered on the screen, but his Nan was in the garden, scribbling rapidly in one of her notebooks. He sat in front of the computer.

'Hey, Aunty Iris. Is everything ok?' Clearly it wasn't, but he couldn't think what else to say,

Iris pursed her lips.

'The trouble with your Nan is that she doesn't appreciate anything that anyone does for her.'

Iris flinched even as she spoke. She found it so hard to control her feelings these days, but letting rip at Tom shocked her.

'I do apologise, Tom. I'm just het up,' Iris paused, 'I only want to make sure my sister is alright. Birdie seems to think there's something wrong with her. Do you know anything? For goodness' sake, Tom, you must see her every day.'

Tom paused. What should he say? That Nan had frightened them, jumbling her memories and places? That for a couple of days she hadn't seemed to know what year it was, who was alive and who had died? That the doctor had given her a course of antibiotics, and now she seemed restored to her old self? If only it were that simple, but who was he to say. He shrugged his shoulders at the screen.

'Um. Maybe I could get her to come inside? She's in the garden right now. I'm meant to be in a seminar. It's just, well. I heard a loud bang.'

'This wretched isolation, Tom. It's driving us all to distraction. Is there something wrong with your Nan? Your Mum is worried sick, you know.'

Yeah, right, thought Tom. His Mum did have a way of making things worse when she tried to help. He shook his head again.

'Um, I dunno, Auntie Iris. Maybe talk to her later. If she's, you know…'

To his relief, Iris nodded.

'Yes, I know. Maybe I shouldn't have called, I just wondered… oh, never mind. Let's leave it. Aren't you talking to Jeannie later? She said you usually Skype on Thursdays? And I've got a catch up with Birdie in my diary tomorrow. I'll send her your best wishes, shall I?'

‘Yeah, of course, heaps of love to Birdie, and tell her I beat Nan at tiddlywinks yesterday.’

In the garden, Hope hadn’t noticed Tom talking to Iris. Her head was low over the notebook, her shoulders hunched as she wrote.

Dearest, dearest Auntie Jane,

I know it wasn’t the reason, but god, you were so lucky not to have people interfering. Bloody Iris. Thing is, I always thought my life’s end would be like yours. My body invaded by not-me-ness, I mean. Your cancer was a goblin, stealing your energy while you watched. Right now, I think I’d be ok with that, though. Afterwards, Birdie used to talk about that last summer, your incredible creativity and the energy you magicked into being. Perhaps you were angry or scared? I’ll never know. She always said that your death was a parting of the ways, a falling out, if you like, between self and body. That makes sense. Like one’s self is not part of one’s body but can be set free after death. Anyway, for years and years I thought it would happen to me, too. No good reason, it just seemed obvious. You, David. Both your parents. Cancer just appeared to be the way of it.

But the thing is, Auntie Jane, it seems that for me it will be the other thing. Like mum. They think there might be empty spaces appearing in my mind. It is not invasion I should fear, but desertion.

And all I want to do is cry. How will I feel the universe dancing if all I have are ragged gaps and flakes of memory. Of course, I know I am not my mind, but how will I find my way without it? It's like. Oh, it's like if my mind gets ragged and torn, and I can't control whatever is left, then I will never experience the divine again.

All this time, it seems, I have been defending myself against the wrong enemy, and I don't know how to start again. Oh Jane, what's to become of me?

Do you remember the story you used to tell. About a huge moth? Someone sees it flying across in the lights of an outdoor performance. A concert, or a play? I don't remember. The idea that the moth is oblivious to the universe of the stage, or the audience. Has its own cosmos. Something written by Loren Eiseley, was it? I've been like that moth, but the stage is also me. Like I've been fluttering cluelessly through my own performance.

Hope put the pen down. She realised how she had been clenching her jaw and stretched her neck to ease the tension.

Anyway. If it's true... Well, I think it is true, you know. And when remember how I tried to believe being pregnant was just an illusion. The pain I caused you. Well, of course I didn't know you were dying. I only know what Birdie's told me. Even though I was there, crowding your serenity with my stupid behaviour. We all have our own forms of dontellitus, do you think? But this time, I won't go about hiding the truth from myself. I'll hang on to me. As long as I can. But I can't bear the way Iris is. Like she wants to stick a label around my neck. I won't tell her. Not until I have no choice.

Love and blisses, H x

Chapter 51

Birdie had been unable to Skype Iris that Friday. She'd felt too unwell. Lying in bed, she listened to Jane's voice.

'The thing is,' Jane was saying, 'I had the clearest sense that knowing about my cancer shouldn't make any difference to how I lived.'

'But it did,' murmured Birdie, 'you're forgetting…'

'That we were scratchy with each other? That our time together became something we fought over? Well yes, there was that. But only for a few weeks.'

Birdie moved feverishly under the sheets on her narrow bed.

'No, darling. I don't mean that. That was nothing. Just a puff of sea fog. Your cancer pushed us into the world. It made us honest, out there. Beyond Flag Cottage. And that has been everything to me. Everything. I've had family, and love, I've stayed close to you through Hope, and now Tom. He has your way of staring intently at a person, you know.'

Birdie hunched her shoulders and bent forward, a heavy cough rattling her like wet autumn leaves, leaving her chest tight and hard. She clenched her jaw to hold the pain at bay, rallying every muscle in her slight frame to combat the virus. Jane sighed through the summer breeze.

‘Pain is just pain, darling girl. There’s no need to fight enemies that aren’t important. Come with me, Birdie. Remember where the waves and the stones dance between the form of water and the form of land. Remember how we used to dance on the beach in the pitch-dark night.’

Jane’s voice grew harder to hear, there was a roaring in the air, the green roar of timeless seas.

Birdie’s dizziness was too much. The pale walls of her room were bright with the glare of sunlight, streaming in the window. Closing her eyes, she could see shapes moving; figures dancing, waves breaking on the shore, sunlight sprinkling the waves. Her limbs were aflame.

‘Poor love. You shouldn’t be alone.’

And with the pain, suddenly, eddies of ridiculous, heart-clenched laughter.

‘Alone, Jane? What, with you telling me what to do at every turn?’

Wearing a face-mask and plastic visor, robed head to foot in disposable scrubs, an exhausted figure passed by the closed door of Birdie's room. Glancing through the small square of glass she could see the patient, her body contorted under the sheet, shoulders shaking uncontrollably. That'll be the sixth one this week, she thought. God save us all.

Chapter 52

For the first time since Birdie's funeral, Tom was alone in the house. Hope's yoga group had started holding classes in the park, and she had left with her mat early that morning. It was kind of weird, he thought, how the house breathed differently when he was alone. The last few weeks had been a bit stressy. He and Hope had been the only ones at the funeral, and Hope was now completely hacked off with his Mum for not being there, and the awkwardness of it all was getting to him. His mum always assumed that he was siding with Hope, even though he kind of got it. The funeral had been like a charade. His mum just didn't know how to deal with that sort of thing. Besides, his similarity to Hope had always been a bit of an issue for her, he knew that. Him and magic Nan had had a kind of secret pact of silliness over the years, which was not silliness at all, but a sort of rebellion against the grain of things. And now he had a ton of work to do for uni. His tutor had given him an extension, because of Birdie, but he still had two essays to write before the end of August. And it was such a pain, doing everything on one screen. He couldn't wait for the uni library to reopen. September, they said.

In fact, the funeral had been worse than he could have possibly imagined. Nan had wanted him to wear colourful, cheerful clothes. He didn't really do colour, so she had lent him a bright scarf, and he wore one purple and one green sock with his mustard sweat shirt and chinos. When they'd got to the crematorium there was a marquee just outside the building. The sort you get at festivals and flower shows, Hope had said. Close up, she'd read the notice on the fence. "A temporary resting place for loved ones." He'd felt an idiot then, and wished he was wearing black. Two of them, sitting like people waiting for a bus, with all that empty seating around them. It had been awful. Afterwards, he'd felt really dark. He sighed and went to sit at his laptop.

His phone buzzed, making him jump. It was Nan.

'Hey, Tom. Do you want me to make you some lunch when I get back? Salad from the garden xx'

He sighed. His fingers hovering over the screen, trying to decide what to say. He didn't want to have lunch with her, but he didn't really want to carry on studying either. He pulled the side of his mouth in between his teeth, chewing on the fold of soft flesh.

'Thanks Nan, but not today. Need to keep going with my essay. How's yoga?'

‘No problem. Interesting. Tell you when I see you. X’

Tom moved his laptop around on the table, flicking between tabs. He hunched forward, and tried to concentrate, managing only an hour’s work before being distracted by a WhatsApp conversation with Jeb. They’d been googling the Dalai Lama and kept texting stuff about radical kindness. Plus, random pictures of airborne plants. He turned back to his coursework. It wasn’t as if he didn’t enjoy it. The course was actually quite interesting, even if he had zero ambition to work for the police or courts, which is what most people with a Criminology degree seemed to do. But maybe Nan was right. Did he have to get a degree?

He picked up his phone again to see if there were any messages or posts he hadn’t read. The only unopened message was one from his mum. Strange, he thought, noticing when he clicked on it that she hadn’t been active on WhatsApp since she’d sent it, the previous morning. “Hey Mum” he tapped, “You ok? I’m having a break right now if you have time to Skype?” He stared at the phone, waiting for the two ticks to turn blue. A message from Jeb flicked across the screen. “Bored. Going into town. Want to meet up?” Tom responded with a thumbs down and the single word "essay", wondering to himself why he kept using uni work as an excuse. It wasn't as if he was actually doing anything productive. Still no reply from his mum.

At nine pm, the light beginning to soften and play slow notes in a minor key, Tom was heading up Lansdown on his own. He'd ended up spending the day messaging friends and even people he just knew from school before going out for a walk. More people were out and about now the rules had changed. Meeting up in small groups. It made his isolation deeper and more uncomfortable. He had to shield, he knew that, but it didn't stop him feeling as if he'd been singled out, forced to be a loner. His phone buzzed.

'Hey, Mum.'

'Sorry I missed your text, darling. Busy day at work, and then I've been out for a walk. There are definitely more people about now. The car park was almost full this evening.'

Jeannie heard the sound of traffic as a bus lumbered up the hill past Tom.

'Where are you? You're not in town, are you?'

‘Don’t be daft, Mum. I’m on Lansdown. By myself.’

‘I’m only asking.’

‘Well, don’t. I’m not an idiot, you know.’

Jeannie sighed. ‘Did you want to Skype for anything in particular?’

‘Well, yeah. Sorry Mum. Actually, I just wanted to say Happy Anniversary. Sorry I didn’t get you and Dad a card.’

‘He’s hoping to get back in August. Fingers crossed. There are no tourists on the island this summer. Should mean that he can get away for a fortnight. We’ll come and see you. Even if we can only meet up outside.’

‘Really? That’d be great. It’s kind of weird not seeing anyone. Except Nan, of course.’

‘Tom.’ Jeannie paused, ‘Look, I am sorry about Birdie’s funeral. I should have been pushier. I’ve got so many memories of her. The fun she bought into my childhood. I should have been more insistent. Perhaps the Crematorium might have let me attend.’

Tom looked out over the city where the sun, sinking into a glorious sunset, was creating a patchwork of light and shade which warmed and cooled the buildings in uneven patterns. He couldn't make out the exact direction but gazed over Twerton as if some recollection of Birdie's departure should be evident from the skyline beyond. The exhausted wail of an ambulance tracked through the invisible streets below him.

'You need to tell Nan that, not me.'

'How are things, at home?'

'Mum…'

'Don't be prickly, Tom. I'm not asking about Nan, I'll talk to her, I promise. I mean, how is it in Birdie's maisonette? Have you thought about staying there, now?'

Tom felt caught, again, in the conflict between his mum and his nan. Of course it didn't help, him staying in Birdie's place. He knew he didn't want to stay there indefinitely. But then, he couldn't imagine going back to his university flat either, even after the pandemic. If there ever was an after, he thought.

'Honestly, Mum. I don't know. It's like, everything is so temporary now. There's no such thing as planning the future, is there?'

Jeannie wished, for the millionth time, that Tom had agreed to come home. She couldn't bear how vulnerable he was.

'Tell you what, Tom. Let's arrange a FaceTime, shall we. The three of us. I'll check with Dad, and text you. How does that sound?' She heard a buzzing sound in her ear. 'What's that? Is it your phone?'

'Yeah, don't worry, it's Jeb. I'll call them later.'

Jeannie's mouth tightened. If she said anything about Jeb, Tom would fly off the handle. There was a long pause while she tried to think of something to talk about. That was even worse. She heard the buzz of Tom's phone again, followed by a sharp gasp from him as he read a message.

'Gotta go. Sorry. Yeah. Good idea about Dad. Let's do it. Sorry Mum. Something's come up. Bye.'

Chapter 53

Sitting in her garden, the evening had darkened before Hope allowed herself to be concerned. Tom was still out, but he was eighteen, she told herself. And the restrictions had finally eased a couple of weeks ago. Why shouldn't he go out? People were allowed to meet outside now. And even the night air was warm. It was, she reflected, difficult for him. He mustn't feel that he had to explain his every movement to her, just because she was there. She wanted to be there for Tom but not get in his way. She wondered how Jane and Birdie had held back, allowing her all the space she needed to make her own mistakes, come to her own realisations. It wasn't easy. She grimaced. Gone ten o'clock now.

Without Birdie in her everyday world, Hope felt a huge sense of loss. She'd never had the chance to talk to Birdie about the way how frightened she'd been when her sense of reality had been so disturbed in the year. Ok, so it was put down to a bladder infection, but at a follow up appointment, the doctor had told her quite firmly that she should be referred to a Memory Clinic. She knew what that meant, and it hadn't really been a surprise. She'd promised herself to be honest about it, but who could she talk to? She would write to Birdie, she decided, that was something she could do now. She felt good today; everything was sharp and clear. Surely, Tom wouldn't be out for much longer. She crumbled a spoonful of last year's feathery dried lemon verbena into a pot and poured herself a cup of tea. At the table, she sat for some minutes, pen poised over the paper.

Darling Birdie,

Since you went, I've realised what I should have known all along. You had such a way, your knowledge and your cosmic sense of fun. I guess they came with you from ancient lives, and now you've returned to the universe again. What's it like, I wonder, having wisdom and laughter and no voice to share it? Not that you're absent, of course. It's just that now I have to pay attention differently. You know that huge beech tree in the park? It's got a lot of you about it. You know. Busy fingering the soil, delving in that sort of ultra-determined way you have and finding the memories and magic and a definite leafy flutteriness.

So, I don't have to put the words on the page for you, but only for me. Bit like when I turned up on your doorstep. Do you remember? It was about to rain, and you were planting carrots or something? It was like you already knew I was pregnant. Even though I had ignored the signs for months. You just knew. And then this year, in April. You saw what was happening to me, didn't you? Back then, it was my body. I can't believe how much energy I wasted building barricades. You know, planning my life as if being pregnant was like, I don't know, a bad cold or a broken leg. I so wanted to be a child of the universe back then. A painter, a mystic, whatever. Just anything that gave me the chance to be me. Even now, smiles and sadness, Birdie. Poor little Hope. So lost.

OK. I'll just write it.

The doctor wants me to get my brain checked out. She reckons that when I got so confused, you know, when I had that UTI, could be part of something bigger. Like my mind going. I mean dementia, Birdie. She wants me to go to a Memory Clinic. So, this time it's not my body, it's my mind...

Hope leant back in her chair, looking at the sheets of paper. She wanted to burn them, and imagined holding them to a candle, watching them catch fire and curl into nothingness. Was that what was happening to her brain, she thought, turning into a heap of charred fragments without coherence, unable to connect to the divine. Tears rolled down her cheeks. Without her mind, how could she be more than an object? A time-bound, physical object that others would have to manage. Fifty years of meditative practice would be as nothing.

... thing is, it wasn't just then. Most of the time, I feel fine, but I also know a sort of absence from myself, as if I'm leaping through time and space like a tiddlywink. And the things I can't...

Hope swivelled suddenly. Tom was standing in the open doorway. Something was obviously wrong. Heavily, he stumbled through the cool night air and sat down. Without speaking, she cleared away the pen and paper, gesturing for him to sit by her.

'Shall we sit out here?'

He nodded.

'I saw you had candles out here. It's nice.'

Hope sat quietly. He needed her to be present, she could see that, but she didn't know if he wanted anything more than that. She didn't look directly at him, but practised a gentle asana, holding her body in a steady position to level out the nervous energy that was coming from Tom. She willed herself to channel a sense of loving kindness in the room, holding her own thoughts and questions in a place far distant. She would see, later, if they were needed. Tom tensed his hands, flexing his fingers like claws on the table.

'Jeb's been beaten up, Nan. That's where I've been. In A & E. They were attacked by some horrible angry stranger. It was awful, Nan. I didn't know what to do.'

Tom lifted his hand to his face as if to imprint the memory of the assault on his own skin.

Hope put a hand on his arm, gently. She could feel the pain in him, a trembling like an aftershock. She wasn't sure he was ready for her to speak yet. There was something more.

'A & E were amazing Nan. So gentle and kind. It was like they were really caring for Jeb. No… you know. No attitude. I was allowed to stay in the waiting area. And then, they discharged Jeb, so I took them home. I feel so bad though, Nan.'

Hope lowered her head, lifting her gaze towards him at the same time with a tentative query.

'It's all my fault.' Tom's voice was ragged then, and she could feel the pain catching in his throat.

'Jeb called me earlier. Said they wanted to go into town. You know, now we're allowed. And I said I wouldn't go because I had too much work to do. I should have been there, Nan. If I'd been there, I could have stopped it.'

He stopped abruptly, searching for breath.

'I mean. It's random idiots who can't cope with the way a person is, you know? Like they feel threatened, or something.'

'Yeah, Tom, you could be right.' Hope spoke slowly, 'But you don't know it's that, do you?'

'God, Nan? Why can't we just accept everybody the way they want to show up. What's wrong with just accepting others, even if you don't get them?'

'How come you've never shown me a photo of Jeb?' asked Hope, 'You must have some on your phone. And I know they are an important part of your life?'

Her question exploded in Tom's head. His face fell as he realised how, at some level, he too acted in ways that limited Jeb's place in the world. Even if he didn't intend to. The result was the same. His eyes filled with tears.

'I never meant. I just thought. Well, you. You might not understand. What about Mum and Dad? They would just use it as one more thing to worry about. And it's not as if…'

Tom broke off, pulling at the skin of his neck until it made an angry red mark.

'The thing is, I didn't think, did I Nan? I just assumed. Just like those evil bastards who beat Jeb up this evening.'

'Not quite like those evil bastards, darling.' Hope looked softly at him, 'You were the one who Jeb called when they needed help. That's pretty awesome, you know.'

'But Nan. I wasn't even really working this morning. I know my course is interesting and all that, but it's not really me, you know.'

'Hey. Slow down Tom… One bear at a time, remember?'

'Birdie.' Tom paused, his shoulders easing, 'I used to love the way she said that. It always made me smile, and it was so wise at the same time.'

Tom pulled out his phone and started flicking through the photos. He found the picture he wanted and held it towards Hope. She looked carefully at the photo, a person with short, riotous curly hair and eyes so dark they looked almost black. Jeb's head was tilted on one side, and there was a look of plain, ordinary happiness as they smiled at the camera. Nothing special, just a perfectly unique human being, like all the others.

'And Jeb is ok, now? I mean. Probably really shocked and emotional, but physically? No broken bones?'

Tom shook his head. 'Just cuts and bruising, the nurse said. Gonna be some pretty intense bruises though.' He yawned, 'God, sorry Nan. It's way later than I realised. You must be exhausted.'

'Well, yes, that's definitely true, Tom. But tomorrow. Or the next day. Whenever you want to tackle one of those bears. Well, you just let me know, ok?'

'Ok, Nan.'

After he'd gone, Hope smoothed out her letter again on the table.

Things I can't – well, something, clearly! Tom's set me thinking about something else and I can't remember what I was going to say. No need for a brain scan on that one... just a manifestation of the man from Porlock that Coleridge complained of, huh? I'm going to be busy, Birdie, so hold on tight.

Love and blisses, Hope.

Chapter 54

In the heat of a mid-August day, Hope caught a bus into the city centre. Nearly everyone around her was wearing masks, and the intense sunshine added, she thought, to the overall sense of unreality. She was heading for an appointment with a solicitor. He'd insisted on seeing her in person before finalising her will, and so here she was, hot and uncomfortable. She was wearing her pale pink harem pants and a T-shirt she'd ordered from Glastonbury Festival, which had been cancelled that year. She was also wearing a straw hat that had once belonged to Birdie. She looked at him irritatedly, feeling that she was being judged. She pulled the hat from her head, setting it crossly on the seat beside her.

'Is this really necessary?' she asked, little puffs of air ballooning under her face mask. She wished she could just pull it off.

'I'm sorry, but given what you've told me, Miss Greenwood,'

'Ms,' she interrupted him.

'My mistake, I do apologise.'

He didn't have an apologetic muscle in his face, Hope thought, wishing she'd asked someone other than her sister to recommend a solicitor.

'Ms Greenwood. I wouldn't be doing my job if I didn't recommend that you get a letter from your doctor, declaring that in their view you aren't suffering from any impairment due to your diagnosis.'

'But I haven't been diagnosed. God, I wish I'd never mentioned it. My GP recommended that I attend a memory clinic in April. I just haven't done it yet.'

From what she could see behind his mask, the man behind the desk remained calm. He looked at her levelly.

'Please don't assume I'm not on your side,' he said, more gently, 'You'll be paying me a fair amount of money to make sure your will is absolutely watertight. You want to leave the bulk of your estate to your grandson. That's not unheard of, but it could be challenged by other, closer relatives.'

Hope stared at him for a few seconds.

'You're right,' she said, 'I'm sorry. It's just…'

'When you know what you want, busybodies in suits seem set on making your life more difficult.'

His eyes smiled, ‘As I said, I do understand.’

‘I’m sorry. I didn’t mean to be awkward. I’ll contact my GP. Though goodness knows, I hardly ever see him.’ Hope paused, ‘In the meantime, I am going to tell my daughter what I plan to do. That’s ok, isn’t it?’

‘I’d certainly recommend it. It will help with your Power of Attorney as well. Good luck, Ms Greenwood. And I look forward to seeing you soon to finalise matters.’

Out in the street, Hope headed towards Abbey Churchyard to meet Mel. When she arrived, Mel was leaning on her walking stick, hovering in the square in front of the Abbey’s huge doors. Hope walked towards her quickly, her arms open for a hug, and then abruptly remembered that hugs were definitely not on the Government’s approved list.

‘This is so weird,’ she said, ‘like I’m not allowed to hug my best friend.’

Mel grinned.

‘Moira’s youngest came round last week,’ she said, ‘and she stood in the garden calling out “virtual hug, Nana, virtual hug.”’

Mel smiled. ‘So, what’s brought you into town?’

'Let's get a coffee. No, actually. Let's go into Parade Gardens. My treat?'

Hope felt Mel's steady brown eyes observing her as they walked the short distance to Parade Gardens and paid the entrance charge.

'Bench?' Hope still preferred sitting on the ground, but she knew Mel wasn't so keen.

'Do you mind?'

Hope sat down sideways, one knee tucked under her. Mel rolled her eyes with mock envy.

'I've been doing yoga for half a century.' Hope shrugged, 'Got to be some pay off. God, this is better than Skype. It is so good to see you.'

Conversation between them moved like a shuttle on a loom, easy, rhythmic and familiar. After half an hour or so, in one of their pauses, Mel took a long, careful look at Hope. The harem pants were smarter than Hope's usual careless baggy trousers, and the straw hat looked fabulous.

'You look gorgeous hun,' she said, 'but tell me. Why are we here?'

Even though it was Hope who had made the arrangement, she had a sudden urge to avoid the conversation she needed to have with Mel.

'Why are we here? Well, Krishnamurthi would say it's to love the world and let go, and Mother Theresa thinks it's so we can help each other die.'

'Come on. Whatever it is, it can't be that bad.' Mel knew she had to be firm with Hope.

'Thing is,' Hope fiddled with the ankle fastening on her sandal, 'you remember I had that UTI a couple of months ago. Before Birdie died.'

Mel nodded, her eyes holding Hope steadily.

'I didn't tell you, but it was more than just an infection. That's why I came into town to see a solicitor. I want to change my will you see.'

Mel took Hope's hand. Hope felt as if a jolt of electricity coursed through her.

'God,' she said, 'oh God Mel. The touch of your hand. That is like pure magic. This bloody virus. It's been so hideous, hasn't it, with no human touch, I mean.'

‘Hope.’ Mel’s voice was low, insistent, ‘I’m holding you here. You know that. What is it? Do you have something wrong with you? Are you ill?’

Hope shivered with a sudden force, her jaw clenched involuntarily as she tried to control a violent trembling. As the panic in her body gripped her, Hope willed herself into a pattern of slow breathing, using her mind to feel her way through and beyond the eddies of panic in her knotted muscles. After a few minutes she lifted her head and looked at Mel.

‘Well, yes. I’m ill. I suppose. But worse than that, Mel. My mind… you see. I had the weirdest jolts and rolls of memory and time when I was ill. Apparently, I thought Jane was still alive, but I was completely unaware of lockdown.’

Reaching forward, Mel enveloped Hope in a long hug. In her arms, Hope felt like a mayfly, fragile and giddy in too much sun. After a long minute, she felt her energy flowing more strongly and started to giggle.

‘Do you think the lockdown police will arrest us? Unauthorised hugging in a public place.’

Mel squeezed her shoulders. ‘Probably, yes. I expect we’ll get five years in solitary.’

Hope pulled away.

'So, Mel, the thing is they want me to go to a Memory Clinic. And I've sort of been putting it off.' She caught Mel's expression, 'No, really. Not like that. I'm not pretending there's nothing wrong. I know there is. It's not extreme like it was in April, but most days. You know, the odd things I can't remember, things I forget I've done. I just don't want to, you know, have a label hanging round my neck like Jane Eyre.'

Hope flinched as Mel frowned, her eyes questioning.

'Am I wrong? Was it someone else. I thought it was Jane Eyre, when she went to that school…'

'No idea, love. But only because I've never read the book.'

Hope laughed with relief and then frowned.

'You see, I don't even trust myself anymore.'

'Honest truth?'

'Of course.'

'Well, you know that school I worked in briefly, about ten years ago?' said Mel, 'the EBD place?'

'I remember.'

'Some of the kids had this kind of haunted look. As if they were empty. Like they didn't know who they were, and they couldn't figure it out. At the moment, I can see something of that in you. It's the look you had when we first met, when...'

'When I knew I was pregnant but didn't believe it.'

'Yeah.'

And she's still the same, thought Mel. She hides from herself and disbelieves the world around her. It's as if she's never trusted things to be what they are. Always on the run.

'So, when you say you know there's something wrong, what do you mean, exactly?'

Hope moved uncertainly, stretching her folded leg out and then lifting both feet onto the bench and hugging her knees.

'Why is it so hard to know what's really true?' she asked, 'You know. I get that suffering is part of being separated from the, you know, the divine energy. Or whatever you want to call it.' she hugged her knees more tightly, 'How can I say what I mean about anything? Bloody labels.'

'You've lost me, hun.'

‘It’s all about stories, isn’t it. We’re empty, so we fill ourselves up with things. Other people, mostly, but times and places too. All we do is tell ourselves stories. Tell each other stories. Then live in them. The stories. Even if they’re not true.’

She felt uncertainty beat around her like a drum.

‘Oh, Mel,’ she wailed suddenly, ‘what will I be if I don’t remember my own stories anymore?’

Mel squeezed Hope’s hand in hers.

‘You’re talking about dementia, right?’

Hope nodded. They sat on the bench, hands locked together. To their left, the river hurried over the weir impatiently, coursing past the stand of trees, mute in the still air. Mel was trying to remember what she knew about dementia. Or Alzheimer's. Were they the same thing? She wasn’t sure. She’d google it later. Her mind turned to herself. She thought about Mike, and George and Moira. Her grandchildren too. What would she feel, if it was her?

‘You know, even when a person can’t remember who they are, it must help having family. And friends. It must, mustn’t it? Everyone who loves you holds a part of you. They can hold you even if you can’t.’

'What do you think you'd have done with your life if you hadn't got pregnant back then? If you'd never been sent off like that?' interrupted Hope.

'Huh?' said Mel, 'Back then? Well, I'd have married Mike and had babies. Just the other way round I reckon. You?'

'I thought I was going to be an artist,' Hope said, 'but that was the dreamy schoolgirl in me. I loved the way painting and drawing made me feel like everything was in harmony. Perhaps I could've been a nun or lived in a Buddhist monastery or something.'

'Yeah' said Mel, 'I can see that.'

She felt, again, unutterably sad for Hope.

'You haven't told me what you wanted yet. Your text said you wanted to ask me something.'

Hope shook her head in surprise. How could she have forgotten?

'The thing is,' she said, 'I'm trying to change my will. And I need to sort out Power of thingy. You know, before I'm dead. If I can't make decisions. I want to ask you to be on both. Executor, I mean, and the other thing.'

‘Power of Attorney’s no problem. And if you want, I’ll be an executor too. Who else are you asking?’

‘Just Tom,’ she paused, ‘and he’s going to inherit everything too. Are you still ok to do it?’

‘Of course.’

‘Is that all?’

‘Why, what else were you expecting?’

Hope laughed. ‘I don’t know. I suppose I thought you’d have an opinion. Say I was doing the wrong thing. You know, tell me off a bit, like you usually do.’

Mel felt hurt for a moment, until she saw the anxious vulnerability on Hope’s face.

‘No, hun. There’s nothing to say. You’ll have your reasons, and that’s good enough for me. And for everyone else, I hope.’

Tears welled in Hope’s eyes.

‘Hey, come on. When have I ever told you off, really?’

‘It’s not that. It’s. Oh, I don’t know. Why isn’t everyone in the world lovely like you?’

'Huh. Have you heard what George calls me to his kids? Grandma Dragon. That's who I am, Grandma Dragon. The cheek of the boy.'

Returning home, Hope felt Mel's friendship keeping her warm, filling her with calm assurance. Suddenly, it was easy to call her GP practice, and the appointment was made. You'd be proud of me, she muttered under her breath. Mel was so good to know, she thought, so practical.

Then, without warning, Hope felt ashamed and guilty. She hadn't been honest. Not really. Mel was so open. So truthful. As was now habitual with her, Hope picked up a pen and paper and started to write.

Darling Mel,

It's awful, now I think of it, how there are still things I don't tell you. Like Jeannie's father for example. I haven't lied, exactly. How can I, when I don't know the truth? I told you there was that boy from the record shop. And the drink and hash cakes. That's all definitely true. He was there, and I was out of it. But at the end of that evening... I don't know if I was awake, asleep, hallucinating or dreaming. So, did I make it up, that it was him, or is it the truth? The thing is, you said that people who get lost in dementia can entrust their true selves to their family. Or something like that. Oh Mel, I'm just scared. You made me think of a horrible conversation I had with Iris. Back in March. She came round in a complete state, panicking unnecessarily about Birdie. And then she suddenly announced that Don's cousin was Jeannie's father. And that apparently, she'd known this all along. Talk about dontellitus. Turned out that Joseph is actually Don's cousin. He's a Professor of Poetry now. Well, she thinks that it was him, not Chris. At that party, I mean. Anyway, Iris has believed this to be true for the last fifty years and because of that, she deliberately kept us apart all that time.

Thing is about this - I can't imagine Iris holding on to a version of me that makes any sense if I get lost in dementia. Nor Jeannie, come to that. I know, I know. Jeannie is a timeless soul. We all are. The really important connections in our lives are with our soul ancestors. They're the ones we need to seek out. Body and breath are just temporary. Gorgeous to have.

And lockdown has made me try to enjoy the sheer delight of the physical world more. But even if I could know what happened, find out who Jeannie's father is, the truth is I wouldn't do it. Her being is too precious for that. I don't even know what to think about Joseph. He's out there somewhere, being real.

And Jeannie does make the oddest comments about her childhood. Like I get that the paternity thing was just too much for her, something she needed to forget about. But some of the ways she remembers me as her mum. She's a bit like Iris, you know. Between them, they have this kind of version of who I am, or who I should be. And they're always nudging me to get me to behave in a different way. More like their idea of me than mine, you know. So, if it comes to it, there's nobody in my family that's going to defend the sort of me I think I am. Well, Tom might try, but he's so young.

It's just you, Mel. And just for the record, Jeannie's biological dad is an unknowable thing. I don't think Iris is right. I don't think she's as certain as she makes out either. And Jeannie told me years ago that she didn't ever want to talk about who her father was. So please, darling Mel, please don't let them damage Jeannie, whatever happens. I'm going to save this letter with the others. I've started putting them in envelopes now and sealing them. Maybe somebody will find them and remember the kind of person I've always tried to become.

Love and Blisses

p.s. I have to tell you how amazing it is to know that Joseph exists. He really exists. We changed each other's lives just by meeting once. Well, he showed me how to be me, anyway. Can you imagine how fantastic that feels.

Chapter 55

August was nearly over, and Iris couldn't understand how everyone seemed to have gone mad. People were behaving like children let loose in the park. Don too. She couldn't understand why he wanted to reorganise his birthday celebration so soon after all those long months of safety in lockdown. He'd only shrugged at her when she questioned him, saying that if the Government said it was safe, that was good enough for him. She couldn't even tell her friends why she was against the idea. Most of them were out and about now, going into each other's houses and even to meetings that could just as easily have been held on Zoom. And she couldn't to talk to Ursula, she was Don's twin, after all.

But if there was going to be another lockdown, and Don was convinced that there would be, then surely it was better to avoid any contact that was unnecessary. Don had accused her of being ridiculous. When he told her he'd started a guest list, and had already invited a few people from work, she almost cried with vexation. It wouldn't be on the scale of the original party, he'd argued, but insisted that he had the right to celebrate his seventieth birthday with his twin sister if he wanted to, even though the party had to be a few months late.

Gatherings of up to thirty people were legal, and he had bruised through her objections, leaving her giddy and nauseous with worry. She refused to get involved with his plans.

Finally, a week before the event, Iris relented and told Hope and Jeannie about the party. How she resented Don for putting her through all this. Tom was to be invited too, and even Peter was back from Scotland. Iris couldn't help herself running through the contacts each of them might have had, the risk that any of the guests would be carrying the virus. Tom was alright, she knew he was still very cautious, and of course Peter saw no-one on his Nature Reserves. But Hope was another matter. She seemed to be out and about nearly every day. God knows how she'd avoided the virus, which in Iris's mind was still bouncing around the streets and buildings like a swarm of invisible sputniks. Perhaps, she thought, the heatwave would break, and heavy rain would mean they had to cancel the arrangements. If only. The weather continued unchanged, with long hot days and blue skies that seemed to have an air of menacing permanence. She was in the kitchen unpacking all the disposable plates, glasses and cutlery that she'd insisted on buying, when her phone rang.

'Ursula. How are you?'

'Sorry. This is a very quick call, I'm afraid. Just about to go to the dentist. We're going to be down on numbers on Saturday. Paul and I are still ok, and so are the girls. But Graham and Jenny can't come. Apparently, Jenny's got a vile cough. She's going to a testing centre this afternoon.

Iris felt the virus circling her, moving relentlessly closer.

'Are you sure you're ok to come then?'

'Gosh yes. Deborah and Jon had the virus months ago, and Lucy, touch wood, hasn't had it yet. I'm not missing our seventieth. And with all the cousins coming.'

Iris gasped sharply in surprise.

'Wait a moment. All the cousins. Are you sure?'

'Didn't Don tell you? Arthur and Felicity are travelling down from Alnwick; they're collecting Joseph on route.'

A swarm of flies started buzzing in Iris's head.

'But Joseph mustn't come. Don told me to invite Hope. And Jeannie. They're all confirmed.'

There was a silence at Ursula's end.

'What am I supposed to do?'

Iris started to tremble.

'Ursula?'

'I've no idea. Perhaps they won't even recognise each other. Look, I'm sorry, as I said, I have to go to the dentist. Sorry. We'll talk later. Bye.'

Within seconds, it seemed, her phone was ringing again. Iris was so distracted that she accepted the call without even checking who it was.

'Iris?'

'Jeannie,' Iris her how sharp her voice sounded, 'how are you?'

'We're very well. Peter arrived home last night. I'm just calling to check you're ok?'

'Of course I'm ok, why on earth wouldn't I be?'

'I mean ok for the party. It's a lot of work for you, isn't it. I thought you might want another pair of hands. Peter and I could come early, if you like? Help get everything ready?'

'No, no. You mustn't do that. You really mustn't. It's very casual. Pop in, of course. Have a bit of cake. But don't feel you have to stay for hours and mingle. It'll really be all Don's family and his work colleagues. Very dull.'

'And you are really ok, are you, Auntie Iris?' Jeannie thought Iris sounded strangely tense.

'Is your mother still coming?'

'Well yes, I think so. I'm afraid there's been a bit of a falling out in that department. I won't bore you with it now. It'll be nice to spend time talking to Don's family rather than my own, to be honest. Present company excepted, of course.'

Iris paused again. There was something wrong. Jeannie couldn't quite identify what it was, but she was sure there was something.

'Are you concerned about the risk of infection? I'm sure everyone will be sensible. And we'll all be outside, won't we.'

'Will you be seeing Hope before the party?'

'No, as I said. We're not really on speaking terms at the moment. Don't worry, we'll be civilised. Or at least Peter and I will be. I can't answer for my mother or my son.'

Wild thoughts darted through Iris's mind. Could she tell Hope not to come? What would happen if she told her the party was cancelled at the last minute? Could she still cancel the whole party? What if she said she had symptoms of coronavirus. Or the weather really did turn nasty. Her heart was beating fast. This must be how a rabbit feels, she thought, with a predator's snout loud and rasping at the entrance to its burrow.

'Iris?'

'You and Peter must have a lot of catching up to do, dear. Now don't fret about Don's do. Well, Don and Ursula of course. First shared birthday party since they were seven, apparently. As I said, it's really going to be a Fellowes family gathering, in the main. We'll see you on Saturday, I expect. I'd better get on now.'

Jeannie sat still for several minutes, staring at the home screen on her phone. Iris always gave the impression of having everything under control. She had lists for everything, listened carefully and never left a conversation in the air. But today she'd seemed really odd. She'd almost told Jeannie not to come to the party but given Jeannie the distinct impression that Hope should be there. Though the idea of Hope making party small talk with Don's friends was so unlikely it almost made her smile. Jeannie was half-tempted to take Iris at her word. She and Hope had rowed bitterly the previous week, and Jeannie was still hurt and angry. On Tuesday, Hope had arrived on her doorstep unexpectedly to announce that she planned to change her will and leave her house to Tom. It wasn't the money. She and Peter didn't need her mother's savings, and it would all go to Tom eventually anyway. She hadn't minded that in the least, even if it was unusual. But the row had erupted when she'd asked Hope why she was in such a hurry to make the changes. Before she knew what was happening, the two of them had fallen out. And when she'd rung Tom that evening, wondering if perhaps Hope had a health issue she didn't want to talk about, she'd managed to fall out with him too. Putting her phone on charge, she told herself that she wouldn't complain if the people in her life could be just a little more predictable.

The day of the party dawned blue and clear. An unreasonable spell of good weather, Iris thought. She'd seen Joseph arrive and had tried to shepherd him to one side of the garden. Joseph, who hadn't seen his cousins since his wife's funeral over two years ago, had quickly fallen into conversation with Arthur and Paul. He didn't seem interested in circulating. Iris breathed more easily. Ursula was right, she thought, there was no reason he and

Hope would recognise each other, anyway. She'd done what she could, she thought; arranged the chairs in small groups of three or four and asked Tom to keep an eye on his Nan, maybe spend time with her. She herself would keep a watchful eye. She could always ask Hope to give her a hand in the kitchen.

Hope hadn't been to Keynsham since the previous Christmas and hadn't seen all the changes Don had made to the garden. She thought she'd have a wander around, see what he'd done. She was surprised to see Tom hovering at her side.

'Are you minding me?' she asked with a smile, 'Does Iris think I'm going to dance on the tables or something?'

Tom looked awkward. He wished he knew why Iris had asked him to stay with his Nan. He felt a spasm of annoyance. Iris was no better than his mum.

'You mean you are minding me. Well, Tom Trenow.'

Tom sighed and shrugged his shoulders.

'So, what is going on here, Tom? Why are you sticking to me like cleavers? Am I a celebrity now?'

Tom didn't want to get involved. I'm not playing their games, he thought with a glower.

'Honestly, Iris just said she thought you'd feel left out. Now you're not talking to Mum again.'

'And you believe that?'

He shrugged again, turning towards the house.

'I'll go and make myself useful Nan, Don's not exactly helping, is he?'

He turned back; there was something he needed to tell Hope.

'Oh, and by the way, Nan, I spoke to Jeb a couple of days ago. Turns out the people who attacked them were muggers. Just muggers. Something else I got wrong, huh.'

'How is Jeb?'

'They're fine, Nan. Cuts and bruises, but they're healing.'

Tom turned and walked away.

Left to herself, Hope stood for some moments, feeling the energy of the earth coursing through her. How she loved life, how even at seventy she was attuned to the constantly changing landscape of the planet holding her with its glorious slow power. She felt more connected to the trees in the distance than she did to the clipped and pruned shrubs in Don's garden. And the people, just temporary blurs of colour and light, moved so fast that it was hard to pay attention to their deeper being. No one seemed to be taking any notice of her, and she decided to stand in tree pose, her right foot lightly balanced against her left knee, her eyes fixed on the distant green of trees on the horizon. Form and being she thought, one existing in time, one beyond it. She closed her eyes for a moment to let the ebb and flow of the party fade and become distant to her.

But in the tangled skeins of conversation across the garden a thread came loose, separated itself and moved towards her. Feeling the presence of joy beside her, Hope opened her eyes.

'Are you a ballerina?' Joseph asked.

'A tree, I think,' said Hope, softly replacing her foot on the ground, 'and I know you.'

Chapter 56

In the first year of their new friendship, Hope had visited York to see Joseph three times, but long car journeys now daunted her. What if she were to get lost, she worried, or forget where she was going? Instead, they'd fallen into an easy rhythm of long video calls, often propping up their screens in their respective gardens. Joseph would always bring a picnic to share with her, and she would scramble together some ragged sandwiches which they offered to each other over FaceTime or Skype. When he could, Joseph would drive down to Bath, finding an Air BnB and exploring the city with Hope. Last time he'd visited, at Easter, they'd played crazy golf all one long windy afternoon, their sides splitting with laughter and silliness.

It was on a late August morning, waking to brilliant sunshine, that Hope had a disconcerting feeling that the weather was somehow different. Tom had told her about it in his bone-cracked way. A drown. Was that it? Something about her garden and not enough water. Yes, Tom had said there was a drown. Funny, she thought, when it hadn't rained for so long. It was morning, which meant yoga. Hope unrolled her mat and lay in corpse pose, waiting for her body to remember what to do. After some minutes, midway through the Sun Salutation, the fragments in her brain quietened into a single voice.

Drought. He'd said drought. Birdie would be upset. Withered plants. Leaves falling from the trees. She wouldn't like that. She'd cried when Jeannie was six, the year her cherry tree had died. Treading carefully as she made her way across her mind, Hope found her route back to the present. It was a different time now. August 2022, she told herself and gave an inward shout of joy. Here she was. She dressed and went downstairs, made her breakfast while listening to Spotify. On her kitchen table she saw that there were some pieces of silk cloth, piled in a glorious array of vivid colours. She looked at them, confident that they were there for a reason. She had learned that leaving a mystery and then, as it were, coming back to it unexpectedly, somehow slant, often helped her find the answers that slipped in and out between the ticks of the clock.

She went to the living room, where her easel was set up, and stood in front of the still life she'd been working on. The perspective was fine, and she liked the way the light source poured over the teapot and mugs she was painting. They were cheap mugs from Sainsbury, and she wondered why she had chosen to paint them.

Didn't she still have the handmade mug Birdie had given her when they sold Flag Cottage? The one she'd kept safe on a high kitchen shelf all through her years in Bristol. Presumably it was here, somewhere? Hope looked about distractedly, returning to the kitchen to open all the cupboards. Then she saw the mug sitting on the table beside the small pieces of silk fabric. She could see the join where the handle had been reattached many years earlier. Hefting the mug in her hands, she felt the solidity of it, hand thrown clay, glazed in cerulean blue. She could see the imprint of the potter's hands in the striations which circled it. Of course, that was what the silk remnants were for.

Closing her eyes, Hope lifted the mug out in front of her as if she were performing a kind of ritual. Then she opened her hands, allowing it to fall to the tiled floor. It made a sound like crickets leaping as it landed, and she opened her eyes to see it had broken beautifully into six different pieces. Carefully, she picked them up and placed them on the table beside the silk.

Because of the heat, Tom had taken to running late in the evening, so he decided he would call round to check up on his nan at the end of the afternoon, while it was still too hot to run. He wondered idly if he should object to the way his mum and great aunt leant on him, expecting him to be their eyes and ears, but actually he didn't mind doing it. Nan was still Nan, and her dementia had a very erratic presence in her life. The hardest bit was actually his mum. She always gave the impression that she was just waiting for things to go wrong, and her anxious vigilance stirred old wrongs in his mind. He arrived at Hope's front door just after five, his tee shirt sticking to his back with sweat. As usual, the door was unlocked, and he let himself in, calling out to her. Instead of her voice in response, he heard a humming cry, as if from a gagged mouth.

'Nan?' He rushed through into the kitchen at the back of the house where he could see her seated, her head bowed and facing away from him.

'Nan, what's up?'

Hope turned her head to him, nodding and smiling with her eyes. She was holding three or four pins delicately between her lips, and her hands were occupied with something on her lap. Nodding again, she freed up a hand and removed the pins. Her movements were small and guarded, and her smile had a vague quality that Tom had learnt to recognise. Today might not be a good day.

'Tom. Here you are. How lovely.'

His heart pointing, he leant over to kiss her.

'Wow, Nan, you gave me a fright. I thought the pirates had been and tied you up.'

'Oh wow! Not seen them.'

Hope held out the small brightly coloured object she was stitching. 'Look.'

Puzzled, Tom took the small item in his hands. It was a tiny pouch made from a scrap of silk with pink swirls on a red background. The stitches were minute. Inside the sac he could feel a hard object, like a piece of broken pottery, and seeing Birdie's precious mug on the table, his heart fell. What had she done? He handed it back, smiling gently.

'Tell me the story, Nan?'

Hope nodded carefully, as if nodding were an action she had only recently mastered, resuming her stitching as she spoke.

'This is the mug which Birdie loved. Me too,' she added, 'it went down,' Hope made the gesture with both her hands, 'and became, um, like when something isn't one thing anymore.'

'Broken?' suggested Tom.

'Broken' Hope nodded again. 'The broken mug was waiting for me. I've been slowing all day.'

She held out the exquisite needlework again.

'Sewing, Nan. Beautiful sewing.'

'Look,' Hope gestured to her lap, where three more delicate silk sacs, each enclosing a broken shard, lay on her knees.

'So, what happens next in the story?' prompted Tom.

'Well, before that, there was another story. The, um, when lots of things fall down.'

Tom knew that he needed to avoid filling in the gaps with his own words. If he interpreted Hope's story incorrectly, she might lose it completely. He used his fingers to give a sense of things falling, like snow, or ash.

'Yes, and at the exhibition they showed what to do with all the things that had… broken.'

She held her sewing out towards him again.

He nodded. 'And in this story?'

'I'm slowing new colours on all the pieces. My fingers are aching and my eyes keep dancing. But Tom,' she looked at him, her gaze suddenly sad and full of doubt, 'the thing is, in the exhibition, about the earthquake in Nepal, and about things falling down. They said it's only broken. Broken isn't the same as lost, is it.'

No, Tom thought, wondering if the mug might be even more beautiful when she had finished her stitching. It wasn't as if the mug was ever used, anyway, it just sat on a high shelf out of harm's way.

She moved her hand caressingly over the remaining pieces of broken mug.

'The thing is, Tom,' Hope spoke urgently, 'It was on a high shelf. That's no good either. Don't put things out of reach, Tom. Not if you really like them.'

Hope flexed her fingers, 'Just look at my poor hands.'

'Time for a break?' suggested Tom, 'Maybe you'd like a glass of water? I think I would.'

Outside, the sun angled sharply over the garden and intruded diagonally into the kitchen. The glare unsettled Tom. The heatwave frightened him in a way he didn't want to put into words. He became aware that Hope was still talking.

'I know what's happening,' she was saying, 'and I'm scared in the night. Thing is, Tom, I want to be me, and I keep forgetting how to do that. They tell me that my mind is broken.'

Her hands were on the table, and she moved the pieces of pottery around, separating those she'd covered with the silk and leaving the other pieces to one side.

'Who are 'they', Nan?'

'Oh, you know, the people. My sister, for example. And Jeannie. Do you know her?'

Hope leaned towards Tom,

'At night, you see, I can hear them tapping on the window, trying to get in. You know, Birdie always hung records in the garden.'

'What for?'

To keep the magpies away. They are frightened of the shininess, you see.'

'Oh, you mean CDs, Nan. Records are big and black. Nice though. Like a bit of retro bird-scaring.'

'Iris gets sniffy, you know.'

It was such an unexpected remark, and yet described his great-aunt so exactly that Tom let out a snort of laughter.

‘Who says “sniffy” in the 21st century, Nan? She’s a bit, I don’t know…’

Tom had been going to say Iris was a bit up herself, but the image of Iris was sadder than that, much sadder. Why did people screw up their lives so much, he wondered.

‘Actually, Tom, I want to ask you something.’

Hope spoke with a low intensity. Tom was struggling to keep up with the shifts and turns in her today. It wasn’t that she seemed lost or confused, just unsettled. Their conversation was like walking along the shore after a storm, surrounded by driftwood and plastic bottles.

‘Can you take me back to my home?’

Tom braced himself. Okay, this definitely looked like a bad day after all, but probably the heat didn’t help. He was glad his mum wasn’t there. She’d flip one.

‘Home?’ he said, ‘don’t you like this home anymore?’

Hope stood up abruptly, angry and suddenly ferociously clear. She shook her head irritably.

‘Don’t “they” me, Tom. I can’t do this if you believe all the crap as well. I wasn’t clear, but that doesn’t mean I don’t know what I’m saying. I was thinking about Iris and me. Where grew up. That’s what I want to do. Go back to my family home.’

‘Sorry. Nan, I’m stupid, aren’t I?’

He wondered how much of the difficulties his Nan faced were like this; from other people’s interpretations of her, and not from her brain at all. She’d always been difficult to follow, he reflected, somehow reassured by the thought.

‘Home, huh. I don’t even have any idea where you grew up, Nan. Don’t suppose you’ve got the address?’

Hope rattled off the address and phone number without pausing to think.

‘You grew up here? In Bath. How come I never knew that?’

‘Well,’ Hope said, picking up a silk-wrapped shard and handing it to him, ‘I guess that’s because today is the first day you’ve needed to know.’

Chapter 57

A few days later, Hope was woken again by the morning light. She'd been in Wales, pregnant, walking on the beach with Spud and her dad. She seemed to remember her dad had been telling Spud that she should take acid if she wanted to experience the sublime. He'd been insisting that psychedelics were the only way to reach beyond the day-to-day illusions of the world. Stretching, she grinned. As if. She flexed the creased feeling out of her body and swung her legs over the side of the bed. The early brightness of the day had music in it, she wished she'd been awake earlier to see the dawn dancing into morning. Glancing at her clock, she saw it was five forty-five. At that time of day, few people would be about. How gorgeous. Dressing rapidly, she hurried to the park with her yoga mat. The trees were glorious and languid in the lull of yellow-green time, as yet uncrowded by human busy-ness.

At the end of her routine, Hope lay on her mat with her eyes closed. Her body felt porous, and the late summer birdsong, muted and less exuberant than spring's melody, flowed through her like an ambling brook. It was several minutes before Hope noticed she was no longer alone. A figure, vibrating with discordant energy, was hovering in her peripheral vision. She turned her head: Iris. Feeling her heart contract, Hope turned and spoke.

'Iris. I didn't expect to meet you here.'

Iris was wearing a plaid skirt with tights and tank top over a long-sleeved shirt. The brown curls of her pageboy cut looked damp on her forehead. She'll be too hot in that get up, Hope thought, trying to feel compassion for her out-of-place sister.

'You went back to our old house, didn't you?' Iris's tone hovered between anger and misery, 'I would have come with you. Why did you ask Tom instead of me?'

'You, Iris? But you hated that house. You couldn't wait to leave, remember?'

Iris stood, her form fixed like a statue, across which the dappling of trees lent the illusion of movement.

'No, Hope. You left me. It was you. What else could I have done? I needed you, you know. I mean, just look at me. Is this who I have to be?'

'The garden had gone, Iris. The house is flats now, with concrete parking and a patio. That's what it's come to. You'd probably approve, but it was hard for me.' Hope sighed. Why did Iris look so unfamiliar? She shook her head slowly.

'The years must have passed differently there. Or maybe the house has just shaped existence in its own way. Like you have, I mean. Our universes are so different. But it's a funny thing, Iris, being old enough to have your own ghosts.'

'You're doing it again.'

Hope stared at the uncertain form beside her.

'Doing what?'

'Dividing us. Don't you see how you exclude me? Every time. You say, "Oh, I am like this, this child of the universe. But Iris isn't. She's a rule-follower," or you say, "Iris has no real soul, she holds me back, but my spirit needs to fly free."'

Iris's eyes were vanishing points of dark intensity.

'How is it that you get to choose who is or isn't part of the divine?'

Turning her head away from her sister's unhappy face, Hope's gaze was caught by the uneven movement of a single seagull skimming above the rooftops. It was etched clear and white against the blue cloudless sky, and as it lifted higher into the air, early sunshine caught and reflected brightly beneath its wings. For an infinity, the bird seemed to be made of molten silver.

As she watched, the gull's form became a dot on the horizon, disappearing from sight. There was a roaring in her head, and she thought she heard the sobbing of a lost child.

'It was fear.' she said, turning to find herself utterly alone.

A few minutes later, Hope's slight figure could be seen, rolled mat held limply by her side, trudging up the hill. She passed the coffee shop, glancing inside where two women were busy preparing for the day, laughing together as they worked. She yearned to go inside, but kept walking, fearful of loss. As she neared her front door, a car came noisily down the street, braking rapidly just ahead of her.

'Hope, Hope!' The figure of Iris emerged from the car, wearing a thin linen blouse and slacks. A light straw hat covered her grey bobbed hair.

'Goodness, you gave us a fright. Where have you been? Poor Jeannie is beside herself with worry. She's been trying to call you since about half-past seven.'

Hope stared. The figures of Iris danced in her mind. Her wild, unreliable mind, she thought, suddenly flattened by exhaustion. How could she know anything, when nothing held its form any longer? She would give in. Iris and Jeannie must do what they wanted with her.

'You'd better come in, Iris,' she said.

There was a dullness in her eyes, and she looked like a defeated child. Iris stared at her, a mix of anger and grief in her expression.

'But where on earth have you been at this time of day?'

Hope gestured at her yoga mat, 'I just got up early. Went to the park for a bit. Sorry, Sis. Come in, you're right, you know.'

'What about?' Iris was startled.

'Oh, pretty much everything, I think. Come into the house. You've got plans for me, haven't you?'

Hope felt a tsunami of fear and tears rising through her.

'I'm scared, Iris. I'm so scared.'

An hour later, on her way home, Iris called Jeannie.

'Look, Jeannie, your mother has decided to be sensible at last. She's going to get an emergency bracelet. And she's promised not to go wandering about early in the morning. I think she has finally accepted that she can't cope alone.'

Iris wondered whether to tell Jeannie of Hope's frightened tears. The way she had hunched her knees to her chest and sobbed. No, not something a daughter should hear, she decided.

'Oh. One other thing, she's agreed to start on the Aricept.'

Iris ended the call. At least Jeannie was pleased, and yes, Hope would be safer now. But Iris felt bereft, as if she had lost something more precious than she had ever imagined. At that moment, she thought, she would do anything to have the old Hope back, even if she were as obstinate, hare-brained and unpredictable as when she was a teenager. Turning into Keynsham High Street, she wondered about stopping for a coffee. It would be nice to have some time alone before she went home. She slowed her car as she approached the turning to the car park and then accelerated again. Better not.

'I'm back, Don. All well,' Iris called out as she opened her front door, not expecting him to respond. She hung her keys on the hook, going to the kitchen to start her day again.

Chapter 58

Tom sat cross-legged on his bed; his laptop perched on his knees while he scrolled through pages and pages of information about becoming a probation officer. He'd worked in a café for six months since his graduation. But he couldn't defend himself against his mum for ever. He couldn't explain, even to himself, why the idea of settling on a career made him want to curl up and hide. Whatever he did, he wasn't join the police, that was for sure. And he couldn't bear the thought of being a post-grad, like Jeb. Not practical enough. He texted Jeb.

'Probation Officer?'

The response was swift, 'Brilliant. Job security, pension and a good salary. Dr P would be so proud.'

Tom sighed.

'So, what about changing lives, supporting people and being empathetic?'

'Nice words.'

'Give me a break.'

Jeb was so difficult sometimes. After a couple of minutes, he received another text.

'You don't really get you, do you?'

Tom didn't reply, turning back to the computer instead to reread the Prison Service website.

Less than ten minutes had passed when his phone rang.

'Hey, Nan.'

'Who's that?'

'Me, Nan, it's Tom here.'

Tom knew he had to give her more information. On her bad days it took her a longer time to get her bearings, and just saying his name was not enough. He cast about for something to say.

'I came round to your house on Tuesday for a cup of coffee and a chat. I like chatting to you, Nan. I used to call you my Cosmic Nan. When I was a little boy.'

'Oh Tom. Good. I'm glad it's you. There's a man outside my house. I think he wants to come in.'

Tom knew, but his Nan clearly hadn't remembered that Joseph was down from Yorkshire. He presumed it must be Joseph, but all the same, he asked Hope to describe the man, helping her along with the words until he was sure.

‘Cool, Nan. Joseph has come to see you. I wonder if he’s brought chocolate this time. Last time Joseph visited he gave you a great big bar of fruit and nut chocolate.’

There was a brief silence at the other end of the phone.

‘Tom?’

‘Yes, Nan?’

‘It’s sweet of you to call, but I can’t talk now. Joseph is waiting for me. You can talk to me later.’

‘Oh, that’s fine, Nan. Say hi to Joseph for me. Bye now, Nan.’

His mum had said Nan had started taking the Aricept a couple of weeks ago. He checked online to see how quickly it should make a difference. Weeks, not days. He knew that the way he felt about the whorls and spirals of Hope’s conversation wasn’t simple. When his mum talked about Nan suffering from dementia, she seemed to assume that protecting Nan was only about fighting for her to have a normal life. For him, it was more complicated. Travelling alongside Nan was important. He wanted to be close, to be able to hold ideas and words within reach for when she wanted them, but there was something else. And he couldn't see why Nan would want the kind of normal life that his mum was set on. Nan had never exactly been like most other people before dementia, so why should she be compliant now?

Tom found himself wondering about Hope as she would have been. When she was his age, for instance. He knew all the facts, how she'd run away to stay with Birdie and Auntie Jane and refused to have his mum adopted, even though it meant she was disowned by her parents. But what had she been like, he thought. Idly, he typed her name into Ecosia and skimmed through the results. Her LinkedIn profile came up quickly, just stuff about her career. What a yawn-fest. Tom scrolled away, wondering how she'd spent so many years as a teacher. Most of the other links seemed to be to various meditation retreats. What about the time she lived in Wales, he wondered. Before the internet, obviously, but why not?

Within seconds, he'd clicked on a link to an art gallery in Cardiff. Jane Greenwood was listed as one of the major artists at a new exhibition, and there were images of several of her paintings.

'Wow, is this for real!'

Tom had only ever seen two paintings by his great aunt, the ones that Birdie had had all his life. He shifted his position on the edge of his bed. He had to get Nan to Cardiff. He really had to. It was like the universe was telling him. Well, that's what Nan would say, he smiled. How to do it? Ok, be practical, he thought. Nan would be up for it, for sure. But it would be easier if someone else came with them. Could he get his mum to agree. She seemed the obvious choice. No time like the moment, he thought, and called Jeannie's mobile.

'Cardiff? No. Have you asked her?' His mum's voice was cautious, 'Well, it's a lovely thought, Tom darling, but your Nan's just not up to it now. We all have to accept that her days of gadding about are behind her.'

'But Mum,' Tom was incredulous, 'surely with two of us. She'd manage. By then she'll have been on the Aricept for a month. And wouldn't you like to see the exhibition too? I definitely would.'

'Well, Tom, I suggest you find a friend to go with, and you can tell me all about it when you get back. But please don't mention the exhibition to Nan. I know you think it's a good idea. but we must be careful that we don't encourage her to do things that might be difficult for her. You do understand that, don't you?'

Tom felt he knew only too well what his Mum meant. She was the Queen of Cotton Wool he thought, keeping people safe from actually living their lives. He wished he hadn't asked her.

'So that's a no?'

'Tom, just leave Nan to me please. Iris and I are trying very hard to do what's right for her.'

Tom felt stupid and powerless, it bothered him that his mum had this kind of miserable smallness that seemed to shape her views. He mumbled something vague and hung up. He needed time to think out what he really felt, to understand why this pinched, reduced version of his Nan's life seemed to him so terribly desolate. If he said nothing, he would be betraying Hope, if he spoke, then his mum would feel betrayed.

Chapter 59

In central Bath, Hope was pointing to a pathway behind the railway station, tugging at Joseph's arm.

'Jacob's Ladder?' he asked.

'Me and Iris used it as a quick route into town. Didn't tell our parents though. They never liked us out. Unless there were pavements. And streetlights. You know. Parks and footpaths were dangerous places. Things might happen.'

Hope led him to the bottom of the steep winding steps behind Bath Spa station which led, so she said, to a divine view of the city in the park at Beechen Cliff. He wondered if they were both mad.

'Well, if we're doing it, let's go. We can always get help from the practical angels.'

Hope turned to him, looking puzzled.

'Ha. Silly joke. Blake painted Jacob's Ladder back in 1799. The angels in that painting are very practical. They're carrying water, books, looking after children. Certain to give a couple of pensioners a helping hand, I'm sure.' He smiled at her. 'How's your balance today?'

‘Good. You just have to tell me what’s up ahead, I’ll be fine. Practical angels. Nice. No trumpets then?’

Joseph looked at her.

‘Trumpets!’ Hope exclaimed, ‘Angels always have them, don’t they? But who decided that angels should play trumpets, of all things?’

‘I’m not sure,’ Joseph said, ‘Isn’t it something to do with Judgement Day?’

‘Is it?’ Hope appeared surprised, ‘I thought trumpets were for something else. You may be right. Anyway, carrying water and books sounds much more useful.’

When, eventually, they reached Alexandra Park, both slightly giddy from the climb, they sat down with relief on a bench. Around them, the beech trees had been wrought into burnished gold like incandescent phoenixes, and the grass was a medley of greens, changing hue and tone where the contours of the ground altered, or where shadows had reached out from the west. Hope half closed her eyes, moving her head slowly up and down.

‘It could be the sea,’ she said, ‘the land is moving like waves, but so slowly that we can’t see it happening.’

‘There’s a field near my house,’ said Joseph, ‘the footpath goes down into a dip in the hill where all of a sudden, you can’t hear the road. You didn’t know you were listening to it until it stops, but then you can hear the silences between the birds’ songs.’

He looked out over the city.

‘Sometimes, when the light is right, or I’m able to give in, I become completely aware of everything moving. The field is energy, moving slowly, the birds’ song, the same energy, but moving at huge speeds. Me, plodding somewhere in between, yet still the same. It’s as if, at any moment, the whole thing could disappear, and if it did, that would be utterly blissful.’

Hope nodded.

‘Do you sometimes imagine that trees create wind by beating their branches to and fro? If you look the right way, I reckon can see them doing it.’

‘No wind today.’ Joseph looked over the city to the smudge of green that was Lansdown and beyond.

‘I used to keep a diary. Now, I write letters instead.’ Hope looked down at her fingers.

‘Who do you write to?’

'Oh, everybody. I keep them in a box. I use them to write about who I am, what's going on, you know, in the universe. I don't want people to forget the real point of me. Well, not before I die, anyway. But there's no point sending them.'

'Hard to change what people already think, you mean?'

'Yeah.' Hope sounded sad.

'Hang on a minute.' Joseph frowned, twisting his head from side to side.

'What are you doing?'

'Just looking for a thought. There's something I meant to tell you. Hang on.'

His head to one side, chin forward, and one hand held out in front of him, Joseph moved his body and arm from side to side. He looked like someone making a speech, but he was silent.

'No. It's gone. Sorry.'

'Not just me then?' Hope smiled wanly.

'Do you want to talk about it?'

'Not really. It's not the most interesting thing about me, you know.'

'You could send those letters. To stop people forgetting who you are while you're still here.'

He meant Iris, Hope knew.

'No good,' she said, 'I don't remember to do that sort of thing very often.'

Joseph felt the grief in her words. 'You need a practical angel.'

From the canopy of fiery leaves, a blackbird sang, sharp and clear.

'You.' Hope turned to Joseph, 'You are my practical angel. I'll give you the letters. Send one, every month. Start on New Year's Eve. Then maybe I won't be so lost.'

Why not, thought Joseph. He was fierce in his defence of Hope's wild ways. I'll send her letters for her. This is something I can do. Every time they spoke, Joseph yearned for the lost years. He was happy that their friendship had started already complete, knowing that in some deep but intangible way they had known each other for all of the last fifty years, and now just happened to be the time for them to share some earthly time and space. But knowing this didn't diminish the anger he felt. He knew he would never ask, but his cousins and Iris, heaven knew why, had clearly been absolutely determined to keep him and Hope apart all those years ago. So, if sending letters on Hope's behalf felt vindictive, well, he didn't care.

'It's a promise. Give me the letters, and every month I will choose one at random, and send it for you. '

Hope nodded at him, enjoying the ease of understanding and magic they shared. After a while, Joseph spoke again.

'What we've got, though, in here,' he pointed at his skull, 'it's paltry. You know Blake had it right. Our human senses are pale imitations of the true senses. It's our true senses that allow us to know eternity.'

'Don't give me any of that crap about the light shining in through the gaps.'

Exhaustion had hit her like a tidal wave.

'I'm not. What I'm trying to say is that even without the gaps, as you put it, our minds prefer familiar thoughts, even if they are small and insignificant, than new ones. We don't like the risk of having to change our perspectives.'

He looked carefully at Hope, realising that she was no longer paying attention, she looked tired, and her face appeared closed.

'Ice-cream?' he asked her, 'And then a taxi back to your house? What do you say?'

It was almost as if he could hear the fizzing and spluttering of the candles in her eyes, Hope thought, nodding thankfully.

While he was buying the choc ices, Joseph suddenly remembered what he had wanted to say. Of course. The exhibition in Cardiff. He must tell her. Returning to the bench, he could see that Hope had her eyes shut, her eyelids flickering gently over her thoughts and dreams. Nudging her back into the present, he handed her the ice cream. He would tell her about the exhibition later, when her mind was less tired.

Chapter 60

A week later, waiting for her train, Hope patted her pocket with anxiety and satisfaction. The small notebook was still there, and in it, she'd written everything she needed to know. Not just the times of the trains and her appointment, but the full address of the railway stations and the clinic. She even had the name of a nearby coffee shop, in case she had time in hand. Funny, she thought, to catch a train again. Trains made her think of her and Iris on the beach; hot days and hard pebbles and the enduring smell of seaweed.

She fumbled the notebook from her pocket, skimming the pages until she found her itinerary. It was all fine, she remembered everything on the list. Her pocket wasn't quite safe though. Perhaps she should she put the notebook in her bag now? What if it were to fall out of her pocket? And there wasn't room for it in the small waist bag that Jeannie had told her to wear. That was just for her tickets, keys and mobile phone. She would put the notebook in her shoulder bag, but it was already heavy with a riot of things she had stored there for safekeeping: Her new paintbrush, a lock of Jeannie's first baby hair in a lozenge-shaped jewelled tin, a small red Philips screwdriver, several blunt pencils and a small purse containing her credit card and £200 in cash. Jeannie didn't know about the cash.

Startled by the train squealing to a halt at her platform, Hope quickly dropped the notebook into the top of her bag. Had there been an announcement? She must have missed it. She wanted to confirm the time of her train again, but there wasn't a moment to spare. She boarded the train, pretending to be confident in case confidence became necessary, and sat in a corner seat looking out as the buildings picked up speed, moving away at increasing speed.

She was soon at Temple Meads, so that was alright. Buoyed up, she got off the train. Her spirits were high, and she would be on time. The appointment was in Redcliffe Street, not far from where she had worked in that boring office, all those years ago.

There were people everywhere, jostling her as they waited to pass the automated barrier. Hope let herself be carried forward and was through the barrier before she realised her bag was missing. Her feeling of hot anxiety returned, jittering her, and she didn't know how to stop it.

A man in a uniform stood nearby, Hope saw with relief, but he was busy answering questions. She didn't want to miss her appointment. She should just check the time. Reaching into her pocket for her notebook and its calm reassurance, she found it too was missing. Had she dropped it? She looked hurriedly about, returning to the barrier, peering frantically to see if it was lying on the platform. The train had gone now, and the platform almost empty. Turning, she saw the station official was alone, and she tapped him on the arm.

'I've just got off,' she said, 'And I think my bag has been stolen. Or maybe I left it in the, um'

Hope wavered. Plane? No, that was wrong.

'Um. I left it. And I need it you see, but I don't have much time because I have to be at the clinic. And I can't find my notebook, either.'

Hope knew that the words were tumbling out of her. She wasn't sure if she was being clear.

'The appointment might be in my bag, you see,' she added. The man looked sympathetic.

'Which train were you on, Madam?'

'The train from where I live, it just arrived at that place where you get off or on – there.'

She'd lost the word, so she pointed to the platform behind the barrier.

The man smiled at her. He was too friendly. Hope began to back away.

'Don't worry, madam. Let's see. Do you remember what time you arrived? My colleague Simon works on the train, and if you give me a description of the bag, then I can get him to help us. He'll find your bag and put it somewhere safe. Now, let's see. Tell me what your bag looks like.'

Hope stared at the man, her mind a blank. She couldn't remember the shape or even the colours of her bag. What was the name for that curved line of colours in the sky? She had had a bag, hadn't she? Yes, because she remembered thinking about the notebook, and whether she should put it in her pocket or the bag. She checked her pocket again, to make sure. No, nothing there but a paper tissue.

The man smiled at her kindly. He was wearing a badge with a blue flower like a large forget-me-not. It reminded her of Jeannie. Her daughter had pinned a badge with a blue flower just the same on to Hope's bag. She said it was lucky charm. Odd, that. Jeannie was always so sceptical. Hope was no longer sure she trusted this smiling man. She turned away.

'Don't go, Madam,' the man called to her, 'I'm sure I can help you. My name is Abdul; I work here at the train station. May I ask you for your name?'

He seemed as if he really wanted to talk to her, Hope thought, wavering. Was he the man with the ice-creams? She stood on tiptoes, trying to place him. It was difficult, because she didn't want to look straight at him, so she gazed over his shoulder, hoping to work out who he was from the corner of her eye. At that moment, the sound of the station Tannoy reverberated above her, and, behind her, a wheeled suitcase clattered rapidly past. She might be knocked down by a rushing tide; she felt herself unbalancing, the world pitching. If she could just steady herself. If she could just grip the unfolding moments and remember how to say the right things. But the day was rearing forward with the curving shape of another huge wave, and she has no time to breathe.

'Do you know Jeannie?' she asked.

She watched her words as they broke on the shore, to where they dribbled away in a thin stream over the pebbles that were bright with glare and glistening in the sunlight.

Chapter 61

Jeannie had rescued her mother from Temple Meads and was now pacing up and down the street outside her mother's house, her mobile held close to her ear as she updated Iris.

'Not today then?' she said.

'Tomorrow would be better. I have to go into Bath anyway. You'll be staying with your mum tonight, I assume?'

'I think I'll have to, Iris. It's not perfect, as Peter's home at the moment. But at least he can see to the cat.'

'Well, my appointment is at ten. Why don't we have lunch together?'

'Will Don be with you?'

There was a pause at the other end of the phone.

'I'll see what I can do. Look, there's a lovely café on Bridge Street. Café Cortado. I'll meet you there. Let's say eleven thirty. Will you be alright until then?

Jeannie sighed.

'Yes, of course. It's not an emergency, is it. She seems quite normal at the moment. But we can't go on like this. You know, when they gave me her bag, there was two hundred quid in it.'

'Lucky the guard found it before it was stolen.'

'That's not the point. What is she doing with all that money in cash? And, for goodness' sake, there was a screwdriver and a paintbrush in the bag as well. I mean.'

'Tomorrow, Jeannie. I'll be there. We'll think of something. Café Cortado. Bye now.'

Making her way into central Bath the following morning, Jeannie moved slowly and awkwardly. She had woken with a searing pain in the left side of her neck which she put down to the stress of being with her mother, the unfamiliar bed, or perhaps her fitful sleep. Crossing the road meant turning her whole body from one side to the other, and even stepping off the pavement triggered a spasm in her neck. Already she could feel the flickers of tense muscular pain in her shoulders and back as her body sought to protect itself by hardening and becoming inflexible. With relief, she reached the café and chose the table furthest away from the noise and bustle of the serving counter. The huge coffee machine gleamed silver, with a presence as if it were the main exhibit in a gallery. Jeannie wondered why cafes made such a performance of coffee these days. The machine irritated her, and the intermittent din of grinding beans and the deafening sounds of steaming water were, she thought, quite unnecessary.

When Iris arrived, Jeannie was relieved to see that she was alone. She would be able to tell Iris every detail, even the things they'd already talked about on the phone. Jeannie needed the conversation to be tangible, to see the impact of her words in Iris's expression, her body language.

Settling over their coffee, Iris and Jeannie that Hope was clearly getting worse. Probably much more quickly than they had anticipated. But the truth had to be confronted, and there was no use pretending things were other than they were. Hope needed looking after. Protecting from herself. Jeannie reminded Iris that Hope had seemed to accept matters after the early morning yoga scare. Jeannie spoke on and on, twisting her hands in her lap, moving objects around on the small coffee table. It was too much. All that early morning yoga in the park. Thank goodness Hope had agreed to stop being so irresponsible. And she was taking the Aricept now.

Iris wanted to talk about Tom having power of attorney, even though she knew that Jeannie was having difficulties with the boy. On top of all the worry with

Hope, it seemed that Tom was refusing to consider his future, start a career, make plans for himself. The boy needed shaking. It was an awkward situation. What should they tell Tom and Mel, she wondered.

‘Mel’s fine. She’ll be practical.’ said Jeannie, ‘she’s always had Hope’s best interests at heart.’

‘But Tom?’ Iris asked, ‘does he have any idea what he’s taken on, agreeing to be her attorney?’

The pain in Jeannie’s neck stabbed at her. It was hard to think straight, what with that, not to mention the unbearable noise in the café, even worse now as it filled up with customers. There was a toddler, whining at the next table. She thought about Tom’s idiotic notion that he could just take his grandmother to Cardiff. To see paintings by an aunt she was probably unable to remember.

‘Let’s leave Tom out of this for now. I had to have a word with him the other day. Nothing, really, just an idea he had to take Hope for an outing. But he saw sense.’

Jeannie didn’t want to discuss Tom’s maverick ideas. She was grateful that he spent so much time with his Nan, but if only he would see things more clearly. She knew that if she told Iris about Tom’s ridiculous suggestion about going to Cardiff, then she'd be forced to defend him, somehow. She'd feel that Iris was criticising her, too.

'You're certain?'

Iris sensed the barricades in Jeannie's reply. There was something she wasn't saying.

'Of course I'm certain. For heaven's sake, Iris, the boy has more important things to worry about. Like getting a proper job. He doesn't need to be involved.'

Chapter 62

Tom sat opposite Hope and grinned at her as the train to Cardiff eased its way slowly out of the city, picking up speed as it started to move across open countryside. She wasn't looking at him, but he grinned anyway. He was aware of a sense of guilty relief that he hadn't had to tell her about the exhibition, as she'd been the one to tell him about it. When she'd suggested going together, he'd been unreasonably, exultantly happy. Hope was also responsible for the invite to Jeb, who was going to join them at Temple Meads.

Hope was wearing a black hoodie. It was too large, but she'd shrugged, telling him she'd bought it on Vinted, and it was fine, she liked baggy clothes. It went well with her black trousers anyway, Tom thought. She also had a ribbed black beanie with a wide brim, and her silky white hair shone in contrast, falling across the contours of her neck and shoulders. Her eyes rested serenely on the view as the fields dashed by at increasing speed. There was no tension in her face at all, Tom thought, she just looked at ease. He wondered what was going through her mind.

Hope felt a sense of balance with Tom today. Between them, time was held in a sort of stasis, as if they were some kind of still point in a universe where everything else, train, houses, fields, hurtled past with a sense of urgency.

'Tell me the names of all the stations again.'

Just as she spoke, the train announcer drowned their silence with the list of stops, as if in answer to her request. She smiled at Tom.

'Now you,' Tom asked, 'tell me again about Great Aunt Jane's paintings.'

'Oh no. Call her Auntie Jane. Great Aunt Jane makes her sound like… you know. One of those furry animals on the television. You know, for children. Before your time.'

'Fine.' Tom was mystified but wasn't to be distracted.

'Auntie Jane. I know about her life. But you and Birdie never really told me about her paintings.'

'Long time ago. I thought I'd be a painter like Auntie Jane. Crazy, huh. Her paintings? Wow. Imagine being in a garden. And then imagine all the scents in the air. Flowers. Baking. Cut grass. Delicious smells. Auntie Jane could turn all that into light and colour.'

'Awesome. Did she paint all her life?'

‘She did. Very lucky. A woman, and she got to study at Art School. No. Not lucky. I think she must have been very determined. When it mattered.’

‘I like that,’ Tom repeated, ‘“when it mattered” What do you mean, Nan?’

Hope paused. The two of them. On a train. The world flowing past them. And them not moving, but still. Life, still a thing of wonder. That intense sense of being, the curiosity and rush of life that had infused her at 20, the precarious joy that had seemingly been drowned in the minutiae of her years as a teacher had now surged back, filling Hope’s heart. She felt Tom’s spirit beside her. As if they weren’t just a young man and an old woman, but two aspects of the same sublimity. Did she like that idea? She wasn’t sure. She shifted forward in her seat.

‘Tom, you know how the waves move in rockpools?’

‘You mean when the tide is coming in?’ Tom asked.

Hope looked uncertain. He tried again.

‘When the waves come up the shore, getting closer and closer to where the people are sitting. The waves are frolicky and fun.’

‘That’s it,’ Hope nodded, ‘and when they go away again. When the sea goes down.’

Tom’s heart was full. ‘I know what you mean. The water swirls about in rockpools like it has a mind of its own. And then everything is quiet and subdued until the tide goes out and jostles everything up again.’

‘Yes.’ Hope nodded, ‘We’re like that. We can really dance in our rockpools when the tide comes in and when it, you know.’

‘Goes out?’

‘Yeah.’ Hope looked as if she was about to dissolve into giggles. ‘Frolicky. I love it. And it’s the best thing ever. You think that you grow out of it. But it comes back. Being old is like being new and frolicky all over again.’

‘Was Mum ever frolicky?’

‘No’ said Hope, frowning carefully. ‘She never was. Perhaps she will be, one day.’

‘Double frolics in her old age?’ A thin smile passed between them.

‘Nan.’ Tom was hesitant. ‘I ought to tell you. Mum didn’t want you to come to Cardiff with me. I asked her, you see. Before you asked me.’

‘Oh. Secrets’ Hope’s voice was barnacle-rough and unhappy, ‘I think secrets are not a good thing, you know.’

‘Yeah, Nan. I know. I will tell her, just when I’m ready. Is that ok?’

‘Birdie liked rockpools. She was always finding things in them. You should have seen the windowsills in their cottage.’

Hope blinked, closing her eyes for a few moments. She could see Jane, standing in the garden with her easel while Birdie hunkered down with her trug, weeding.

‘You know, she used to tell me that sometimes her paintbrush trembled with delight. And when it did, she knew the painting would come out right.’

Had he done the right thing? Tom felt the seriousness of what he had done, what they were doing. His mum would blame him for sure. And if anything went wrong... The train was slowing again, as they drew close to the station. He looked up.

'Bristol already. This is where Jeb gets on the train. You haven't met Jeb before, have you Nan?'

Chapter 63

After an hour at the exhibition, Tom thought they should leave. Hope's mood had changed from vibrant to exhausted as if on the flick of a switch, and he knew that often meant she would start to struggle. He too was feeling disoriented. It was something about the experience of seeing paintings though, he realised. They had brought Auntie Jane to life for him, but seeing her life and work curated in the vast white spaces of the gallery had also made her feel less like a real person, less like someone who had been part of his family, someone who belonged to him.

Jeb eyed them both.

'Hey both, we passed a café on the way here. Welsh cakes and scones. Earl Grey and Darjeeling. What do you think? We have time before the train.'

The interior of the café looked as it might have done in the 1950's. White tables and dark wooden chairs. Tom and Hope looked at each other in dismay.

'Different.' said Tom, 'Nan?'

Hope made a face.

'There's a courtyard out the back,' Jeb said, 'let's have a look there.'

Outside, the tables and chairs were enclosed on three sides by white painted walls. Pots and plants were huddled in random groups. The fourth side was open to a vacant plot of land, so long abandoned that weeds and wild plants had filled the space. The afternoon sunshine was low and had become tangled in the early autumn's remnants of Rosebay Willowherb, which sprawled and spread across the empty ground. Its long seed pods had split, creating a cloud of white that hovered above ragged green foliage. In places, there was still a sense of pink, as if the flowers, or at least the memory of them, still lingered.

'Perfect.'

Hope sank onto one of the chairs, pulling her beanie over her ears before drawing her feet up so that she could hug her folded legs. She rested her head on her left knee, angled so that she could look out away from the courtyard, from Jeb, and most of all, from Tom. She didn't want to talk about the paintings. One in particular, a jug of spring flowers sitting next to a broken cup on a deep windowsill, the background a smudged medley of green and sunlight, had torn at something inside her, something she didn't recognise.

She half-listened, half-dreamed while Jeb and Tom talked about a gig they'd been to, the difficulty of finding a job, a person they both knew who was, it seemed, dying. She tried to make out the shapes and the colours of their conversation, Jeb's voice had an ultramarine tone to it, drifting between violet and blue. Tom's was more… she searched for the colour… it was usually more of a yellow ochre, but just now it had a deeper resonance, more like a dark mix. It resonated like an antique violin, burnt sienna perhaps, or even heavier. He was probing some reticence Jeb had, and his words brooded between them. Hope tuned into their conversation. Their dying friend wanted to arrange a living funeral, and Jeb was uncertain.

'It feels totally ghoulish,' Jeb was saying, 'it may sound wrong, but I'd kind of rather help her get through the next few weeks. I've only ever been to one funeral. But isn't it better to do it after someone is dead. You can remember them like they used to be then.'

'It's not about memory,' Tom said, 'it's about being. She gets to say how she does that, more or less, while she's still here.'

He paused, glancing at Hope, who looked steadfastly into the distance.

'Nan talks about ancient atoms. Well, Leah's atoms are still hers right now. And I think that means she has the freedom to have a party, if that's what she wants. Funerals,' he glanced at Hope again, 'well sometimes the one person who is absolutely missing is the one you want to say goodbye to.'

He was thinking of Birdie, Hope knew.

'Can we do this another time?' Jeb was defensive. 'I get what you're saying. I'm just not there yet.'

Tom moved restlessly, his hands rearranging the cups and plates on the table while his right leg seemed to be out of his control, jerking rapidly up and down on his heel as he sat.

Unexpectedly, Hope found herself standing up. She walked to the open edge of the courtyard, her eyes scanning the wilderness intently.

'Hey Nan?' Tom's voice was shaped like a question.

She held her hand up behind her like a stop sign. There was something she needed here. The cloudy white froth of silken seed capsules. What was it? Like the glint of dew on an early morning lawn, recognition dawned.

'Listen Tom.'

She returned to the table and sat down.

'Do you know that plant, the one over there?' she pointed at the smudged white haze.

'Sorry, no. It's some kind of wild plant, isn't it. There was loads by the railway track.'

Hope was insistent. 'Yes, yes. I know it. Rosebay Willowherb. But it has tall spires of pink flowers in the summer, and the colour, it's so intense. And when you look at them closely, in the summer I mean, each small flower is a kind of poem. Very precise, you know.'

'So, what makes them special?'

'Look. The petals are just memories of pink now, no form left. You just have to look in a different way, then you'll see them. And those puffs of cloud,' Hope waved at the tall weeds, 'they look random, but they're not. They have hundreds of seeds ready to fall through time.'

'I don't get it. Do you think Auntie Jane's paintings are like petals then?'

The direct challenge unsettled Hope, clouds scudding across her face. She didn't like that Tom hadn't understood her. Had she used the wrong words, or perhaps what she thought she saw wasn't there at all. She stood up, ready to walk away.

'Hey Nan,' Tom realised what he'd done, 'Come back. I love listening to you talking.'

Hope shook her head. Tom was a long way off. And the other person was there, moving towards her. Was that okay? She watched the stranger lay a gentle hand on Tom's arm.

'What I'm getting,' said Jeb quietly, 'is that you can't see the flowers in that wild froth. Fair enough. You can't see the seed capsules when the flowers are growing either. But the different forms don't matter. Memories are there, even when we can't find them.'

Hope looked at Jeb, caught between gratitude and disappointment. That was what she had been trying to say. The presence of absent things. But she'd wanted Tom to see something. He hadn't followed her thoughts, and now she'd made him anxious. His phone buzzed, and she watched him glance at it. He glowered and then turned the handset off. Jeb raised an eyebrow.

Hope sat at the black table, feeling helpless, following the pattern on the metal surface with her eye. Below the table, three sparrows were hopping about and pecking at invisible crumbs, heads cocked to one side as they scavenged.

‘It’s not just memories,’ Hope interrupted the silence, ‘they’re no different to bodies. They only make sense when we live in time, not in the moment.’

‘Hey. Hold a moment.’ Jeb scrolled through their phone, face obscured by clouds of curls. ‘Yep. Here it is; “to live in this world you must be able to do three things, to love what is mortal; to hold it against your bones knowing that your own life depends on it; and, when the time comes to let it go, to let it go.” I saw this the other day. Mary Oliver.’

‘And when the time comes to let it go, to let it go.’ repeated Hope, ‘That’s exactly what Blake thought.’

‘I wish my Mum knew that.’ Tom knew he sounded like a teenager.

Hope could see Tom clearly again now. The way time and place were knotting him into a single way of thinking, damaging his future before he’d travelled far enough to break free. She could see the ancient souls that whispered beyond time and place were trying to liberate him.

‘Never mind Jeannie,’ she said suddenly, ‘I want to ask you something awesome. The other day, Joseph asked me who I would be in the world, if I had absolute free choice. He’s clever like that. So, I thought I’d ask you.’

Tom hesitated.

‘Actually. I do know. Well, I know what I want to do, and that’s related to who I am, isn’t it? I’ve known ever since Birdie died. I just haven’t got the words right yet to tell people.’

Tom seemed to be speaking to the ground, but then he raised his head.

‘I want to work… no, I want to be with the dying. I think I can be trusted to be there while they let go.’

‘What do you mean, the right words?’ Jeb was curious.

‘You haven’t met my mum.’ said Tom, ‘It’s just, well sometimes she…’

‘Sometimes she starts by worrying. Dragons at the gate. All that.’ Hope offered.

‘Nice one, Nan.’ said Tom, ‘Yeah. It’s like you have to find words that have the right weight and heft.

Build something she can believe in. I don't want to keep falling out with her, you know,' he gestured towards his phone, 'I just need to be prepared. It's harder when she rings me unexpectedly.'

Chapter 64

Back home, Tom relaxed, realising how nervous he had been about the day. But the trip had been a success. Nan had had a great time, and Jeb was completely wowed by her. He smiled. He switched his phone back on. Predictably, he thought, there were three missed calls from mum. No messages though. She usually left a message if he didn't pick up. He would seize the moment. Tell her what he'd decided to do with his life. He grabbed a piece of paper and drew a rough line down the middle. In note form he jotted down, on the left, the skills and knowledge he had from his degree, and on the right, his thoughts about how these were the ideal skills for working with the dying. Sitting on his bed, he propped the sheet of paper on his knees to Facetime her. He was ready, so ready that the certainty inside him was solid, so immense that even Mum would realise he was doing the right thing.

'Hey Mum, how was your day?'

Tom felt happy. He didn't have to be her version of him anymore. He knew who he was meant to be, and that was everything.

'My day? Well, what do you think, Tom?'

Her voice was slow but guarded. He had forgotten something important, he thought. Should he know what she'd been doing that day?

'I'll tell you about my day.'

Jeannie's anger cascaded like a rockfall. A loose stone, dislodged, and now a thundering mass hurtling towards him.

'I've been talking to Dad about Nan. I told him that you had agreed to act responsibly.'

Jeannie's voice was icy.

Tom felt the boulders falling around him. He didn't know if he could stay on his feet.

'Hang on Mum, just listen a minute.'

'And after that, I checked my phone to see where Nan was. Just to make sure she was safe and secure at home.'

'Look Mum, you've got it wrong.'

How could he have forgotten that his Mum tracked the whereabouts of everyone in the family on her phone. Why was he so stupid.

'I've got it wrong? No Tom, you have no idea what you're doing. You gave me your word that you wouldn't take Nan to Cardiff. For heaven's sake, it's only two weeks since Iris and I had to deal with the aftermath of her getting lost on a train. You didn't think about that, did you?'

'Getting lost? What? I didn't know about that. You never tell me anything.'

'But you knew about the mug she smashed, didn't you. Birdie's favourite mug, and apparently you encouraged her to throw it on the floor.'

'Mum, no. Honestly, I just said I liked how she'd stitched it together again. It's up to her what she does with her things. Look, I'm sorry I didn't tell you before we went. But honestly, it was her idea. Joseph told her about the exhibition. And she had the best of days. She really did.'

As his footholds gave way, Tom felt himself falling. He was the boy who hadn't been able to cope with other kids at school. The odd one. The one whose body gave in to arthritis and turned on itself. The one who hid himself like some half-baked hermit, scaring himself sleepless about everything.

'Nan is a sick woman, Tom. She's desperately unstable underneath all her pretence, and she can't make good decisions, not even about herself. Especially not about herself. When are you going to realise that your Nan is not the person she used to be?'

As if watching himself from a great distance, Tom knew he must speak. He couldn't pretend to misunderstand Jeannie any longer. He breathed deeply.

'And when are you going to realise that she is?'

He paused, letting the question steady him for a moment.

'You and Aunty Iris. You're both trying to force her to let go too soon. She's still here, and I so wish you could see that.'

Chapter 65

'I've come to see my mum.'

Hope spoke loudly to the nurse. She didn't mean to, but the desk he sat at was broad, impersonal and as implacable as a battlefield. He looked like he might be in charge. A broad strip light above the desk flattened the shapes of pens, plastic water bottles and piles of paper, making them shadowless. The desk must be new, Hope thought. She didn't recall having seen it before. Even the layout seemed unfamiliar. Had that long curved corridor been there before? She could see a row of pastel-coloured doors, each bearing a printed name card. Presumably that of the occupant? Hope supposed her mum wouldn't care, what with her forgetting pretty much everything these days.

'Hope.' The man had a gentle voice, but Hope tutted, annoyed.

'No, not Hope, Elizabeth. I'm Hope. I've come to see Elizabeth, you see. She was admitted in…'

Hope tailed off as she realised she didn't know exactly when her mum had been moved out of her home.

The nurse came out from behind the desk, lifting a blue face mask over his mouth and nose as he approached her. Behind him, a phone continued to ring.

'Why don't you come with me, Hope,' he said, 'I can get you a cup of tea?'

Alarm bells started to ring in Hope's mind. Was this, in fact, the same ward? There seemed to be more locked doors than she remembered, and now she looked harder, the pastel-coloured doors seemed ominous, somehow. No passion. People without souls.

On the right was a courtyard garden. Someone had tied off the daffodils, bending the stalks over so that the browning flowerheads were pointing towards the soil. Hope supposed her mother must have one of these rooms. Weird how it all looked so different. If only the nurse would just give her directions. Hope pulled at the loose threads on the sleeve of her cardigan. A fawn cardigan, she thought, is that really mine? She peered at the nurse's name badge.

'Tom' she said out loud. 'You've got the same name as my dad.'

She was tired. She guessed it must be from the long journey. Last time, Iris had bought her. Shame she wasn't here now.

A buzzer sounded behind the long desk, and the nurse glanced up the corridor, where there was a door with a large glass pane. A woman wearing a pale blue face mask stood waiting to be admitted. Hope turned her head to the door, and the woman began waving at her. Hope tutted again and tugged one of the threads from her sleeve so hard that it broke.

'Here I am, Hope. Is everything ok?' Iris could see that Hope was arguing with the nurse.

Hope stared.

'Look, I just want to see my mum. But they won't tell me where she is.'

Iris exchanged glances with the nurse.

'Well, I'm here now,' she smiled, 'we're just two sisters together. I think we'll go out into the garden shall we. That's as good a place to look as any.'

She turned to the nurse.

'My name is Iris. I'm Hope's sister. I can take over from here, I think?' The nurse nodded.

‘I’m Tom’ he said, pointing at his identity card. Let me know if you need anything.’

‘Tom?’ said Hope, sharply, ‘I thought you were David. My father isn’t called Tom, he’s called David.’

She glared at the nurse before linking arms with Iris.

‘Ridiculous,’ she muttered as they walked past the pastel doors, ‘why did he say he had the same name as Dad?’

Iris sat on the bench next to her sister. She pulled out her phone and glanced at it briefly. Two thirty. How long would Jeannie be now?

‘Hope, love,’ Iris patted her sister on the arm, ‘Jeannie will be here soon. She’s just having a little chat with the consultant.’

Hope turned and glared at Iris.

‘Don’t be vague, Iris. You were never vague. Jeannie’s talking to the consultant to see what’s left of my mind, isn’t she? That’s not a little chat. You think I can’t understand what’s happening to me.’

Hope took a long breath, filling herself with air from her belly up to her sternum. Desperately, she tried to recall what it was like to be centred and still. She wanted to sob with loss, but she couldn't quite think what it was she wanted to mourn. She fixed her eyes on Iris.

'Thing is, about coming to see mum. You know, what I said to that nurse. Even when I was saying it, I knew it wasn't real. It was just, like. I suppose it was the best stab at real that I could come up with in that moment. It's horrible, but it's not all the time. It's worse here, because none of this is believable.'

She spread out her arms, gesticulating vaguely at the safety glass windows through which they could see nurses and lost people sitting in a semi-circle with institutional cups and saucers held in blue-veined hands or balanced on wads of paperwork.

'I'm right, aren't I?'

Hope jumped to her feet and started pacing the narrow-paved path in the ridiculous garden. The whole area looked neglected, with dandelion leaves and couch grass struggling through the gaps between the stones. Would she know the dandelion, when it flowered? The thought made her drop to her knees. She reached out a hand. It looked like the hand of an old woman, not hers. She caressed the knotted winter-worn weeds and started to cry. Her sobs lurched into the air like soapy bubbles, swaying erratically and then ceasing to exist. The old hand in front of her was exploring the abandoned border now, grasping the dry stem of a sprawling mahonia. Iris looked around, embarrassed, and reached down to pull Hope to her feet. There were tears on Hope's cheeks.

'I'm not ready to let go. Can we go back, Iris? I want to go back home.'

Iris felt the calming atmosphere of the Assessment Centre. Here, she could see more clearly the dementia that was gouging holes in her sister's brain. She was sad, but her sense of relief was stronger here. The locked doors and hovering presence of medical expertise comforted her, helping her understand how Hope's life must be, from now on. She patted Hope on the shoulder. Hope jerked away at her touch.

'Don't you get it, Iris. I want to go home now. I don't want to be here.'

Hope recoiled from Iris's calm sympathy. Anything, She would run, climb, break down doors, do anything to escape all this sympathy. Iris and Jeannie disturbed her; she hated the way they wanted to stop her being free. Around her, the petty shrubs and tired foliage of the Assessment Centre looked as if they had given up.

They panicked her, and she desperately wanted to go home.

'Home? Yes, of course.' Iris decided to play along, 'We'll go back inside and find our way together.'

They went into the large communal area, and Iris closed the door behind them.

'Now, let's see. We need to go down this corridor, I think.'

Iris led her sister along the curving passageway that would, in fact, simply lead them back to the same place, hoping that by the time they'd walked slowly round, Hope would have forgotten her demand to leave. She wondered how much longer Jeannie would be. The corridor was punctuated by open doors, each leading to rooms that tried to combine medical uniformity with personal mementoes pinned to identical noticeboards. At her side, she could feel her sister's restlessness.

'Look at those rooms.' Hope said abruptly, 'All the same. All with the same people staying in them. All being forced to lead the same lives. Don't they feel trapped?'

Poor Hope, Iris thought. She'd always been like this; so critical and hostile of ordinary life. If only she'd accepted the world for what it was. She could have had a more comfortable existence. Iris couldn't remember a time when she hadn't been provoked and irritated by Hope's refusal to settle.

'I don't think that's true, dear,' Iris spoke clearly, 'I expect people staying here feel really fortunate to be looked after so well.'

Iris knew her sister better than she knew herself. It was her duty, she thought, to be there for Hope, stop her getting into any more scrapes. That was something, however tragic the circumstances. Her annoyance was mixed with compassion and pity.

'It's an illusion, you know,' Hope waved her arms at the window, 'none of this is real. You especially. 'You'll see. You know, I wish you could see it, Iris. All that stuff you believe in. None of it is real. And you think my heart can't be trusted, but you're wrong. You've always been wrong about that. Blake said there are doors you know. Between the known and the unknown…'

'Not Blake again, please.' Iris cried out like a trapped animal.

'Come on,' she said, steadying herself, 'let's go and find your daughter. I can't take any more of this.'

Neatly dressed, her bag held tight, Iris strode over the sanitised hospital floor. Beside her, Hope took each step with careful thought, observing and letting go of the impressions and emotions that scudded around her. The moments of their lives divided them still; each so separate from the other.

Chapter 66

The weeks passed. For Iris, each was bound in neat parcels of practical activity, while for Hope, time billowed like curtains in a breeze. By March, a sharp spell of winter weather had come and gone, and in Hedgemead Park the leaf-bare oak tree choreographed the wind, a brown dance of bare boughs. Most mornings, Hope could be seen at dawn, sitting about twenty metres from the tree, her blue yoga mat unrolled as she prepared her familiar ritual.

Today, the last day of her life, she was there even earlier, sitting on the ground as she watched the dark umber around her separate into distinct shadowy presences; the oak tree, the rolling shapes of shrubs like Hogarth's revellers, and, further away, the angular forms of play equipment. As usual, she was struggling to dismiss Iris from her thoughts. Iris would be furious if she knew where Hope was, but she'd told nobody, not even Tom.

It was too early, yet, for birdsong, and shivering slightly she knelt on the mat, folding her body close to the ground in Child's Pose, her arms stretched towards the oak. Like this, she could feel the heat of her belly snaking through her shoulders and hips towards her fingers and toes. Her body knew the rhythm of the Sun Salutation as well as the dawn knows its chorus, and she rose slowly to move into prayer pose. As she went through her asanas, easing out the tension in her legs and back, she felt as if she were calling the day into being. While the dark early morning clouds disentangled themselves from trees and shrubs on the horizon, the bruising purples of her now familiar confusion melted away and she knew that this was one of those mornings where her being would surrender itself.

It was like this for her sometimes, especially at that time of day, when the universe was undifferentiated, when earthly illusions and the clouds of unknowing in her mind combined in peace, not fear. Standing tall in the middle of her salutation, dry scraps of thought faded like fragments from a dream, and she was as one with the air and the trees. The wide-eyed robin gave a first, exploratory trill, its melody resonating like ancient starlight.

Hope had stepped aside from the movement of time. But as she bent into a deep fold, a sudden dizziness assailed her, and she staggered forwards, wrenching her ankle hard. She stretched out her arms as she fell, gashing her wrist on the sharp edge of a broken bottle hidden in the long grass. At first, she felt nothing, and then the loud beat of her heart tunnelled through her skull as the shock of pain set in and time rattled backwards like a train.

There was Iris, running across the open ground, her arms waving, and her eyes looked full of fright. Hope shook her head. Not now, her mind urged, fearing the way her sister always misunderstood the truth of a situation. Not now, she thought, while my thoughts breathe in the robin's song. But Iris came closer. She was dancing, not waving, and her eyes were large with light.

Time snapped like a twig underfoot.

The trees in the park must have grown a foot while she'd waited. Her sister was still on the swing, her mouth set wide in a grin as she swung higher and higher, leaning back as the swing lifted to the trees behind her and then, at just the right moment, flicking her body forward and lifting her legs out straight in front of her, toes pointed.

'I'm going to let go. Mind out of the way!'

Her sister had long dark hair, just like her own, and with each forward movement it streamed out behind her. She watched her sister as she flew off the swing and landed on the ground, laughing.

'Again!'

'No, it's my turn.'

She pushed her sister aside as they both dived towards the swing, which rocked erratically like a broken pendulum.

'I'll tell Mummy if you don't let me go on it now. It's my turn.'

They glared at each other. Her dark eyes were fiercer. Her sister gave in.

She fumbled her fingers on the hard burnished chains. The swing tried to spin away from her, and she pulled hard to make it slow down. The links were as big and cold as shiny pebbles from the sea.

Reaching to the ground with one toe, she pushed herself into motion, building up speed until she was swinging high. She was thrilled and terrified. The chain flexed like a muscle. She tipped her head back like her sister had done, laughing and yelling into the wind-chopped sky above her. She reached the top of the arc, feeling the inevitable shift in direction. A pause. Shuddering her whole body into the effort, she made herself like an arrow, stretching toes first, into the air in front of her. She wanted to fly. Should she fling herself into the air like her sister? Could she? She wriggled on the seat, moving the grip of her hands on the cold chain so that it would be easy to let go. She wanted Iris to see her soar.

But then she was on the ground, breathless and disappointed. Her body thrummed with the motion of the swing, but here she was, flightless, still earthbound and full of yearning. Envy lodged itself in a blind corner of her mind, effacing her confidence in hope, even as she yearned to soar.

'Again.' The voice was in her head. If Iris could do it, then so could she. And again. Why didn't she fly? She could feel no feathers, nor the silky movement of air over taut wings. And now the effort of swinging higher and higher had become a chore. Her heart ached and she had cut her wrist. There was grit in the wound, and it stung.

With thanks

So many people have offered me encouragement, help and advice as I scribbled my way through the pages of this novel.

I'd like to thank my writing friends, Min Hodges, Mary Graham, Fiona Bunn, Sue Lilley, Patti Carter, Tiffany Jolowicz. Lorna Taylor, Susan Ronald, Michelle Callus, Helen Francis, Shaun McDonald, Helen Lucey, Steve Leighton, Jackie Llewellyn, Jill Rossiter and Andre Bremer. Each in their own way has challenged and encouraged me, helping me shape my characters and their stories.

Other friends who have generously shared their thoughts and comments include Rachel Celia, Brennie Barnett and Heather Ford. Thank you for sharing your friendship, expertise and general good sense.

Thanks go to gin majka, the fabulous photographer who generously let me use one of her beautiful images for the cover of the book.

Finally, heartfelt thanks to my mum, Judith Thomas, and my sister, Liz Wilson-Chalon, who have been supportive in so many ways, and who offered me steadfast encouragement through my many moments of doubt.